M000113859

TRAIN

L.J. Woolfe

MINDSTIR MEDIA

Train
Copyright © 2023 by L.J. Woolfe. All rights reserved.

This is a work of fiction. Names, characters, places and incidents are products of the author's imagination or are used fictitiously and should not be construed as real. Any resemblance to actual events, locales, organizations or persons, living or dead, is entirely coincidental.

No part of this book may be used or reproduced in any manner whatsoever without written permission, except in the case of brief quotations embodied in critical articles and reviews. For more information, e-mail all inquiries to info@mindstirmedia.com.

Published by Mindstir Media, LLC
45 Lafayette Rd | Suite 181| North Hampton, NH 03862 | USA
1.800.767.0531 | www.mindstirmedia.com

Printed in the United States of America
ISBN-13: 978-1-960142-42-9

Little Darling
Words and Music by Anthony Waddington and Arthur Bickerton
Copyright © 1975 Arlovol Music and WC Music Corp.
Copyright Renewed
All Rights for Arlovol Music Administered by Penny Farthing Music c/o Concord Music
Publishing
All rights Reserved   Used by Permission
Reprinted by Permission of Hal Leonard LLC

Teeny Bopper Band
Words & music: Bergman/hessing/Duiser/Eggermont/Mol/van Prehn/Veerhoff
© 1974 New Dayglow B.V. administered by Nanada Music B.V.

Train
Words and Music by Leo Sayer and David Courtney
Copyright © 1974 SILVERBIRD SONGS LT. and UNIVERSAL/MCA MUSIC LTD.
Copyright Renewed
All Rights for SILVERBIRD SONGS LTD. in the USA and Canada Administered by ALMO
MUSIC CORP.
All Rights for UNIVERSAL/MCA MUSIC LTD. in the USA and Canada Administered by
UNIVERSAL MUSIC CORP.
All Rights Reserved   Used by Permission
Reprinted by permission of Hal Leonard LLC
* 'Just a boy' Album

Don't Let The Music Die
Words and Music by Eric Faulkner
Copyright © 1977 by Complete Music Ltd.
Copyright Renewed
All Rights in the United States Administered by Universal Music - MGB Songs International
Copyright Secured   All Rights Reserved
Reprinted by permission of Hal Leonard LLC

CONTENTS

Track 1: "Train" – Leo Sayer 1

Track 2: "Rocket" – Mud 16

Track 3: "Lonely This Christmas" – Mud 23

Track 4: "Tiger Feet" – Mud 33

Track 5: "Hell raiser" – The Sweet 47

Track 6: "Cherie Amour" – The Rubettes 52

Track 7: "Funny, Funny" – The Sweet 62

Track 8: "Slow Down" – Shabby Tiger 72

Track 9: "Forever and Ever" – Slik 83

Track 10: "Teeny Bopper Band" – Catapult 97

Track 11: "Little Darling" – The Rubettes 111

Track 12: "Juke Box Jive" – The Rubettes 119

Track 13: "Hot Love" – T. Rex 127

Track 14: "Moviestar" – Harpo 135

Track 15: "Your Baby Ain't Your Baby Anymore" – Paul Da Vinci 145

Track 16: "Rose Tint My World" – Richard O'Brien 153

Track 17: "Daddy Cool" – Boney M. 176

Track 18: "Fancy Pants" – Kenny 187

Track 19: "Teenage Rampage" – The Sweet 204

Track 20: "Blockbuster" – The Sweet 227

Track 21: "Tessie (I Love You)" – Left Side 240

Track 22: "The Cat crept in" – Mud 250

Track 23: "If I Had Words" – Scott Fitzgerald and Yvonne Keeley 256

Track 24: "Eloise" – Barry Ryan 266

Track 25: "Crazy" – Mud 270

Track 26: "Don't Let the Music Die" – The Bay City Rollers 278

Track 27: "Little Darling"(Reprise) – The Rubettes 286

This book is dedicated to Mom...and only she knows why.

"These indeed had turned out to be the happiest, saddest, wettest, wildest, and most extraordinary years of my life, and I did not want them to end."

—Patricia LaPlante

PREFACE

Is it really true you can't go home again?

Maybe. But could returning to a time and place when our adolescent minds were free to explore the boundless possibilities of the future evoke the zealous person we once were?

Perhaps summoning the years of our unconstrained youth and the many "firsts" it brought us could whet our appetite for risk again.

More importantly, could a shattered soul desperately searching for resolution find the answers on a journey back along the tracks?

TRACK 1

"TRAIN" – LEO SAYER

APRIL 2018

T he only sounds in the room were the rhythmic ticktock from the antique schoolhouse clock on the wall and the soft, drawn-out rustling of paper.

Louisa LaPlante sat in her attorney's office shoulders slumped, steadying her cramped hand around a pen. She was signing the last of her divorce papers from a marriage she thought would last forever: "Until death do us part."

Now fifty-something, Louisa marveled how the small, insignificant task of a signature could erase a life that had taken twenty-two years to build. As her tears welled, she quickly wiped the first droplet away on her sleeve, refusing to give in and let it roll down her cheek.

Once the final line was signed and dated, she sighed heavily and shook her hand to get the blood flowing again.

Ruth Weiss, who sat across the table, leaned forward in her chair. "As your attorney and friend, I can assure you—you *will* get past this, and life will go on," she said gently, patting Louisa's hand. "Remember that it's not the end. It's the beginning of something new."

1

Louisa's body clenched, and she grimaced as she did whenever she heard that annoying phrase. *What a cliché.* It's like someone saying, "Money can't buy happiness." *Really? Baloney! Of course, it can.*

If she had all of the money in the world, she'd head right now to the docks in New York to board a luxury world cruise, booked in one of those royal suites with floor-to-ceiling marble in the bathroom and a Schimmel baby grand in the living area. That would make her *very* happy after all she had endured lately.

Glaring at her attorney, Louisa snorted, conveying her discontent.

Ruth's expression of compassion morphed into one of authority. Coming from the city, she had a pit-bull-like, New York temperament. "Go, Louisa," she instructed. "Get on with your life and stop wallowing."

That was the kick Louisa needed to get out of her chair. Minutes later, for the final time, she descended the porch stairs of the Victorian townhouse where Ruth's office was located. The place had begun to feel like her second home over the last few months. Birds melodiously chirped in the early April sky. On a bare gray branch of the maple tree in the front lawn, she spotted what she thought was a fresh green bud bursting open. It held a feeling of promise, bringing the first flicker of optimism she'd had in a long time.

Was it just her imagination, though, since she was anticipating spring and warmer weather? She squinted her eyes to get a closer look. *Nope.* It was only her wishful thinking toying with her again. Spring hadn't arrived.

Crestfallen, she trudged off to her car, muttering under her breath. "Anything else you want to throw at me, God? Just one measly green bud is all I'm asking for."

Once in the car, she flung her purse on the passenger seat and settled in on the driver's side. Through grief-swollen eyes, Louisa caught sight of her bare ring finger resting atop the steering wheel. The big void her life had become was finally settling in. Now what?

She sobbed quietly. How would she ever start again? Was there a *Dumped for Dummies* instruction manual out there? There had to be something to give her life enough meaning to get up and breathe every morning.

Her cell phone sounded off an air raid siren, startling her out of her despondent moment. She'd programmed the earsplitting ringtone for whenever her mom was calling. For a second, she considered letting it go to voicemail. Sharing the moment-by-moment details of the final day of her divorce was *not* what she wanted to be doing.

What she really wanted was to crawl into bed, pull the covers over her head, and shut the world out. But Louisa couldn't bring herself to ignore the call. Her parents were getting older, and she knew she needed to answer—just in case.

Swiping her finger across the banner, she prayed the conversation would end quickly. "Hi, Mom. It's done, and I really don't want to talk about it anymore."

"Oh, honey," her mom said in that tone reserved for mothers, the one that's a soothing balm. She had used the same tone whenever Louisa was sick as a kid, and the sound of her sympathetic voice was almost medicine enough by itself. But her mom's next words ruined it. "Well, just remember. It's a new beginning."

No. No more of that stupid advice. Louisa's thoughts sounded childlike, as if her hands were cupped over her ears and she were chanting the words "peas and carrots . . . peas and carrots" to herself to block out her mother's words of "comfort."

Everyone loved Louisa's mom, Patty—even though she didn't know the right thing to say at times. When Louisa had been a teenager—the age when parents were considered the archenemy—her friends had always taken the time to chat with her mother. It seemed like they loved to hear Patty's humorous stories about everyday dilemmas, like what had happened to her at the store when she'd forgotten her wallet and the tall, burly truck driver behind her in the checkout line had paid for her pantyhose.

Or the time she'd neglected to put one of the main ingredients into the chocolate soufflé for an important, elegant luncheon for twenty, and the result was a soupy chocolate pudding. There was even the story of how a police officer had pulled her over after catching her driving eighty-two miles an hour in a fifty-five zone, and she'd told him a little white lie: that her medicine was kicking in and she needed to get home to the bathroom *very* quickly.

Her mom was probably the most adventurous and spontaneous person Louisa had ever known. She respected that and loved her for it. Still, it meant trouble. Her mother had gotten into "predicaments" all of Louisa's life.

"I know this hasn't been a good day for you, Louisa," she said. "But I have a *huge* surprise, and it couldn't have come at a better time. I want you and your sister to come over on Saturday and I'll explain."

Louisa rolled her eyes. She hadn't ever liked her mother's idea of a surprise. She strongly believed they didn't agree on what the word meant.

"Really!" Her mom's tone was pressing. "It'll be great! And I think it'll get your mind off things. We can get a pizza, some wine, and make a night of it. What do you say? How long has it been since the three of us had an outing together? Or an 'inning' is more like it."

Too tired to rebel against "Patty's good idea," Louisa gave in. It seemed like the easiest way out—even though it wasn't an out. "Okay, okay, Mom," she conceded. "But you call Judy and talk her into coming."

Saturday soon came, and Louisa arrived at her parents' split-level ranch in the laid-back town of Danbury in Connecticut. When she entered through the front door, she spotted her father, Lyle, relaxing in his gray corduroy recliner in his "dad den" downstairs. He was mesmerized by the ballgame on the television. A retired chemical engineer, Louisa's father wasn't a man of many words. He thought methodically and was mindful of what he said. Giving a quick, breezy answer to a simple question was hard for him. Whenever he spoke, it was a struggle for him to get his point across.

Louisa had long suspected fifty years of marriage to her mother had made him a highly prudent man. Her parents always reminded her of the *I Love Lucy* show. She could still hear her dad's booming voice, like Ricky Ricardo, echoing in her head: "Patty! What have you done now?"

Louisa chuckled. Her father was so focused on the game he didn't notice her approaching. She bent over and kissed him on the cheek. "Hi, Dad. Whatcha watching?"

He startled. "Oh! So you're here for your mother's surprise?"

"What, no, hello?" she asked sarcastically. "Don't you wanna know how the single life is treating the newbie divorcée?'"

He glared at her, his eyes dark, and mumbled something she couldn't make out.

"All right, Pops." Louisa patted him on the shoulder. "At ease. Back to your game."

She crept upstairs to the living room, slowing once she neared the top step. Her guard was up over her mom's "big surprise." Knowing her mother, things could go either way.

It could be a new exotic recipe she wanted to try out on Louisa before she served it to a big group at church. Or she could be playing matchmaker and arranged for one of her friends' son who had never been married before at age fifty-something to meet her. *Ugh.*

Louisa held her breath, and she entered her parents' formal living room, which was like a miniature version of Windsor Castle filled with antiques from their world travels. Period pieces from France, like the dainty glass side table with gold-finished Queen Anne legs, sat next to the blue paisley Venetian armchair. Nineteenth-century hand-painted porcelain lion candelabras from Japan were perched on top of the Italian marble mantel of the faux mahogany fireplace.

Louisa's sister, Judy, sat on a Wedgewood blue velvet couch, smiling slyly at her. Louisa was close with her sister, but the similarities in their gregarious personalities had them fighting like schoolgirls constantly.

Louisa, much shorter than Judy, kept her hair long, blond, and wavy. She didn't often decorate herself with bling or accessories and had more of a casual "just-got-off-the-beach" look. Judy, however, was the beauty of the two sisters and always had been. Her rosy cheeks were highlighted by her short, dark, shiny hair. She was edgy and chic, always dressed to be seen. Louisa had always thought her sister had a porcelain "Snow White" look about her.

All her life, she had seen boys captivated by Judy's looks. Even when her sister's first marriage had ended a few years earlier, word had gotten around town quickly, and suitors were knocking at Judy's door before the ink on the divorce papers had dried. Judy had seemed to enjoy the attention for a while until finally meeting her Mr. Right and was now engaged to be married the following year.

Patty elusively wandered into the living room, with her hands behind her back and sat next to Judy on the couch. At eighty-something, Louisa's mom was in remarkably good shape. She was tall like Judy and kept her slender figure by going to the gym three days a week. With her mom and sister both having a statuesque, model-like presence, it always irked Louisa why she had drawn the short straw between the three LaPlante women.

Suspicious, Louisa glanced around the room to see if anything was amiss. Her eyes fell upon a bottle of champagne in a silver ice bucket on the coffee table, surrounded by three tall Waterford crystal flutes. What was going on? Her mother never took out the Waterford.

"Champagne?" Louisa asked. "Well, what is it? What's up with the funny looks on your faces? Did you already start drinking without me?"

Rising to her feet, her mom pointed to the empty Venetian chair. "Sit," she commanded. Louisa quickly lowered herself into the chair. She spotted a copy of the memoir her mother had published earlier that year sitting next to the champagne bucket. A single-stemmed red poppy in a glass tumbler sat on top of the book. Louisa had received an autographed copy from her mother three months before but still hadn't read it. She'd been waiting until the divorce drama had settled down and she was in a better frame of mind to appreciate her mother's accomplishment.

In the 1970s, her father's job with Union Carbide had transferred him and the family to Antwerp, Belgium, for four years. Patty's book covered that period, sharing the family's follies as they adjusted to a different life in Europe. The title—*Does Anybody Here Speak English?* —foreshadowed the humor the reader could expect within its pages. Patty had spent the last three decades writing about her experience in Belgium. During that time, the book's creation had become almost part of the woodwork. In a way, it was like her fourth child.

Louisa had seen the birth of the book, from handwritten notes on paper to the hen-peck clicking of a typewriter to a Commodore word processor, then finally to a desktop computer. The day the manuscript was complete and her mom had written the words "The End," she right away developed something akin to empty nest syndrome, as if her last child was going off to college. Louisa, however, had pacified her by introducing her mom to social media, which had occupied her spare time ever since.

Patty filled the flutes with champagne and passed two of them to Louisa and Judy. "Well, you know how I've been playing on that Spacebook thing you taught me, Louisa?"

Louisa sprang up in her chair. "Mom! It's *Facebook*." She knew her mother was famous for inventing her own words and no doubt had confused Facebook with Myspace.

"Whatever," her mom went on. "Facebook, then. Anyway, I started reaching out—you call that 'tagging,' right?'" She turned her head toward Louisa as if to see if she would correct her again before continuing. "So I started reaching out to some of the people in the administration building over at the school you went to back in Antwerp. I was trying to get in touch with the parents of the kids you were friends with so I could wink at them on Facebook."

"Friend request, Mom!" Louisa cut in, explaining slowly. "You send a friend request to someone on Facebook. You wink at someone when you're flirting on a dating site."

Staring blankly at her, her mother nodded as if she understood. "So one thing led to another, and I started explaining to the secretaries at the school that I had recently published a book about living in Antwerp back in the seventies."

While she continued her story, Louisa glanced over at her sister. Judy's tight-lipped smile hinted she already knew what the surprise was. "Do you know what this is all about, sister?" she interrupted again, narrowing her eyes.

Judy gestured with her hand, miming that her mouth was zipped shut and the key thrown away over her shoulder. That was followed by a forced sigh, as if to tell Louisa to be quiet.

Their mom, noticeably irritated by Louisa's disruptions, spoke louder and faster now. "So word about my book got around at the school. The American Women's Club found out—remember them? They've invited me to speak at a luncheon in Antwerp and do a book signing." She turned to Louisa again, wide-eyed and waiting for her reaction.

Louisa paused, aware she needed to respond. She could see this meant the world to her mother, but she'd been unable to feel a stitch of enthusiasm about anything for ages. Being excited would be a lie, so she'd have to fake it. "Mom . . . wow," she eventually said. "This is great. See? All your hard work has paid off."

Judy scowled at her. "You sound like you just walked out of a morgue, Louisa." She turned to their mother. "This is a big deal!"

Louisa gulped down some champagne and let out a muffled belch before attempting to brighten her tone. "When are you going, Mom?"

Patty eagerly scooched to the edge of the couch. "Well, this is where the *real* surprise comes in. They want to hold the luncheon at the end of next month, and I want to book airline tickets for you and Judy to go with me on a mother-daughter trip. Just like the old days, when we had our girls' outings."

Snatching her glass, Louisa could feel her adrenaline flow as she took a larger gulp of champagne. She was petrified of airplanes and flying. Fifteen years earlier, on a short flight from New York to Washington, the pilot had hit some turbulence. In the panic of the moment, Louisa vowed to herself, "That's it! Never again!"

Ever since, she'd ignored several events that required air travel. She had been invited to a wedding in Tuscany and a fiftieth wedding anniversary in Hawaii but didn't go to either one. She had also passed on a ski trip to Argentina right after finding out the flight was over ten hours long. The only words that had rolled out of her mouth in response were *No way. No how*! Boarding a stable cruise ship an hour's drive from the house out of New York was good enough for her, regardless of whether it took longer for the boat to get her to her destination.

"Mom, you know I don't fly," Louisa whined. "Can't we just . . . take a ship there? Or . . . ." Her voice trailed off. It was ridiculous even to suggest it.

Judy shook her head. "Louisa, you need to get over this. You've been grounded for too long."

"You know I'm somewhat of a control freak, and flying isn't in my control." Louisa's pitch was rising. "Accept it. This is the way I came from the factory."

"You work in the aerospace field." Judy waved her finger at Louisa. "You sell the darn bearings that go into the planes. Shame on you for not standing by your product!"

Louisa smirked and folded her arms across her chest defensively.

Sighing heavily, Judy walked over to the TV. "Well, if words won't convince you, we'll just have to go to plan B." She picked up the remote, pressed the button to bring YouTube up on the screen, and typed "mud" in the search bar.

Louisa wasn't sure where her sister was going with this, until multiple videos from the 1970s popped up at the bottom of the screen. She leaned in for a closer look—and *bam!* It was as if someone doused her with a glass of ice-cold water. Everything became clear.

A rush of nostalgia flooded Louisa as she recalled her unbridled obsession with the British pop band called Mud. She and her family had moved abroad during the tail end of the glam rock movement that had come out of the United Kingdom. The trend's wild spirit was a novelty to Louisa and most Americans that had first moved there because in the States, pop music had more of a conservative, softer rock sound. The dynamics of glam rock didn't catch on in America until later in the '70s.

Her memory of Mud and other similar bands was of young men with a unique dancing style, flashy attire, and fanatic teenage girls for their audience. One thing that had always puzzled Louisa was why these glam-boy bands from Europe had little or no fame in the US. In her opinion, it was preposterous and America's biggest loss.

"Okay, sister, do you remember this one?" Judy asked, pulling up a video.

Louisa moved to the edge of her seat as the image on the TV came into focus. All four members of Mud were dressed in matching fitted red pantsuits and metallic platform shoes. The guitar player's earrings hung like silver Christmas ornaments, dangling from his earlobes to the tops of his shoulders. The lead singer, Les Gray, wore tinted aviator glasses and an elaborate, oversized belt buckle, looking like he'd won a WrestleMania championship title. His ultra-thick sideburns grew down his jawline.

Their dramatic ensembles were entertaining, but it was their spirited dancing in unison to the spritely music and the campy way they played to the camera that captivated Louisa. It was nothing like the somber performance of pop bands nowadays. They were laughing, smiling, clapping, dancing, and goofing around.

"Oh, my God!" Louisa leaped to her feet. "I forgot about Mud." She scratched her head. "How could I have forgotten?"

As the video continued, the three women clapped loudly, stomped their feet, and laughed at every move the band members made. Then a man's deep voice bellowed from the den downstairs as if they were little kids horsing around. "Settle down up there!"

Louisa exchanged a surprised look with Judy, and they both broke out laughing even harder at their father's sudden outburst.

When the tune ended, Patty sprung from her seat. "Hey, Judy, put on that Leos Sayers guy," she grinned, theatrically batting her eyelashes. "I always thought he was a real cupcake."

"Mom, it's *Leo Sayer!*" Louisa yelled. "He's not plural. There aren't two of him."

Judy clicked around the screen using the remote and brought up Leo Sayer. Once more, the '70s vibe was obvious in the video, right down to Leo's huge afro. While she watched, Louisa noticed an awkwardness about the singer. His dance moves were limited to jerky lateral and vertical movements as if he were a puppet and someone were pulling his strings. Was that the way they danced back then? It seemed so funny to her now. Maybe what happened in the '70s should *stay* in the '70s.

"More!" roared Patty when the song ended. "Do some more!"

"Okay, Louisa," Judy said. "I've been saving this just in case everything else failed to convince you to get on the plane with us." She rubbed her hands together. "I know The Rubettes were one of your teenage idols. In fact, I believe you had the band's poster right above your bed when we lived in Belgium." She walked over to the bucket of champagne and filled Louisa's glass to the rim. "You're going to need this."

Judy switched to another video. In this one, The Rubettes were onstage together, wearing tight-fitting black suits with white piping on the lapels and a white ascot cap on each member's head.

The camera closed in on the lead singer, Alan Williams, as he clapped his hands above his head to encourage the audience.

"Oh!" Louisa cried out. "I forgot about The Rubettes. I loved them too!" She wriggled in her chair, holding her cheeks with her hands, feeling like a raving teenage girl at a Beatles concert.

"I would give up one of my offspring for that lead singer," Judy said, closing in on the TV to get a closer look at Alan Williams.

Louisa leaned to one side of her chair, giving her sister a puzzled look. "What are you in a tizzy about? You never listened to their music when we were in Belgium. That was my gig!"

Judy turned to her. "Girl, that was then. This is now."

"I don't know what the fuss is about him." Their mom stood, crossing her arms over her chest. "The lead singer looks like Renée Zellweger. Leos Sayers is much cuter."

Once the song ended, Louisa leaned back in her chair and stretched her arms above her head, fulfilled. "I needed that. I feel like I should go have a cigarette, and I don't even smoke the darn things." She glanced over to see Judy's self-congratulatory expression. It was obvious her sister thought she'd won. Louisa scowled. "However, music or no music, I'm still not getting on a plane."

Judy stuck her tongue out at her. "Keep this in mind, sister: my alternate plans go all the way to Z."

Louisa swore her head would explode from the pressure. It was exhausting. She thought if she gave her sister and her mother something, they would leave her alone for a while. In time, she'd figure out a clever excuse for not going. "All right, let me think about it. Just give me a few days to let this all settle in. Is that good enough for now?"

Patty let out a grunt of frustration.

"Okay, Mom, don't worry." Judy nodded. "We have progress here. It's a start. We knew it wouldn't be easy."

Louisa left her parents' house, energized from revisiting the music of her past. It had been a long time since she laughed like that, let alone smiled. Nonetheless, it didn't take long for her to fall back into gloom. Ho-hum. Nobody loved her. It was like she'd turned into Eeyore, all sad, pessimistic, and gray.

The next few days passed, and Louisa still struggled to find a reason to avoid going on the trip to Belgium. She genuinely wanted to go and be there for her mother, but her fear of flying was getting the best of her. By that point, she was also anticipating a call from her mom or Judy about it, so she was even more on edge. When she got home from work that evening, she still hadn't heard from either of them. Could it be they'd both forgotten and she was off the hook? But with the way her life was going, she knew she wouldn't be so lucky.

Louisa settled in for the night and fed her two cats, Spencer and Jasper. The minute she'd walk through the front door, they would remind her they were top priority. After she took care of them, she started cooking her lonely dinner for one, turning the heat up on the stove to boil water for pasta then dragging herself into the living room to wait on the couch while it got up to temperature.

The house was quiet, and the only sound was the burbling from the stove. The still atmosphere brought on a profound weariness, and Louisa dropped her head in her hands, letting the depression consume her. It had been over a year since she'd moved into her condo for one. Since then, she had spent her free time decorating her new home in a Key West tranquil fashion, with plantation shutters, airy earth tones on the walls, and lots of tropical plants. She had hoped the resort style would rid her of her loneliness, yet it still visited her frequently.

After a few minutes of wallowing in self-pity, Louisa sat up and lightly slapped her cheek, scolding herself. She realized she was acting like the depressing friend no one wanted to be around. The harsh advice Ruth had given her rang through her head. "I refuse to be a Debbie Downer," she rebuked.

Leaning over, she grabbed the remote control off the coffee table and turned on the TV to catch the news, hoping it would get her out of the dumps. After the first two headline stories—a bombing in the East, and an eighty-five-year-old woman robbed and beaten—she turned it off again. "Seriously? This isn't gonna work."

The water on the stove was boiling furiously, so she headed back to the kitchen and turned the heat off. Lingering on the spot, she stood motionless. The heavy feeling of despair drained her once again, pulling her down. Fighting it seemed useless, so she gave in and let the misery submerge her. A feeling encompassed her like she was lost in her loneliness at the bottom of the dark ocean floor with no escape. She had been there before and knew she might be there for a while.

Moments after plunging into the abyss, though, an enigmatic warm sensation crept up from her stomach, lifting her out of the darkness. Bright images of the colorful, eccentric outfits and the humorous way the UK glam-boy bands would parade around onstage flashed in her head.

Louisa regained her composure and peered around the corner into the living room. The TV stood tall, luring her in. Anxious, she clicked away on the remote, found The Rubettes on YouTube, and hit Play. First the camera zoomed in on the hunky drummer, John Richardson, who comically made silly faces into the camera. Next, the screen focused on Alan Williams as he sang and ogled the audience, making the young girls scream in the front row. Eventually, some of the metaphorical dark clouds above Louisa's head were clearing, and her spirit was lifting.

"Gosh, if this is all it takes to cheer me up, I could bottle these guys up and sell them at the local depression clinic," she chuckled. "I could make a fortune."

When the song ended, she glanced down at Jasper, who had crawled into her lap. "Okay, buddy. Let's do another one, shall we?"

She found one of her mom's favorites: "Leos Sayers," as her mother had called him. While browsing through the video list, she found a clip for his song "Train." Cocking her head to one side, she mumbled, "That's odd. I don't think I've heard that one before." The video's still picture of skinny Leo Sayer and his dark corkscrew hair, which stood about twelve inches high, made her smile. She hit Play.

The music started with a slow tempo and bleak vibe. Louisa realized she *did* recognize the song but hadn't heard it since her days abroad. As Leo continued singing, something bizarre happened. His face developed a frozen expression, and Louisa couldn't take her eyes off him. At first, she didn't pay attention to the lyrics and focused more on his startled look. But once she listened to the words, she became completely engrossed by its message.

The music soon picked up speed, and its tone brightened. Yet Leo continued staring bug-eyed into the camera. It was so compelling to Louisa, though she didn't know why. Her eyes were fixed on his. It was like he was looking right at her, into her soul. The only thing she could do was stare openly back at him with her mouth gaping.

> Running through my life
> Like a river, like a song
> Train keeps pushing me
> Right back to the place where I belong . . .
> Back along the tracks
> Fly a million years
> Right across my path
> Train moves on, ringing in my ears . . .
> Come on board
> Come on board
> Train, oh train, take me back again
> I remember, I remember, take me back
> Train, oh train, the journey ends and starts again

I remember, I remember, I remember
I've been up all night, trying to get this down
Now I'm hallucinating
Staring at the wall, look what I'm creating . . .
Look at the clock, I'm twelve hours old
So many more remain
Way up ahead, I know I see a train . . .
Come on board
Come on board
Train, oh train, all those memories, all over again . . .

When the number ended, Louisa sat there in disbelief. What had just happened? Had she had an epiphany? What was an epiphany anyway? Had she ever had one before?

She was utterly undone. It was as if hundreds of butterflies fluttered around inside her. A few seconds went by, but the feeling didn't pass, and it prompted her to jump to her feet. Her fingers balled into tight fists. She threw her arms above her head and yelled, "I'm going to do this!"

Flying off the couch, her cats made a mad dash out of the room. At first, Spencer couldn't get a grip on the hardwood floor as he tried to flee. Sliding sideways, he ran in place for a second until he got enough traction then shot out of the room like a cannonball. Louisa laughed heartily. It was a good laugh—and a much-needed one—like the laughter she'd experienced the other night at her parents' house.

A wave of exhilaration rushed through her body. She ran over to her purse, pulled out her cell phone, and called her parents.

"Hello?" Her mother answered.

Louisa hesitated, then shrieked, "Mom, book me a ticket! I'm on board—take me back."

TRACK 2

"ROCKET" – MUD

MAY 2018

The weeks leading up to the trip to Belgium passed quickly. Louisa was still nervous about the flight, but her fear of getting on a plane was battling her anticipation of a new adventure in Antwerp—and the excitement was winning. She decided she might need more assistance than a stiff drink to board the plane—but she didn't want to take anything that required a prescription for her anxiety, so she went to a natural supplement shop a few days before flying out.

The store's shelves were packed with bottles of every color and shape. Baffled, Louisa muttered to herself, "Isn't there just something that says 'anti-aerophobia' on the label?"

A young man who appeared to be college-age and was dressed like he'd walked out of a Woodstock concert asked if she needed help. Louisa paused a moment and wasn't sure if he had addressed her as "man" or "ma'am." She proceeded to explain while she rocked side to side, fearing that she'd look foolish. She was surprised, though, when the young man bobbed his head up and down. "Yeah, dude," he said. "I know exactly what you need."

Louisa followed him as he scuffed down the aisle and rummaged through the packed shelves of merchandise. Did this hippy even have any shoes on below his long, flared indie-style pants? She leaned over curiously and caught a glimpse of his gnarly, long, hairy toes peeping out from underneath the frayed hem of his pants.

Soon enough the young man pulled out a small brown glass bottle with a dropper. "We call this 'yoga in a bottle,'" he said, handing her the vial. "Just one dose under your tongue every four hours, and you'll be at peace with the world, man."

He snickered nasally and all Louisa could think of was Sean Penn playing the perpetual stoner in *Fast Times at Ridgemont High*.

When she realized he had been addressing her as "man," her face brightened with relief. At her age, she would rather be called "man" than "ma'am" any day.

The night before the flight, Louisa tossed and turned in bed for hours. So many things ran through her head. What would it be like, going back to her old stomping grounds in Antwerp? She could hardly remember the four years she had spent there. It seemed like she'd already lived a lifetime since her family moved back to the States forty years ago.

Her mind wandered back to the wild days of her twenties—living a fun single life, blowing all of her money on summer trips to the shore and winters skiing. She had no savings, no care for tomorrow, and was loving it. In her thirties, she had married and was ready to settle down, take on responsibility.

Looking back, she realized she'd taken her role too seriously and let it alter the free-spirited, happy-go-lucky person she'd always been. She'd mapped out how she wanted her marriage and life to fall into place, all the way to her retirement years. Now that she was divorced, one of her biggest struggles was letting go of those plans.

Louisa had had a vivid picture of her future, and once it was gone, she was devastated. Her whole life's purpose was stripped from her and she was left naked and alone. All her friends and family were busy with their aspirational lives. Her mom was marketing her book, her sister getting married. She wanted some of what they had but couldn't find the motivated person she once was.

The days felt aimless, like she was wandering, searching for anything to restore her spark or sense of purpose. What did she want from the future now? She couldn't even see it.

Louisa rolled onto her back and stared at the ceiling. Her mind drifted back to her lost innocence living in Belgium when life was so much simpler. Those thoughts brought a warm, comforting feeling to her. Perhaps this trip would be a good distraction from her woes. She wasn't sure what the pivotal question was that would lead her out of this eternal funk she was in, but maybe she'd find the answer in the trip.

Eventually, she dozed off, exhausted from her contemplation.

Louisa and her family arrived at JFK in the late afternoon. She sat in the back seat of her father's car and watched plane after plane take off. Each one appeared so calm, silent, and peaceful as it lifted into the sky and disappeared. Louisa knew it was an entirely different experience inside the aircraft, though: the engine's loud noise, the adrenaline rush when the plane tipped its nose up to what felt like forty-five degrees, the sounds of carry-on luggage shifting in the overhead compartments.

Next, anxiety would follow as she'd wonder how the plane could possibly get airborne with all the people and their luggage inside. And why did the passengers always get so quiet during takeoff, as if it was D-Day and they were all about to jump into no-man's-land?

Once their suitcases were loaded on a cart, the ladies said goodbye to Louisa's dad and made their way to the check-in area. After passing through security, they continued toward their gate.

"Well, that was quick," Judy griped, looking at her watch. "We still have over two hours."

Louisa, on the other hand, had a complacent smile and was relieved they had so much time. She anxiously scanned the airport for a bar, in search of her liquid Xanax. Down the long corridor, she spotted a fluorescent art deco sign in the shape of a martini glass. "I'm going in for a drink while you two shop. I've got two hours to get a glow on; I'm going to start the process."

She bolted to the bar, hopped on a stool, and pulled the vial of "yoga in a bottle" out of her purse. After filling the dropper with liquid, she squeezed the droplets under her tongue. The taste was bland and did not seem to have any medicinal properties. Would it really do the trick? She figured these things usually had to taste nasty to be effective.

Nibbling at her thumbnail, she was getting ready to dose herself again with more droplets when a tall, dark bartender moved toward her, whose easy stride reminded her of a Jamaican man she had met once when she was on a cruise.

"Don't like to fly now, do you?" His baritone voice was gruff but warm. "I'll take care of you." The corners of his mouth curled upward like the Grinch as he smiled. "Just relax now. What is your pleasure? Do you want a pretty little pink drink with an umbrella in it?"

Frustrated, Louisa rolled her eyes and grumbled to herself. Did she look like she needed a girly drink? She needed a *man's* drink for this situation.

She leaned over the bar, glaring at the bartender intensely. "Listen here. I want a double Beefeater martini, straight up. I want extra olives, extra cold, and leave the extra dividend in the shaker here. And when the glass looks like it's near empty, bring me another one!"

The bartender stood back, clearly astounded by her request. He snapped her a sharp salute, then walked away to make her drink.

An hour later, Louisa's glow was beaming bright, and her worries mellowed when Judy and her mom showed up. "Where have you been?"

Judy rolled her eyes. "I lost Mom in the jewelry shops."

The bartender came over to ask them what they wanted to drink. Patty looked at Louisa, then at the drink in her hand. "I'll have a ditto," she said, pointing to the martini.

Judy grunted with a look of annoyance. "Just a water for me. Someone has to be the designated adult here and get us on the plane."

"One ditto, coming up," the bartender shouted as he walked away.

Time flew by, and it was time to board the plane. After two grand martinis and half a bottle of yoga juice, Louisa was satisfied the prescription she wrote for herself worked.

"Hey, sister," she called out to Judy as they made their way to the back of the plane. "I call the window seat!"

Judy smiled at her and patted her on the back as if to appease her.

Still, Louisa felt like she needed to rationalize her demand. "It's like this: I want to see how the pilot is driving. If he starts going too fast or hitting those speed bumps in the air, I'm gonna ask him to pull over."

As the three women settled into their seats, Louisa felt her phone vibrating in her purse. She pulled it out and saw it was her best friend, Donna, calling.

Already giggling when she answered, Louisa recalled a nickname she gave her friend in their college years. "It's Donna-do-you-wanna! Are you calling to wish me bon voyage? Or to read me my last rites?"

Donna had been Louisa's closest friend for three decades. They had gone through their roaring twenties together and stayed close after they both got married. Louisa depended on her company, and Donna was her lifeline when tedium got her down. Neither of them had children, so it was easy to act on a whim and go on an impulsive weekend getaway or a night on the town.

"Okay, Louisa," Donna asked her. "How much did you have to drink?"

Louisa thought about her answer for a moment. "Two Martians—I mean, martinis . . . I think."

Patty, who was sitting next to Louisa, leaned into the phone and shouted, "I had a ditto!"

Louisa pulled the phone closer to her mouth and lowered her voice to a whisper, her tone serious. "Donna, if the plane goes down and I don't make it, I already cleaned my bathroom and did my laundry. So you don't have to deal with any dirty undies when you're sorting out what I left behind in my hamper."

The plane made its first movement indicating they were preparing for take-off. Louisa finished her conversation with her friend. "Goodbye, bestie.

I'll call you when I get across the Pond." After turning off her phone, the reality started to sink in that they were taking off. Subtle waves of fear ran through her, pushing aside the numbness from the drinks and yoga juice.

The plane turned onto the runway, and the lights dimmed for take-off. She could almost hear the clashing cords of suspenseful music playing in her head. The aircraft picked up speed as the tension built, and Louisa squeezed her mom's hand tightly. She closed her eyes, taking a deep breath. *This was it. No going back now.*

As usual, the plane became intensely quiet. The only sound Louisa heard was the screaming engine as the plane rolled faster and faster down the runway. Everything was loud and chaotic for what seemed an eternity. Finally, when they were in the sky, the lights came back on, and everyone continued talking. It was business as usual.

Louisa looked out the window as the pilot banked the aircraft to the right. A beautiful view of the New York City skyline, silhouetted against the sunset's silky bursts of magenta. The plane headed out to the boundless Atlantic Ocean. Gradually, they ascended above the clouds, and a feeling of peace came over her. Breathing normally again, she bent over to get her bag out from under the seat and pulled out her copy of *Does Anybody Here Speak English?* It was time to finally start reading her mom's book.

She turned her head toward her mother, who was engrossed in a movie on the screen in front of her, and nudged her. "It begins, Mom."

Patty looked down at the book and smiled. "Have a good time with it."

A few chapters in, Louisa could no longer focus on reading. The excitement, anxiety, and stiff drinks had caught up with her. She peered out the window to the heavens and reminisced about her days living in Belgium. What she recalled was completely different from what her mother had shared in the book so far. The memoir was humorous, but it focused on the family's sophisticated cultural adventures, which she barely remembered.

Louisa chuckled to herself. If her mother only knew what she recollected about living in Antwerp. A foggy image of her and Judy sneaking into her parents' liquor cabinet in their house in Belgium, filling a tall glass with a pour from every bottle they could get their hands on, came to mind.

Nope, her parents should *definitely* never know about the reckless things she did when they were there.

She plugged her earbuds in and started the Mud playlist she'd made on her smartphone for the trip. The band's rowdy music blared in her ears—their big hit, "Rocket"—and it launched her mind back to those "reckless" days living abroad. The gentle, steady vibrations from the plane's engine lulled her as it took her across the ocean to her past. A heavy fatigue set in, and her eyes closed.

Louisa wondered what lay ahead of her on this trip. Would those outrageous adventures of her adolescence come back to her once she was in Belgium? And what about present day? What would Antwerp have in store for her now?

The book fell into her lap, and she fell into a deep sleep.

TRACK 3

"LONELY THIS CHRISTMAS" – MUD

OCTOBER 1974

I t was late afternoon on a mild fall day, and a splash of sunlight still lingered on the horizon. Twelve-year-old Louisa lay wriggling in a large pile of raked leaves on her front lawn at her family's Westchester County home. The crunching sound as she moved, and the leaves' sweet musky smell, had her bursting with anticipation for Halloween to arrive.

Louisa was a middle child and somewhat of a misfit. She was tiny for her age, and her long, straggly blond hair always had a golf-ball-sized knot at the nape of her neck that she never could manage to brush out. She certainly didn't have her sister Judy's looks or her brother Teddy's intelligence. Her only special skill was gymnastics—but even at that, there wasn't any future for the gold.

Born partially deaf, Louisa endured several surgeries over her childhood to correct it. She finally reached a normal hearing level at the age of ten. Because of this setback she was scholastically behind her peers, which meant her social life was very quiet. Not to mention her short attention span, making it almost impossible to have any meaningful aspirations.

Her eyes were fixed on a flock of birds perched in the birch tree above. She pondered on what she'd dress up as for Halloween. For two years in a row, she'd been the impetuous genie from the sitcom *I Dream of Jeannie* and was thinking it was time to throw away the headpiece and veil. Maybe, the ever-so-cool Fonzie from *Happy Days* would be her next fetish. But would that be too radical? She wasn't sure if her mom would allow it. Her thoughts shifted to Butterfingers—lots and lots of Butterfingers. It was her favorite candy bar, and the thought of a trick-or-treat bag full of them made her deliriously happy.

The low humming of an engine and the sound of tires rolling into the driveway broke her trance. Louisa's dad had arrived home from work. She watched as he exited the car and sauntered up the front path, his brown suede briefcase in hand. Lyle was a well-clad slim man, dressed in a formal fitted navy blue suit. His dark undertones were from the family's French side, and his thick, dark mustache was groomed almost to perfection.

Louisa suppressed a giggle. He hadn't noticed her in the pile of leaves when he passed her. He seemed preoccupied, and she heard him mumble. "Do I want to blurt it out when they won't expect it?" He halted in the walkway and raised his finger as if he had a good idea. "Maybe I'll be cute and place a waffle in a box with a red bow."

Before entering the house, he paused to gaze at the dusky sky. He inhaled a deep breath, went inside, and closed the front door.

Moments after, a loud, piercing shriek rang out from inside the house, causing the birds Louisa had observed to take off from the birch tree. She sprung up from the ground, flustered. Leaves were stuck to her hair and clothes as she ran into the house to see what the uproar was about.

Stepping into the foyer, Louisa found her mom screaming ecstatically, running room to room. "My prayers are finally going to be answered." Patty cheered. "I'm finally going to see the world. Wheee!"

What was happening? Louisa had never seen her in such hysteria before. Her eyes followed her mom running to the phone in the hall to make a call. Despite her mother's chaotic state, she still looked put-together. In Louisa's opinion, she had a classic *June Cleaver* look and was always impeccably dressed. Even on the days when she never left the house, her dark blond hair was perfectly styled into a comb-out after setting in pink sponge rollers overnight, and her frosted "strawberry forever" lipstick went on every morning right after her first cup of coffee.

Once the commotion settled down, Lyle summoned the kids into the living room and sat them down to explain the news. "Kids," he began, struggling with what would follow. His face went blank, followed by silence. Louisa knew that whenever her father was going to deliver news of any real importance, he had a hard time with his presentation. She eagerly moved to the edge of her seat, preparing herself.

Eventually, Lyle appeared satisfied with what he would say and raised his chin. "We're going to be moving to a place called Belgium in December."

Belgium? Louisa had never heard of it before. Was that in New York? And what was her mom's big deal about it anyway? They moved all the time.

Patty ran into the room and stood there for a moment, speechless. It appeared like she was going to say something. Instead, she turned, darted out, flailing her arms in the air, like she had won the New York lottery.

"Dad?" Louisa asked. "What's wrong with Mom?" He shrugged and turned his head back to them.

Teddy's reaction to the news was "Meh." He acted like the whole Belgium phenomenon had no real significance to him. It was just another place, right? Louisa's brother was ten years old and took after the family's Irish side in looks, with red hair and freckles. Like his father, Teddy had a quiet brilliance, and just by talking to him, you could tell he might someday be an engineer, just like his dad. Teddy spent most of his free time in his bedroom like a crazed scientist in his lab, always mixing up some experiment he'd read about in a science book.

Judy, the beauty, was the oldest and boldest at thirteen. She wore her silky dark brown hair down to her waist and spent all of her allowance money on fashion. Out of the three, she was the one who was hit the hardest by the news. At that point, she had her first steady boyfriend, which made moving the end of the world. She acted like she was leaving her future husband.

Of course, Louisa had seen her sister's interest in boys dating way back. When Judy was just ten, the family had gone on a cruise to the Caribbean. Judy developed a serious crush on the ship's elevator porter, who was from London. She would bring him candy bars every day and hang out in the elevator with him. On the day the LaPlantes finally disembarked, the young man came running off the ship to meet them at Customs. He gave Judy a flower and her first boy kiss on the lips to say goodbye.

It didn't take long for Judy to forget about her shipboard romance and return to her everyday life. A few months later, though, Louisa's father picked up the phone to hear the operator saying they had a call coming in from London. The elevator porter hadn't forgotten Judy. Since then, Louisa had seen her sister's relationships with boys give her parents more than a few premature gray hairs.

The next seven weeks were hectic as the family prepared to leave. Moving boxes were stacked throughout the house and hallways, making the whole scene look like a hoarder's house from hell.

Louisa was still not sold on the whole idea of this Belgium thing and continued to wonder why the news had put her mom into such a frenzy. Throughout the grueling work of packing, her mother had a perpetual grin, lifting heavy boxes like she was invincible. She kept chanting, "This is truly a labor of love."

One day, giving in to her curiosity, Louisa asked, "Mom, we already moved from Buffalo to Austin, to Chicago, then to Somers. What's the difference?"

Her mother took her by the hand and sat her on a packed box of books. "This one is different, honey," she explained, exhilaration radiating on her face. "It'll be like the first time you saw Disney World." With firm conviction, she vowed: "This experience will change your life forever. *Mark- my- words.*"

That night, as Louisa lay in bed, her mother's words echoed in her mind. Her enthusiasm always had a way of making everything magical. So Louisa started to welcome the idea. What did she have here? Nothing really.

With no popularity at school and only two friends, escaping her humdrum life in Westchester County sounded like a good plan. She even fantasized about the possibilities, marveling at what would be waiting for her when she got to Belgium that was supposed to "change her life forever".

Weeks before the move, Louisa's dad was on a mission to educate the family on their new world in Europe. Although he was running the show, even he needed to pay close attention and learn what they were studying—everything from locating Belgium on the world map and which countries surrounded it to which languages they'd hear there.

Arriving home from work one evening, he summoned the family into the kitchen as if he was a commanding drill sergeant. All three kids stood at the table, books under their arms at attention, looking like the von Trapp children ready for their daily inspection.

Patty wandered into the kitchen and stood in the doorway. That evening, though, she made a late appearance as a protest; the night before, Lyle had given her a hard time in class when she couldn't remember the capital of Luxembourg. So he'd made her sing "Frère Jacques" for five minutes straight.

Louisa's father glared down at them as they sat at the table. "If you did your homework and studied what the animals are called in French, like I instructed, then you should be able to handle this next exercise." He put the *Learn How to Speak French with Alfred* cassette into the recorder. "When I play the recording of the French word for each animal, I want you to make the sound of the animal you hear. Simple and fun, right?"

He pressed Play. In French, a woman's voice said, "*Le chien.*" He stopped the tape and pointed at Patty. Rolling her eyes, she brought her hands up to her chest, like she was a dog begging, "Roof-roof."

"Correct." Louisa's dad pressed Play on the tape recorder again. This time, a man's voice said, "*La vache.*"

He pointed to Teddy next, who hesitated. "Dad, he's saying cow; I know that. But how does a cow moo in French? You didn't teach me that yet."

Judy stood up, acting like she was the teacher. "Teddy, the French cow goes like this, *meuh*." Her upper lip curled upward as she demonstrated the noise. "That's how a cow moos in French. The emphasis is on the letter u."

The lesson continued for another hour until the kitchen sounded like Noah's Ark on the way to the French Riviera.

When the day came for the family to start their journey to a new world, it was Friday, December thirteenth—and coincidently, Patty's birthday. She wasn't going to let any silly superstition rain on her parade, though. All day long, she thanked Lyle for "the best present anyone could ask for."

They arrived at Kennedy Airport in the late afternoon and went through security. Afterward, Lyle guided them over to the lounge for the Belgian airline, Sabena, and he smiled at Patty. "Surprise! We're going first class, courtesy of Union Carbide. That means *free* champagne."

Patty looked flabbergasted and she kissed him on the cheek. "First I get to finally quench the wanderlust I've been building for years!" She looked at the kids, her hands clenched in prayer at her chest. "Now I get to wash it down with a glass of bubbly!"

Inside the lounge, funky-patterned contemporary art hung from the walls, and the furniture had clean, modern lines. A sign read, "No one under eighteen years of age at the bar." So the three kids were directed to sit by the window while their parents went to the bar to get their champagne.

Louisa trudged toward Judy, annoyed. "What's the big deal about this first-class thing if we can't even go to the bar?" She was trying to show off in front of her big sister, acting like she even knew what champagne tasted like.

To pass the time, Judy and Teddy started a game of I Spy. Louisa sat across from them, sprawled out on a bench and draped over her carry-on bag, watching one aircraft take off after another. She had never been on a plane before, let alone traveled to another country. And where was each airplane going anyway? They kept elusively disappearing into the sky.

Her attention dropped to the twenty-sided Christmas ornament made from greeting cards dangling from her finger. She had made it in art class before leaving school that day. Since it was the only festive decoration her family would have for the upcoming holiday, she was not taking any chances putting it in her carry-on bag and risking it getting crushed.

Louisa spun the ornament around on its green yarn hook and admired the rim's gold glitter. The rumbling roar of another plane taking off prompted her to look up again. As the aircraft ascended into the clouds, her fear and jitteriness kicked in. She'd soon be going up into the clouds and disappearing too. Fearful, she looked over at her parents for reassurance. They were at the bar, talking and laughing with another couple.

Watching her mom breezily having a good time without a care in the world soon put Louisa at ease and the alarm bells in her head stopped. There was always something soothing about her mother's laughter. It was like a warm blanket sheltering her from harm.

Glancing back at the ornament around her finger, Louisa wondered what Christmas would be like in this place called Belgium. Did they even celebrate the holiday there?

After boarding the Sabena aircraft in style, a first-class flight attendant was waiting for the family at the top of the ramp to escort them to the front of the plane. When they got to their row, Louisa eyed the window seat as if it had her name written all over it. That was her seat. She was sure of it. Judy apparently had her sights on it too. In a matter of seconds, the sisters started a commotion, squabbling over who would get to sit there. Eventually, Teddy stepped between them. "Here, I have a quarter. Heads or tails, Judy?"

He tossed the coin up in the air, and Judy yelled. "Tails!"

The quarter dropped to the plane's floor. Louisa shoved her sister aside and closed in to see the result. George Washington's profile was facing up—in her favor.

Feeling smug, Louisa scooched her way over to the window. She was in first class, had the best seat in the house, and beat her sister out. It was like she was on top of the world, and they hadn't even taken off yet.

Her self-satisfied air soon turned to terror, though, when the plane headed down the runway at full speed. Louisa's heart raced as she gaped out the window, petrified as the world sped faster and faster past her. She slammed her eyes shut to make it all go away.

Meanwhile, Judy and Teddy made a carousing clatter during takeoff, acting like they were on a roller coaster at an amusement park. Her brother kept giggling during their steep climb into the sky. Whenever the plane hit a bump of turbulence, he yelled "Neato!" in a shrilling tone.

Louisa didn't get their excitement at all. And what was up with the funny feeling as her stomach dropped during takeoff? She soon found herself envying her siblings. Why didn't they share the same horror she was experiencing?

Once the aircraft reached cruising altitude and the adrenaline rush was over, Louisa pried her eyes open and caught a glimpse of her frightened reflection in the portal glass. She stared obstinately at her dilated pupils and pale, trembling features. She knew then, this was one ride she did *not* want to get on again.

The following morning, the Sabena aircraft prepared to land at the airport in Brussels. The lights came on, waking the passengers, and the smell of fresh coffee filled the air as the food carts rolled out with a quick breakfast.

Louisa woke and saw the early morning dismal sky out her window. She squinted at her watch, which read 1:00 a.m. Confused, she counted on her fingers. Had she only been asleep for a few hours? And if it was one in the morning, why was it light outside?

"Don't worry about it," her father said. "I'll explain the time change later—once I've had my coffee."

After a smooth landing, the family made their way down the ramp and past the gate. Once they turned the corner, they were in the airport. Everything was dazzling, with festive strings of red and green lights blinking everywhere. Louisa could feel her excitement bubbling up when she saw Christmas trees lined up like soldiers down the corridor, as if they were saluting the travelers who had just arrived. Maybe her mom had been right; maybe the *whole country* was like Disney World.

She and Judy hit the bathrooms to freshen up from the long flight. When they returned to the terminal, Lyle stood with Teddy waiting—and Patty was nowhere to be seen.

After half an hour of searching, they found her in a small airport jewelry shop. Louisa watched as her father stormed inside and dragged her mother out as if she was a kid on the loose. Patty swung a small shopping bag from her hand, grinning from ear to ear. She pulled Louisa and Judy aside, reached into the bag, and whispered, "This is a starter." Hanging from her fingers were two sterling silver chain bracelets, each with a single charm of a Sabena airplane. Louisa had never had any *real* jewelry before and could almost feel her eyes sparkle like the trinket's radiant silver.

Once the family retrieved their luggage, they continued following the direction the crowd was headed, which eventually led them out of the terminal. Louisa glanced up at a green sign that read "Sortie." Another thrill rushed through her, and she jumped up and down, pointing at the sign. "I know what that means! It's the exit. This way, c'mon, c'mon! This French thing is going to be easier than I thought."

The LaPlantes made their way out of the airport and hopped onto a train. When they arrived at Antwerp's Grand Central Station—or the GSC, as the locals called it—Louisa was the first one to step off the locomotive and into the city she'd now call home. She stood silently on the platform, suitcase in hand, absorbing the ornate station and her intimidating surroundings.

The high vaulted ceiling was made of glass and iron, and straight ahead of her was a magnificent clock sitting on a noble foundation of gold as if time was royalty looking over its loyal subjects. She had never seen anything like it before. It was nothing like Westchester County.

Even the smell in the air was unusual as she inhaled deeply through her nose. A distinct scent of fried fish and sugary Belgian delights meshed with cigarette smoke in the cold, damp air. Her eyes shifted back and forth nervously at the sound of chitter-chatter in foreign languages that buzzed past her. Over the intercom, an unfamiliar, heart-rending tune called "Lonely This Christmas" echoed throughout the station. The melody carried a feeling of desolation from the dinging somber notes and added to Louisa's uncertainty.

The rest of the family joined her on the platform, standing in wonderment. Lyle looked down at them with raised eyebrows tugging on his earlobe. "Well, kids," he said, "I don't think we're in Kansas anymore."

TRACK 4

"TIGER FEET" – MUD

JANUARY 1975

A few weeks later, Louisa's dad loaded the family into their tiny rental car and drove them from the hotel in Antwerp to their new house in the quaint suburb of Schilde a few miles away. The day was typical Belgian weather, with a colorless sky and a fine cold drizzle making it hard to shake off the chill unless you took a long, hot soak in a tub afterward.

While driving through the town of Schilde, Louisa peered out the window, analyzing every element of the peculiar world they were in. The houses and other buildings were nothing like their American counterparts of man-made materials and vinyl siding. Everything was built of sturdy red brick or stucco. Amused, she giggled at the tiny cars parked along the curb reminding her of windup toys, their trunks seemingly the size of her lunch box.

They passed all the essential places, including a food market called the GB. The store marked the beginning of the downtown area of Schilde. Out in front stood several rows of bicycle racks for its patrons. Louisa had never seen this type of prime accommodation for cyclists back home. She soon realized that everywhere, people of all ages were cycling in the streets, taking care of their daily chores on bikes, even in the middle of winter. An elderly woman that could have been her great-grandmother vigorously pedaled away from the GB on her green cycle with a cart in tow filled with grocery bags. Her frail skinny legs pumped up and down as if she were fleeing a crime scene. On the opposite side was a distinguished businessman in a three-piece brown suit. He buoyantly rode his fire-engine-red bicycle with his briefcase strapped snugly on the back of the bike.

Continuing through the village, a small colorful novelty shop prompted Louisa to sit up straight. Its storefront had a variety of showy knickknacks on display: pink parasols hanging from the ceiling, dainty teapots with matching cups in a periwinkle flower pattern, and gift bags filled with soaps wrapped in pink cellophane and tied at the top with glittery purple bows. The entire display oozed with magical splendor, warming her all over.

That feeling disappeared quickly, though, as her face hollowed in alarm. The next shop could have been a scene from the horror TV show they watched back in the States called *Creature Features*. Dangling on hooks in the large window were freshly skinned carcasses of chickens and pigs. She couldn't even identify what the largest one was, whose ribs she swore were the size of an elephant. Nope. That was definitely not on her list of favorite things in Belgium.

Thankfully the bloody scene ended, and next on the agenda was a music shop and a café with more bike racks for patrons. A few men sat out in front, smoking cigarettes at a bistro table. They were chatting intensely— probably about the *voetbal* match. One man was not participating in the smoking, but with the cold air, it still looked like he was as he spoke to his friends. The misty fleeting cloud streamed out of his mouth with every movement of his jaw.

Why would he be out there suffering in the cold if he was not partaking in the smoker's club? To Louisa, it was weird. The raw winter weather didn't seem to bother the locals, between them cycling everywhere and joyfully shooting the breeze outside. It was like they thought it was a warm, sunny spring day.

A few blocks down, a towering, majestic church almost kissed the low clouds in the sky. Louisa's curiosity, though, was drawn across the street from the church, where a dilapidated white shack barely stood. A line of people with eager looks flowed into the street.

She looked over the entrance and the sign read "Frietkot." Struggling, she tried to pronounce the word but couldn't put together its phonetics. "What's a frar-a-taats-kot, Mom?" she asked, pointing to the sign.

"Kids, I read about this." Patty turned to them in the back seat. "These are frites stands, and they're one of Belgium's claims to fame."

Teddy let out a high-pitched cackle. "What a dump!" He pressed his nose to the window to get a closer look at the stand. "These frites shacks don't have a prayer to stand on."

Their mother's eyes flared. "Yes, Teddy, but these little huts of heaven make the best French fries you'll ever eat. You'll see."

Louisa studied the shack as the car slowly drove past it. What could be so different about these frites—or fries, or whatever they were called in Belgium? She usually shied away from what she didn't know, but her mom's enthusiasm was infectious, and she found the anticipation to try them brewing.

After touring the village, the family headed to their new home. A large stone square pillar sat on the corner of their street. On the side of the column was a gold plaque engraved with the name Bremboslaan. The street itself was quiet, located two blocks off the busy Turnhoutsebaan, which was the main road leading into Antwerp.

A grand Victorian cast-iron mailbox painted in hunter green greeted the LaPlantes at the entrance as they pulled into their driveway. Lyle turned the ignition off, and the family remained seated, intently examining their new home. The single-story, L-shaped, white stucco house was accented with dark brown shutters on the tall French windows. A long walkway from the driveway led up to the front door.

Patty was the first to hop out of the car wearing a purposeful look as she paraded back to the cast-iron mailbox and tried to hoist open the heavy iron top to retrieve the mail. "Lyle! We're going to have to do something about this, or I'm going to need a forklift to get the mail every day."

Once her dad opened the front door, Louisa zoomed under his arm and inside. She was on a quest to pick out her new bedroom. Entering the elegant formal foyer, her breath drew in at the sight of the lustrous marble floor and the chandelier embellished with teardrop crystals hanging overhead. In front of her was a long built-in coat closet and to the left a small guest bathroom.

Louisa looked both ways, unsure which way to head first. She finally decided to venture off to the right and found a set of doors that opened up into a large room that appeared to serve as the dining room, living room, and family room combined. The extensive living space was wallpapered with a busy moss-green floral pattern. Lined up across the front and back of the room were eight sets of French doors; the four in the back led out to the gardens, and the four on the opposite side looked out on the front lawn. The abundance of natural light gave the area a warm, cheerful atmosphere.

Backing out of the room, Louisa headed to a long hallway to the left of the foyer, where she discovered four bedrooms. After she opened the door to each of them, she picked the bedroom with pastel pink roses scattered throughout the wallpaper that had a girly feel. She stood silently imagining where all their things would go when the movers got there. The room was much smaller than what she had in the States. Or maybe it only seemed that way because there was no furniture. She scanned around for a closet and didn't see one but found the oddest thing next to the set of French doors: a sink. In the bedroom? Even funnier was the bidet in the bathroom that she discovered later. That posed many questions.

The first night in their new home was somewhat of a strange experience. After finishing her dinner, Louisa wandered away from the table as the rest of her family continued eating. Peeping out one of the living room's French doors, she was curious to see the new neighborhood in action. To her surprise, the neighbors across the street were out in front of their home theatrically running to close their shutters. The house next to them had metal coverings that motored down electrically from above over each window.

Further down the street the same devices covered the windows of a brick house and a large one lowered over the front door as well.

What was happening? It looked like Armageddon was coming to Bremboslaan. She backed away from the window, scrunching her brows. "Dad, are we going to have a hur-hur-hurricane?"

Her father chuckled. "No, they don't have hurricanes in this part of the world." He rose from the table, and the rest of the family followed to get a glimpse of the excitement. Teddy, who was on a Teenage Mutant Ninja Turtles kick, darted out of the living room, then ran back in moments later, dressed in his camouflage army costume from Halloween, a hard helmet, and goggles.

"Cowabunga!" he hooted, with a toothy grin and his fists raised in the air. "Don't fear—Teddy is here!"

The next evening after dinner, Louisa's dad dragged the entire family outside to join their neighbors in the evening ritual so they would look like locals. Everyone took one side of the house and closed the tall shutters on the French windows as if they were preparing for the storm of the century.

To adapt to their new life in Belgium, the family made many expected adjustments—and a few unexpected ones. Days after moving into their new home, Louisa's father came back from work in a foul mood. "Well," he announced to the family, "I just found out why we couldn't understand the locals for the last few weeks. Their language isn't French—it's Flemish!"

"What's a Flemish?" Louisa asked, tilting her head.

"It sounds like something you cough up," Teddy joked.

Their dad shook his head. "Flemish is a dialect of Dutch, which is *nothing* like French." He turned to leave the room and swung around, raising a finger. "It's going to be survival of the fittest from now on!"

Louisa and her family quickly learned that the English language wasn't commonly spoken in Belgium in the 1970s. This meant daily tasks like going to the market were a struggle, especially in the meat and dairy departments. Everything was labeled in a different language and had no pictures to help with interpreting. During the first week in their new house, Louisa's mom cooked a couple of steak meals, and the beef was so tough it was like gnawing on a dog's leathery chew treat.

One night, the family was gathered around the table like lab rats, waiting for their mystery meat dinner.

Patty waltzed out of the kitchen, as if she were Julia Child, with the main entree on a silver platter above her head, "Bon appetit everyone."

Louisa started eating her bite of steak as normal. Soon enough, her pace slowed, and her jaw locked—she couldn't chew anymore. The same look of distress was on her siblings faces. Desperate, Louisa surveyed the table for a place to dispose of her mouthful of meat. No way was it going down her chute.

The search seemed hopeless until finally she spotted the antique lamp on the dinner table's back end. Its base was a large cast-iron teapot. Her eyes landed on the teapot's open spout and she muttered, "Problem solved." That was going to be the drop site for her mom's disaster meal when her parents weren't looking.

The beef dilemma felt like it had consumed the whole family. It was all they could talk about. A few days later, Patty explained the situation over a cup of tea with Gail Marquette, who was from the French Quarter of New Orleans. The two women had met shortly after the LaPlantes arrived in Belgium, and Gail's husband worked with Lyle. She had become Patty's American mentor on the dos and don'ts of living in Belgium.

Louisa sat with her mom and Miss Gail, as this was how she asked to be addressed from the young ones. Her mother took a sip of tea then stormed off to the kitchen, grabbing the package out of the refrigerator, she handed it to Gail. "See? It looks like a nice steak, but you could play hockey with it!"

Curious about the outcome, Louisa's eyes were glued to Miss Gail as her mom's friend carefully read the label while shaking her head up and down. Seconds later, Gail erupted in a shriek of laughter. Struggling to gain her composure, she roared in her southern New Orleans twang, "Why, honey, that has the word *chevaline* written on it. That translates to 'horse'!"

"What?" Patty's nostrils flared and she crossed her arms over her chest. "Lyle never taught us the word for 'horse' in his French farm animal class. So he's to blame for this fiasco." She turned to Louisa, "Don't you be telling your brother or sister about this, or you'll have to deal with me!"

Louisa sunk into the chair with a small grin. Her disgust that she ate a horse was overcome by arousal. She loved it when she had a secret to keep. It always gave her a feeling of empowerment that she knew something others didn't.

Finally, the day came for the kids to start class. Lyle and Patty registered them at the Antwerp International School, known to the Americans as AIS. It was a multicultural English-speaking institution, but most of its students were from the United States.

The morning of their first day was dark and dismal. A heavy wind blasted through as Louisa climbed the steps with her mother, Judy, and Teddy to the noble-looking kastel administration building. Glancing around, Louisa examined the two other small buildings on the school campus, then up at the red brick mansion where they were headed. The wind whipped her long blonde hair around, and an eerie chill ran through her. Between the creepy weather and the old building, the whole scene felt like she was ascending the stairs to Bran Castle, where Count Dracula would be waiting for her.

In the weeks that followed, though, Louisa discovered the school wasn't scary at all, but rather exceptionally friendly and small. There were only 290 students all the way through from first to twelfth grade. This made the whole experience more intimate, like a family instead of an institution.

The first few months at AIS went by fast for the three LaPlante teens learning the ropes. They certainly had no problems making new friends. Since they were the new kids on the block, everyone eyed them as soon as they joined class like they were fresh inventory rolling in.

Teddy developed a friendship with a French student named David. In no time the two boys became almost glued at the hip. Judy, whose striking beauty turned heads wherever she went, made many friends—and boyfriends—fast. Louisa thought it was funny her sister had forgotten so quickly about the boy she'd thought she was going to marry back in Westchester County. In only two months, her sister became one of the most popular girls in her class. On the other hand, with only thirteen students in her grade, was that really something to boast about?

For Louisa, socializing with her classmates was easy. But ever since she was little, she would hide behind her big sister whenever they were together. She let Judy take the lead and speak for both of them, especially around people who were older than her or ones she didn't know. She wasn't shy, but she still hadn't developed a sense of self-assurance yet. And after moving to Belgium, given she was in unfamiliar and foreign surroundings, she hid behind her sister more than ever.

Penny Hallsworth was Louisa's first friend at school. Her father—a renowned heart surgeon—was from the United Kingdom, and her mother was from the States. On Louisa's first day of school, her teacher, Mrs. Grannis, introduced her to the class. Silence fell over the room of fifteen students eyeballing her as she stood on display by the chalkboard. The stillness in the air soon broke when Penny, who sat up front, boldly hopped out of her seat and marched up to Louisa inches away from her face. She raised her hand over Louisa's head and measured it to hers. They were the exact same size. Penny's smile widened with fulfillment. "Good," she uttered. "Now there are two of the shortest girls in the class."

Despite Louisa's friend having the confidence that she lacked, there was a resemblance between them. Both girls trained in gymnastics and had dirty long blond hair as well as tiny, petite builds. Whenever they were together, a certain pint-size, teenybopper cuteness radiated from them—or so Louisa thought.

One day, she was sitting at her school desk, eating her lunch, when she bit into her sandwich and nearly gagged on it. Her mother had cut a banana in half and put one half in the same plastic bag as her ham sandwich. So the sandwich, the chips, the cookies, everything for lunch tasted like a banana! Miffed, she ranted. *What's the matter with Mom? It's bad enough dinner is always a mystery. Couldn't she at least get lunch right?*

Penny walked over to Louisa's desk. "Louisa, are you and Judy coming to the school dance next Friday?"

Louisa leaned her head to one side. She had never been to a dance before. "My Uncle Jack taught me how to do the Alley Cat. Do they do that at the dance?"

Penny shrugged. "I don't know the Alley Cat. Is that like 'Tiger Feet'?"

Tiger Feet? Louisa was mystified. What was this "Tiger Feet" dance her friend was talking about?

"Don't worry." Penny giggled. "It'll be fun. You can be my date. Besides, you have to come so I'm not shrimp girl, all by myself."

The prospect of going to a dance intrigued Louisa. Maybe this would be her first real adventure in Belgium. She slid to the edge of her seat. "How does everyone dress?"

Penny gave her the once-over, as if Louisa had no fashion sense. "Ask your mom if you can come over next week before the dance. We can look in my closet for something you can wear."

Thrilled with delight, Louisa fantasized about going over to her friend's house and how the invitation would take their friendship to the next level. Maybe it would elevate her status with the other students when word got around she had gone to Penny's house. Could the day have finally arrived when she actually mattered? After all, Penny was the most popular girl in her class, and every girl wanted to be her. When Penny came to school with the new trendy bang flip, within weeks all of the girls were styling it with the coif. And when Penny came back after mid-winter break in the Canary Islands with bronzed skin and pierced ears, it didn't take long before the female classmates ran to the drug store for tanning cream and begged their moms to get their ears pierced.

After Louisa got home from school that day, she snuck into her parents' room to see if she could borrow anything that would help her stand out from the crowd at the dance. She wasn't sure what she was looking for—a necklace, makeup, perfume, anything. As she rummaged through her mom's drawers, she came across a box of "frost and tip" hair bleach. Her mom had purchased several kits in the States before the move to Belgium. Louisa raised her finger to her cheek. How daring would it be to go to her first dance in style—with blond streaks in her hair!

Her satisfied grin gleamed as she snatched one of the kits from the drawer. "I'll bring this to Penny's house next week," she said to herself. "She'll think I'm so cool."

A few days before the dance, Louisa's mom dropped her off at Penny's house. When the front door opened, a maid greeted her wearing a gray dress and a ruffled white apron. Louisa was in awe; she'd never known anyone before who had had a servant.

She walked into the foyer and was even more amazed at the enormous size of the house. It was decorated in old-world European charm, with a long sweeping staircase leading to six bedrooms. Two grand fireplaces in Italian marble with a lustrous sheen and swirly earth-tone veins stood out when she walked into the living room.

Louisa quickly became apprehensive. Looking around at all the extravagance and wealth, she wondered why Penny took a liking to her—at the end of the day, she was a nobody compared to her friend. What could she offer to someone who lived like this? How were they even in the same league? Then she started to worry that something was wrong with Penny. Perhaps her friends head wasn't screwed on straight.

Penny grabbed Louisa's hand and led her up the massive staircase. Her bedroom wasn't breathtaking like the rest of the house. Still, Louisa was impressed with the en suite bathroom, since she had to share one with Judy and Teddy.

Penny locked the door behind them. "Just in case my little brother wants to come in." She skipped over to her closet, which ran the whole length of one wall, and pulled outfits for Louisa to try on.

"So, Louisa, what do you think of Collin Wright from our class? Isn't he a fox?"

Louisa wasn't sure how to respond. A fox? Why was Penny calling Collin a fox? She didn't know what it meant or even how to respond. She stared vacantly at her friend for a second and realized the best thing was to go along with it and not look dumb. "Sure."

Changing the subject quickly, she pulled out her mother's "frost and tip" kit. She was eager to educate her friend on something for once, since she was so often the one who was being told about fashion trends. "This is what all the girls are doing in the States these days. See? Do you want blond streaks in your hair, like the lady on the front of the box?" Penny studied the packaging and then smiled in approval.

The two girls read the directions on how to mix up the bleach. Once the first step was complete, they agreed not to pull their long hair through the holes in the frosting cap, for even distribution, that would take too long and be too painful. Instead, they both took smatterings of the bleach mixture and applied it in globs to different areas of their hair. Once that step was done, they tied a plastic cap over their heads and waited.

Time seemed to drag as Louisa's anticipation built to see the finished results. Visions flashed in her mind of her mother's blonde-streaked hair, which sent thrilling tingles to the tips of her toes.

After a long half hour, it was back to the bathroom, where they washed their hair in the sink and wrapped towels around their heads like turbans to speed the drying process. While they waited, the girls rested on Penny's bed lying next to each other, admiring the blond-streaked hair of the woman on the front of the bleaching kit box.

Louisa sensed that her friend was impressed with her vast knowledge of salon products. Penny turned her head toward her. "Louisa, do you want to be my best frien—"

"Yes!" Louisa blurted out. She could hardly contain herself. She was best friends with the most popular girl in her class—a girl whose family had a maid and lived in an enormous house and who had a closet full of outfits from the finest stores in town she could borrow anytime. Who cared if Penny had picked her for her best friend because she didn't have her head screwed on right? She wasn't going to tell anyone.

Penny's focus returned to the lady on the box again. "It looks so beautiful!" she roared. "I can't wait any longer!" Jumping off the bed, she ran into the bathroom.

Louisa eagerly trailed her. "Okay, Penny. On the count of three, take off your towel. One . . . two . . . three!"

The girls whipped the towels from their heads. Louisa instantly gasped as a lump swelled in her throat. Large white and bright orange spots were scattered throughout her hair as if she were a Day-Glo leopard. She glanced over in the mirror at Penny, who had the same shocking results. Silence filled the room as the two teens stood next to each other with their hands cupped over their mouths.

Penny was the first to speak. "Cripes! What will my Mom say?"

When Louisa's mother arrived to pick her up later that day, she and Penny's mom agreed the girls would have to live with their mistake—which meant no trip to the beauty parlor to fix the mess they had created. That would be punishment enough for not asking for permission to color their hair.

Being the leader in fashion, though, Penny cleverly wore a designer bandana on her head to school the next day. The following day, half the girls in class hopped onboard the headscarf fad. After all, Penny the fashion maven had spoken: head scarves were now the "in" thing.

Finally, it was the night of the dance. Louisa sat on the bed in Judy's room carefully studying how her sister prepared herself for the big event. She noted every detail, from the way her sister applied her makeup to the finishing touch: a spritz of Cachet perfume. Once Judy appeared pleased with her look, Louisa took off to her room and copied everything her sister had done. When she finished her own makeover, she glared in the mirror above the sink. "*Stome*," she muttered.

Stome was a Flemish word that meant "stupid," and one of only three words Louisa knew of the local language—the other two were curse words. She grabbed her hot pink hairbrush, which she hadn't cleaned in months and looked like a sheep in need of a shave. Brushing her speckled hair to the other side, she hoped it wouldn't look as drastic but soon realized it was no use. Letting out an exasperated sigh, she dropped her hands to her side, still sneering into the mirror. *Good grief.* Going to her first dance, at her new school, in her new life, looking like the bride of Frankenstein was not what she had fantasized it to be like.

When it was time to leave Louisa stood in the doorway of the foyer, with slouched shoulders, and a down-turned smile, dressed in Penny's fitted plaid teal pantsuit. Judy, on the other hand, blissfully twirled around in the center of the room, showing off her low-rise flared seersucker pants and a yellow button-up blouse. But it was her sister's flawless sleek hair bouncing and swaying as if she was in a shampoo commercial, that had Louisa bolting out of the room in one last attempt to not look like a freak show.

She returned with her mothers' silk, art-deco print, Hermès Carré scarf wrapped around her head and a look of confidence. Why hadn't she thought of that earlier? That Penny really knows what she is doing.

The girls arrived fashionably late at AIS, where the dance was being held. Louisa inspected the empty halls when they came through the doors and realized everyone else must already be in the gym, so she and Judy walked through the lobby and headed down the long hallway to the auditorium.

From behind the gym's closed doors, Louisa could hear the muffled music and the heavy thumping of drums. The pounding grew louder and more intense as she drew closer. Her blood pulsed as a sense of dread took over. Something dawned on her that she had not thought about before. Would she know how to act at a social event that boys were at? What if one asked her to dance? She was *definitely* not ready for that.

Biting down on the inside of her cheek, she slinked behind her sister, grabbing onto the back of her coat. The locker-lined hallway made her feel like she was walking down the magisterial corridor leading to the great and powerful Oz. All she wanted to do was bail out like the Cowardly Lion and jump through a side window.

Once they reached the end of the hallway, Judy turned to her. "Come hither, sister." Her nose tilted up. "Let's do this!" And with a forceful thrust, Judy flung the gym doors wide open.

Louisa froze in place. Inside the auditorium, the students were all on their feet, exuberantly dancing in unison to the song the DJ was playing. With their hands rolled into firm fists, her classmates chopped their arms up and down freely while jutting out their buttocks. This was followed by a gliding box step. Next, they shook their legs in an iconic Elvis "rubber legs" dance move.

Some were on the bleachers; others were on the stage. Some even danced on the refreshment stand. They were oscillating in such a hearty manner, it was as if the dance were outlawed and the gym was some secret basement speakeasy where they could cut loose to the music.

The scene was sheer pandemonium—but Louisa soon realized her amazement was not so much at her classmates, but the music they were dancing to. The explosive sound coming from the speakers was like a wild electrical storm blowing in. She could practically see sparks flying around the room as a hard, bouncing bassline filled the gym and the singer playfully sang out the lyrics. She soon realized the song was "Tiger Feet," the one Penny had talked about the week before.

A broad smile stretched across Louisa's face. What was this extraordinary sound the DJ was playing? She didn't know music could be like this. If she could taste the melody, it would be a mouthful of fizzy pop-rock candies followed by a couple of atomic fireballs.

Standing motionless, she could feel the effervescent rhythm sending jolts to every nerve ending in her body. It was at this point, Louisa was certain, she had stumbled upon something that was going to be massive in her life.

TRACK 5

"HELL RAISER" – THE SWEET

MAY 1975

Louisa sat with her mother at the kitchen table, still in a tizzy over the dance the night before. "Mom, I never heard music like that before! It was so different from our slow stuff in the States," she raved. "It's funny and fast and . . ." Her face went vacant briefly, searching for the right word. "So wild. That's what it was." She took a deep breath. "Yup, I'm gonna save up all my allowance and buy lots and lots of it."

Louisa fell silent, after she caught a glimpse of her mom raising her eyebrows at her. She knew her mother had always been overprotective of her, given her hearing disability earlier in life. She didn't want her thinking she had developed a new impairment with her mania for this music. What kind of surgery would that require?

Weeks after the excitement of Louisa's first dance, Teddy invited his AIS buddy, David, over to the house. It was a leisurely Saturday afternoon when his classmate arrived at the front door with a bouquet of yellow tulips and politely introduced himself to Patty and gave her the flowers. David was a tall boy for his age, with thick, curly dark hair mounding on top of his head, adding another five inches to his height. Louisa was always baffled by her brother's friend; sometimes he would act the way teens his age did, yet he was also like an adult at times and extraordinarily intelligent.

He seemed to enjoy conversations with grown-ups and would gravitate toward adults if they were in the room. At AIS, he could always be found in long, deep conversations with the teachers during recess instead of playing with his friends. Louisa could never understand why anyone would want to speak with an adult, other than their parents, unless they had to.

While the boys made themselves scarce, the sisters sat in the living room with their mother, who was explaining her plan for them for the day. Patty had proclaimed after they moved to Belgium, the three of them—only the girls—would have a monthly outing together.

"Well, I want to take you girls on a surprise afternoon today," she said. "It's a concert. It'll be just like the *American Top 40* that you used to listen to in the States. Afterward, we can stop at that music shop that you wanted to go to in town, Louisa, and get your Dirt album."

Crinkling her nose, Louisa wondered. The Dirt album? What was her mom talking about? Eventually it registered, and she jumped off the couch, riled up. "It's *Mud*, Mom. Not Dirt!"

Judy, who teased Louisa all the time about her obsession with Mud, rose from the couch too and mocked her by singing one of the band's song "Hypnosis." She gestured in a creepy back-and-forth wave, like she was casting a spell, and chanted the lyrics in a cackling, witch-like voice.

While Judy harassed her, David came out of the guest bathroom in the foyer and walked into the living room, watching her sing. "Hey, that's Mud!" he exclaimed as he stood in the doorway, interrupting Judy. "I love them. They were just on *TopPop* the other night."

That sparked Louisa's curiosity. She whipped her head around to face him. "*TopPop*?"

David bounded over to the couch and sat with them. "Yes. AVRO's *TopPop*. The show is on every Tuesday night. They do the top twenty songs in the Nederland each week. That's the Netherlands' hits parade."

For the next ten minutes, Louisa grilled David about the show. "What bands?" she asked "What channel? What time?" Her heart pumped rapidly—she needed to know everything.

Later that day, Louisa and her sister discovered their mother's idea of a "surprise afternoon," which was nothing like the *American Top 40*. The concert she took them to turned out to be a sixteenth-century Baroque symphony at the Rubens House Museum. After more than two grueling hours, Louisa climbed into the back seat of their car in a huff, followed by Judy. It was clear no one wanted to sit up front with their mother after the stunt she pulled.

Judy leaned over to whisper in Louisa's ear. "So much for Mom's girls' day outing. I almost died in there. Well, at least there was a foxy violin player to look at."

When they arrived back in Schilde, their mom parked the car on the side of Turnhoutsebaan, which was also Schilde's main street. Patty walked to the GB Foods a few blocks away, while the girls ventured up the street to get Louisa's album.

Passing the town's establishments, the girls approached the butcher shop with the dangling horror show display in the window of various meat products. Louisa paused when she came upon the gory scene, her mouth filling with saliva. She was going to have to do something about this. The world was clearly not big enough for the two of them. Grabbing her sister's hand, she yanked Judy swiftly past the shop to their destination.

Upon entering the music store, they were greeted by sinister screaming and a piercing electric guitar riff, blaring through the sound system: a rock anthem called "Hell Raiser."

Louisa's eyes feasted on every detail of the room. To the left of the front door was the checkout counter made from dark oak wood. Straight ahead of her were several rows of long tables with bins on top, full of albums. Hanging on the walls, gold and silver glitter almost jumped out of posters displaying rock and roll bands with long, wild hair and tough-boy smugness. In the back of the store a small candy section was tucked away.

As Louisa followed closely behind Judy, she felt the hair on her arms stand up from the sharp buzzy music. It was the same heavenly high she'd had at the dance when she heard Mud for the first time. Her head bounced freely as she became engrossed by the powerful sound of 'Hell Raiser'. "After two hours of *moms* 'greatest hits' of the sixteenth century, this song is my reward," she joked to Judy.

After they'd been strolling around the store for a while, Louisa tugged on the back of her sister's coat. "Can you ask someone to find me the record *Mud Rock*?"

Judy snarled. "No, you do it."

"But they don't even speak English. How am I supposed to ask?"

Crossing her arms, Judy angrily stared down at her. "Figure it out, little sister. Don't be such a pest."

Louisa continued badgering her sister, and their quarreling grew louder.

Eventually the store's owner, a man in his fifties with messy dark hair and black-rimmed Coke-bottle glasses, hastily moved toward them. "Ja, can I help you?" he asked.

Judy stepped aside, leaving Louisa to ask for help. The store became deathly still. The other patrons stopped what they were doing, and all eyes were on Louisa. She hesitated as nausea surged through her.

Finally, shaking like the faint-hearted Oliver Twist asking for more porridge, she stuttered, "Please, sir, do you have Mud?"

The owner scratched his head. "Mud? What is this Mud?" His accent was so thick and heavy that Louisa wasn't sure how to respond. His Ws sounded like Vs, and the way he said the word "this" made it sound like it began with the letter D and had a few hard Ss.

She opened her mouth to respond when someone tapped her on the shoulder from behind. Turning around, she found a young man about her age with shoulder-length sandy hair and a radiant face, holding a copy of the album *Mud Rock*. The boy smiled, revealing a dimple on his left cheek.

Louisa stepped back, mesmerized. As their eyes met, a maddening electricity crackled inside her. Never feeling an emotion like this before, she marveled. Could this be what that "fox" thing was all about?

She continued to gape at him and soon realized he stared back at her with the same dazed expression.

"Ah, Mathis, good boy." The store owner struggled with the letter G so much that it sounded like a K. "You found it." He looked at Louisa and Judy, then nodded toward the young man. "This is my son."

Mathis's father waved his hand in front of his son's eyes which were still locked on Louisa and laughed. "My son does not speak Engels."

The shop door swung open, and Patty entered with a few bags of groceries in her arms. "There you are," she hollered. "You were supposed to meet back at the car in five minutes. Are you two ready to go home?"

Louisa jolted out of her delirious state turning away from Mathis. "Mom, I found my album. I just have to pay."

She took the record to the front counter and pulled out her little change purse, which contained her life savings. Mathis followed her and helped ring up her purchase. The whole time, Louisa watched his every move.

Meanwhile, Patty fell deep into conversation with Mathis's father about a piece of classical music by the French composer Saint-Saëns. The store owner was clearly smitten with her. He introduced himself to Louisa and Judy as Mr. Janssens but told their mom to call him Maarten. He even took the shopping bags from her arms and carried them out to the car.

As they exited the store, Louisa glanced back through the window and saw Mathis watching her the whole time as she disappeared down the street.

That evening, Louisa climbed into bed and gazed at her fiber optic waterfall night light with happy thoughts bouncing around in her head. She was thrilled over her new Mud album and the discovery of the music shop. The store was like her own little rock and roll playground. The musty smell of old collectors' albums behind the register and the edgy glam rock atmosphere came back to her as she lay making her giddy inside.

Then her mind wandered to Mathis. She could still picture his face through the music store window. Smiling coyly, her anticipation for the next Mud album took on an added importance.

TRACK 6

"CHERIE AMOUR" –
THE RUBETTES

LATE FALL 1975

Louisa's fascination with Mud intensified through the months. Most evenings, she'd retire early and lie on her bed, spinning the album over and over again while fantasizing about the band. Her make-believe encounters with the group were a little far-fetched, but she couldn't help herself. One of her favorites was of her sitting in class at AIS and the four members of Mud appearing unexpectedly at the door, clad in coordinating light blue suits with glittery silver lapels, waiting to take her on tour with them.

Another part of her Euro glam rock education was when Tuesday nights arrived. She would religiously sit on the floor in front of the TV, watching *TopPop* and taking notes on everything about Mud and similar bands she discovered. Most of her allowance, birthday, and babysitting money was spent on teen magazines. Some were in Dutch, so she'd stare at the photos for hours, idolizing the bands without understanding the articles.

Meanwhile, Judy was on a persistent quest to meet European boys. She had been practicing Flemish and French, since both languages were spoken in Belgium, depending on which region you were in. She told Louisa one day cheekily, "I want to cover all my bases for my future romances."

Teddy, however, was a mystery. It wasn't clear to Louisa if he'd picked up any new crazes. But he was spending more time in his bedroom than he ever did in the States, trying to create his next big invention. Probably homemade stink bombs.

Louisa's dad was too smart to take on any silly obsessions, so he remained the same stable person he'd always been. Louisa figured somebody had to be the sane one in the family. Patty's wanderlust, on the other hand, was compelling her to see as much of Europe as possible. For weeks, she'd been bugging Lyle to take her to the Rijksmuseum in Amsterdam. He finally gave in one Saturday morning that fall and told the family to prepare for a day trip to Europe's "Sin City."

After a two-hour drive, they arrived in the city of Amsterdam. The mood in the car grew tense as Louisa's dad became irate about maneuvering their brand-new blue Peugeot wagon around the busy streets. Adding to the tension, her parents started a shouting match about where to park.

Eventually, though, they found a place to leave the car, and things became pleasant as the family walked around the Netherlands capital town. Louisa found herself in dreamland at the leaf canopy along the tree-lined canals. She imagined the giant parasol effect was a mystical tunnel. Yet it was the quirky, narrow brick houses nestled up against one another and how they edged the cobblestone streets that had her pretending she was walking through a real-life fairy-tale book.

Once they had strolled several scenic blocks, the family arrived at the Rijksmuseum. Glancing up at the massive arched entrance, Louisa quickly became reluctant. Did she really want to spend the entire afternoon in a stuffy old place full of boring paintings and sculptures? The streets of Amsterdam seemed much more appealing and exciting, and she wanted to do some more fairy-tale fantasizing.

Her sister apparently had the same thoughts. "Dad, the tickets are so expensive. Think of the money you'll save if Louisa and I don't go in," Judy begged. "We'll wait over on the benches. We won't even move."

Lyle deliberated for a few moments. Louisa knew when it came to spending money, he was always trying to save a penny or two. Even on the long car trip there, he made all three teens split *one* can of soda.

"Okay," her father gave in. "But I want you to stay close to the museum."

Their parents and Teddy disappeared through the entrance, while the girls walked across the street and settled on a bench to people-watch. Louisa felt like she had her own little museum in front of her, or maybe it was more like a circus. Either way, Amsterdam was loaded with all kinds of entertaining, colorful, artistic people who kept her head turning like she was watching a tennis match as they passed her.

Once the show grew old, the girls started a conversation about boys. "Judy, the other day, some kids pushed me into the gym, and they held the doors shut so I couldn't get out. No one but Kevin was in there." Louisa lowered her head into her hands, distressed. "I had to talk to him. It was horrible."

Kevin was a student in Louisa's class. The rumor was he had a crush on her and wanted to ask her to go steady with him. Louisa had avoided him for weeks. She was frightened to death of being anyone's girlfriend. Even the thought of it made her uneasy. That was one of the reasons why she liked seeing Mathis at the record store: she didn't have to talk with him about going steady; she didn't even have to talk to him at all, given he didn't speak English. It was so much easier to glance at him, get her thrills, and go on her merry way without interacting, holding hands, or doing any of that gross stuff.

Judy explained her own dilemma about an American boy she was going steady with. "He's such a fox, Louisa, but I really want to meet a European. I love their accents. Anyone would do, tu sais?"

While Louisa continued chatting with Judy, she noticed out of the corner of her eye a cyclist had ridden up and hopped off their bike a few feet from them. Louisa sensed the cyclist's presence to her right, but she kept looking at her sister, listening to her boy dilemma. After a few minutes passed, she realized the cyclist was lurking and moving in closer to them. Finally, she turned her head to see who it was.

To her horror, an elderly man was making a spectacle of himself, opening his long gray trench coat for her and Judy—with *nothing* at all on underneath. His skin was weathered and wrinkled. Long, wiry white hairs on his legs and chest seemed to stand out twelve inches. He had an empty look in his eyes as he stood teetering.

The only thing Louisa could compare this to was the Winter Warlock from the movie *Santa Claus Is Comin' to Town*; but in this movie, he was in a trench coat with nothing on underneath. She felt on the verge of a panic attack, nearly paralyzed with fear.

Meanwhile, Judy was still going on and on about her boy problems, oblivious to the scene in front of her. Louisa nudged her hard in the arm, and her sister turned to the man. Judy's eyes practically rolled right out of her head. She grabbed Louisa's hand, and they ran as fast as they could, screaming like banshees. Once they reached the Rijksmuseum's entrance, both girls were out of breath.

"That was disgusting," Louisa cried. "Is that what old people look like under their clothes?" Her head dropped as she flinched from the image that kept replaying in her head.

Louisa never told her mother and father about the events of that day. It always seemed that whenever something went wrong, it was somehow her or Judy's fault, and this was one situation she didn't want to be accused of provoking.

As the months passed, everyday tasks brought more life lessons and culture clashes for Louisa. However, it was the 1970s, and she witnessed the entire world being swept up in a big, noisy shared moment since she had moved to Antwerp. Television and radio had brought everyone together like never before. Something could become popular back in the US and make its way to Europe almost overnight. Because of that shared pop culture, life for her in Belgium could be similar to life in the States at times. But as a nationality,

Louisa found it easy to distinguish between Americans and Europeans in a crowd, just by their appearance. She soon developed a talent for spotting families from her homeland anywhere they went in Europe.

American moms were typically chic, with pixie-shag hairstyles and Sears jumper dresses. Dads often had thick sideburns, mustaches, wearing the latest polyester leisure suit. Teens were the easiest to pick out. The boys kept their hair on the unruly side and wore fitted sweater vests, Sears Toughskins jeans, with white leather belts wrapped around their waist. The girls parted their long straight tresses down the middle and could often be found in football jerseys, elephant bellbottom jeans, and caramel-colored Earth Shoes. The popular shoe had a thick sole in the front and a thin heel.

Another difference between the two cultures Louisa discovered was puzzling—and the locals were oblivious to—was the necessity for telephones. Ever since the family moved to Schilde, her parents had been trying to get the service company to install a telephone line at their house. Every month, Lyle called, but the company always replied, "Ja, ja, we will be there in a few weeks." But they were never there a few weeks later—or even a few months later. Almost a year had passed and still no phone.

Apparently, it was something of a shared running joke among the American families living in Antwerp: nobody got their phone installed until they did their time. It was almost a form of initiation for newcomers, and now it was Louisa and her family's turn to pay their dues. But as the months passed, Patty insisted Lyle get a line of communication for the house so her loneliness during the day, while he was at work and the kids were at school, wouldn't drive her crazy.

One evening after work, Louisa's dad told the family that one of his American coworkers went through the same "initiation" a few years back. He suggested they get a car phone. "And instead of installing it in the car, we can have it installed in the house," Lyle said, turning to Patty. "Will that pacify you?"

The next day, the communication lines were open, and the LaPlantes were connected to the outside world. However, the process of making a call wasn't easy. Once they picked up the receiver, they had to dial the operator in Brussels—who spoke *only* French—and provide the phone number they wanted to reach. Louisa attempted the process once to call Penny Hallsworth. But the minute the French-speaking male operator said, "Oui, bonsoir," she panicked and hung up. And this was supposed to be progress?

It seemed to be a breeze for Judy, however, since it allowed her to practice the French she was studying in school. After months of talking mostly to male operators so she could call her classmates, Judy developed an "acquaintance" with one specific operator named François. Soon enough, he was calling the house, asking for Judy.

Every afternoon when they walked through the front door after school, Louisa watched her sister dash to the family room where the car phone sat on a hutch, to practice her French with the male operator. One evening, though, the phone rang during dinner. Lyle picked it up. "Hello." Silence filled the room and his pupils dilated into large black endless holes. He shouted into the phone, "Non!" and slammed the handset down. He turned to Judy, who sat at the dinner table. "Who's François?" he demanded. "Why is he asking for you?"

Sinking into her chair, Judy wore a sneaky smirk.

Lyle shook his head. "Never mind. I don't want to know."

The day the phone company finally arrived to install the LaPlantes' "real" telephone line was a happy time for the family—except for one person, of course. Still, Judy was determined to meet a French beau despite their father's interference. She told Louisa one day, "I don't know why, but I have strong feelings about the je ne sais quoi of the French culture." It was then, Louisa detected a determined look in Judy and suspected her quest would eventually lead to some kind of a "la catastrophe."

Life in the LaPlante household finally became free from chaos. All was well in her world one afternoon when Louisa arrived home from school, skipping through the front door. The glorious *bree-breeing* of a real telephone sounded making her smile, in hopes it was Penny calling. She headed over to the hall desk to answer the call, only to watch her mom whiz past her and beat her to it. The whole family had become so thrilled with having a real line of communication, it was like a steeplechase every time it rang.

Patty picked up the call. "Hello." It was silent for a moment as she listened then she shrieked, "What?" The handset fell out of her hand and dropped to the floor, and she ran toward the kitchen in a frenzy. Louisa, startled by her mom's outburst, followed her to see what the mayhem was about. "Your father is to entertain Union Carbide's director of North American sales!" she cried out. "The bigwig and his wife are visiting from the States, and he is bringing them here—in *one* hour! He instructed we'd have drinks and appetizers here, then go out to dinner." She frantically pulled food from the fridge to make hors d'oeuvres. "I don't have enough time to pull this together. Something's gonna go wrong. I feel it in my bones."

Seeing her mother's stress, Louisa wrapped her arms around her mom's middle and squeezed her tight. "It'll be okay, Mom. I'll help."

"Your father is never going to hear the end of it for this fast one."

Promptly an hour later, the front door opened, and the Union Carbide top executive and his wife walked through with Louisa's dad. The prideful way the couple carried themselves seemingly put Patty on edge. When Lyle made the families' introductions, Louisa handed the executive's wife a small bouquet of azaleas she had picked from their backyard, and the woman gave her a look as if she had handed her a bunch of dried-up weeds. Judy, on the other hand, proceeded to show off in front of the persnickety couple, speaking in French. "Je m'appelle Ju-dee." The executive and his wife each shook her hand, appearing impressed but still holding their disdainful composure.

Once the small talk was over, Judy was the first to exit. She sashayed out of the room, waving goodbye to the couple, "Au revoir. I'm going to go *douche* myself now. Nice meeting you."

A loud abrupt gasp erupted from Patty like she was choking on her saliva. The room fell silent, and all four adults stood with their mouths hanging wide open. *What was going on?* Louisa wondered. What had her sister said that made her mom choke like that? In her opinion, Judy's graceful display of the French culture was brilliant.

The next day, all was revealed when their mother educated the sisters on what the shocking scene from the night before was all about. Apparently in French, the word douche only meant "shower." But as for Americans, the term had an entirely different meaning and usage—one both girls were oblivious to.

It took Louisa's parents a long time to recover from their embarrassment over Judy's misuse of the French language. Eventually they appeared at ease and it was safe to bring her out in public again. Lyle accepted an invitation from one of his colleagues, Jan Verstraete. He and his wife, Noelle, were native Belgians and invited the LaPlantes to their house for a small get-together.

Upon the family's arrival at the Verstraetes' home, Jan greeted them at the door. "Welkom," he said in a bouncy tone. His eager-to-please smile extended from ear to ear.

Louisa was charmed by him, even though he was a stranger to her. She found his warm, loveable air made her want to run up and wrap her arms around him as if he were a fluffy teddy bear.

The two Verstraete children came down to meet the family moments later. Anneke and Harry, who were both in their mid-teens, were formal and polite as they introduced themselves to Louisa's parents. They were fluent in English, but their accents were thick, and their word choices didn't always make sense. Yet they conversed with the adults in a sophisticated way, showing off their intellect and maturity. This made Louisa feel less significant. In her mind, she and her siblings appeared like toddlers next to the two astute Belgian teens.

While Anneke struggled with what she wanted to say in English to her mom, Louisa studied the Belgian girl. She wore her black hair wavy at shoulder-length. She had thick dark-rimmed glasses that immediately reminded Louisa of the brainy Velma Dinkley from *Scooby-Doo*.

"Mees LaPlante, please let me take your coat to the closet," Anneke's eyes shifted back and forth in an overly cautious way as she spoke.

To Louisa, she seemed way too responsible for a teen. Harry, on the other hand, was quiet and kept to himself. He had neatly groomed dark hair, a short physique, and muscular legs, perfect for soccer. He seemed disinterested in the American teens, like he had better things to do with his time than entertain the kiddies.

After the introductions were made, all the teens went up to Anneke's bedroom. As they entered, Louisa could not believe how everything was orderly, spotless, and staged perfectly. The bed was meticulously made. Not one article of clothing was on the floor or draped across a chair. No messes were shoved under the bed. Was this really a teenager's room? It looked like a guest room that no one ever slept in. Louisa wanted to find something that would tell her more about the girl, but what was in front of her was a big mystery.

She continued searching for something when her quest ended abruptly. Anneke and Harry stood at the far end of the room studying her and her siblings as if they were a biological rarity. Looks were exchanged in an intense stare-down between all of them. As the tension built, Louisa could almost hear the familiar two-note melody of a flute resembling a coyote, whistle in her head. *Was this what a Mexican standoff felt like?*

She couldn't take it any longer; it was downright creepy. At last she averted her gaze, and spotted Anneke's record collection in the corner of the room. Hints of a smile in the corner of her mouth signaled her excitement. She had finally found the camaraderie she was looking for with the Belgian girl over their love of music.

Wandering over to the collection, Louisa pulled an album out to play. Anneke darted over and was right under her nose. "You need to be very careful holding the music so you don't get any damages," she said condescendingly.

Louisa stared starkly at her. This girl had *definitely* never been yelled at by her parents.

Later, the afternoon turned into a smorgasbord when the Verstraetes served food in the living room. Mrs. Verstraete had prepared several courses of Belgian delights for the LaPlantes.

First came stoemps: a dish filled with mashed potatoes, vegetables, and bacon. Next, they brought out steak tartare, the classic raw beef—which Louisa stayed clear of, and so did the rest of the teens. Vol-au-vent, bite-size pastries with creamy chicken inside followed. In between the feedings that came out of the kitchen, the Verstraetes had an array of snacks and Belgian-style dips elegantly displayed on the coffee table.

Louisa hadn't seen so much food since the holidays at her grandparents' house. Did the Verstraetes eat like this every day? Maybe that's why the Belgians bicycled everywhere—to work off their daily Thanksgiving dinners.

As the time approached 8:00 p.m., Louisa was so stuffed she wasn't sure she could walk out the door. She saw the same overindulgent expression on her parents' faces. Her dad even struggled to stand up out of his chair to signal it was time to go home. He trudged over to the closet, grabbed his coat, and thanked the Verstraetes for a lovely evening.

Jan sprang from the couch, his eyes lit up like an overworked pinball machine. "What, Lyle?" he exclaimed. "What are you doing? We haven't had the main course yet. Sit down."

When the LaPlantes eventually returned home that evening, Louisa thought she was ready for a stretcher and maybe some medical assistance. She didn't want to eat ever again. While she lay on her bed—on her back, because it hurt to lay on her full stomach—she was surprisingly intrigued by the prospect of having a Belgian friend. She and Anneke liked the same bands, which was the most important thing. Having a straitlaced friend like the Belgian girl might also help her stay out of trouble.

Of course, she knew she wouldn't want that all the time. She needed to live life on the edge as well. But there was something more to Anneke than she was letting on. Louisa couldn't put her finger on it, but there was something about the way she cast her wary eyes around all the time that said she was hiding something—and Louisa was determined to find out what it was.

TRACK 7

"FUNNY, FUNNY" – THE SWEET

DECEMBER 1975

The holidays were fast approaching. The local American Women's Club organized a trip to the festive Christmas market in Nuremberg, Germany, and Louisa and her family were signed up for the event. Teddy even invited his sidekick, David, to come along and keep him entertained while everyone else was shopping.

On the day of the trip, the LaPlantes met eight other American families at AIS to catch their chartered bus to Germany in the morning for the six-hour drive. One of the families, the Kowalskis, were originally from Chicago, and their two girls—Fran and Debbie—were Louisa's and Judy's ages, respectively, so Louisa was excited about having a sidekick for the weekend.

They arrived in Nuremberg right after sunset. The pale sliver of a moon dangled low in the twilit sky. Louisa pressed her nose against the bus window, fascinated. It was like she was driving into one of those magical, feel-good Christmas movies. Multicolored lights twinkled everywhere. A gentle dusting of snow lay on the trees and rooftops throughout town. Christmas—in traditional German fashion—was everywhere she looked.

The driver parked the bus along a side road adjacent to the main square, which was packed with hundreds of craft booths decorated for the season. At the far end of the market stood a medieval cathedral. Its striking Gothic architecture, complete with pointed arches and ribbed vaults, also had been graced with a layer of snow.

The timing was perfect. As everyone hopped off the bus, bells chimed musically from the cathedral. The crisp air was laced with the aroma of fried onions, grilled hamburgers, and freshly baked apple strudel, making Louisa's mouth water. She was loving this town called Nuremburg already, and they hadn't even started yet.

The hotel where they were staying was located on the market square. It featured traditional Bavarian half-timbered construction. Part of the building overlooked the busy festival; the rest had a view of the side street.

The plan was for Louisa and her siblings and David to sleep in one room on the fourth floor that had a set of bunk beds, while her parents would have their own room down the hall. Louisa was the first to check out the teens' accommodation. When she walked inside, she was slightly disappointed their room was small and plain. She knew her father must have reserved the "el cheapo" suite for the kids to save money. It was nothing like the rest of the festive hotel—not one Christmas decoration could be found anywhere. To the left of the door was a vanity with two large sinks. A set of large French windows were to the right of the sinks, overlooking the streets below. A dormitory-style bathroom was directly across the hall from the room.

While she and Judy unpacked their things, placing their clothes in dresser drawers, David and Teddy stormed in, tossed their duffle bags into one corner of the hotel room, and darted off, laughing. Louisa shook her head, knowing for sure the boys were up to no good and probably searching for potential victims for their future pranks. She wondered what kind of mischief she and Debbie would get into. Hopefully something for a good story to bring back to her friends at AIS.

Once she and Judy finished unpacking, they left their room to meet up with the two Kowalski sisters in the common area on the fourth floor.

When they approached the lounge, though, Louisa saw their parents and other adults from the travel group sitting with cocktails in their hands. It must have been time for the aperitif before dinner. Judy nudged Louisa, giving her a look that said, "Let's get out of here." They took off down the hall, and that was where they ran into Fran and Debbie and invited them back to their room.

Fran, who was in Judy's class, was tall for her age and wore her platinum blond hair in a short wedge. Her scheming—compared to Judy's—was on a whole other level. "When our parents go to the restaurant," she whispered with her lips spread in a sly smile, "let's see if anyone left any of their drinks so we can try them."

Louisa's ears perked up. She'd never had an adult drink before. She turned to Judy, whose eager expression told her they were game.

Debbie, who was in Louisa's class, didn't want anything to do with the plan. Short and chubby, she parted her shoulder-length red hair straight down the middle; her large-rimmed eyeglasses took over her face, reminding Louisa of those wide-eyed tarsiers she'd studied in science class. "That's not a good idea," Debbie warned her older sister, "if Mom and Dad find out, you know what'll happen."

Despite Debbie's objection, the majority ruled: the girls would invade the common area for their own little aperitif party. They huddled closely together, whispering about their plan.

An unexpected knock on the door made all four teens jolt up straight. As the door opened, Louisa's mother came inside. "Girls, are you ready for dinner?"

"Mom, we'll be down in a minute," Judy said, clearly stalling for time. "We're still getting ready."

Once their mom left, the teens conspired together and continued outlining their plan. "Debbie, go check and see if they're gone yet," Fran said. "We'll stay here and wait for your signal."

Louisa eagerly chimed in. "I'll keep an eye on Debbie to make sure she stays safe," she whispered, acting like her role was courageous and put her in the line of fire. It made her feel like a real daredevil, and that she would shine in the eyes of her sister and Fran. She followed Debbie out of the hotel room, watching from the threshold of the open door. Eventually, Debbie glanced around and waved to her.

Louisa grabbed Judy and Fran, and they tiptoed quietly to the lounge. Inside the sitting area were three long couches surrounding a solid oak coffee table, flanked with matching side tables. Various highball and wine glasses were scattered throughout.

Fran inspected the sitting area, but no open bottles had been left behind. That didn't stop her, though. She sat on a couch and drank the last few sips from one of the parents' drinks. Judy followed Fran's lead.

Louisa picked up a glass and swirled the amber-colored remnants around examining it, and wondered what was so great about this alcoholic beverage the grown-ups seemed to love. She brought the glass to her mouth apprehensively and took a swig. Right away her eyes flooded with tears, feeling like they were on fire. This was followed by the feeling that her throat was closing up. The next glass she drank from was even worse—the burning sensation was almost unbearable. What could she do? She didn't want to look like a prissy and stop drinking. She eyeballed the area and spotted a few glass steins that had a little bit of foamy beer left over on a side table. Discovering it was far less painful, she decided to make it her go-to beverage of the night.

Once the girls polished off every drop of booze the parents had left behind, Fran grabbed a lighter off the coffee table and picked her way through an ashtray packed with butts until she found a used cigarette still long enough to light. She took a puff, put it out, and moved on to the next one. Louisa watched in disbelief as Fran continued her frenzy until she'd gone through the whole ashtray.

"Come on, they're going to get suspicious," Debbie cried.

Louisa pressed her lips together, annoyed that her classmate was trying to end their mischievous adventure. Her accomplice was surely no criminal. Why was she stuck with the runt of the litter?

Eventually the girls made their way downstairs, where they found their parents sitting at a large table. The hotel restaurant was like a cozy grandparents' living room. Family pictures of the owners hung everywhere, and earthy-scented peat burned in the rustic stone fireplace.

Louisa sat down next to Mr. Kowalski and picked up a menu. It was strange the drinks hadn't had any effect on her. Although, she wasn't sure what to expect. One time she'd had a cold and been given a capful of some blue stuff that made her mind hazy, and she'd had an overwhelming urge to practice handsprings afterward. She wondered if that was what being buzzed felt like.

Once the main course was served, everyone busied themselves with eating. Louisa glanced at her plate of sauerbraten—marinated beef slathered with gravy—and mashed potatoes. At first, she thought she saw one scoop of potatoes, but after she blinked her eyes, she could have sworn two appeared. What was going on? She sat for a moment, stumped, then something welcoming and warm coursed through her veins.

"How do you like your sauerbraten, dear?" Mr. Kowalski asked.

Louisa opened her mouth to answer him. Out of nowhere, laughter bubbled up inside, and all she could do was giggle. Worried her parents would suspect what she had done, she attempted to stifle herself, but it only made things worse, and her cheeks puffed out like a baby blowing raspberries.

After dinner, the American group continued to congregate in the restaurant. Lyle entertained everyone by pounding out Christmas tunes on the piano kitty-cornered at the far end of the room. He was a classically trained pianist but had never taken up his talent professionally. Instead, he preferred to show off his gift to small, intimate audiences of family and friends. He had tried teaching Louisa years before, but between his lack of patience and her hearing impairment and short attention span, his attempts hadn't lasted long.

As the Christmas tunes continued and everyone sang along, Louisa's head felt almost too heavy to hold up. She could no longer keep a straight face, acting sober. She slipped out of the restaurant quietly before her parents could suspect anything.

Arriving back in her hotel room, she hunted for a washcloth but couldn't find one. Was that a European thing? Were facecloths not allowed? Or maybe she was worse off than she'd realized, and they were right under her nose.

She examined herself in the mirror, her nose inches away from her reflection. Her eyes seemed to be bulging and out of kilter, which reminded her of the wide-eyed comedian Marty Feldman. At that, she nodded laughing at herself. Is this what she looked like when she was buzzed?

Despite the humor of it all, she had to find something to blot her flushed face with, so she ran across the hall to the bathroom and brought back a roll of toilet paper. After wrapping a large wad around her hand, she turned on the faucet and ran it under the cold water in the sink, creating a makeshift washcloth. A peacefulness came over her seconds later as she blotted the back of her neck.

Louisa stumbled over to the window and opened it for fresh air. The street was still bustling below, and angelic singing from a children's choir drifted in from the main square. She embraced the frosty winter air and sedate music.

A loud thump came from the hallway, making her jump. The bedroom door flew open, and Teddy and David barged in, out of breath and howling with laughter.

"What's so funny?" she asked.

The boys didn't let her in on their joke. Instead, David walked up to Louisa at the window and stuck his head outside to see the activity below.

"Come on, guys," she begged. "Let me know what's so funny."

While she pleaded with them, her wrapped hand accidentally bumped against David's. The saturated heavy clump she was using for a washcloth broke off and dropped down into the crowded street below. She watched as it plummeted like a torpedo toward a well-dressed woman with a tall Cossack hat. To her horror, the wad struck with precision, knocking the woman's hat completely off her head.

Louisa gasped, stunned at what had occurred. She turned to David, who appeared shocked as well. They both swiftly ducked out of sight and sat on the floor for a minute, speechless. Finally, David reached up his arm to shut the French windows. Once all was clear, they wailed with laughter.

A few minutes later, Judy and Fran blew into the hotel room. David repeated the whole story to them. His animated expressions and body language made it even funnier than when it had first happened.

"Let's get some more toilet paper and do it again!" Teddy cried, all pumped up.

"I'm on it." David ran across the hall to the bathroom and came back with several rolls of toilet paper.

Judy and Fran made the new projectiles at the sink while Teddy and Louisa opened the French windows again and searched for victims in the crowd below. Beautiful Nuremberg was under attack from toilet paper bombs falling from the sky.

After the teens raided the streets below for over an hour, they eventually ran out of energy—and toilet paper. Calling it a night, they conspired to meet back in the room the next night after dinner to continue with fresh targets.

The following morning, the group of Americans hit the Christkindlesmarkt for some shopping. Strolling around with her mom, Louisa was fascinated by all of the booths and displays. Each was packed from the ground to the ceiling with colorful, festive merchandise. It was hard for her to focus on any one booth because another one would come along and steal the show.

In one merchant's stand, Patty found the handcrafted wooden Erzgebirge Christmas pyramid she'd always wanted. "I've been dreaming of this day for a very long time," she told Louisa, pleased as she paid for her treasure.

After a traditional bratwurst lunch at one of the food stands, Patty took the girls to a jeweler off the main market to buy them new charms for their bracelets. "I want that one." Judy pointed to the silver nutcracker dressed in a red coat.

Louisa let out an agitated grunt. She wanted the nutcracker charm too and didn't want hers to be the same as Judy's. For her whole life, whenever she and her sister had gotten presents from relatives, they had always received the same gifts as if they were twins. Yet they were over two years apart. It was like everything she owned was a duplicate of Judy's or the same but in a different color.

Louisa desperately searched and searched for something unique in the crowded display case until finally, there it was—the charm she knew she had to have. One representing a "first" for her from the night before.

She slyly giggled to herself while the merchant attached a traditional German beer stein to her bracelet.

That night, Louisa, Judy, and Fran snuck into the sitting room again after the parents' aperitif hour and drank the last drops of leftover alcohol. For a finale, along with Teddy and David, they resumed sabotaging the Christmas shoppers with toilet paper bombs.

Once the antics fizzled out for a second time, the boys took off, most likely seeking a new adventure. The three girls, however, remained in the hotel room with one last freshly saturated toilet paper wad. Judy, looking tired of the game, casually flung the clump out the window without even looking for a target. All three girls swiftly ducked down and took cover, to be safe.

When Louisa thought all was clear, she poked her head out of the window followed by Judy and Fran. The street was quiet by then, and only a few people were walking around. Louisa scanned the area and her gaze shifted below them. There stood two young men in their late teens leaning against a car, arms folded as they smirked up at her and the others. Louisa's breathing halted.

Judy had a knack for turning a bad situation into a good one, though. "Oh, pardon moi," she said, pretending like the whole thing was an accident. Luckily for her, the two Germans spoke French.

"Bonsoir, mon ami." Fran stood up straight, tossing her shoulders back to exaggerate her bust. The young men kept smiling and proceeded to converse with the girls in French.

The chatter and laughter was still flowing after fifteen minutes, leaving Louisa out of the interaction. Not that she wanted to have anything to do with the strange boys in the street anyway. She eventually backed away from the window, crawled into bed, and watched her sister in action. Judy's facial expression became theatrical as she playfully ran her fingers through her long hair several times.

Louisa rubbed her chin bewildered at what was going on. How did Judy entice the young men as she did? It was as if the boys were intoxicated by her beauty the way their eyes sparkled looking up at her. Was it a magical spell? Did she have some of that alluring magic and not know it? Even worse, would she even know what to do with it if she did?

The next morning, it was time to head back to Antwerp. While the bus warmed up outside, Louisa lingered by herself in the hotel room after everyone had vacated. She opened the French windows for one last view of the street below. Their amusing weekend antics kept replaying in her head, and she found herself laughing about it all over again. Once her reminiscing stopped, she stood quietly, savoring the warmth flowing through her body.

The feeling of pleasure prompted her mental record player to spin The Sweets bubblegum hit song "Funny, Funny." The engaging music had her joyously swaying back and forth. She was in her own little la-la land looking over the streets of Nuremburg with not a care in the world.

Her utopian vision quickly vanished, though, when right below the window she spotted a big commotion around a car. The automobile must have been parked there all weekend, and it was inundated with dried-up wads of toilet paper. It looked like a papier-mâché creature from another planet—and three German police officers were standing around it, poking at the dried wads with their batons. One of them jumped back, startled, as if the lump had moved.

The officers scratched their heads looking like they couldn't make sense of it. One of them looked up at the hotel, most likely to see where the objects could have fallen from. Quickly, Louisa ducked and crawled across the floor, away from the open window. Her body quivered in fear as she grabbed her bag and ran downstairs to join the other Americans getting on the bus. Once she was safely on board, she headed to the back seat and sat with Debbie, in case the police came looking for the culprits. She would probably be safe sitting next to the good one.

Soon, the bus pulled away from the hotel and drove down the old streets, away from the beautiful Christmas market. Louisa, now relieved, turned to look out the back window. The village looked silent, serene, and calm, as if Nuremburg was at peace once again.

TRACK 8

"SLOW DOWN" – SHABBY TIGER

EARLY SUMMER 1976

With no fixed timeline for how long the LaPlantes would remain in Antwerp, Louisa's parents seized every opportunity to see as much of Europe as possible with the three teens. They vacationed in Germany, France, Austria, and Switzerland. They even went on a cruise of Europe's western seaboard.

Early that summer, though, Patty planned her own adventure—without the family. She announced she was taking off for a week of shopping in London with her girlfriend Cook Cole, a Canadian who lived a few houses down on Bremboslaan. Lyle readily gave her his blessing—and his credit card. Whenever the LaPlantes had an opportunity for a sabbatical from "Patty's wanderlust," they were all for it.

After her mom left for London, Louisa went on summer break from school with her siblings. The tranquil, lazy days of the season had her relaxed, and she felt free from impromptu day trips, which her mother was notorious for springing on the family.

One morning, breaking the serenity she was enjoying, Louisa woke with an unusual sickening feeling all through her body. She'd never felt that way before and wanted to pull the covers up over her head and stay there all day. Determined to fight it, she rolled out of bed and dragged herself into the foyer bathroom.

Moments after she entered, Louisa darted out again, terror-stricken. She slammed the bathroom door shut behind her and leaned her back against it. Her hands were clammy, and her eyes were moist behind her closed lids. *This couldn't be happening. Make it go away.* She pressed her body harder against the door, hoping what had just happened in there would stay in there.

Judy had experienced the same awful "happening" a few years earlier. When her sister told their mother about it, their parents had celebrated it like they were going to have a parade and roll out a cake. Louisa had vowed never to endure that kind of humiliation. Ever since she was little, she'd hated it when anything drew attention to her. Once, when she was ten, she was riding on the back of her cousin John's bicycle when her foot got caught in the chain, and the bike fell hard on the pavement. To avoid the attention, she had hobbled away with a sprained ankle and hid under a neighbor's porch until it was dark outside.

Louisa rubbed her upset tummy, her thoughts racing. Why couldn't things just slow down? She didn't want to go on to the next phase in her life. She liked being the cute baby girl. Did this mean she wasn't cute any-more? She often felt like Peter Pan, but was the *girl* who wouldn't grow up. Her friends would always profess they couldn't wait to live like an adult and marry a boy—but Louisa was quite content where she was, in her safe little-girl world.

She flung her foot backward and kicked the door. She'd never go into that stome bathroom again. It had ruined things for her.

Her torment continued, and eventually she ran down the hall to her sis-ter's room, screaming all the way. Louisa laid her head in Judy's lap as they sat together on the bed. Judy gently stroked Louisa's hair to calm her down.

"Don't tell Mom when she gets back from London." Louisa rubbed one of her teary eyes. "I don't want to have a party for this."

Judy showed her compassion and educated her on what to do next. Louisa felt more at ease—and thankful her big sister was there. Judy's warmth and caring manner almost made her glad the "happening" had happened. Her calmness didn't last long, however, when her sister teased: "Louisa, guess what? Now you can have babies."

Sirens blared in her head so loud, she could almost feel the color draining from her face. She flew out of her sister's room and back to hers, jumped into bed and pulled the covers over her head to shut out the world. She should have stayed there all day, as she'd originally planned.

A few days later, Louisa had recovered from her rite of passage and accepted she was in the big girls' club now. It was time to move on. So she invited her new classmate—Barbara Benton, whose father was in the US military—to the house.

Louisa was always amazed at how quickly students came and went at AIS. She never got bored with anyone because they were never around long enough. She also considered herself a seasoned AIS student and knew the ropes—or so she thought. Barbara was an amateur, like she'd been once, so she wanted to show off her abundance of knowledge and instruct her new friend on the current fads in Belgium. She felt it was her American duty to mentor Barbara on everything she knew.

Upon Barbara's arrival, Louisa gave her friend a tour of the house before they made their way to her bedroom. Once there, Barbara walked around the room, examining her surroundings. Louisa watched her friend's eyes casting from one thing to another. It was like she was sightseeing. To the left of the doorway, a large framed Holly Hobbie poster hung on the wall over her dresser, displaying the famed country girl in her oversized bonnet. Above Louisa's bed was her shrine to the rock gods she idolized. A pin-up of Mud was front and center, of course.

The band was dressed in coordinating yellow and brown outfits. To their left was a poster of The Rubettes, also in matching outfits with white caps. Next to The Rubettes was the colorful glam rock band The Sweet, with their long hair, garish makeup, and eccentric attire. The band's music always brought out the bad girl in Louisa, making her want to do something shocking, like pierce a second set of holes in her ears. One time she'd asked her mother to take her to get it done at one of the jewelry stores in Antwerp and was flatly refused. "One hole is radical enough, Louisa!"

She especially loved The Sweet's lead singer, Brian Connolly, and the way his blond hair swept forward on the sides and over his forehead. While all of her friends were trying to imitate the Farrah Fawcett-Majors flip-back that had just become popular, she was doing the anti-Farrah, styling her hair in the opposite direction.

Louisa's entertainment cabinet stood by the bedroom window. The treasured turntable that played the music she worshipped was proudly perched on top of an oak stand like royalty on a throne. Underneath was a shelf where she stored her vast music collection.

Sitting down on the floor next to it, Louisa pulled out a handful of records for Barbara. "Now, this is my favorite band, and they're from England." She held her head high, acting like she was some kind of Europop prodigy. "I've been saving up for *Mud Rock Volume II*. I'm almost there, just a few francs to go."

Barbara nodded, looking like she was hanging on every word Louisa was saying. She picked up the *Mud Rock* album, examined its cover, and bashfully smiled at Louisa, her mouth full of gleaming braces. Barbara's metalwork was the focal point of her face. She had Dutch-boy bangs and wore her hair in a short pixie. Louisa thought of her friend as the "ugly duckling" ever since she'd met her. But she knew one day, once Barbara got her braces off and tried a new haircut, she'd shine up like a brand-new penny.

Barbara pulled out one of the seven-inch vinyl records from the pile of albums. "Louisa, can you play this one by Shabby Tiger? I like that name."

Louisa was thrilled. Barbara was catching on and taking an interest in her collection. She jumped up, placed the record on the turntable, and hit Play. The music started with a slow, erotic rhythm, followed by a deep male voice half-singing and half-groaning lustfully. Drifting into another world briefly, Louisa absorbed the guitar's sly, seductive rhythm. It had always reminded her of a prowling panther in the wild.

Halfway through Barbara turned to Louisa, her face puckering sourly. "Oh, I don't think I like that. What's wrong with the singer? Is he hurt?"

Louisa burst out laughing. "Barbara, it's the song 'Slow Down.' You'll get used to it. We'll just have to listen to it a few times."

Over the next couple of hours, Louisa played Barbara all her records, educating her new friend on her favorite bands and everything she knew about them. Eventually, they became hungry, so Louisa took the cash her father had left on the kitchen table for them and skipped out to the backyard. "Judy, we're going to the frites stand!" she called out.

Her sister appeared to be in another world, sunning herself on a lounge chair. Instead of her bathing suit, she wore her maroon AIS gym shorts that were falling apart at the seams and a white cross-your-heart lace bra. Her skin was slick with baby oil and a sheet of foil under her chin. "Okay," she replied dreamily while her eyes remained closed.

The two teens hopped on their bikes and pedaled into town. It was a beautiful day—by Belgian standards. As Louisa discovered in the past year and a half, Mother Nature didn't bless the small country with the sun often. So whenever one of those unexpected things called a "sunny day" came around, it was surely a reason to celebrate, or at least to be duly noted.

Riding along, Louisa was feeling full of herself. Not only was she entertaining her new friend, who was like putty in her hands, but she was also going out independently, without her older sister to hide behind. It felt good to be the leader for once.

The girls arrived at the frites stand and racked their bikes. Louisa led Barbara into the little shack and up to the counter. An extensive menu was posted on the wall, and a large display case below showed off various accompaniments. One could order a stoofvlees, which was a Belgian beef stew, or a currywurst sausage, and choose from a wide variety of condiments in almost every color imaginable.

"Wat wil jij hebben?" asked the older woman behind the counter.

Louisa wasn't sure what the lady said, but she knew how to order her French fries with mayonnaise in Flemish. She raised her chin. "Twee frites met mayo, alstublieft."

When the frites were ready, the girls took their orders outside and headed for the picnic tables in the back of the stand. All the tables were empty except one where a group of young men was hanging out. They were a few years older than Louisa and had a rock- and-roll edge about them with their long, shaggy hair. Louisa stiffened, feeling intimidated.

After a moment of hesitation, she reminded herself she was the leader for the day, and to just deal with it if she was going to make an impression on Barbara. After all, they were only boys. How bad could it be? She stood tall and marched past them to sit at another table.

The girls opened their bundles and started their frites fest. "Louisa, you're right," Barbara said, with a small dollop of frietssaus on her lip and her mouth full of fries. "This mayonnaise is great." The two teens leaned into each other and chatted about the boys at AIS, periodically letting out a girlish giggle simultaneously. As their conversation deepened, Louisa noticed one of the young men from the other table strutting toward them.

The way he bounced in his strides, like he was king of the world, gave him a pompous air. His layered shoulder-length blond hair was streaming in the warm summer breeze, and he wore his blue denim shirt half-buttoned up, exposing his bare chest. Around his neck dangled a chunky shark tooth strung from a black leather cord.

Louisa tried not to make eye contact with the young man, but he was forthright as he approached them. "Oh, you guys spreken Engels. Where are you from, London?"

Louisa felt a cold sweat coming on. She wasn't sure how she should respond. How would her suave sister have reacted? Although what worked for Judy might not work for her. She realized she would just have to improvise. "We're Amerikaans!"

The other three young men sailed over to the girls' table as if she had told the first one they were Hollywood stars. Not that people from the western hemisphere were like royalty to the Belgians, but in the 1970s, it was unusual for the locals to come across people from the States. Tourism in Antwerp wasn't conventional yet, so whenever Americans popped up, they were kind of a novelty.

The four lads huddled together, hovering over Louisa, smiling broadly. "Hi, I'm *Bub* Dylan." The pompous one extended his arm for a handshake. His friends started laughing.

Louisa tilted her head to one side, still unsure of the situation, but shook his hand anyway. She had no clue if he said Bub or Bob from his accent, but after consideration, he must have meant Bob.

The next Belgian had red hair that hung loosely over his eyes. He pushed Bob Dylan aside. "Hi, I'm Jerry Garcia," he said with a goofy, crooked smile. The other boys chuckled quietly.

At that point, Louisa was wondering if these were bogus names they were giving her. Why would they lie about who they were? Whose names were these anyway? And why were they all laughing? Maybe they were on some of the "funny stuff." Nevertheless, she introduced herself and Barbara cautiously and continued the conversation to show Barbara she was a fearless leader. She turned to the one who called himself Bob Dylan. "I'm from New York."

The young man moved closer, squinting his brown eyes as he studied her face. "You are going to be very pretty when you are older."

That caught Louisa off guard. No one had ever said she was pretty—Judy, for sure, but not her. Something was definitely wrong with this group. Yet she did find relief because the young man appeared to think she was too young for him, so she was probably safe from his advances. The whole situation gradually became less frightening, and she settled back in her seat.

Just when her confidence was building, Bob Dylan went down on one knee in front of her and playfully serenaded her with Shabby Tiger's lustful hit "Slow Down."

He sang in a deep voice, just like on her record. Louisa struggled hard to keep a poker face while he teased her, but heat flowed to her cheeks nonetheless. The steamy lyrics he was singing were about an older man being tempted by a girl much younger than him. She knew she had to do something quickly to take the spotlight off her. It was sheer agony being the center of attention. "I have a sister!" she proclaimed, jumping up from the bench. "She's almost fifteen, and she's beautiful."

The redhead, who called himself Jerry Garcia, shoved his friend aside. "Waar is she?" he asked wide eyed.

Louisa hesitated. If she brought these boys home for her sister, maybe Judy would like one of them and finally live her dream of having a European boyfriend—and Louisa would win points with her big sister. Her face brightened at the thought. "She's at home. It's very close." Her smile was driven by her ambition. "Do you want to meet her?"

Barbara nudged her sharply in the ribs, but Louisa ignored her. For the first time, she felt like she might not have been a lost cause. "Follow me," she said to the Belgians.

The boys agreed. Everyone got on their bikes, and the girls led the Belgians like the Pied Piper as they rode off toward Bremboslaan.

When the six cyclists arrived at the LaPlantes' house, the girls hopped off their bikes and ran to the front door. The boys trailed after, riding their cycles all the way up the front walkway. Louisa fumbled in her pockets a minute realizing she had forgotten her house key, so she rang the bell repeatedly. She was antsy to show her sister the Belgian boys she'd caught for her. "Judy, open up!" she desperately called out. "I have a surprise."

Finally, she spotted Judy through the side window, heading into the foyer. Her sister flung the door open in a huff. "You dummy! You're such a spaz!" Judy's scowl quickly disappeared as her jaw dropped, looking straight ahead at the four eager boys with their long rock and roll hair, standing behind the two girls.

Louisa turned her head back and saw the boys with the same shocked expressions, their eyes glued on Judy. She was still in her tattered gym shorts and bra. Her face, flame red, and eyelids had swollen into slits from the foil-under-the-chin experiment. On top of her head, sticking straight up, was her frayed ponytail, looking like a broccoli spear. Some beauty queen—she looked more like a Dr. Seuss character gone wrong.

Judy flushed, darted out of the foyer, and returned with an oversize blue rugby jersey on.

One of the quieter lads introduced himself as Rory Gallagher—the famous Irish folk musician. He was tall and thin, with dark brown hair that hung past his shoulders and short blunt bangs across his forehead giving him the trendy rocker look. His smile was quiet but not boring. From the way he and Judy ogled each other, Louisa could almost feel the heat radiating between them. They later learned his *real* name was Gui.

After the boys and Barbara left that day, Judy dragged Louisa into her bedroom and stood towering over her with an icy glare. "What's the matter with you doofus? You saw what I was wearing when you left the house. Is there anything upstairs in that head of yours?" She shook her head at Louisa in disgust. "Badly done, sister." Then her angry face softened and she wore a hint of a smile as she bounced merrily out of the room.

Louisa knew very well what that expression meant. Judy was secretly grateful for the boy she brought home to her. Her mission was a success after all.

One Sunday afternoon a few weeks later, Gui invited Judy to attend a dance with him and his pals at a venue outside of Schilde. Louisa, hearing about this, pleaded with her parents to go as well.

"No." Her dad was firm. "You are too young to be going to a public dance."

The blood rose in Louisa's cheeks. Fleeing to her room with her arms swinging forcefully, she slammed the door so hard her framed Holly Hobbie poster came crashing down.

Broken glass flew everywhere. She stood, eyes bulging, hand over her mouth, looking down at the chaos she'd caused. Instead of cleaning up the mess, she plopped on her bed sulking about not going to the dance.

Judy came into her room, all empathetic and consoling. "Louisa, I'm sorry you can't come with me today. But you can someday soon. You'll see." She sat down and wiped away the single tear rolling down Louisa's face. "Hey, when I come home from the dance, I'll come in and tell you all about it."

That evening, Louisa waited patiently for her sister's return. As Judy had promised, she came into her room and told her gripping stories about her adventure at the dance that day. She was a great storyteller and emphasized every detail about the venue, the dance floor, the people who were there, and what they wore. It created a vivid picture in Louisa's mind—it was almost like she was watching a movie of it in her head. The exhilaration and hunger to go to one was boiling over inside her.

Judy explained the event was called a "Belgian popcorn dance." The music played was R&B from the 1960s, but the Belgians put their own spin on it—*literally*. The DJs modified the records, changing the speed and tempo, and put their own label over the original record label. Louisa absorbed every word and counted down the days to when she would be old enough to go. Although she was not sure she'd be able to wait until that day, an inexorable yearning was brewing.

Judy's relationship with Gui continued through that summer. He and his friends started popping over to visit her in the middle of the night, knocking on her window as if it was midday. "Of course, I was sleeping," Judy told Louisa one afternoon when they were talking about her midnight callers. "I still got up when they knocked, quickly brushed my hair, and brought a chair over to the window so I could sit while we talked." She tilted her face upward so her nose was in the air. "I felt like a queen on a throne, and the boys outside the window were my faithful servants, at my beck and call for anything I wanted."

To Louisa, though, Judy was a queen. She had always admired her sister's confident persona and her daring pursuit of pleasure, which she knew she lacked and might never have. At times, Louisa wondered how she and her sister came from the same mold. Judy was charging into adulthood and had been since she was ten. Meanwhile, she was on the opposite end of that development and running from it. Could it be her parents weren't telling her something?

Louisa woke one morning to the loud sound of her father reprimanding Judy in the kitchen. His voice was muffled, so she wasn't sure what was going on. Once the commotion stopped, Judy flew into Louisa's room, laughing as she told her what it was about. The night before, her midnight callers had stopped by for a visit. Apparently, the noise had woken their father.

"Dad opened his window," Judy giggled. "He saw Gui and Bob Dylan around my window. He yelled and shooed them away like they were stray dogs."

Despite the mishap, Louisa knew her sister was walking on air. Judy *finally* had her first European boyfriend. It seemed like all of her dreams were coming true until one Sunday when she went to a popcorn dance with her friend Allison, who was a real merrymaker. Judy, caught up in the moment of her friend's pleasure-seeking ways, had too many beers and let Bob Dylan woo her into a kiss. Gui caught the two of them together in a lip-lock in the middle of the dance floor, and that was the end of another romance for Judy. She passed it off, though, like it was nothing. While telling Louisa about the unfortunate incident, Judy's hands flew up in the air as she chuckled, "C'est la vie."

TRACK 9

"FOREVER AND EVER" – SLIK

AUGUST 1976

T oward the end of the summer, Andre Chensoy, a coworker and good friend of Lyle's from the Paris office, offered the LaPlantes his apartment in the French Riviera for a week. Unfortunately, Lyle had to go back to the States on business. Since the summer was ending, the rest of the family took the trip without him.

One of Patty's good ideas was to take a road trip to the South of France instead of flying. It was a ten-hour drive, which she said she could do easily in two days. "I've always dreamt about driving through France's wine region," she exclaimed to the family a week before they left. So she mapped out a route, taking the back roads to enjoy the scenic French countryside. She even let Teddy invite David, who spoke fluent French, just in case they needed a translator—or a guardian angel.

Another good idea Patty had was to go camping on the way down to the seaside. On the morning of their departure, everyone loaded their sleeping bags and crammed the twelve-person tent they'd brought from the States into the Peugeot wagon.

Louisa hopped into the car, excited about their adventurous road trip and going to the beach. Once she looked around, though, and saw the cramped interior packed to the ceiling with luggage, as well as camping equipment poking out everywhere, she shook her head. Two days of this? *Ugh.*

As the car headed down Bremboslaan, Louisa turned her head toward the rear window and peered through a tiny opening between poles and bags. Her father was standing at the front door, waving goodbye. It was the first time they had vacationed without him. She had never seen him look so uneasy before. Did he know something she didn't? He stood rubbing his chin with an unsettled expression, as though this might be the last time he'd ever see his family.

Morning turned to afternoon, and a sprinkle of rain turned into a drencher. The Peugeot stormed across the flatland of Flanders and approached the rolling hills of the French wine region. Patty had packed two days' worth of lunches for everyone, intending to picnic in the vineyards. She told the group of teens the photos they'd take there would be lovely. However, the torrential downpour meant the photo shoot wouldn't be happening that day. So she pulled off to the side of the road, and they all ate their lunches in the crowded car.

Soon enough, one meal led to another. For dinner that evening, Louisa's mom gave the teens reprieve from their cramped traveling accommodations and stopped at a small café, where everyone had more elbow room and a quick meal.

After dinner, they scouted for the campground that was circled on Patty's map to pitch the tent. While they searched and searched, the downpour continued, and it was getting dark. In Louisa's opinion, getting out of the car and setting up a tent in these conditions would be a total nightmare. Would they even know how to do it? Their father had always orchestrated that task when they camped in the States. Did her mother even think of that?

Time seemed to drag as they hunted for the site. Wherever it was, they weren't able to find it. Patty eventually pulled the Peugeot over at a roadside rest stop. Louisa sat in silence, waiting with the others to learn what their next move would be. "Okay," her mom said, her eyes looking heavy. "We're just going to have to sleep in the car tonight."

The night was long and restless with the rain thumping nonstop on the car roof. Even worse, Louisa woke to another miserable day of the wet stuff—and it didn't look like it was about to let up. She wondered how much longer she'd be able to endure being in the car. This was not a part of the deal. They were supposed to be having memorable moments picnicking in the countryside with the warm sun beating on their faces and fun evenings, sitting around the campfire roasting marshmallows and singing. She certainly did not sign up for this train wreck.

An uneasiness filled Louisa as the hours slowly went by. The only sound was the irritating wipers squeaking back and forth and the rain clacking like a million tap dancers on the roof. She soon realized a part of her angst was there hadn't been any music playing in the last twenty-four hours. Her mother said it was too distracting while she was driving. Louisa's torment, though, became unbearable. "This is agony, Mom. Please turn on the radio. I need some music to drown out the sound of the rain."

David, who was sitting up front, leaned over and turned on the radio. It was a struggle; the only stations coming in were French talk shows. After searching up and down the dial, David said, "We may have to wait for some music. We're in the middle of nowhere."

When they stopped for lunch later that day, everyone remained in the car to eat again because of the inclement weather. Thankfully though, after hitting the road, the heavy rain dissipated into a fine drizzle.

While they drove along the desolate back roads of France, Louisa observed the gray, wet scenery for hours, noticing they passed through one little deserted village after another. Each one consisted of small stone houses nestled up to the road and no sidewalks. She laughed to herself—they were so close to the road, one could almost knock on the front doors from the car as they drove by. But something strange became evident: all the shutters were closed in the middle of the day. They were like ghost towns. No sign of life was around.

Teddy let out one of his animated, high-pitched cackles. "Where are all the people?"

David, being French, understood what was happening. "They're taking lunch. And many are napping." He went on to explain that stores and businesses in that part of the country would shut for several hours every afternoon.

The reason didn't matter to Louisa, though. The deserted villages still felt creepy, like that scary movie where the evil children with their red eyes took control and ruled the adults.

Between each town were miles and miles of vacant, untouched countryside. Periodically there were abandoned old farmhouses tucked into the lonely, rolling hills. Their stone exteriors were crumbling, and they had half-missing shutters, glassless windows, and overrun vegetation growing everywhere. Spooking herself, Louisa imagined ghoulish scenarios and what frightful things might be lurking around inside. Her mom, however, was clearly fascinated. "Oh, let's stop and explore," she said whenever she spotted one of the ramshackle houses.

Louisa couldn't believe she was hearing this from her. Really? Who was the adult here, anyway? She laughed it off, hoping her mother was only kidding.

Finally, though, Patty pulled the car over to see one of the dilapidated homes not far from the main road. She turned around to face the three teens in the back seat. "I just want to see what it looks like inside," she said grinning.

They all hopped out and headed over to the house—or what was left of it. Patty was the first to the front door, and tried pushing it in, but it wouldn't budge. Her face hardened as she looked around and headed to the back of the house. The rest of the group followed. It was there she found a window large enough to fit through. "Okay. I'm climbing in. Anyone want to join me?"

Judy and David began stammering. "Ah-ah-ah-b-b-but—"

"Okay, Mom," Teddy volunteered. "I'll go in with you."

All Louisa could hear ringing in her head was her father yelling at her mother like Ricky Ricardo. *"Patty! What did you do now?"*

Her mom headed toward the window. Teddy trailed behind her, rubbings his palms together. She peered into the house and cleared some broken glass on the ledge with the sleeve of her London fog raincoat. Louisa stood back and observed as her mother hiked one leg up to the ledge, then the other, and slowly lowered herself inside. Judy ran over to help boost Teddy up and over. Then the two disappeared into the darkness.

Soon the sound of Teddy's voice echoing through the house could be heard. "Wow!" he shouted at first, then "Neato!" His words didn't tempt Louisa to see what was so exciting, though.

"I'm going to check on the car. We left all the doors open when we got out," David said.

Not long after David disappeared, the sound of an approaching car on the dirt path they drove in on came from the front of the house. Judy looked at Louisa with wide-open eyes and she ran around the corner and disappeared too.

Seconds after, she reappeared, running full tilt past Louisa to the broken window. "Mom, come out! Quick! The police are here!"

David returned to the back of the house, escorted by a short middle-aged man, sporting a thick dark mustache and wearing a gray uniform with a matching cap.

Teddy popped his head out the window first, flashing a mischievous look. He climbed out, their mother right behind him. They were covered in soot on their faces and clothes, looking as if they'd been sweeping chimneys.

The police officer spoke to them in French, directing his eyes on Patty. No one understood him, except for David, who replied in French. While their discussion continued, the vertically challenged officer waved his hands up and down, looking up at David. His expression was tense, and his voice grew louder. Eventually, David waved his hands around while he spoke. As scared as Louisa was observing this, she found it funny that even though David was a teen, he towered over the officer and appeared to dominate the conversation.

Meanwhile out of the corner of her eye, Louisa noticed her mom stealthily slipping an object into her raincoat pocket. She was curious what her mom had confiscated from the house but was too intimidated by the officer to ask her about it.

Once David's heated conversation with the officer ended, the policeman briskly walked up to Louisa's mother and stood on his tippy toes, inches away from her nose. "Go!" he shouted bluntly in English, spraying spittle in her face.

Louisa, frightened by the officer's harsh demeanor, grabbed her mom's hand. The group bolted as fast as they could to the Peugeot.

Back on the road, they traveled in silence while the police officer followed them in his car. Whenever Patty glanced at the rearview mirror, Louisa would turn around and peer through the luggage in the back window to see him. Finally, after several nerve-wracking minutes, her mother let out a heavy, relieved sigh. The officer was no longer behind them.

Patty pulled the car over to the side of the road. "What did you say to the policeman?" she asked David, who was sitting in the passenger seat.

"Oh, don't worry, Mrs. LaPlante." David smirked. "I took care of it. I just told him you were crazy."

David never told Louisa—or anyone else from her family—what he and the police officer said to each other that day. Still, Louisa knew he'd gotten them a Get Out of Jail Free card, which was all that mattered.

Early that evening, they stopped at a charming bistro painted in a Van Gogh–esque yellow with hunter-green shutters in a small town called Roussillon.

As they entered, Louisa found the interior was just as quaint as the outside, with country-style blue-and-white-checked tablecloths and fresh lavender bouquets in small, flared Picardie glasses on each table. Everyone ate the same thing for dinner—croque monsieur avec pommes frites—thanks to David, who ordered for the group.

After dinner, they still had to scout for the campground on Patty's map and set up the tent. However, as Louisa and the group stepped out on the bistro's terrace, it started raining again. Which quickly turned into a down-pour; it was as if they had entered a drive-thru car wash on foot.

By the time they piled into the Peugeot, they were drenched. Patty brushed off the excess water and turned to them, rain still dripping from her hair and trickling off the tip of her nose. She wore a distressed look Louisa knew all too well. Nodding her head listlessly, Louisa prepared herself for another night of agony sleeping together cramped in the wagon.

When morning finally broke, Louisa found herself in a state of complete misery after a second, long night of trying to sleep upright and the sound of incessant rain. No one else looked like a happy camper either. Teddy had kept elbowing her all night long for more room. Judy sat scrunched up sitting behind David, who had pushed his seat back because of his long legs. Patty, with drooping eyes, was clearly exhausted from two days of driving in the rain.

Louisa, however, saw a small glimmer of hope: it wasn't raining. It wasn't sunny, either, but at least the rain had stopped.

"Okay, kids," Patty said. "We're less than two hours away. We can do this."

After freshening up at a small rest stop, the group hit the road again for the last leg of the trip. As they drove along through the green, plush vegetation, Louisa observed how the landscape's colors grew more dramatic. The purples of the lavender fields and the yellows of the towering sunflowers rolled right up to the road. Blue patches of sky broke through the clouds. She could finally see the sky-piercing French Alps in the distance from the clearing visibility.

Roused by the brightening scenery, the good feeling reminded Louisa of the music she loved. "David, could you please try the radio again? There has to be something by now." Her imaginary radio wasn't cutting it any-more. She needed the real thing.

David fidgeted with the dial but still got nothing. "It will come in even-tually," he explained, leaving the radio on. "I know this station from when I drive down to the Riviera with my parents for holiday."

Silence had filled the car for some time, rolling along until Judy screamed from the back seat. "Stop, Mom!"

Patty slammed on the brakes. She glanced back at Judy, who had already flung the car door open, jumped outside, and run across the street. Louisa watched as her sister hurried toward a drove of donkeys grazing in the grass. "Donkeys!" Louisa cheered, sprinting out of the car to follow her sister, leaving her door wide open. The rest of the crew soon followed.

"Mom, can we feed them?" Louisa asked. "We have some apples left over from lunch yesterday."

They retrieved the apples from the car and the group went over to the fence to feed the *anes*, as David called the donkeys in French.

"The markings on the ane de Provence are unique to the region." David's deeper adult-sounding voice emerged as he educated his audience.

Once the group had gotten their donkey fix, they piled back in the car and continued on their journey. A few kilometers down the road, they approached a farm tractor with a trailer of hay in tow, moving at a snail's pace. Patty drove the Peugeot up behind the tractor to try and pass it, but the road was too winding. The elderly farmer turned his head around to look at them. His messy gray hair poked out above his ears as he smiled warmly, tipped his beret to them, then turned forward again.

For the next twenty-five minutes, they inched along. The edginess was noticeable on all of their faces. They were so close to their destination, yet they would have made better time walking briskly.

Louisa wondered if all these obstacles were meant to prevent them from reaching the beautiful French Riviera. Had she done something terribly wrong before the trip she was being punished for? Maybe God was mad at her for the time she lied to a priest on her first confession. She'd been preparing for her Sacrament of Reconciliation at the English-speaking catholic church they attended in Antwerp earlier that year. For weeks she scrutinized what she was going to say once she got in the confessional booth. There was no way she was going to tell Father Riando any of the deepest sinful acts she had committed, fearing she might be struck dead right there in the church. Then she remembered one wrongdoing that didn't seem so bad and he probably wouldn't make her say too many Hail Marys in penance. She'd ask for forgiveness for the time she stole her sister's Aerosmith 'Toys in the Attic' album and hid it in the back of her armoire. She never liked the sound of it blaring through Judy's bedroom door and was certain that the heavy metal rock music was not healthy for her sister. On the day of her first confession, Louisa sat in the booth telling Father Riando about what she had done. The priest asked her if she had given the album back to her sister and Louisa told him she had, so he wouldn't be too harsh on her. But that was a lie. The album still remained in the same place, buried under a pile of clothes in her armoire so Judy couldn't play that distasteful music.

A sudden burst of static from the radio broke the silence that lingered in the car. Soon it became muffled flashes of distorted electric guitar and eventually turned into beautiful clear full-blown music.

Louisa moved to the edge of her seat. Not only did she have her tunes back but the song playing was "Forever and Ever," the latest hit by the Scottish band Slik. She was so excited that she belted out the song's lyrics along with the radio. Everyone laughed at her. Even Louisa chuckled over it, knowing very well she had a horrible singing voice. She always blamed it on her years of having a hearing impairment.

Right when "Forever and Ever" ended, the tractor pulled off onto a dirt road. By then, it almost seemed like the farmer was an old friend or a relative whom Louisa had known for years. When they passed the tractor, David hung his head out the window, waving his hand while shouting the words musically to the Bay City Rollers' hit song "Bye, Bye Baby."

A few more kilometers ahead the car approached a hairpin bend in the road. Louisa's eyes followed straight past the curve, and it looked like the edge of the earth. Nothing but the open sky. She squinted, struggling to see what could possibly come next. Her mother downshifted to negotiate the tight curve and as they slowly rounded it, Louisa looked down from the sloping mountain. Directly in front of her, in all of its breathtaking glory, was the wide-open Côte d'Azur. The sea looked endless, a scene from a postcard—and to Louisa, it felt like she had reached the promised land.

Once they descended from the hills, they finally arrived at their destination in the Provençal seaside town of Carry-le-Rouet. The idyllic village was everything Louisa had expected from the stories her mom told her about the South of France: old stone houses with Mediterranean blue shutters; small cafés surrounding the main square; plenty of boulangeries and souvenir shops; and elderly men sitting in rows on park benches, smoking, chatting, and looking like their wives had banished them from the house while they cleaned for the day. Straight ahead of the main square was a marina, the beach, and the deep blue sea. Louisa was pleased with this little piece of heaven. She felt it was worth the last couple days of misery—well, almost.

The blissful feeling continued every morning with David running to the corner boulangerie for a warm, just-baked baguette in the morning. Afterward, it was time for fun in the sun, then lunch at the apartment or one of the little cafés in the main square. In the afternoon, they would stroll around the village and wander in and out of the souvenir shops. It was a perfect end—in paradise—to what had begun as a wet and wild trip from the flatlands.

David was their entertainment in the evening. Louisa found herself fascinated with the stories of his family history. Hearing about his Czech grandfather—who had run a renowned circus before World War II—really piqued her interest when David explained how glamorous the entertainment under the big top was back then. Sadly, he also spoke about how the family eventually went underground to escape the Nazis and lost the circus.

Following suit with his grandfather, David had his showman's talent. One evening after dinner, he spontaneously hopped onto the sturdy coffee table in the apartment. Swiveling his hips in large circles like Liza Minnelli in *Cabaret*, he sang, "Money Makes the World Go 'Round," while holding up his hands as if they held a million jingling coins. His tall and husky physique made for some awkward dancing, and he had everyone in tears laughing. No doubt, David was beginning to feel like family. Something about his congenial character made Louisa feel like she had known him her whole life.

On the final night of the trip, they ate an early dinner at a café on the main square. Patty announced they would drive straight home in the morning, with no overnight stays. She would be driving the shortest and fastest route as recommended in her travel guidebook. Camping had sounded like fun in the beginning, but after their drive down to Carry-le-Rouet, the thought scared Louisa. She and camping were through.

The sisters strolled over to a bench overlooking the marina after dinner, taking in the view of the approaching sunset and chatting about "girl things." Judy wasn't a typical older sister. Even though she sometimes yelled at Louisa, she wouldn't shoo her away when she wanted to tag along with her and her friends. She'd always include Louisa in her adventures. Judy would also confide in her whenever she did something their parents would disapprove of. So there was always lots to talk about.

Plenty of light was still left in the early evening sky. The girls continued to share stories and laugh about anything and everything. It was at that point Louisa spotted two young men walking across the beach toward them and she noticed her sister's attention had shifted. When the young men approached, Judy locked eyes with the taller one. "Bonjour," she said looking up at him through her eyelashes.

Louisa sighed. *Oh, boy. Here we go again.*

Judy conversed with the young men in her limited French while Louisa clammed up, hoping the boys would go away soon. The second, shorter lad, Victor, tried to engage in small talk with her in English, but it was more Fren-glish. Louisa had no idea what he was saying and wasn't sure she wanted to.

The taller one, Antoine, inhaled the last of the cigarette he was smoking, flicked the butt down, and crushed it with his foot. Judy threw her chin over her shoulder, behaving flirtatiously. "Avez-vous une cigarette?"

Puffing away, Judy continued the conversation in French. After some more small talk back and forth, her face lit up. "D'accord . . . Okay." She turned to Louisa and whispered, "They have motorcycles parked over there. They want to give us a ride to the lighthouse to see the sunset."

"Are you asking me?" Louisa blinked. "Or are you telling me we're doing this?"

Judy gave the two young men a once-over. "They look harmless. Besides, it's our last night. We should do something we can brag to our friends about when we go back to AIS."

Louisa was apprehensive. How would she ever be able to pull this one off? She could barely talk to boys. Still she agreed, and they walked over to the motorbikes with Antoine and Victor. Louisa had been on a moped before, but never a motorcycle. They always seemed so loud and monstrous to her. She watched as Victor hopped on the bike first. Following his lead, she hiked up her short leg. After a bit of struggle, she finally fell in behind him. It was very awkward, being so close to a boy. Her whole body was wedged up against his back.

The French men revved their engines, and they took off. Louisa kept her eyes ahead, planted on Judy and Antoine's motorcycle, ensuring her sister was in sight at all times. She already knew she wasn't enjoying this adventure and they had hardly gotten started yet. The things she would suffer through to be popular back at school.

The windy village roads soon led them out of the town and to the open coastline, where they drove about a half mile before parking the bikes at the entrance to a small, rocky peninsula. At the end stood the lighthouse, which wasn't impressive at all; the red and white tower was only about eight feet tall. To Louisa, it looked more like a light *hut*. And she'd straddled a boy on a motorcycle for this puny thing?

The group hopped off the bikes. Judy followed Antoine up one side of the rocky peninsula, and Victor led Louisa to the opposite side. Flustered, Louisa frowned. She couldn't see her sister anymore. Why had Judy parted from her? She didn't know what to do but knew she had to continue to not look prudish. Cautiously, she followed Victor.

The small dirt path leading to the tip of the peninsula became narrower. Louisa peered down to find the blue swells of the Mediterranean smashing against the rocky coast and rolling back out to sea. The spray from the waves misted her face, and she could taste the water's briny salt on her lips.

She rubbed the ocean's mist from her eyes and lips and noticed Victor kept glancing back at her with an edgy look on his face. Was it to make sure she hadn't fallen off the path into the water? Or maybe he was worried that she would run away?

By the time the two neared the end of the peninsula, the sun looked like it was about two minutes away from hitting the water and exploding onto the horizon. Victor spun around and took Louisa's hand. He turned her so her back was against the rocks and she was looking out to the sea, then stepped in front of her so they were face-to-face. Louisa braced herself—she knew what was coming next. Pleading with herself, she prayed that it wouldn't be too disturbing.

He leaned in, put one hand around the back of her neck, and pulled her up to meet his lips.

Louisa squeezed her eyelids shut, giving in to him.

What followed was worse than she could have imagined. Her stomach turned, and she nearly gagged. She thought she would vomit right in his mouth. The Frenchman was like a hungry iguana. Is this how kissing is supposed to be? He can't be doing it right. What's up with the slobbering and the drooling? And what was he doing with his tongue? Still, she let Victor continue the horrible kiss despite her nausea.

Eventually, she was saved by Judy's boisterous laughter as she made fun of her first kiss. Louisa pushed herself away from Victor and swiftly ran to her sister's side, practically attaching herself to her sisters' hip. The look she gave Judy said "lets get out of here *now*."

Once the sun set, the girls said their goodnights to the young Frenchmen. As they trekked back into town, they talked the whole way about Louisa's experience.

"Louisa. It's French kissing," Judy chuckled. "Everyone's doing it."

"I don't care," snapped Louisa in disgust. "It was like a wrestling match started in my mouth!"

Judy shrugged. "Hey little sister, when in France, you have to do like the French."

The next morning, the group bid adieu to Carry-le-Rouet. As they drove away from paradise, Louisa hung her head out the car's back window for one last glimpse of the deep blue Mediterranean and its sulphury scent. Rehashing the events from the night before left her disappointed and worried about her experience with Victor. Was she regressing instead of progressing? And what was the big deal about kissing anyway? Maybe the whole world was playing a funny joke on her.

TRACK 10

"TEENY BOPPER BAND"
– CATAPULT

SEPTEMBER 1976

The new school year brought new friends, new teachers, and new fashion. On the first day back to class, Louisa saw a total transformation in her classmates over the summer. It seemed like every girl's coif had gone from Dorothy Hamill's trendy short wedge to a long, feathered lioness mane. Meanwhile the boys had traded their Sears Toughskin jeans for Levi's 501s. Times were a-changing.

One afternoon, AIS held a pep rally to get the students into a spirited mood. Louisa wandered into the noisy gym and spotted Barbara way up in the back of the bleachers, saving her a seat—a look of sheer excitement on her friend's face. Standing upright, she eagerly sprinted up the bleachers to get the lowdown.

Arriving at the row where Barbara sat, she struggled not to fall as she maneuvered around several students. Barbara continued waving to her anxiously to hurry, making the situation even more nerve wracking. Finally reaching her seat, she let out an exhausted sigh as she plunked down.

Before she could even open her mouth to ask her friend's exciting news, a crash of electric guitars split the air as the resident AIS school rock band called Exodus started jamming on stage. All the students erupted, screaming, stomping their feet on the bleachers and whistling as the sounds of rock and roll filled the gym. Conversation became impossible. Barbara's news would have to wait until the band finished their set.

Three numbers later, the music finally ended. Louisa could wait no longer, despite the continuous screaming and whistling filling the air. She turned her head to Barbara and shouted in her ear, "What's going on? What happened?"

Barbara attempted to explain but Louisa couldn't make out her voice. "What?" she yelled, her frustration building. "I can't hear you!" Her friend continued talking, but Louisa could barely make out what she was saying over the crowd.

"What?" Louisa screamed again, hanging off the edge of her seat.

Barbara took a deep breath and bellowed, "Guess who's coming to town in December?" Her face turned beet red. "*Mud!*"

At the same instant, the other students had quieted down in unison as Principal Dubois took the stage to make a speech. Louisa, shocked, looked down from the top of the bleachers. The principal and the entire school had their heads turned up at them, pointing and laughing uproariously.

Normally, Louisa would have suffered for weeks from embarrassment over being the center of attention. But Barbara's news was like Christmas morning. She'd dreamed about this day for a *very* long time.

At home that evening, she pleaded with her parents to go with Barbara and see Mud in concert. It wasn't easy, but her mom and dad eventually gave in—but in return, she had to stay out of trouble and not give them flak about day trips or weekend sightseeing anymore. Were they nuts? Of course, she'd agree.

The months leading up to the big day were monotonously boring, and Louisa was doing everything in her power to stay away from any shenanigans that would jeopardize her going to see Mud. Her mother, on the other hand, was behaving questionably, and Louisa witnessed her taking off for hours on end. She didn't have to ask where her mom was going; she knew her mother was like a real-life Nancy Drew seeking secret adventures. But she also knew her mom would have to do some serious "splaining" if her father came home from work at the end of the day and she was still out gallivanting.

Many evenings, she came home just in time before he walked through the front door. One night, Louisa overheard her father sharply laying into her mom in their bedroom about where she had been, what she was doing, and how she'd managed to accumulate fifteen parking tickets and traffic violation charges from all over the country—all within *six* months.

"I've already talked myself out of eight tickets," her mother shouted at one point. "So you should be happy that I saved you from paying those."

Of course, that was when her father's temper really exploded. Louisa quietly giggled at them from behind her closed bedroom door. Better mom than her in trouble. Nope, she would be a perfect angel.

That November, after the height of fall's magnificent colors had passed, Louisa and Barbara took a bus to Antwerp one Saturday for some early Christmas shopping. They were browsing for gift ideas in Sarma, a store carrying everything from apparel to household products. While they shopped, they ran into Jean Erickson, one of their classmates.

Jean, who was with two Belgian girls who didn't go to AIS, was tall for her age and big-boned. She was known for her intimidating, angry scowl and constantly teased and tormented everyone in their class. Louisa and Barbara never dared to stand up to her and always referred to her as Mean Jean.

The bully stood tall and glared down at them. "Hey, have you guys ever stolen anything from a store before? We do it all the time."

Louisa flashed back to when she was five years old and she had lifted a plastic treasure chest for her turtle cage when she was shopping with her mother at the Grants department store. She'd gotten away with the crime, but once she and her mom were back in the car, she'd pulled the stolen merchandise out of her coat to show her mother, and everything hit the fan.

Her mom dragged Louisa back into the store and brought her to the manager. She must have asked the stern man to put the fear of God into her because he'd taken Louisa to a dimly lit room and interrogated her, explaining what happened to shoplifters. Louisa knew she was not the brightest, but she never heard of five-year-old girls going to prison before for shoplifting . . . or anything for that matter. At the time, she suspected she had a few more years before her mischief would ever get her into any real deep trouble.

Jean glowered down at them, "Go on. You two should try it. See those fancy jars filled with licorice? They'd make a nice present for someone in your family."

Louisa didn't know what to do. If she and Barbara got caught, the police would come. And for sure, she was now old enough to go to jail. Even worse, her parents wouldn't let her go to the Mud concert. But if she did lift the jar, maybe Mean Jean would leave her alone for good.

She turned her head to Barbara, who looked terrified. Louisa knew her friend was even more intimidated by Mean Jean than she was. So often, Louisa called the shots in their friendship, but this was one decision she did not want to make alone.

"Okay, Louisa," Barbara whispered, half stuttering. "Le-let's do this—and quick."

They slowly made their way over to the candy display on the table and each picked up a jar. Louisa's eyes shifted around to see if anyone was watching them. Trembling, she slipped the candy inside her coat. Barbara did the same. After, she looked back at Mean Jean and her friends, who stood laughing and mocking them.

Louisa grabbed Barbara by the arm. "Let's get out of here before we get caught!"

They ran to the store's stairwell, which led up several floors. A sickening feeling rumbled in Louisa's stomach. She second-guessed what she had done. "Barbara, I don't like the way this makes me feel," she cried out as they climbed the stairwell. "My stomach hurts. Let's go put the jars back!"

Right as she turned to head back down, a male security guard took her by surprise, yelling at her from the top of the landing. His strong voice echoed through the stairwell in Flemish. Barbara let out a high-pitched scream, which made Louisa's heart thump so hard she thought she could see it pounding through her thick down snorkel coat. At that moment, the crisp clicking of dress shoes sounded in the stairwell from behind them. Louisa spun around and found her science teacher, Mrs. Peterson, climbing the stairs. Her teacher, who spoke fluent Flemish, stopped to converse with the security guard. The whole time Louisa dreaded what would come next. It was judgment day, and her life was on the line. The security guard glanced at the two teens, let out a snort, and disappeared down the stairs.

Once he was gone, Mrs. Peterson held out her hand for the loot the girls had taken. Louisa and Barbara opened their jackets and gave the jars to her. "This will never be spoken about again," the teacher said, straight-faced. "Let's just say you got an early Christmas present today, but I hope there was a lesson learned."

For days afterward, whenever the phone rang, Louisa would fret. Maybe Mrs. Peterson had changed her mind and was calling to tell her parents about the incident after all. One night when the family was gathered around the table for dinner, the telephone rang. Louisa bolted upright in her chair, fearing again it was her teacher.

Her mom answered the call. "Louisa it's for you. It's Barbara."

Louisa picked up the receiver to find her friend crying hysterically on the other end. "Louisa we're moving back to the States in three weeks; my father's been reassigned to a new position."

Louisa was heartbroken. Her friend was moving away—but a bigger disappointment loomed. What about the Mud concert?

She went to bed that night without telling her family the news and how lost she felt. For hours she pondered the possibility of not seeing Mud. Her anxiety made sleep impossible; she needed to do something to occupy her mind. Eventually, Louisa turned to her music collection and busied herself making a new mix tape. Her homemade cassettes were never good quality because she didn't record directly through the stereo. Any other noise in the room would be taped along with the music if she wasn't careful. Still, she lay in bed with a small cassette recorder in one hand and her transistor radio in the other, waiting hours for a song she'd been hunting down.

She was about to give up and call it a night when the familiar sounds of a reverberating bass in an animated, springy riff streamed from the radio. It was "Teeny Bopper Band" by the Dutch glam rock band Catapult—the song she'd been waiting for.

Louisa slammed her finger on the red record button. Those musical bolts that she would always get charged through her veins. She was so amped up and wanted to scream out. It took everything within her to refrain from singing along. These lyrics were her own personal anthem and spelled out everything that this music represented to her:

"What's going on?
Is there something wrong
In the rock scene of today?
If you're looking good
Wear a glittersuit
you'll make it anyway
The kids are gonna scream and shout
Do they know what this is all about?
Oho, teeny bopper band, teeny bopper band
Oho, teeny bopper band, teeny bopper band
A big hand for a teeny bopper band
A big hand for a teeny bopper ba—"

Louisa's bedroom door flung open. She jumped up, almost swallowing her tongue. Her father stood in the doorway, scowling—likely because she was still awake on a school night, blaring her music at 11:00 p.m.

"What do you think you're doing?" he shouted. "Turn that racket off and go to bed now!" He turned smartly on one heel, slamming the door behind him.

Louisa sat on a bench on the grounds at AIS the following day, waiting for Barbara. It was a dark, murky November day and knowing her friend was leaving made the grave weather even more oppressive. Her portable tape recorder sat in her lap playing the mixtape she made the night before, in hopes it would lighten her mood. The recording of the Catapult tune was on low volume as her foot tapped to the beat. When the chorus played "A big hand for a teeny bopper ba—" it was sharply interrupted by the sound of her bedroom door swinging open and her father bellowing at her. Miffed, Louisa mumbled to herself. "No, Dad. *You* go to bed and let me do what I need to do."

Barbara trudged over to her with a long face. "Louisa, I can't believe I'm leaving and we're not going to see Mud together."

Louisa stood up and hugged her friend. "Now I have them all to myself." They both giggled, and Louisa sat back down on the bench, taking Barbara's hand to hint that she should sit next to her. "I'll write to you and tell you all about the concert. I just don't know who I'll get to go with me."

Barbara reached into her purse. "Oh, yeah, I forgot. Here's my ticket. My parents told me to give it to you. You might get someone else to go."

Louisa's face lit up. "Do you need money for this?"

Barbara laughed. "I could always use money, but my mom said I couldn't accept it."

The extra ticket left Louisa conflicted. She had mentored Barbara well, teaching her to love the band wholeheartedly. She knew she probably couldn't go alone, but she wanted to be there with someone who had the same appreciation—no, devotion—for Mud.

At dinner that evening, Louisa finally told her family about the concert situation. Her mother named a list of Louisa's friends from AIS she could ask but none would do. She had very high standards for whomever she would ask.

Judy finally spoke up. "If you want, I guess I'll go. That is, if you can't get anyone else."

Louisa sensed her sister's lack of enthusiasm. "No!" she sneered. "I need to go with someone who knows the songs and loves the band. You listen to that hard rock stuff, like Led Zeppelin."

"I'm all you have, Louisa. Take it or leave it."

Louisa sat for a moment, deep in contemplation about what to do. She knew her sister was probably her only hope. Then an idea came to her. "Okay. You can go with me, but you need to go to Mud boot camp. You gotta learn the songs, the band members, when their birthdays are, how old they are, and—"

"Okay, okay," Judy said, cutting her off.

Louisa gave her sister a deadpan look. "We start tonight, soldier," she commanded. "Finish up your dinner! We have a lot of work and very little time."

The uplifting holiday spirit welcomed the LaPlantes to another Christmas season. It was two days before the Mud concert, and Louisa was in Judy's room as they figured out what they would wear to the show. Their winter Sears, Roebuck & Co. catalog order hadn't come in yet from the States, and they were both bored with their wardrobes.

"Oh well," Louisa sighed. "I'll just have to wear my Bay City Rollers pants." She rolled over on Judy's bed and stared up at the ceiling. "It's just that I wanted to wear something new to my first concert."

The Bay City Rollers, a Scottish band, became an overnight success earlier in the year. The word was they were the biggest thing since the Beatles. The "tartan teen sensation" had even found a spot on Louisa's rock shrine above her bed. She had begged her parents for Bay City Rollers pants for her birthday. After she'd unwrapped the box—which even had a plaid bow—she had worn the pants every day for two months. The high-waisted, flared white trousers had a built-in red tartan cummerbund and matching tartan cuffs at the bottom. She loved the Scottish group, but it seemed disrespectful to wear another band's trademark to the Mud concert. So she contemplated what her plan B would be.

Twirling a lock of hair around her finger, she watched Judy rummaging through her drawers. Her torn thoughts bounced around until Mathis and the record store popped in her head and interrupted her dilemma. She hadn't been to the shop in months, and a sudden pining to see the owner's son swelled inside her.

"Please, please come with me to the music store," Louisa pleaded to her sister. "I need to see if there's any new music for me to buy." What she really wanted, though, was a dose of Mathis's smile and the way he gazed warmly into her eyes making her feel like she was the only person that mattered.

Judy gave in, but when they headed out the front door, their mom shouted, "Take your brother with you. He needs an airing out; he's been in his lab all afternoon."

Minutes later, the trio cycled into town. Teddy's bike had a flat tire, so Judy let her brother ride on the back of hers.

They entered the record store to find it filled with caroling music and decorated with bright gold and silver Christmas trimmings hanging from the windows and ceiling. Teddy darted off to the back of the store, looking for the candy section, leaving the two sisters in the doorway.

Louisa's hopes fizzled when she glanced around, and Mathis was nowhere to be found. Stalling for time in case he came in, she wandered over to the record rack under the letter M and waved Judy over. It was time for some Mud training.

Louisa pulled out the album *Mud Rock Volume II* and cleared her throat. "Now, what year was this album released?" she asked, acting like she was the teacher.

Judy rolled her eyes at Louisa then looked at the cover. "The year seventeen ninety-five," she said clownishly.

Louisa snarled and went through the rack again, pulling out a different album. "Judy." She clenched her teeth. "Which one of these songs was their first hit?"

Her sister studied the list on the back of the album and put her finger on her cheek. "Hmm. 'A Fifth of Beethoven'?"

Louisa could feel her blood boiling. All the hard work and time she'd spent training Judy on the band and their music—and now she was making a joke? How could anyone make a joke about Mud? She glared menacingly at her sister while her rage built.

Laughing, Judy stuck her tongue out at her. "Take a chill pill, little sister."

Louisa finally had enough of her sister's irreverent behavior. She didn't know what to do but wanted to inflict some sort of pain to teach her a lesson. It couldn't be just name calling; it needed to make a statement that said she meant serious business. Nobody messes around with her Mud. On an impulse, as if possessed, she grabbed Judy's arm and firmly sank her teeth into her sister's hand.

"Ow!" Judy tore her hand away from Louisa's mouth. "I can't believe you just did that. How old are you, ten?"

Mr. Janssens flew over to them to break up the argument. "Hello, my Amerikaan friends. How are you today?"

Judy looked at him and wept. "Look at what my sister did!" She nodded toward Louisa. "She bit me." Judy held her hand up to show him. The imprints of Louisa's teeth were clearly visible.

The shop's owner stood there, his mouth half open, as he stared at the girls. The store was silent for a brief moment, then the back door swung open. Mathis stood in the doorway, a backpack slung over one shoulder, large as life.

A sinking feeling of panic swept through Louisa when she saw him. She needed to make amends with her sister fast so Mathis wouldn't know what she had done. "Judy, I'm so sorry! I didn't mean to do that. It was . . . an accident."

Judy stared at her coldly, then gave her a Cheshire Cat grin. "I think a Kriffy candy bar will make it better."

Louisa felt the tension drain from her and was able to breathe again. She ran to the back of the store, where Teddy was still pawing through the candy, and grabbed the peace offering Judy had requested. When she made her way to the counter to pay for it, Mr. Janssens followed. Mathis cut him off, though, whispering to his father before zipping to the register to help her.

As Louisa's eyes met Mathis's from across the counter, she could almost hear the loud thunder of fireworks exploding in her head. That was funny because he always had a quiet, elusive way about him—or maybe he only seemed that way because he didn't speak English. Either way, his demeanor was an enigma, and she loved not knowing what this was between them.

Teddy darted up to the counter. His arms were full of assorted candies, from salted licorice to Côte d'Or bars. "Here, get this for me." He pulled a plastic sandwich bag loaded with coins out of his coat pocket and handed it to Louisa. "I think this is enough."

Louisa's hand shook nervously as she opened the bag in front of Mathis and poured out the coins, scattering them everywhere. Some rolled off onto her side of the counter, and some fell onto Mathis's side. They both scurried right and left to catch the runaway change and eventually shared a laugh about the chaos. Once the last coin was retrieved and the situation under control, their eyes met again in an intense gaze.

Interrupting the heated moment, Judy approached them. "See what Louisa did to me?" She laid her wounded hand on the counter in front of Mathis.

He smiled at Judy and lowered his head to count Teddy's change.

Judy sighed heavily, clenched her hands, and propped them on her hips. "Your girlfriend is a demon child."

Mathis's face remained blank to her rage. He bundled up the candy and handed Louisa a brown bag. Then he turned his back, and Louisa caught a glimpse of him sliding something into a second bag before giving it to her. Puzzled, she tilted her head at him.

"Dag, Louisa." Mathis's smile broadened, exposing his one dimple. "Very Christmas."

It always gave Louisa a sense of importance the way he pronounced her name. His S sounded like a hard Z, and it sounded like he was saying *La-wee-za*. No one else in the world addressed her in that unique manner.

She took the bag without opening it. "Goodbye, Mathis—I mean, dag—ah, I mean, Merry Christmas too." Embarrassed, she ran out of the store without looking back.

Louisa jumped back on her bicycle and headed home with her sister and brother in the lead. Off in the distance, she could hear Teddy complaining to Judy she was hitting the bumps too hard. "That hurts. Why are you aiming for them?" he cried.

Louisa, however, was riding at a much slower pace. She was daydreaming about Mathis and what he'd put in her bag.

Once they turned onto Bremboslaan, she spotted a small furry lump in the road up ahead. "Watch out, Judy!" she yelled. "I think there's a dead animal in the street."

She knew whenever Judy saw anything dead on the road while in a car or bicycling, her sister would pray for the unfortunate creature.

As they passed the furry corpse, Louisa heard Judy finish her prayer out loud. "The Father, the Son, and the Holy—eeek!"

Louisa stared in horror. Her sister had lifted an arm to cross herself in prayer and lost control of her bike—with Teddy still on the back. They wobbled to the right as Judy attempted to bring the bike upright. But it went down to the left, hitting the pavement hard.

Teddy crawled out from under the bike, his face flaming with anger. "You're a space cadet! Why would you pray when someone's on the back of your bike?"

Judy lay still on the street for a moment. When she lifted her head, her eyes were clenched shut, and she cried out in pain. Her right arm had somehow ended up under her when they had fallen, and it was swelling up like a balloon.

Louisa ran over to help her up.

"I think it's broken!" Judy shrieked.

Louisa panicked momentarily over her sister's situation. What followed in her mind was: who would go with her to the Mud concert if Judy's arm was broken?

Their home was only a few feet away, so Teddy walked Judy's bike back to the house while Louisa ran ahead to tell their mom. By the time Judy arrived, the bone had almost popped through her skin. Frantically, the family piled into the car and rushed her to the hospital.

Two hours later, Judy came out of the examining room, her right arm bandaged and in a sling. She had broken it in two places, according to the doctor. Looking down at her sister's arm, Louisa's eyes widened in fear; the teeth marks were still on Judy's hand. Luckily, she saw her sister was so doped up from the painkillers she probably didn't remember what she had done—or if she did squeal on her, her parents would just think she was high from the drugs.

When they arrived back from the hospital, Louisa sat in the living room with her parents, trying to decide what to do about the concert dilemma.

"Well, you may have to call off your concert on Saturday. Your sister can't go in her condition. Unless you want to go alone." Her father appeared to have no compassion.

Tears of disappointment built up inside Louisa, but she tried to hold them back. First Barbara couldn't go to the concert because she'd moved away. Then she'd done all that hard work to prepare Judy on such short notice. And now this happened—all because of a dead animal on the street?

"Who does that?" she exploded with anger. "How can anyone be so stome that they pray for roadkill with someone on the back of their bike?"

"Your sister is in a lot of pain, so I'm sure this is a lesson learned," her mother said quietly, so as not to wake Judy, who was already fast asleep in her bedroom.

"I have to go to this concert, or I'll die! I won't have any reason to live if I don't go." Louisa's breathing became labored.

Her mom patted Louisa's hand. "Hey, I have an idea. Why don't you ask Anneke Verstraete to go? You both like the same music."

Sinking in her chair, Louisa brooded over her predicament. She knew Anneke was far too prudish for her. It would probably be no fun to go

109

with her. Would she be able to let loose and go wild at the concert with the mother hen there telling her to calm down and be careful? On the other hand, the concert was only two days away, and this was her only option: either stay home and die or go with someone who never broke the rules.

Maybe, though, she could unravel whatever Anneke's secret was. There *had* to be more to the girl.

TRACK 11

"LITTLE DARLING" – THE RUBETTES

DECEMBER 1976

Louisa sat next to her brother on the school bus on their way home from AIS the following afternoon. She was bursting with anticipation at that point. It was Friday, and the Mud concert was tomorrow. All day, she had pleaded with the Universe not to let anything else get in the way of her going to the show. Considering who she was going with though, she figured she was safe. Anneke was too careful to screw this up for her.

Louisa stared intensely out the bus window as one schoolmate after another hopped off. She dreamily thought about what seeing Mud in person would be like. Nothing else seemed to matter. Then something surfaced in her head she'd forgotten all about, making her shoot straight up in her seat.

She'd never looked in the bag to see what Mathis had put in there yesterday. Everything had been so chaotic the night before, between taking Judy to the hospital and the stress of who would go to the Mud concert with her, that she'd left the brown bag from the music store in her bicycle basket all night. How could she have forgotten? The poor brown bag was by itself in the cold garage all night long.

The bus ride seemed to take forever, and the anticipation was burning inside her. When they eventually arrived at the end of Bremboslaan, Louisa darted off as soon as her feet hit the pavement.

"Where are you going in such a hurry?" Teddy yelled behind her.

She didn't respond. Instead, she bolted down Bremboslaan toward home.

As usual, her mom had left the garage door open, so she rushed up the driveway and inside. The bag was still in her bicycle basket. She grabbed it, ran into the house, dashed into her bedroom, and slammed the door shut. Catching her breath, Louisa sat a moment on her bed until she could breathe again.

Her guessing was all over the place as to what it could be. Finally, her hand slid in the bag, and she pulled out a 45-rpm vinyl record. The label read "The Rubettes," and the title of the single was "Miss Goodie Two-Shoes."

Louisa slumped. She didn't know what to make of it. Was it possible Mathis knew Anneke? But why would he have given her this record? Was that what he thought of her? Did he even know what the phrase "Goody Two-Shoes" meant?

Her arm dropped to the bed in disappointment, letting go of the 45. She rolled over onto her stomach, propped her chin on her hands, and gazed up at the posters of the bands above her bed. Whenever Louisa's parents grounded her or she was upset about something, this was often her ritual. She'd fixate on the posters like they were a higher power. It calmed her down when she was stressed, knowing she had these bands in her life and that they would never disappoint her, make her angry, or leave her crying.

A few minutes passed, and Louisa rolled back over and stood up from her bed. The Rubettes record fell to the floor. Bending over to pick it up, she noticed the record's A side was face up and labeled with a song called "Little Darling." Underneath the title was a drawing of a heart with a handwritten note inside that read, "Voor jou, Louisa."

For a moment, she blinked at what Mathis had written. She'd never heard of the song. Was it new? Filled with excitement, she whipped the record out of its paper sleeve, put it on the turntable, and hit Play.

It began with the gentle strumming of an electric guitar, leading into a sweet, engaging melody. Once the singing started, Louisa knew she could not live without it. A thrill passed through her that was almost unbearable, causing her to lean forward and hold her stomach. She was emotionally torn between an urge to cry and the desire to laugh. Whenever she drew in a breath, rapture swarmed over as if her head was filling up with happiness helium. She was taken to another world as she listened to every lyric:

"Don't you know I love you
Little darling?
Want the world to know now
Little darling
Can't live without your precious love
Can't do without it anymore
Little darling
Ah
Little darling
Put your arms around me
Little darling
Tell me that you want me
Little darling
Can't live without your precious love
Little darling
You showed me how
Gave me true loving now
So don't let's change it
Or rearrange it"

Louisa sat in silence after the song ended, blown away by the conflicting feelings she'd experienced. She eyeballed the record on the turntable and read what Mathis had written again, focusing on the heart he'd drawn. A shriek of exhilaration poured out of her, as if it had been bottled up inside her all her life. She needed more of it. Fast.

Leaning over, she pressed Play to start the song again, pretending Mathis was singing it to her. If only he spoke English—that would have made the fantasy complete.

The morning of the concert, Louisa woke to a surprise dusting of snow outside. It was lying gently on top of the brown blades of grass through the French doors in her family's yard when she walked out into the great room.

Her eyes sparkled at the six-foot illuminated Christmas tree her mother had lavishly decorated a few days earlier standing in the living room. At the top was a large hand-painted gold foil angel called a Rauschgoldengel. Her mom had picked up the heavenly ornament at the Nuremberg Christmas market. The angel was accompanied by strands upon strands of berries and popcorn underneath. Tinsel and handmade beaded and sequin bulbs in every color imaginable dangled freely on the evergreen's branches. The icosahedron greeting-card ornament Louisa had brought over on the plane from the States to Belgium had the best seat in the house, though. It hung in the center at the front of the tree proudly, to be seen by all.

Louisa waved "hi" to the Christmas tree, acting like it were a friend she was passing in the hall at AIS, and skipped into the kitchen, singing the lyrics of "Little Darling." She'd played the record Mathis had given her at least twenty-five times before she'd gone to bed the night before, so now she knew the words by heart. After grabbing her cereal bowl, she sat at the table where her mom was drinking coffee and reading the GB Foods ad for its weekly specials.

"You're in a good mood today," her mother said. "Are you getting used to the idea that Anneke will be going with you to the concert?"

Louisa smiled. "Today is the greatest day ever!"

"Well, Louisa, what's going on with the sudden mood change from the concert dilemma a few nights ago?"

Louisa looked up from her bowl of cereal grinning ear to ear, then dropped her head and resumed eating.

Mr. and Mrs. Verstraete dropped Anneke off at the LaPlantes' house a few hours before the concert. Before the girls left for the big night, they sat at the kitchen table to snack on peanut butter and jelly sandwiches that Patty had made for them. Anneke gracefully placed her napkin in her lap like she was sitting down for an elegant meal fit for a queen. She pried the sandwich open, and her dark unruly brows drew inward.

"Mees LaPlante, what is this brown stuff?"

Patty came in from the kitchen. "You never had peanut butter before?" She joined the girls at the table. "This is a real American gourmet delicacy. I picked it up the other day at a market that imports this from the States."

Louisa often went with her mom to the American specialty food store whenever they needed something that said "home" to them. But she knew this shop connecting them with their homeland came at a hefty price. All her fellow American friends nicknamed the shop "The Robber Lady" because the ticket price included the exorbitant cost of shipping from the US.

Louisa scoffed. It was a waste of her mother's money to feed such expensive "brown stuff" to someone who didn't even know what it was. She turned her head and studied Anneke while she fussed over the sandwich. The Belgian girl was probably a picky eater, like she never tried anything unless she knew exactly what she was eating and where it came from. Her friend surprised Louisa, though, when she politely asked her mom, "Please, Mees LaPlante. Something to crack it open with?" Once Patty handed her a knife and fork, Anneke slowly cut the sandwich into eight tiny squares, picked up one of the corners with her fork, and took a bite.

The Belgian teen was silent as she carefully chewed . . . and chewed . . . and chewed. Then her eyes shot open. "Oh, Mees LaPlante, this is a very *special* sandwich. I never had anything like this before. We don't have this pee-nus butter in Belgium."

Louisa couldn't control herself and broke out laughing at her friend's pronunciation of "peanut butter." But a swift kick to the leg from her mother silenced her right away. Louisa cleared her throat and sat up in her chair.

Patty dropped off the girls in front of the large concert hall in Deurne, a small town outside Antwerp. "Have fun, girls! I'll meet you here after the show! Don't get into any trouble!"

Louisa frowned and scooched out of the car. She doubted very much that she and Anneke would get into trouble. It was like she was bringing her own mother to see Mud.

Once they found their seats all the way up in the venue's nosebleed section, they plopped themselves down and settled in. Anneke continued to rave about the "special" sandwich they ate at the house, and it didn't seem like she was going to let up anytime soon. Louisa, tired of hearing about it, finally decided to change the subject. "Hey, Anneke, what's your favorite song by Mud?"

The Belgian girl's face illuminated. "Oh, Louisa, I like them all, but 'Crazy' is my favorite."

Louisa turned away from her and held in a laugh. Crazy? That was an odd choice. Did she even know what the word meant?

Eventually the lights dimmed, energizing the mostly female audience who began screaming. Louisa straightened up in her seat, squinting to see the stage that was so far away. She quickly realized a part of the problem was clouds of cigarette smoke had emerged from the row in front of her, distorting her view. Looking down at the back of their heads, every girl looked like their own individual smokestack. As soon as they sucked their cigarette down to the filter, they'd extinguish the butt on the floor and light up another, without a moment to spare. It wasn't too long before a thick fog of fumes rolled in from the rows behind Louisa, becoming one large mass with the smoke in front of her, making it nearly impossible to see the stage. What was going on? She griped. How will the band sing with all this pollution in the air?

She elbowed Anneke. "Can you see the stage with all the smoke—"

At that same moment, Anneke reached into her coat pocket, pulled out a pack of Bastos cigarettes, and lit one up. Confounded, Louisa eyeballed her friend as she sucked half the cigarette down in one puff. Even the prim and proper girl was in the fleet of smokestacks.

Eventually, the lights brightened on stage and blazing electric guitar flooded through the hall. Mud opened the show with their smash hit "Dynamite." This stimulated the screaming girls further, as if someone had cranked the volume up on them. Two teens behind Louisa were wailing in her ear like a colicky baby crying. And everyone in the row in front of her was out of control, whipping their heads from side to side and jumping up and down as if a swarm of bees was attacking them.

Halfway through the first number, Louisa pulled from her purse a pair of binoculars Teddy had let her borrow, hoping she could see better. It was still hard, but she spotted a teenage girl running toward the stage, struggling to climb up the scaffolding to reach Mud. Security came in and quickly dragged the teen off like a common criminal. Louisa was beginning to worry if this was the only form of entertainment she would be getting from the concert.

The smoke and gyrations from the unrestrained girls only intensified a few songs in. Adding to the lunacy, Anneke slipped her hand into her coat and pulled out a can of beer. Flipping the lid, she guzzled down a huge gulp. Louisa elbowed Anneke, who then turned to her with an annoyed look that said, "You dummy, this is what Belgians do when we go to a concert." Then she pulled out another beer from her coat and handed it to Louisa. Afraid of being caught, Louisa slumped in her seat and discreetly sipped the beer. This evening was not going how she expected, and the biggest surprise was that she now felt like the straitlaced "Miss Goodie Two-Shoes."

Time only brought more absurdities and surprises as the music played, distracting Louisa from the main reason she was there. At that point, determination took over, driving her not to let the surrounding situation ruin things. She held the binoculars up in a firm grip to her eyes again, fighting to find the band. Eventually she was able to zoom in on her target. And there in clear sight, as if they were standing right in front of her, were the four people who provided her life with meaning: Mud. A shiver rippled in her, as she clenched the binoculars tighter. The band spoke to her in a way that none of the crowd seemed to understand as the girls continued to scream hysterically, not even listening to the music. In her opinion, she was the only one taking the band seriously and really got them on a spiritual level.

Silent, serious, and intent, Louisa hung on every lyric, note, and movement while they seemingly performed just for her. She found herself in a mystical state. All of the chaos around her became background muffled noise and it was only her and Mud. Just the way she always dreamt it would be.

Back home, Louisa climbed into bed and pulled the blankets around her, still in a flutter from the evening. She felt like she had achieved the only goal that mattered to her. She wondered, though, what would be in store for her next? Was there more to life than Mud?

TRACK 12

"JUKE BOX JIVE"
– THE RUBETTES

APRIL 1977

espite all the trips Louisa and her family had made throughout Europe, Antwerp itself was a destination location. Unlike the tourists, though, Louisa had absorbed the history and grandeur of the city in a different way—the way almost any American teen would.

Whenever she visited Antwerp with Judy and friends, their day in the City of Diamonds would start when their bus arrived in front of the GSC and they met up with their classmates. Their first stop was Antwerp's version of Fifth Avenue, called the Meir. It was home to all sorts of posh department stores and unusual knickknack shops. Next, they'd hit up a frites stand for lunch. After eating, they would try to take advantage of Belgium's legal drinking age of sixteen.

Louisa, her sister, and many of their friends would doll themselves up fashionably, hoping they would appear of age to get into the clubs. Their eyelids would be painted in a trendy sky-blue eyeshadow, their cheeks highlighted with pink blush, and they would spend hours tweezing their eyebrows into razor-thin half-moons.

The latest hairstyle was the most important part of their preparation. They'd make sure it was styled to perfection in whatever the current fad was in the States. Perms were popular again, so the wild, curly Peter Frampton–style locks were all the rage; but any one of the signature coifs from *Charlie's Angels* would do as well.

Most Belgian girls under sixteen, Louisa had learned, didn't seem to care as much about the whole dance club scene. Pubs and discos were on almost every street corner, so there probably was no thrill in the forbidden quest. Belgians had been brought up with small amounts of wine and beer at the dinner table, so trying alcohol wasn't a big deal for them; they'd learned to appreciate it from a young age.

Most American teens, on the other hand, were raised not being able to touch alcohol until they were of legal age, which made drinking exciting to them. So Louisa, along with Judy and their American friends, had an ongoing quest to defy their parents by going out and sneaking into bars—something they *never* would have been able to do in the States given the drinking age was at least eighteen years of age and strictly enforced.

One Saturday afternoon, during a trip to Antwerp with Judy and her friends, Louisa invited Jackie Seaman, a new student in her class at AIS who had come from San Diego. Jackie had the typical California-girl look, with sun-bleached blond hair, a deep tan, and well-developed curves for her age. Although she looked like a ten out of ten on Louisa's attractiveness scale, she was bashful. Louisa often joked with her family that Jackie was Barbara's replacement model. She had gone through the same efforts as before, training her timid new friend on what bands and music to listen to and learning the ropes around town. Jackie appeared to hang on to Louisa's every word like it was the golden truth, just like Barbara had.

After the group of girls left the shops and grabbed some frites met mayo, they moseyed up to Statiestraat where rows and rows of small discos and bars were located. Louisa and Jackie were trailing behind Judy and her friends when they approached all the excitement. "I got into a bar in

Schilde once with my sister and her friend Allison, and they were able to buy me a beer," Louisa bragged.

Statiestraat buzzed with liveliness even in the middle of the day. Lights flashed everywhere in bright psychedelic colors: *disco, nightclub* and *dance*. Judy and her crew strutted up to the large doorman sitting on a barstool outside a disco called 2001. Pausing, Louisa stood back and watched as her sister presented herself with the utmost assurance, lifting her head and walking past the doorman into the club, followed by the rest of her class-mates, who had the same attitude.

Louisa, however, didn't share the same confidence. As she and Jackie approached the entrance, the doorman dropped his arm like a toll booth boom gate in front of them. He didn't say anything, but the look on his face as he shook his head said that his decision was final.

Louisa paled. She grabbed Jackie's arm and dashed away, pulling her friend with her. Embarrassed, she put on a false smile, trying to act like it was nothing. "I really didn't want to go in there anyway. They play disco, and you won't hear *our* kind of music in there."

The look of disappointment on Jackie's face, however, told Louisa she needed another plan—stat! She glanced down to the GSC, which was at the end of the street. The historical railway terminal had an alluring aura about it, puzzling Louisa. She hadn't been inside the station since the day she and her family had arrived in Belgium, and she found it odd she was drawn to it that day.

"Hey, Jackie, I have an idea. Do you want to go to the train station?"

Jackie shrugged. "What's the big deal in there?"

"I think they have a restaurant inside." Louisa was making it up as she went along hoping her friend wouldn't catch on. "And maybe they'll serve us a beer. It's worth a shot."

Jackie shrugged again. "Cool beans." She stepped aside to let Louisa lead the way.

The GSC was a work of art with its eclectic architecture. The epic dome in its center was as glorious as the stained-glass windows of the Notre-Dame cathedral. Louisa walked in with Jackie through the main entrance, her head tilted up in awe at the vaulted ceiling. Her eyes landed on a spectacular grand staircase sweeping up to the next level. Two more staircases forked off, going up each side to a mezzanine that overlooked the entrance, which swarmed with people coming and going from the tracks.

Louisa scanned the area desperately looking for a bar or restaurant, but none were in sight. Her attention gravitated back to the grand staircase. "Hey, let's go up to the next level and explore."

They climbed the first set of stairs and then the second. At the top, the crowds had thinned out, and only a few people were around. The two girls leaned over the railing, looking down at the activity below.

Jackie nudged Louisa's shoulder and pulled out a cigarette from her purse. "Do you want to smoke? I snuck one from my mom's pack."

Louisa surveyed their surroundings to ensure no older people were nearby who might say something to them. The coast appeared clear. She looked down at the cigarette. "Do you have any *stekskes*?"

Jackie cocked her head.

"*Stekskes* are matches. That's what Judy and her friends call them," Louisa explained.

Jackie extended her arms, opened her empty hands, and shook her head.

Louisa glanced over the station again, searching to ask someone for a light. On the other side of the staircase, she caught sight of a young man. He appeared to be about sixteen years old and was dressed well in fitted flared denim jeans and a matching high-waisted jacket. His skin, slightly darker than hers, was almost the same color as his large, rounded, curly hair. He seemed harmless and young enough that he wouldn't lecture them for smoking.

Louisa knew she had to make it up to Jackie for not getting them into the disco. If she went up to the guy and asked for matches, that would make her shine again in her friend's eyes. "Do you dare me to go over and ask him for a light?"

Jackie smiled. "You don't have the guts."

Louisa huffed, turned, and walked away, with Jackie following behind. They descended the second flight of stairs and went up the other side.

When they approached the young man, Louisa's stride slowed, and she pursed her lips. Could she really do this? He's a boy—and one she doesn't even know. The young man held a small portable radio and swayed his hips to the music playing. He turned his head, draped his chin over his shoulder toward the girls, and flashed them a bright, glowing smile.

Louisa decided she had to press on and get it over with. She knew little Flemish, only what she'd learned from TV programs with English subtitles underneath. Her pronunciation wasn't perfect, so she hoped she'd say what she wanted to say correctly. Her eyes met his. "Hebt ye stekskes?"

He nodded. "I can tell you are not from Belgium," he said in perfect English. "Where are you from?"

Louisa's posture loosened in relief. "We're American," she boasted.

The fellow seemed curious about them and introduced himself as Said. "I am Moroccan. I moved here a few years ago." He leaned over and lit Jackie's cigarette.

Louisa acted like she knew what a Moroccan was—or even where Morocco was. "So we're in the same boat, living in another country." Feelings of hope and optimism swept over her. She could not believe she just said that to him. And so eloquently too. Was she actually having a mature, intelligent conversation with a boy? Spiritedly, she complimented Said on how good his English was. Judy had said that to a French boy once, and Louisa had waited years to use the line.

The three conversed for a few more minutes before Said glanced down at the main entrance and spotted someone he knew. "Yo!" he yelled to three young men in the lobby below, proceeding to say something in Arabic to them. Said's friends looked up at him—at Louisa and Jackie—and in a mad scamper, they hustled their way up to the next level.

When the other Moroccans approached, Louisa noticed the first two appeared to be around her age. One of them had a round face splattered with chocolate brown freckles over his dark complexion. The other, who was quiet, intrigued her. His shoulder-length curly dark hair was greased with a fixative making his corkscrews shine, and his stunning light blue eyes stood out against his bronzed skin.

The last of Said's friends appeared a little older than the others. He wore a fitted white-and-black pinstriped suit. Louisa thought he seemed very pleased with himself and appeared to be the group's ringleader, the one who called all the shots. He swaggered over to the girls and snapped his head up to swoosh his sleek feathered coif back, then stopped inches away from Louisa's face. "We love Americans. What are you doing here?"

Intimidated by the older one, Louisa stepped back to give herself some space. "Well, my father's company in the States transferred us here, and we've been living in Belgium for—"

"That's not what I mean," he said, cutting her off. "What are you doing here at the train station?"

Louisa turned to Jackie. The two girls covered their mouths in a muffled giggle. Jackie appeared to be gaining the same confidence as Louisa when she boldly asked the Moroccans, "We're looking for a bar. Is there one in here?"

The younger lad with electric blue eyes leaned over and whispered something in the ear of his pinstripe-suited friend. The two looked back at the girls. "Yes, my friends," the pinstripe-suited one said. "Indeed. There's a restaurant on this floor, on the other side of the clock."

Louisa stood back and studied the four Moroccans. How far should she and Jackie take this encounter with the boys? This was already a big step for her. Should they just walk away and let it mellow? Or would she have a good story to bring to AIS on Monday? After standing a moment in silence, she decided "a good story" for her friends was the favorable choice. "We met Said," she nodded. "But what are your names?"

The other three introduced themselves. Still, the only names Louisa could pronounce were Said and Cointreau, the younger one who had caught her eye. The names of the others were too hard for her to pronounce or remember, so she and Jackie secretly gave them nicknames: Freckle Face and Striped Pants. Those were much more manageable.

The two girls promenaded into the restaurant, escorted by their very own entourage of young men. Pleased, Louisa quickly checked out her surroundings. Straight ahead of her was a circular bar in the middle of the high-ceilinged room where a few elderly men sat on stools, each with a goblet of beer before him while they smoked cigarettes. Three long windows let light in from the restaurant's left side. The ambiance wasn't lively like Statiestraat, but Louisa knew beggars couldn't be choosers.

Once the group sat at a table, Striped Pants, who was legally old enough, ordered a round of beers for them. "My new American friends," smiled Stripe Pants as he handed Louisa and Jackie a chalice of beer. "Tell me about yourselves."

Louisa found the interest and special treatment from them much more bearable than in the past. Maybe it was because she was the leading lady now, no longer her sister's understudy. But whatever it was, she was beginning to like it. A lot.

The conversation flowed, and it wasn't long before Louisa's short attention span kicked in. Her focus wandered away from their table and to the other patrons. As her eyes surfed around the room, she was pleasantly surprised when she spotted a jukebox in the corner. She had seen a small one once in the States, mounted on the wall of a diner booth. Yet this jukebox was much larger, and radiant. In her opinion, it should have been on its own noble foundation of gold, just like the enormous clock out in the station. She sprang up from the table as if something pulled her toward the box.

Once she was in front of the machine, she flipped through the selections, one after another, trying to find the perfect song. Soon she found herself torn between two selections. But she only had a coin for one and wanted to impress the Moroccans with her impeccable taste in music, so she had to make the perfect choice. No mistakes.

While the battle in her head continued, she suddenly felt warm breath heating up the back of her neck. Someone was right behind her. She spun around and found Cointreau standing there, inches away.

Louisa tensed. Should she talk to him? What would she say? No, she wasn't ready for a one-on-one conversation.

She spun back, facing the jukebox, trying to ignore the young Moroccan, yet she sensed his presence still there. Eventually, he leaned over her shoulder and tapped on the jukebox's glass. "Play that one."

Louisa looked down to where Cointreau was tapping. It was a song by J. Vincent Edwards. She looked back at him and considered not putting on his choice with her only coin, but the intense look in his blue eyes reminded her of the Mediterranean Sea, when she had been in Carry-le-Rouet with her family. She fed her coin into the machine and punched in the song's code. A steady drumbeat began, followed by a cheerful, bouncy melody reminding her of skipping through a plush green meadow on a warm spring day. She turned back to Cointreau and found herself swimming in the swells of his sea-filled eyes.

The engaging melody continued while the song's chorus "Love Hit Me" rang out through the room. Maybe she really was ready for this. *Quick, say something to him—now.*

Interrupting the tension between the two, Jackie yelled out, "Get over here quick, Louisa. Said is telling us a funny joke."

When Louisa got home later that day, she was elated at her discovery of the train station and the Moroccans. Even though she hadn't mustered up the courage to speak privately with Cointreau, she felt like she'd achieved something big that day—like this was a turning point in her life. She and Jackie had independently lured their new friends in without Judy's help, and that brought on a confidence she had never had before.

After that trip, the two girls continued visiting the GSC on Saturday afternoons to see their new friends. Meeting the Moroccans was never arranged, though. Louisa simply knew when she and Jackie walked through the station's impressive main entrance, one of them would be hanging out on the other side by the grand staircase. Yet she often pondered if the attraction was really for the Moroccans on their own accord or if was she trying to do something outrageous to one-up her pretty, popular sister.

TRACK 13

"HOT LOVE" – T. REX

OCTOBER 1977

Another fall had arrived, and Louisa's parents announced they would be traveling to Paris for a long weekend to enjoy the vibrant autumn foliage in the French capital's magnificent gardens. The teens were to stay home, though with a sitter. Her mom had arranged for Joan the gym teacher, who was very popular among the students at AIS, to stay with them while they were away.

Louisa was thrilled with the prospect of taking advantage of her hip young babysitter, who didn't know all of her parents' strict rules and regulations. She saw it as a golden opportunity to finally go to one of the Belgian popcorn dances Judy had attended with Gui, since her parents still hadn't given her permission to attend. She was desperate to satisfy her curiosity about this underground music scene and had to find a way to go. Surely the DJ would have a huge collection of rare bootleg music by Mud. So she brainstormed a plan with Jackie for the two of them to go.

The day her parents left for Paris, Louisa worked on her sales pitch right away. Her gym teacher sat on the living room couch while Louisa stood in front of her, fidgeting while she made her plea.

Joan was an American and had worked at AIS since her family arrived in Belgium. Short, chunky, and in her late twenties, her full red cheeks matched her jolly character. She was known as an entertaining jokester and was always playing practical jokes on the students in class. Louisa was quite comfortable with her since she was her gymnastics coach, and they traveled together on many school competitions.

"Joan, my mom and dad let Judy go all the time, so it should be no problem," Louisa explained.

Even though her teacher was less intimidating than most adults, she anticipated a flat-out refusal, knowing her luck. Joan paused, though, and contemplated it for a minute. "Well, I guess it's okay."

Louisa's heart quivered.

"But Judy will have to go with you," she added.

Hearing this, made Louisa sneer in disgust. All hope fell by the wayside. Not that she didn't want her sister to go, but Judy was still deeply embarrassed about Bob Dylan kissing her at the popcorn dance. She told Louisa after she and Gui had broken up she'd never go back to that place again. She was too nervous she'd run into one of the boys. Louisa found Judy's unexpected concern for the situation very puzzling, given her usual composed manner. Perhaps her sister wasn't as indifferent as she came across.

When Jackie arrived at the LaPlantes' house late Sunday morning, Louisa broke the bad news to her friend. "I can't believe it. My one chance to go while my parents are away. I'm so cranky right now I could scream."

"No biggie." Jackie shrugged it off. "It's cool beans."

Louisa's face brightened, "Hey, let's go listen to records. Music will make us feel better."

As they headed down the hall, the front doorbell rang. Teddy ran out of his "lab" to answer it and let David in.

The four teens ran into each other in the hallway. David's eyes practically doubled in size as he ogled Jackie. He appeared starstruck by her shoulder-length wavy blond hair, tan skin, and white teeth almost glowing in the dark hallway.

Louisa knew her friend's looks could turn heads, but she was never envious. She would have hated it if everyone gawked at her and drooled like they wanted to devour her for dinner.

Jackie took no notice of David and pulled Louisa away by the arm, appearing anxious. Once they were inside Louisa's room, Jackie shut the door and faced Louisa. "You won't believe it. There was a whole van of Moroccan workers behind our school bus for the longest time on the highway. I tried looking through the back window to see if I knew any of them but couldn't tell. And when they exited before my stop, I was so sad."

Jackie nudged Louisa and pulled her pant leg up. On the side of her calf, she'd drawn a big heart in blue pen. Inside the drawing, she'd written the words *Jackie and Louisa + all of the Moroccans.*

Louisa applauded her friend's homemade tattoo and gestured for Jackie to sit down on the floor close to her entertainment center. After she hit Play on her turntable the funky, sexy rhythm of T. Rex's "Hot Love" poured out of the speakers. Closing her eyes blissfully, she let the melody take her away while she rocked back and forth on crisscrossed legs. As with all of her music, she'd analyze the melody by breaking it down, fixedly listening to each facet separate, from the rolling drum patterns to the intervals between each chord. Each layer would evoke a distinct feeling of intense rhapsody.

Louisa was sure her dramatic swaying from side to side looked silly, like she was under a demonic trance, but she didn't care. Besides, she knew Jackie would understand—she had taught her friend well about the allegiance to their music. When the sing-along coda started, Louisa signaled Jackie to follow her lead, and they both spiritedly raised their arms and waved them back and forth as they sang "La, la, la" over and over.

The music eventually faded to an end, leaving Louisa invigorated. "See?" she crowed. "I told you music would help."

The bedroom door flew open, startling both girls. Louisa turned her head as David stormed in. There was a look of fierce determination on his face and his bugged eyes almost made her burst out laughing as he sat down close to Jackie. "Where are you from?"

"I'm from California." Jackie smiled.

While David and Jackie small-talked, Louisa sat quietly, concocting a plan. If she asked David to escort her and Jackie to the popcorn dance, Joan might reconsider and let them go. David was one of the smartest boys in school and came across as a mature adult when he wanted to. Plus, his height meant he could act like their bodyguard.

Louisa had never been good at negotiating with her parents. However, when Joan said yes after she presented her case, she was thrilled about how this might open up a whole new world of persuasion for her in the future.

Joan took the three of them in the Peugeot wagon to the venue, an old farmhouse converted into a dance hall located on a remote dirt road. As they rolled into the parking lot, people everywhere were dancing freely on the grass surrounding the building and on top of cars. The wild scene made Louisa's toes twitch with excitement. She glanced over at her teacher to see if she noticed the chaos and sensed a look of regret in Joan's eyes.

Once the car stopped—and before Joan had a chance to renege—Louisa yanked Jackie's arm hard and dashed out of the car with her friend. "Thanks, Joan!" she yelled quickly. "Goodbye!" They hit the dirt road and headed to the entrance, with David running to catch up, following Jackie like her shadow.

The teens walked into the venue after plowing through the rowdy dancers outside. Louisa closely observed the interior. She wanted to capture every detail of the extraordinary scene Judy had raved about. The place was a little run-down, but the vibe was swanky. On the dance floor, couples danced in a lavish swing style. The café was a mix between a sock hop, cabaret theater, and dive bar. The people appeared liberated, open, and friendly. Some patrons were dressed flamboyantly and en vogue. Others were casual, wearing blue jeans and T-shirts.

Standing a few feet away from Louisa was a flashy-looking man in his twenties, with hot, pink-rimmed eyeglasses studded with silver sequins. On his head was a purple felt fedora. His long paisley green coat fell just far enough to expose his shimmering pink platform shoes.

Louisa had never seen a man dressed like that in person, only on TV or on the posters of some of her favorite bands. She couldn't take her eyes off him. Intrigued, she jabbed Jackie with her elbow to get her attention. Jackie turned her head to look, and she lit up with wide-eyed excitement.

The glitzy fellow returned the stare while the girls openly gaped, and he strutted over to them. Louisa was taken aback when his deep voice didn't match his eccentric appearance as he spoke to them. "Bonjour, mon amie. Ça va?"

Louisa knew some French but wasn't sure how to respond. "Do you speak English?"

The young man lowered his head dramatically, tipped his pink-rimmed glasses, and slid them down the bridge of his nose. "Of course, smiley. Where are you from?"

Jackie stood tall, with a focused gaze and stepped in front of Louisa. "We're from the States. Where are you from? What's your name?"

Pushing his glasses back up his nose, he flung his hand open, palm up. "My love, I am Hugo, and I am from Paris."

David's face hardened, as he puffed his chest like he was the girls' protector. He stepped in between them and Hugo.

"And who is this?" Hugo asked, playfully brushing some lint off David's shoulder. "Your husband?"

Louisa giggled. "No. He's David, and he speaks French."

Jackie moved in closer to Hugo, trying to regain his attention. "Do you come here from Paris every week?"

"Non, mon amour." Hugo's focus remained riveted on David as he spoke to the girls. "Only once a month."

David appeared uneasy at Hugo's flamboyant manner. He exhaled, backing away a few steps.

Louisa was getting the feeling their new friend was more interested in David than the beautiful blond who kept saying "cool beans." She stood back and watched, amused. While David stared at Jackie, Jackie gawked at Hugo, and Hugo ogled David.

The laser-focused stare down finally ended when David snapped. "I'm going to take a walk around." He strode off angrily.

Hugo raised his hands, looking puzzled at David's departure. Letting out a snort, he turned his attention to the dance floor.

Louisa pulled Jackie's arm. "Let's go see if the DJ will play something we can dance to."

They walked up to the booth where the DJ sat. He was preoccupied, browsing through his music library and preparing for the next number, taking no notice of them. Louisa studied him and could tell he was tall even though he was sitting down. He had a severe face and wore black Poindexter eyeglasses and a tall cowboy hat.

The girls stood in front of the booth, waiting to be noticed. But he never looked up at them. Instead, he remained buried in his work. After a while, Louisa grew restless. What could she and Jackie do now? She flung her hands up in the air, waving them to get the DJ's attention. "Hey!" she yelled, jumping as high as she could. "Hello! Dag!"

The DJ slowly tilted his head up. His eyes were barely visible under the wide brim of his hat. He waved them over to the side of his booth.

When Louisa approached him, her smile widened as if he was a rock and roll superhero. "Hebt ye 'Hell Raiser' by The Sweet?"

The DJ shook his head in a cool, reserved way. His eyes returned to his turntable.

Maybe it was only a fluke he didn't have anything by The Sweet? Baffled, she tried again. "Hebt ye 'Tiger Feet' by Mud? How about that?"

The DJ snarled, mumbled something without looking up, and shook his head again.

Could it be he didn't understand her Flemish? Otherwise, it was certainly a crime he didn't have any of her music. "What about a little 'Hot Love'?" Louisa asked slowly in English, hoping he'd understand her. "Do you have that? By T. Rex. Do you?"

The DJ was silent for a second. Slowly, he propped his hands on the arms of his chair and rose to his feet. Louisa's eyes were glued on him as he towered over her and Jackie like a dark cloud passing over the sun. "Née!" he snapped. "No 'Hot Love' for you today!"

A cold shiver ran down Louisa's spine. Unnerved, she grabbed Jackie, and they fled from the booth, back to their spot on the edge of the dance floor where Hugo was still standing.

"What's wrong with this place?" she asked Hugo. "They wouldn't play Mud, The Sweet, or even T. Rex. What kind of joint is this?"

Hugo laughed and put his hand on her shoulder. "Amour, this is not that kind of establishment. Don't you understand? People come from all over Europe to hear and dance to this special music the DJ mixes."

Louisa's disappointment almost brought tears to her eyes. All this time, she'd fantasized about this day. And it turned out the hype was a myth. *What a rip-off.*

By the time they had to leave, the café was packed. Most of the people that were outside earlier had moved inside. Louisa made her way out with Jackie and David, weaving through the thick crowd. The diversity still fascinated her, despite her disappointment in the music. Her head swiveled to the left, to the right, up high, and even down low, when a few female dwarfs passed her with bright red boas wrapped around their necks, flowing in their wake.

As they continued on, Louisa's attention was drawn to someone dancing she thought she knew. The person's familiarity mystified her—she had to get a closer look. She navigated her way through to the edge of the dance floor.

Once she found an opening, she saw a girl standing gracefully in the middle of the club, wearing a low-cut, mermaid-style black lace tango dress. Her hair was slicked back in a small bun, and on one side a large red poppy was tucked in front of her ear. Dark eyeliner swept up from the corners of her eyes, giving her a cat-eye look, and ruby red lipstick enhanced her mouth. She extended her sleek arm seductively to her dance partner, who appeared to be in his twenties.

Louisa strained to get a better look at her, but the dimmed lights made it hard. The two dancers continued their routine, the heat radiating between them as the girl wedged her body so close to him they appeared as one. They circled the floor in sync with the rhythmic music. The crowd cheered at their erotic dancing.

What was so familiar about her? Soon, the female dancer peeled her body off the man, nodded to him, and smiled—that was when all was revealed. The erotic girl dancer was Anneke Verstraete.

Taken aback, Louisa stood hand over her mouth. Should she approach her friend? What would she say to her anyway? The whole situation seemed awkward, like she'd caught Anneke in a questionable act and did not want to embarrass her. She was sure of one thing, though: Mr. and Mrs. Verstraete would disapprove.

Anneke's character was like a chameleon. First, she seemed like an over-cautious prissy, then a smoking, beer-guzzling "pee-nus" butter and jelly lover, and now this—Mata Hari? What would be next? Who was Anneke Verstraete really?

TRACK 14

"MOVIESTAR" – HARPO

NOVEMBER 1977

As fall continued, Louisa's world spun fast, and everything and everyone kept evolving into something new. Teddy was still best buddies with David, but the boys had grown from their youthful pranks—like stink bombs and itchy toilet paper—to more mature endeavors, like running away after ringing a stranger's doorbell or spiking the punch at school dances. Judy had dated a Texan boy who was attending AIS—but only for a few months until his father got orders to return to the States. Weeks after his departure, she started going steady with a young man from Great Britain at school named Ashley. She told Louisa it was the best of both worlds because he still had an accent, but she didn't have the language barrier problem.

Louisa had also been evolving. She had moved on from her main addiction for Mud to The Rubettes. Mud was her first love, and she'd never forget them. Maybe it was the "Little Darling" record Mathis had given her that played a small part in her choice. Either way, there was a giant ocean of music that waited out there for her, and it was time for something new.

One burning question lingered with Louisa, though: how long would her family be staying in Belgium? Her dad was vague about that detail, but one day he simply implied, "It's possible that we could be staying four years or even longer." Her mom's shriek of delight that followed echoed off the walls. Louisa never really understood her mother's wanderlust. All the same, she knew her mother never understood her obsession for the bands she loved.

One evening, Lyle came home from work and announced some big news. "In three weeks, we're going to be entertaining the Mexican ambassador to Belgium for the night." He turned to Patty. "You'll have to get your game on."

"What an honor," Patty said solemnly, holding her hand over her heart. "I'm up for the challenge."

Louisa hardly knew what the role of an ambassador was, let alone *where* Mexico was located. But her mom apparently did, and she told Louisa and the rest of the family she'd go all out and host a dinner party at their house. She would invite Belgian acquaintances from their father's office and some of her local American friends.

Through the days leading up to the dinner party, Patty's excitement made her noticeably uncertain and fickle. Louisa didn't understand what the big deal was. It reminded her of when her father had first told them they were moving to Belgium. Her mom's big dilemma was what to prepare for the meal, and she drove everyone in the house nuts with her indecisiveness. First she said it would be a Mexican dish, to make the ambassador and his wife feel at home. But she reconsidered. "Everybody must do Mexican food for them. It's hardly a unique experience." The next day, she announced, "I know! I'll do a Belgian dish. But is that elegant enough to serve His Royal Highness?"

Finally, she had a brilliant plan and told the family that since the party would be at the end of November, she'd prepare a *traditional* American Thanksgiving feast. She would cover all bases and present an authentic culinary experience for the ambassador, his wife, and the Belgians from Lyles's office since they'd probably never celebrated the holiday before. And their friends from the States would no doubt be happy, to just have a little taste that said "home".

"Everyone will be impressed!" Patty said, adding that she would "need only the best." So she arranged for a twenty-six-pound turkey to be flown in from the US, along with stuffing mix and cranberries. Most of the traditional fixings were hard to find in Antwerp—or, worse, something would get lost in translation. And Louisa's mother, as she told the family, didn't want *any* surprises.

"This is it, Patty," Lyle shouted one night at the dinner table with the family, clearly disgusted at the expenses she was racking up. "This meal you're making doesn't just count against this year's budget. It's gobbled up this family's next three Thanksgivings."

Patty said she didn't care if they'd be eating peanut butter and jelly sandwiches at Thanksgiving for the next five years to come. The sacrifice would be worth it if she could present an elegant meal to El Embajador.

A week before the party, the turkey still hadn't come in from the States. Louisa's mom was in hysterics that it might not arrive on time. She had been yelling at the entire family all evening long. Finally, Lyle sat her down on the couch to try and calm her. "Patty, you'll have to have a backup plan, just in case something goes wrong with the shipment."

Louisa sat in the kitchen doing her homework, witnessing her father's attempts to console her mother. Her speculation from past experience was confirmed: her dad had no talent for finding the right thing to say to put someone at ease. His words sent her mom into an explosive rage.

"Now I have to mentally prepare for *two* meals?" She stormed out of the living room, and her parents' bedroom door slammed shut seconds later followed by a click.

Thankfully, just days before the party, Mr. Turkey arrived, saving the family from further hysteria.

Louisa was thrilled when her mother said she could be her sous-chef for the big event. She set her alarm for 6:00 a.m. to help her mom put the bird in the oven the morning of the party. The plan was to cook it ahead of time so they would have the whole evening to socialize instead of spending it in the kitchen.

In the early afternoon, the time came to take the turkey out of the oven. The whole LaPlante family gathered in the kitchen. It was like the unveiling of the Statue of Liberty when Lyle opened the oven door to reveal a perfectly cooked turkey—and the mouthwatering smell that followed. Everyone oohed and aahed at the sight.

Patty bowed, appearing pleased with what she had created. Next the teens followed as their dad brought the turkey into the garage to cool down on the workbench. After everyone else went back inside, Louisa, playing the serious role of the sous-chef, stayed by the bird like she was its faithful protector.

Teddy had begged their mom a few days earlier, asking if David could come to the feast, since he had never had a traditional Thanksgiving meal before. When his friend arrived that afternoon, Louisa dragged David into the garage to see the twenty-six-pound bird. "It's amazing that he was able to lift himself up and fly here from the States," David joked.

Patty popped her head into the garage while the two teens admired the bird. "Louisa, I'm going to need a few things before the party. Could you run to the GB for me?"

"I'll go, too," David jumped in. "What do you need?"

Patty had a small list, then hesitated before handing it to him. "You know what? I think I'll go. There are too many things you might get wrong. Why don't you two come along and help? It might be quicker."

On the ride back from the GB, Louisa's mom preached the importance of that evening's guest of honor. The lecture seemed to go on forever while Louisa stared blankly at her lap. Once they turned onto Bremboslaan, David, unexpectedly broke out in roaring laughter. Louisa, startled, looked back at him and followed his eyes to see what was so funny. Further ahead in the street, an enormous Great Dane ran toward the car along the side of the curb with something huge hanging out of its mouth, flopping back and forth. At first, Louisa couldn't figure out what it was. But as the dog came closer, she feared the worst. "Mom, did you close the garage door when we left?"

Her mother, clearly unaware of the dog ahead, continued driving and carrying on about the importance of tonight's guest.

They eventually crossed paths with the Great Dane, and Louisa's eyes ballooned when she got a closer look. Their twenty-six-pound turkey was hanging from the dog's mouth. The Great Dane trotted proudly like he'd caught the bird himself.

"Mom, he's got your turkey!" Louisa shouted.

David's laughter ceased as the car pulled into the driveway. The garage door was open, and the workbench empty.

"*No!*" Patty's scream was so loud it must have traveled all the way down Bremboslaan. Her horrified look morphed into one of firm resolve. She jammed the stick shift down, stiffly yanking the car into reverse and backing it out of the driveway. The Peugeot wagon flew down Bremboslaan after the dog.

"Mom, what are you doing? We can't catch that dog! And even if we could, you can't serve the turkey after it's been in a dog's mouth!" Louisa cried.

Veins bulged in her mom's forehead. "I don't care!" she yelled. "I'm getting that bird back! He's mine."

Up ahead, Louisa saw the huge Great Dane merrily trotting along the side of the road. How could he carry such a massive thing in his mouth? As they approached, the large dog jumped off the pavement and headed into a cornfield.

Patty pulled the car over to the side of the road, flung her door open, and gave Louisa and David a threatening look. "Don't just sit there! Come on. We have to follow the dog." She ran over to the cornfield and dove in, rustling through the tall stalks.

Louisa turned to David. "I'm gonna run around to the other side and see if I can catch him when he comes out. Go in and keep an eye on my mom."

Reaching the opposite end of the field, Louisa stood back and saw the stalks moving in several places from above. She kept her eyes on the movement that was deepest in the middle—that must be the dog.

"I hear something ahead of me," her mother shouted from somewhere inside the thick stalks. "Almost caught up to the little devil!"

"I can't see, but I can hear him moving," David called out. "Louisa, it sounds like the dog is headed out."

Louisa moved in closer and squatted, preparing to jump on the Great Dane. The prospect, though, of tackling such a large animal terrified her, making her nerves rattle.

Crouching low, she stared intently as the cornstalks slowly parted, revealing what they were chasing in the field. Out hopped a humongous rabbit—one as *big* as a dog. Shocked, Louisa fell on her butt and screamed as the animal passed her, hopped down the hill toward a small barn, and disappeared through its open doors.

Louisa bolted upright. What had just occurred? She couldn't comprehend what was going on. Had that been her *Alice in Wonderland* moment? Or maybe more like her *Go Ask Alice* moment?

Her mother ran out of the cornfield with David trailing. "Did you get him?" she panted, trying to catch her breath.

"Mom, that wasn't the dog. It was a rabbit—a big one!" Louisa realized how funny it sounded, but she was sure she wasn't imagining things. "He went down to the barn," she added, pointing down the hill. Their eyes followed. At the same time, a farmer came out of the barn doors. The giant rabbit was in his arms. He held the oversized animal like he was cradling a baby. Its long legs dangled below the farmer's knees as he carried him.

"I don't know where the dog is, but that's not what we were chasing," Louisa said, disappointed.

"Well, let's ask that farmer if he knows about the dog," her mother headed down the hill to the farmer.

Being fluent in Flemish, David did the talking, going back and forth with the old farmer. Louisa watched the rabbit in disbelief as the farmer stroked the animal. It looked soft and gentle, but she was still intimidated by its size and didn't dare reach out to pet it.

David turned to Louisa and her mom. "He doesn't know whose dog we're asking about. He has a small one in the house, but it has only three legs and doesn't get around fast."

Louisa headed back up the hill with her mom and David, dragging her feet. Once in the car, she tried to brighten things up by changing the subject. "I can't believe the size of that rabbit! I didn't know they could get that big." David cleared his throat and his tone deepened, explaining it was a vlaamse reus, known as a Flemish giant rabbit. "They're typically domestic," he went on to say, "and common in Belgium."

Patty turned her head to David, fury still burning in her eyes. "Enough with the rabbits," she snarled. "I need a turkey! I'm in a big bind here. I have guests arriving in *three* hours, and I don't have time to make another meal." Almost in tears, she dropped her head on the steering wheel and everything went silent.

Louisa stared at her mom and the pitiful state she was in. The stress her mother had endured throughout the day and the past few weeks made Louisa dwell once more on the whole "course of nature" thing and the growing-up process. She was torn, as she wanted some adult benefits like getting into a disco and having her own car. Yet it was a scary thought to be burdened with responsibility and having to make crucial life decisions. Things were so much easier when her parents did all of that stuff for her.

David leaned up front. "Mrs. LaPlante, my uncle owns a rotisserie in the city. He'll be able to help. Take a left onto the Turnhoutsebaan and head into Antwerp."

An hour later, the trio came through the front door with six huge rotisserie chickens freshly cooked to perfection. David had saved the day once again. The birds went perfectly with the Thanksgiving sides Louisa's mother had prepared to go with the turkey. It wasn't what she'd planned, but as she told everyone, "I'll just keep everyone's glasses of spirits full at all times."

At 6:00 p.m., Louisa peeked out from the hallway door into the great room to see the festivities. Her parents stood at the front door and were busy receiving their guests. Beautiful energy flowed throughout the house, with lively chatter, soft background music, and the wonderful aromas of Thanksgiving wafting from the kitchen.

Louisa closed the hall door and went back to her room to listen to her new Rubettes album for the millionth time. When she'd gone to the music store the week before to get the record, she hadn't seen Mathis. She was disappointed, yet her head was preoccupied with her new adventures in Antwerp, the train station, and her new Moroccan friends. She still hadn't decided whether she liked Cointreau, but she'd admitted to herself something was there—though she wasn't sure what it was.

Maybe the real attraction was the attention Cointreau and the other Moroccans had paid her and how they had put her and Jackie on a pedestal. Could that be why she kept going back to the train station? To feel like royalty? Like how her mom treated the Mexican ambassador?

She stood up from the floor and pulled out a 45 record called "Moviestar." The backing vocals reminded her of an old Esther Williams movie she'd seen, in which a pool full of synchronized female swimmers floated under a waterfall. The glamorous Hollywood fantasy gave her a luxurious feeling inside like a warm bath filled with scented oil bath beads.

The music softly flowed through her room, as she grabbed her fuzzy hot pink hairbrush and walked over to the sink. Gazing into the mirror, she turned to one side, raised one shoulder, and tossed her chin over it. She held the hairbrush to her mouth like a microphone and sang along with the record, swaying from side to side: "Moviestar, movie star. I'm such a movie-star!" A cluster of straggly long blond hairs poking out from her brush kept tickling her nose. She brushed the fuzz away and continued singing.

Halfway through the song, someone nudged her from behind startling her. She let out a high-pitched screech and turned around to find her sister standing there.

"It's time, silly Louisa, to make our appearance." Judy chuckled. "There must be at least twenty-five people out there."

Totally embarrassed, Louisa dropped the brush in the sink and gave her sister a funny grin.

The girls headed down the hall, and as they passed their brother's "lab," howls of laughter came from inside the room. Louisa poked her sister, and they knocked on Teddy's door to investigate. "What are you guys doing in there?" Judy asked suspiciously.

David opened the door. He stuck his head out into the hall and looked both ways, then waved for the girls to come in.

Teddy's room was a hodge-podge of things. A large wooden wall unit packed with "how to" books had a built-in desk and ran the whole length of one wall. His full-size bed was unmade on the opposite side. Two bright yellow beanbag chairs were on the floor by a set of tall French doors. Hanging from the ceiling were multiple model airplanes he had assembled from kits. Swirly brown and orange wallpaper gave the room a quirky fun-house feel.

Teddy stood by the wall unit and opened the cabinet under his desk. On the shelf were rows and rows of unopened beer cans.

Louisa was puzzled. "Where did you get this?"

Teddy shrugged as if it was nothing. "Oh, Louisa, Dad had so much beer in the garage for this party. I just took a few cans each day this week, so he wouldn't notice it all missing at once, and loaded them in my room."

David pulled two beers out of the cabinet and gave one to Teddy. The boys faced each other and bowed like they were performing a ritual. Louisa's brother stared intensely at his friend. "One, two, three—go!" he shouted.

They lifted the cans to their lips and guzzled down the beer. Foam poured out from the corners of their mouths as their Adam's apples bobbed up and down.

Louisa smirked at Judy. It looked like fun, but the sisters opted out of the boy's frolics. They left Teddy and David to their own ambassador party and went out to play their roles as dutiful, well-behaved daughters—at least, that's what they'd make the crowd think.

The dinner party appeared to be a success so far. Everyone was mingling, and Louisa's dad was playing the piano. The lively melody of Scott Joplin's "The Entertainer" filled the great room from the Baldwin upright.

As the evening went on, Teddy and David kept blending into the crowd for a while, then disappearing, before returning to the party moments later with suspicious looks. Both of them jumped back into the crowd, interacting with the adults in a refined manner. Louisa, observing the boys for over an hour, concluded they must have had at least four beers each. She envied how they stayed sober. She was always a silly mess after just one beer.

The party was still going strong after dinner. Louisa followed her mother around the room, passing out pumpkin pie while her mom made sure everyone's cocktails were filled to the rim. As they walked into the living room together, an audible gasp erupted from Patty. Louisa, surprised, followed her mom's wide-eyed look across the room to the Mexican ambassador, who sat on the loveseat. Next to him sat Teddy, passed out cold, sitting upright. His jaw hung wide open, a string of drool stretching from the corner of his mouth down to the top of his chest. Louisa's eyes moved down further, and she spotted a huge wet stain on his denim jeans, starting at his crotch and spreading down the right side of his leg to his shoe. *Oh my god!* Her brother had peed himself.

Louisa turned back to her mother, who was visibly mortified—surely from seeing Teddy looking so disheveled, sitting right next to diplomatic royalty. The ambassador appeared to be oblivious to Teddy's situation. Instead, he leaned forward in his seat, engrossed in a deep conversation with Gail Marquette. Luckily, the ambassador's wife waved her husband over to the other side of the room to meet someone. Once he left, Louisa and her mother swiftly ran to the loveseat and carried Teddy off to bed.

Later, Louisa and Judy were in the kitchen with their mother, putting the last few dishes away once the last guest left. "Well, girls, you know there's an old saying—whatever can go wrong, will go wrong. Let's hope you two will never have to experience that." Their mom chuckled. "C'mon, let's go to bed."

TRACK 15

"YOUR BABY AIN'T YOUR BABY ANYMORE" – PAUL DA VINCI

JANUARY 1978

O ver the winter, Lyle had made several business trips back to the US. While he was away, Louisa's mother was clearly taking advantage of her newfound freedom, spending her days in Antwerp's Diamond Quarter with a small group of American girlfriends. Several times, Louisa saw her mom walk out the front door first thing in the morning, lavishly dressed in her finest designer clothes, decorated in cubic zirconia, and pretending she had all the money in the world to spend in those sometimes-shady diamond shops.

Louisa wondered what her mother was up to. Once, she even asked her why she was all dressed up. The only explanation her mom gave her, as she giggled like a young teen, was she just wanted to be as close to "a girl's best friend" as she could.

One day during winter break from AIS, Patty went off on one of her daily adventures, leaving the three teens at home. With all their friends on vacation, either skiing or someplace warm, they were bored because they had no one to play with.

"Hey Louisa, let's go into Antwerp for the day," Judy suggested.

They arrived in town in the early afternoon. As they hopped off the bus in front of the GSC, Louisa felt the train station's alluring entrance calling her and considered dragging her sister inside to meet her Moroccan friends. But Judy already had an agenda. "Louisa, there's this bar I know that would serve you a beer. It's a few blocks down from the 2001."

They hustled over to Statiestraat, passing all the lively blinking disco lights until they reached a small unpretentious café. A simple white sign above the entrance read "BAR." Louisa looked up at it, disappointed. She'd hoped her sister would take her somewhere colorful and fun, somewhere that would make a good story to tell her friends at school after winter vacation.

The café's interior was just as nondescript as its exterior. When the girls walked in, a few patrons were standing at the bar, while others sat at tables scattered throughout the room. The only activity in the subdued atmosphere was a jukebox playing the Paul Da Vinci number, "Your Baby Ain't Your Baby Anymore."

Judy directed Louisa toward a table, while she walked up to the bar to get their beers. Louisa sat by herself on edge, twirling her hair, with her head hung low. She feared someone would spot her and ask if she was old enough to be in there. How embarrassing would that be if she was asked to leave? The plaintive lyrics about breaking up coming from the jukebox only added to her stress. "Your baby ain't your baby anymore" harped on her like a pesky mosquito. She clamped her hands over her ears to make it all go away.

When Judy finally returned, she had two De Koninck beers, followed by two young men she'd met at the bar. What followed was the same story as ever. The Belgians wanted to know all about the two American sisters.

Fifteen minutes had passed, and Louisa was no longer sitting at the table. Instead, she and Judy were joyfully mingling with the crowd. Everyone was interested in speaking with them. Even though their new friends didn't speak English well, they knew enough to make small, simple conversation.

At one point, Judy introduced herself to a fellow, and he instantaneously exploded with laughter. "Is dees like Judy van Daktari?"

Recognizing the name *Daktari*, even though he spoke with a thick accent, humored Louisa. It was a 1960s American TV series set in Africa that her father had always watched. Judy was the name of a chimpanzee from the show. The name must have stuck in the young fellow's head. He probably thought it was amusing anyone would name their daughter after a monkey. Louisa always found a level of pride when Belgians associated her with American entertainment—be it a musical group, a TV show, or an actor. Pop culture from the States was so prevalent in Antwerp; it was almost like a language they both understood.

Judy grabbed Louisa by the arm, "Hey, let's do that thing we practiced last week."

"That thing" Judy was referring to was a choreographed dance routine the two arranged at home based on the disco moves they'd seen on *TopPop*. Many of the hit songs were played with the show's resident team of dancers performing alongside the musicians.

Louisa hesitated at the thought of dancing in front of everyone. This would mean she would be the center of attention. Was she really ready for that? She knew her dance skills weren't any better than her singing ability. Teddy always teased her that she needed medication for what ailed her when she performed her disco moves in the room.

Nonetheless, the attention from the Belgians that day had gone to her head. All she had to do was not look at them when she was doing their routine and find something to focus on in the room. "Let me see what's on the jukebox first. We need a song that'll wow them."

Louisa skipped over to the jukebox and flipped through the pages, in search of her debut dance tune. After careful contemplation, she found it— "Let's All Chant" by the Michael Zager Band. She fed the machine a coin and ran back over to her sister, pumped up. "Okay. I got one. Let's do this."

Judy walked out first through an opening between the tables and the bar. Meanwhile, Louisa quickly ran back over to their table and took a huge gulp of beer, hoping it would steady her nerves. She closed her eyes and felt the song's intro—a heavy drumbeat—work its way through her hips, guiding her on the rhythm. That was followed by squawking, which sounded like a bird's mating call. When the first line, "Let's all chant," blared from the jukebox, it was her cue. She ran over to Judy, and the girls started their routine back-to-back.

In unison, they each got down on one knee, spread their arms open, and moved their fingers in a rippling, wavelike motion. Next, they stood up and did a small, jerky box step, followed by another round of rippling with their arms and kneeling again. Louisa kept her eyes fixed on the ceiling at the back of the bar, silently chanting positive reinforcement. *You are great. You're just like one of TopPop's beauty queens.*

Eventually, the birdlike squawking and chanting ended, and so did the dance. Judy was down on one knee, and Louisa—ever the gymnast—was doing a handstand next to her sister.

Louisa rolled to her feet and looked out at the crowd, waiting for their reaction and applause. But none followed. She and Judy made their way back over to the table where they had left their beers. At that point, the other patrons had turned their backs on them and seemed uninterested in any further conversation.

Judy gulped her beer down and gave Louisa a puzzled look. "I guess they didn't like our dance," she shrugged. "Let's go to another bar."

Louisa didn't have her sister's nonchalant attitude, though. Feeling like their dance routine must have looked like a comedy skit from the 'Laugh-In' show, she walked out of the café with her shoulders slumped and her head down. For the first time, she willingly allowed herself to be in the direct spotlight and managed to make an embarrassing mess of it. *Ugh!*

They made their way back up Straitstraat past the blinking disco lights and found a pub across from the train station. Right as they entered, Louisa spotted Cointreau and Striped Pants standing at the bar. Her spirits soared at the sight of familiar friendly faces, especially after she and Judy had been shunned at the café. She nudged her sister. "Those are the guys I was telling you about. They're right there."

They walked over and Louisa introduced the two Moroccans to her sister. Striped Pants' eyes widened as he fixated on Judy. He took her hand, brought it up to his lips, and kissed it. "Nice to meet you." Then he bowed to her as if he were greeting the Queen of England. "You're awfully nice."

Judy's jaw dropped as he fussed over her. Certainly she must have thought he was a real player.

Louisa stepped back and stood with Cointreau. She was anxious to see how her perfect sister would react as Striped Pants put the moves on her. A slow churning in her stomach, though, halted her speculation as saliva filled her mouth. She hadn't eaten all day and drank beer on an empty stomach. A flash of nausea prompted her to bolt outside.

She stepped onto the front terrace, hoping to catch some crisp winter air. After a couple of deep breaths, she settled on a window ledge in front of the bar. Her thoughts turned to Cointreau again and her indecisiveness about her feelings toward him. These things were supposed to come naturally, from what she had heard, and the whole situation with him seemed like too much work. She didn't feel that "it" thing. But what was "it," anyway? And how was she supposed to act with a boy she liked? Would she ever figure that one out? Her jaw clenched. The conversation with herself was only adding to her out-of-sorts state, making her dizzy.

A high-pitched creaking sound of the bar door opening made her jump. Judy came out and headed toward her, followed by the two Moroccans. Striped Pants was playfully serenading Judy with "Miss Wonderful," a song by Dutch pop singer Wally Tax. He schmoozed her with the flattering lyrics and slunk his way in front of Judy to get her attention, but she stepped around him and rolled her eyes.

After a few minutes of his romantic efforts, he gave up and threw his hands up in the air. Sitting next to Louisa on the ledge, he pulled a bag of tobacco out of his coat pocket and proceeded to roll a cigarette. Louisa wasn't sure what he was doing. She had never seen anyone roll their own tobacco before. Maybe this was some of that Moroccan hashish Judy's friends had talked about?

Striped Pants lit the cigarette he had rolled and puffed away. Louisa wondered why he didn't ask her if she wanted some. She thought it was meant to be passed around like a peace pipe. Was he a greedy Gretchen who wanted it all to himself? Frustrated, she reached over, grabbing the cigarette from his hand. Since this would be her first experience tasting what she thought was hashish, she had no clue what to do. She'd only heard stories from Judy's friends. Louisa looked at her sister, then the two Moroccans, making sure everyone was watching her. She took in a huge gulp of the cigarette and held the smoke in. The hot air funneled down her throat and flooded her lungs. It was sheer misery, but she knew she had to look cool. She held it in for as long as she could until the urge to exhale became over-whelming. Her lungs pushed out her breath, her eyes filled up with water, and a coughing fit followed.

Once she got her breathing under control, she looked at Striped Pants, her cheeks flushed to a tomato red, and her eyes filled with tears. "Good—ahem. This is—ahem—good stuff, man."

Judy and the two young men looked at each other, then back at her, and cried with laughter.

Why were they so amused? Louisa raised her palms. "What? What's so funny?"

"Louisa, that was only a cigarette," Judy explained. "Come on, bone-head. We should be heading home. It's almost dark out."

The Moroccans escorted the girls to the bus stop and waited with them. Striped Pants was persistent with Judy; it was obvious he wanted to know more about her. He took her hand and led her a few feet away so he could continue to entice her in private, leaving Louisa with Cointreau at the bus stop post.

Louisa grew silent at that point. She didn't know what to say to Cointreau. The whole situation was uncomfortable, and she kept looking over at her sister, hoping she'd come back.

Breaking the stillness in the air, Cointreau leaped in front of her and firmly planted his lips to hers.

Louisa swiftly pulled away. Cointreau was determined, though, and he eagerly leaned in again with his lips puckered. Contemplating it, Louisa paused a moment and watched him standing with his eyes closed. He looked like an inflated blowfish and was inches from her mouth. *Yuck!* She found nothing appealing about the situation. Still, she slowly leaned in and decided to explore to see if that "it" thing was there—or something, anyway.

Her lips touched his, and she discovered the kiss wasn't as disturbing as her first experience in Carry-le-Rouet. She at least knew the boy, and his tongue wasn't like a wild bull in a cage. While they kissed, though, she still didn't feel her knees going weak or her heart pounding, like they said in the movies. Something was definitely missing.

Louisa heard the bus come up along the curbside followed by the compressed air releasing as it stopped. She kept her eyes closed, though, and continued kissing him, hoping this failed science experiment would be over soon. She only needed to hang on a little longer to see if it got any better.

Interrupting her concertation, she felt a light tap on her arm. "Louisa?" Judy said in a hushed voice. "Louisa."

Everything was silent for a moment, and Louisa did not hear her sister say anything more. Eventually she'd had enough. It wasn't any use; no fireworks here. Opening her eyes, she stepped away from Cointreau and looked over at Judy. Her sister's eyes were wide open, her expression alarmed. Louisa cautiously glanced around and when she discovered what Judy's dismay was, every inch of her body hardened.

Mathis stood a few feet away from her.

Their gazes met, but the single-dimpled smile that always made her melt was missing. Breaking their locked eyes, he bowed his head as if he had been defeated, then turned his back to them and walked away down the street.

Louisa's heart plummeted with a deadening thud.

Grabbing her arm quickly, Judy guided her onto the bus. Louisa could barely climb the steps, her legs shaking in fear. Once the girls settled in a seat, she slowly came out of her shock and began interrogating Judy. "What happened? How long was Mathis there? Did he see me kissing Cointreau?"

The look on Judy's face made it clear that she understood what her little sister was going through. The dismay Louisa felt was probably no different from what Judy had felt when she'd kissed Bob Dylan at the popcorn dance and deceived Gui.

"He got off the bus and saw me first," Judy explained. "Then he immediately looked around to see if you were with me. He saw you and Cointreau kissing. He stood there a few seconds, and he looked so sad. I'm so sorry."

A rush of adrenaline pierced through Louisa's beer buzz. Embarrassment, remorse, and pain bundled up inside her stomach and heart.

When they arrived home, Louisa fled to her bedroom, flopped on her bed, and buried her face in her pillow. Thoughts of what had happened in Antwerp ran through her head at full speed. She felt like she had wronged Mathis. With one foolish mistake, the innocence of what they'd had was gone. Reliving it over and over again was agonizing. She knew he would never look at her the same way again and felt like damaged goods.

She swung out of bed and dragged her feet over to the turntable, putting on the 45 Mathis had given her. When it ended, she hit Play again, repeating the tune over and over. Finally, Louisa set the turntable on Autoplay, climbed back into bed, and lay listening to the words she'd always fantasized Mathis would sing to her.

"Little Darling" played all night long, as she cried all the way to morning.

TRACK 16

"ROSE TINT MY WORLD" – RICHARD O'BRIEN

APRIL 1978

For months, Louisa struggled to forget what had happened with Mathis. Her exciting life of going to Antwerp and the record store had disappeared. She spent her free time hiding in her room, escaping the pain through her music. As soon as her record player would spin, those glorious songs would flow out of her speakers, lifting the dark cloud over her head. How she wished she could stay in her room forever with her bands and live in the only world that mattered to her.

On an early spring morning, she opened the French doors in her room to get some fresh air flowing after a sad long rainy winter. Outside was a stone terrace and gardens. Louisa wandered into the backyard, taking in the first evidence of spring. The sweet music of birds singing in a nearby chestnut tree and a single tulip poking up through the ground stimulated her. She inhaled a deep breath of nature's fragrance and felt renewed. Her awakening had arrived; she had been in seclusion long enough.

A few weeks later, she signed up for a class trip to London during spring break.

The sky was still black as night at seven in the morning when Louisa kissed her mother goodbye and hopped out of the Peugeot. She headed up to the big red coach parked in front of the kastel building at AIS, her suitcase in hand.

Lingering in the line to get on the bus, a nervousness grew in her. Louisa realized she didn't have a sidekick for the trip to London. Going solo on the bus was awkward and lonely. She'd always had a friend attached to her hip. Jackie had moved back to the States a few months before, and she still hadn't found her replacement.

She hiked up the steps of the bus, dreading the moment when everyone would look at her and wonder who she'd sit next to. Once she approached the aisle, her eyes darted forward. All the students glanced at her from over their seats. An empty spot was available up front behind the driver, next to Cindy Wallace, but that made her cringe. Cindy had a bad reputation for picking her nose in public and examining her finger afterward. The chubby girl wore colossal spectacles hiding her face, and her dandruff-infested, mousy brown hair always appeared greasy, like she never shampooed it. Sitting next to the girl would not do. Besides, the front of the bus was where all the nerds sat anyway. Desperately, her eyes scanned to the back, where she spotted a friendly, eager face smiling at her and waving.

"Louisa!" Penny Hallsworth yelled. "Over here! I saved you a seat."

Louisa's mood lifted as she quickly made her way to the back of the bus. She and Penny never had a falling-out or a fight. Rather, Penny had started going steady with a classmate from Peru a few years back and became one of those friends who dropped everything for the man in her life.

Louisa plunked herself down next to her friend, and they hugged. Shortly after, the bus's engine revved up and the AIS class headed to the Belgian coast, where they would catch the hovercraft to England. Along the way, the two girls chatted nonstop.

"My Carlos is gone," Penny cried. "I miss him so much. I write him letters every day, but I think he's found someone else." Her eyes dropped down to her lap. "I haven't gotten a letter from him in *three* whole days."

Pouring out her heart, Louisa told Penny about Mathis and the terrible way things ended between them. "I wouldn't know what to say to him even if I saw him again," she moaned. "Wait! He doesn't even speak English, so I couldn't say anything to him anyway." She and Penny giggled at that. By the time the bus arrived at the port in Ostend, the girls were best friends again.

The hovercraft was an air-cushioned vehicle and wasn't nearly as luxurious or smooth as the ocean liners Louisa's parents had taken her on. The wild waters of the English Channel crashed against the side, tossing the craft around like the S. S. *Minnow*. Thanks to Louisa's and Penny's past nautical travels, they weren't affected by the motion, unlike some other students, whose faces were turning green. The two girls moved to a small sitting area at the front of the vessel to avoid being seen with their classmates getting sick into the brown paper bags the crew had provided.

After a rough two-hour voyage, the captain finally announced over the PA system their arrival in England would be in twenty minutes. Louisa peered out the window stained with water spots and salt residue. What she had once seen as a blur on the horizon of the English Channel had formed into the towering White Cliffs of Dover. The mounds looked like they were standing guard, proudly protecting her nation.

An arousing spark within Louisa brought on a tenderhearted smile when it dawned on her this was the homeland of her favorite musical groups. Running into her bands while the class was touring the streets of London could be a real possibility. She could actually be breathing the same air as them. The thought was almost too hard to handle.

"Louisa, what are you thinking about? You've got a funny look on your face," Penny asked.

Louisa jolted out of her fantasy state, embarrassed. "Oh, nothing. I was just thinking of a funny joke my brother told me."

In Dover, a chartered bus was waiting for the class. It brought them to the center of London, where they disembarked at a dormitory-style hostel in a renovated two-hundred-year-old courthouse run by a husband-and-wife team. The couple greeted the class upon their arrival and escorted them into a large reception area. Louisa strolled in, looking up in wonderment at the gloss burnt copper ceiling. The walls were paneled in deep mahogany and various bright-colored abstract art hung, giving the lobby a turn-of-the-century art deco character.

Penny and Louisa darted over to sit on a four-panel 1900s oak bench for two across from the reception desk. The rest of their classmates piled in and sat on the floor. Some placed their bags in front of them. Others were lying down, using their luggage as pillows. Louisa chuckled to herself when she saw the whole scene. It looked like stranded passengers at an airport. But lucky her had a first-class ticket up on the bench.

Mr. Scott cleared his throat to get everyone's attention and started reviewing the itinerary for the week. He was the English teacher at AIS and the trip's organizer. Louisa thought he was a regal man the way he stood with his hands palm-in-palm behind his back. He wore a three-piece green plaid suit with a white cravat around his neck tucked snugly into his shirt. His dark hair was slicked back, with wide sideburns billowing out like black cotton candy.

The English teacher instructed that there would be five groups, each one consisting of four students and one chaperone. Louisa crossed her fingers, hoping she and Penny would be together and have Joan, the gym teacher, as their chaperone. Joan was funny, fun to be around, and more like an older sister than an authority figure.

"Okay, group D will be Joan's," Mr. Scott announced. He looked over at the bench. "Penny Hallsworth, come stand behind her."

Penny grabbed her bag and sprang up from the bench. She gave Louisa a wistful look and flashed her crossed fingers.

"Cody Conlon, you're also in Joan's group." Mr. Scott nodded at the boy.

Louisa watched when Cody rose from the floor, looking confident with his shoulders held back. He was tall and had curly dark brown hair, a chiseled face, and a long, strong jawline making him appear older. He wore fitted blue jeans and a well-tailored tweed jacket over a beige turtleneck. His whole look was avant-garde. Louisa thought he was a fox—and no doubt the other girls in her class thought so too. Cody had even been voted Most

Handsome in the yearbook that year. He was ahead of his peers, though, in maturity and didn't bother much with the naive, inexperienced girls in class. Rumor was, he spent much of his weekends on Schippersstraat, better known as the red-light district in downtown Antwerp.

"Louisa, you can go over to Joan's group as well," Mr. Scott directed.

Louisa's heart swelled as she leaped from the bench, knowing her group was super cool. She stood with Cody, Penny, and Joan, trying to conceal her excitement.

"And the last one in Joan's group is . . . Cindy Wallace," Mr. Scott announced.

Louisa's smile dissolved into a frown as Cindy moseyed up to them, her hands behind her back, looking pleased and smug. The girl must have known she was ruining it for the cool group and was loving every minute of it.

After they were assigned their rooms, Louisa, Penny, and Cindy went up to drop their bags off and check out their accommodations. The three single beds lined up a few feet apart had Louisa thinking she was sleeping in a military barracks. She recalled when her cousin Alan had visited the family a month before they had moved to Antwerp. He was attending the prestigious military school, West Point. He explained to her and Judy in detail about the tight corridors of the sleeping accommodations. He also boasted about his precarious adventures sneaking out of the cadet barracks for some space and late night fun after the night watchmen inspected their room. On several occasions he was caught in the act. His punishment was spending his weekends of free time marching endlessly back and forth for hours in the dark secluded courtyards of the grounds on West Point.

Hopefully, Louisa smirked, if she got caught in any funny business on this trip, she wouldn't find out what the "disciplinary article 10 code" her cousin spoke about meant.

The first night's itinerary brought them to a medieval-themed dinner banquet set during the rule of Henry VIII. Louisa was thrilled by the restaurant's old atmosphere, from the low wooden ceilings to the stone walls.

She loved anything allowing her to fantasize about "what was" long ago. The actors were dressed in period costumes, performing jousting demonstrations and comedy skits, and rallying the patrons to join in on various competitions. At one point, the character Henry rose from his hand-carved wooden throne and challenged two tall, well-built German men in the audience to see who could finish a yard of ale first. The Germans stood in front of the king, held the giant test-tube-like glasses filled with beer, and guzzled them down.

Louisa was impressed at the size of the yards and how the Germans could drink them so fast. Her father had once let her have a *whole* beer when the family went to Oktoberfest in Munich with the Kowalski family. She had guzzled the pilsner down in one gulp, trying to show off, and slammed the stein on the wooden picnic table feeling all ballsy. Alarm bells followed, though, when she tried to breathe. The beer had hit a traffic jam in her throat, and she felt she might drown. Eventually the liquid made its way down, and air flowed into her lungs again. She knew then her guzzling days were over.

As the two Germans continued swilling their beer, the rest of the group cheered them on, as if betting on who'd win. The whole restaurant sounded like a boxing arena. Louisa took notice that Cindy, who sat next to her, was expressionless and not chiming in on the fun. At one point, Cindy turned to her and let out an exasperated sigh. "So immature."

Louisa, disgusted, rolled her eyes and scooched as far away from the "annoyance of group D" as she could. How had they gotten so unlucky?

London was full of notable structures Louisa was familiar with, whether from movies, music, or books. The school seemed to be on a mission to cover every inch of these iconic places. Despite all the awe-inspiring, symbolic monuments, she was most fascinated by a small, less significant spot known as The Old Curiosity Shop. The tiny sixteenth-century bookstore stood on an unpretentious side street, nuzzled in between tall, modern architecture. The sloping red-tiled roof, crooked Tudor framing, and old creaking floorboards made her feel like she was walking back in time and that "what was" fantasy returned to her.

Mr. Scott stood proud as he educated the class about the shop immortalized by the beloved English writer Charles Dickens. Louisa could tell her teacher was in his element, being an educator of English and a literary enthusiast. He practically acted out the whole story of how the young, morally virtuous Little Nell had lived there with her grandfather.

Louisa knew her mom had a collection of antique Charles Dickens works on the living room bookshelf at home. Surely she had a copy of *The Old Curiosity Shop* there. Except for music, not much captured her attention artistically. Yet listening to Mr. Scott's storytelling about the adventures of the fourteen-year-old Little Nell gave her an unusual connection with the Dickens character. She was not sure what the attraction was and considered it might only be the angelic and infallibly good character Little Nell represented, that Louisa lacked in. Or maybe it was that they were the same age. Either way, Louisa knew she needed to explore more.

Later in the day, Mr. Scott gave the teens some free time to explore the surrounding streets of their hostel in the Kings Cross district. It was a gray afternoon, with a dull sky suggesting rain was imminent. Louisa strolled along with the rest of group D in a trendy neighborhood lined with Victorian streetlamps, slumped-over blossoming trees, and small souvenir shops. Periodically a red double-decker bus would pass, adding to the London experience.

The streets seemed endless, and each one brought new scenery different from the previous. At one point, Louisa spotted in a window of a souvenir shop a whole army of miniature Queens guard charms for her bracelet. Drawn into the store by the display, she made her way to the sparkling jewelry. When she turned around to ask Penny which charm she liked best, no one was behind her. Her pulse raced and she ran out of the store looking for her group. Frantically, she glanced around the narrow, pedestrian-congested sidewalk. As she looked off in the distance, she caught a glimpse of her classmates disappearing around a sharp bend in the road. Further panicked, she contemplated yelling out for them. But that would be too embarrassing if it brought unwanted attention. She bolted down the street. Once she approached the bend out of breath, she was relieved to see her class waiting for her on the other side.

Louisa marched up to them, swinging her arms angrily to give them a hard time for not waiting. Her gaze, though, drifted over their heads and landed on one of the most impressive sights she had ever seen—a huge billboard advertising The Sweet's new album *Level Headed*.

She stood marveling at the giant photo of the band. It was like she had stumbled upon one of the Seven Wonders of the World.

Anxiously pulling out her camera, she snapped one shot of the billboard after another. Unsatisfied, she realized she needed more. "Here, get some of me standing with my boys, Penny," she directed her friend. "Take as many as you can."

She could sense her classmate's amazement but was undeterred. After going through all the film, Louisa knew twenty-four shots of The Sweet was *clearly* not enough. She spied a store across the street where she could get more film. But just as she started to walk over, the first droplet of what proved to be a heavy downpour hit the tip of her nose, ending that idea in a flash.

Group D charged back to the hostel, fleeing the area screaming as if Godzilla had taken over London.

The whole trip felt like a nonstop party for Louisa, touring with her classmates. Even so, she found her patience wearing thin at Cindy's annoying ways and continuous sneering comments. Louisa had discovered her classmate was an only child, and she constantly boasted that her *mommy* bought her whatever she wanted and that her *daddy* said she was the most beautiful girl in the whole world. In Louisa's mind, this girl needed a little humbling to set her straight—or *something*.

On their last day, the class was ambling toward a craft fair in Hyde Park. Before they entered the royal grounds, Mr. Scott warned the group about pickpockets and asked them to keep vigilant. Louisa had her guard up; she found the whole situation intriguingly scary, knowing she was susceptible to a little danger as she walked along suspicious of every stranger she passed.

The mystique of being in harm's way diminished quickly, though, when a high-pitched primal scream came from behind her. Louisa's heart raced as she whipped around to find Cindy standing alone. She had one hand on her head and was looking down at the other, which she held in front of her. Absolute horror was all over her face.

"A bird pooped on me!" Cindy cried while she stomped her feet.

A roar of laughter exploded from the other students as they pointed at her; Louisa couldn't help but join them.

"Okay, class." Mr. Scott said, appearing to suppress a laugh. "Let's take a rest here for five minutes."

"She sure got hers," Penny said to Cody and Louisa, chuckling.

Cody smiled but remained nonchalant, acting as if he didn't want to fraternize with the help. He strode away from the girls and sat on a bench by himself.

A scrumptious aroma wafted through the air, enticing Louisa while she lingered with the group, taking a break. She realized it was the Yorkshire puddings, which Mr. Scott had told them about made of beef dripping, egg, flour, and milk. "I'm going to get one of those thingies," she said to Penny. "They smell so yummy. Don't you want one?"

Penny shook her head and brushed her hand across her belly, as if to say she was watching her weight.

Louisa skipped over to wait in line at one of the truck vendors selling the British treats. As she stood there, her attention turned to Cindy, who was sitting at a picnic table by herself, head down as she moped. Her hair was wet and matted to her forehead after being cleaned of the bird droppings. She was mumbling to herself, causing her glasses to fog up, and snot ran down to lip.

A lump of sadness swelled in Louisa's stomach. The poor girl was all alone with no friends to comfort her.

"How many, love?" the round-faced British woman who was selling the popovers asked.

Louisa smiled, looked back at Cindy, then back at the vendor. "Two, please."

She walked away with the Yorkshire puddings, and the savory aroma drifted back to her, making her salivate. She was on a mission, though, and did not stop to indulge yet. She walked up to Penny. "C'mon. Let's go see if Cindy is okay."

Louisa sat on the bench on one side of Cindy and Penny on the other. "Here, Cindy," Louisa said, handing her one of the Yorkshire puddings. "This will make you feel better."

Cindy's head slowly rose. Her glasses were so fogged she could barely see and struggled to take the popover. Louisa leaned over and pulled the spectacles off to clean them for her. To her surprise, Cindy had large, almond-shaped eyes that were green like emeralds. Her complexion was flawless, and her high cheekbones gave her face a Sophia Lauren look. Louisa had never noticed before how pretty she was under the large rim of her glasses and her annoying attitude.

She nodded at Penny, signaling for her to get a look at Cindy. Surely she could see it as well.

"Cindy, I'm sorry we laughed." Louisa smiled. "It was just so funny. I remember once when my sister was sunbathing in the backyard in a bikini, and a bird dropped a load smack in the middle of her belly button."

"Really?" Cindy's slumped posture perked up.

Penny ran her fingers through Cindy's hair, studying the girl's unkempt coif. "Hey Cindy, since it's our last night in London, let us dress you up for the night."

Louisa and Penny gave Cindy a thorough makeover back in their room, which took most of the afternoon. The most challenging part was tweezing her unibrow. While Cindy was lying on the bed, Penny did the plucking and Louisa held Cindy's hands down to prevent any unexpected punches.

"See?" Louisa stood with Cindy in front of the bedroom mirror once the transformation was complete. "You look so beautiful."

Cindy squinted at herself in the mirror and reached over to the end table and grabbed her glasses. "I can't see a thing without them!" she cried.

"Cindy, keep them off. We'll be your eyes tonight." Louisa reassured her that she and Penny would stay by her side *all* night.

Penny drew in close to Cindy's face. "Listen, Cindy. You look beautiful, but don't open your mouth and talk if it's something stupid." She walked over and opened the door. "And for heaven's sake, keep your fingers out of your nose!"

The two girls guided Cindy to the reception area. Louisa stood tall, proud of her and Penny's work, like it was something she had created in art class. All the students turned their heads when the three girls walked in. Cindy's hair was shampooed and fluffy, and Penny had wrapped her silk psychedelic pink scarf around Cindy's head and tied it in a bow on the side, giving her a 1920s flapper look. The makeup accented the best features on Cindy's face; her electric-green cat's eyes were hypnotizing. Louisa also took Cindy's long, flowing button-up blouse that looked like a maternity shirt and wrapped it around her waist, making her appear less frumpy. Finally, she and Penny had placed bangle bracelets on Cindy's arms and several strands of Louisa's Hawaiian puka shell necklaces around her neck. It was truly a triumph.

On the last evening in London, Louisa and her classmates were headed to the West End—London's version of Broadway. They would be seeing a new musical called *The Rocky Horror Show* at the King's Road Theatre.

"I love spooky movies," Louisa whispered to Penny and Cindy. "I hope it'll be scary."

Cindy's pupils dilated, fear evident on her face. She was about to say something—probably something stupid—when Penny cupped her mouth with her hand to stop her.

Mr. Scott gave a brief lecture on the importance of arts and theater and how operas and plays were people's main forms of entertainment many years ago.

"Mr. Scott, what's the show about?" Penny asked.

The English teacher looked out at Louisa, Penny, and the other students, who were all sitting on the floor. "Well, I'm not sure. We got a good group discount on the tickets. It's a fairly new musical, but it won many awards when it first started to run." He rocked back and forth on his heels, then stood evenly on both legs and tilted his shoulders back. "It is truly a privilege and will be an excellent educational experience for you all. I'm sure of it."

Inside the lobby at the King's Road Theatre, several banners hung from the ceiling and walls advertising the show. On one of the posters was a black and white illustration, displaying a lady who wore a horrified expression on her face. Louisa stared obstinately. It looked like the woman's eyelids were propped open with toothpicks and her mouth hung open so far, Louisa could almost see the tonsils in the back of her throat. Underneath were the letters "The Rocky Horror Show," and dripping from them was splattered blood. Louisa reckoned, the class was in for a little frightful fun, although she'd never been to a musical before. Her parents had taken her once to see the opera *Carmen* in Brussels. She had no idea what it was all about, and they didn't even sing in English.

She remembered a blunder that happened during the performance: as the supreme diva Carmen sang a wild gypsy song about dancing and seduction to a rowdy tavern crowd, one of the patrons' long peasant skirt dropped to the floor, exposing her "real" undergarments. The actress, surely embarrassed, ran off stage in a flash, carrying her costume. Louisa giggled to herself. Since Rocky Horror was live, what kind of surprises would the show bring to the stage tonight?

The class entered the dimly lit theater, and Joan handed Louisa and the others their tickets. Taking in the ghoulish surroundings, Louisa's eyes shifted around as she followed the group to their seats. The backdrop was unlike anything she had ever seen before. Scaffolding ran up the side of the stage, with metal stairs leading to multiple platforms. The scene felt cold and futuristic, yet an old Gothic mansion was in the center with a warm glow coming through the windows. Louisa couldn't help but feel an ominous dark cloud hanging over her head. What was this show going to be about? One thing for sure, it would be nothing like her parents' boring *Carmen*.

Group D sat in the last row of the theater. Cindy settled into an aisle seat, Cody next to her, and Penny and Louisa followed. Mr. Scott and his crew were in the row in front of them.

While Louisa sat eagerly erect, eyes on the stage, waiting for the show to start, heavy breathing emerged from the open space behind her. At first, she figured it was an usher or a stagehand. As she turned to investigate, Cindy broke her focus and leaned toward her and Penny, squinting. "I can't see the stage at all. I can barely see you."

"If it's anything like *Show Boat*, then you're not missing anything," Cody snarked.

The lights soon flickered to signal the show would be starting. The audience quickly quieted down, and the only sounds were a few whispering classmates.

Louisa, still feeling uneasy that someone had been in the open space behind her, turned around. An eerie green glow cast over the dark space from the Exit sign above the door. Once she closely examined the area, nothing appeared menacing and she settled back in her seat.

Moments after, the weight of something heavy plopped onto her left shoulder, sending chills through her. She craned her neck back, and her eyes slowly tracked left, where to her horror she discovered a large, boney hand resting on her. She spun all the way around and there stood a character wearing black clothes and a creepy green alien-like mask. Slowly tilting her head up, a set of glaring eyes peered down at her through the mask's holes. Fear overtook Louisa as she screamed, prompting most of the audience to whip their heads around and look at her.

That was when she learned the opening for the show had begun, and she was a part of the act. Even more embarrassing, she knew she probably looked like the lady with the shocked face on the poster out in the lobby.

The lights dimmed further, and the room was almost black. Slow, pulverizing keyboards resounded in the orchestra pit. From the back of the theater, a character dressed as an usherette slowly promenaded down the aisle singing. A bright spotlight shone down on her, making her the center of attention. Her frilly pink uniform-style dress, black stockings, and a lacy headband gave her a classic French maid appearance. In front of her, she carried a concession tray of strawberry treats.

"What just happened?" Cindy yelled.

"Shh," Mr. Scott hushed from the row in front.

Once Louisa regained her composure she settled back in her seat and focused on the stage. The usherette's squeaky, high-pitched singing sounded like a dog's rubber toy being squeezed. She kept referring lustily in her song to scary beasts like King Kong, killer triffids, and giant tarantulas. At that point, Louisa's yearning had diminished for any further frightful fun. Enough was enough. Where was this all going anyway?

Soon after, the musical took on a bizarre spin when the scientist character, Dr. Frank N. Furter, erotically revealed himself in a corset, leather briefs, fishnet stockings, and high platform heels. Louisa glanced around at her peers and teachers. Was anyone else taken aback by this unexpected turn of events?

The show's strange journey soon introduced her to something she'd known nothing about: promiscuity. She was still trying to get the whole kissing thing down, so this caused her more concern and left her with a list of questions to ask Judy when she got home.

Despite Louisa's bewilderment, one favorable aspect from Rocky Horror *had* captured her attention: the wild, energetic music. And in the end, wasn't that what it was all about? It was like her glam rock bands on steroids. It had Mud's quirky edginess, The Sweet's raw eccentricity, and The Rubettes' soda-shop doo-wop sounds. All her favorite bands in one show. *Now that was something to applaud.*

As the show continued, Dr. Frank N. Furter stepped down from the stage and strutted up the aisle to the back of the theater like a peacock, singing. He approached the last row where Cindy was sitting, kicked his long leg high, and slowly lowered it to rest his foot on the arm of Cindy's seat as he continued his song. Cindy glanced up at him, squinting.

Everyone's heads were turned toward the actor so they could watch his performance. He was only a few feet away from Louisa, and she couldn't help but notice every detail about this bizarre scientist, from the outrageous women's lingerie he wore to the sweat beading on his forehead. She studied him while he sang—and soon noticed while the actor stood there with one leg perched on the arm of Cindy's seat and the other on the floor, his stance left things wide open in the pelvic area. Her eyes zoomed in for a closer look, and creeping out from the main antagonist's fitted leather bikini briefs was something that was either a fashion faux pas or a part of the show.

Louisa leaned over to Penny. "Do you see what I'm seeing?" She nodded toward the actor's briefs. "Is that one of his man parts coming out of his undies?"

Penny looked back in the direction of Dr. Frank N. Furter's crotch. She bent over immediately, holding her stomach in laughter. What was even funnier to Louisa, though, was Cindy's nose was right under "it," and the girl was just smiling up at the actor, oblivious.

Eventually, Dr. Frank N. Furter lowered his leg to the aisle, and the peep show was over.

When the play was nearing the end, the actors lined up on the edge of the stage and sang a song called "Rose Tints My World." The melody was infectious, but Louisa found herself perplexed and once again had questions. Rose Tints My World? What were they singing about? The lyrics made no sense to her. She always tried to figure out the message of each song she listened to because it helped her connect to it more deeply. Even with silly, simple lyrics and melodies, she almost always found the song's soul inside. But was this Rocky Horror poking fun at something? Or was it only a meaningless fantasy? Either way, the show's charade was making her feel quite apprehensive.

Proceeding the encore, Mr. Scott asked the students to remain in their seats until the theater emptied. "Each group must stay with their leader once we get into the lobby," he directed, "because it will be crowded for a few minutes, with everyone leaving." He appeared nervous and on edge, and his eyes darted over the students. "But once it thins out, you'll have an hour of free time to buy souvenirs, go to the bathroom, or get refreshments until the bus takes us back to the hotel."

As the theater emptied, Louisa, standing next to Joan, overheard Mr. Scott whispering in the gym teacher's ear. "I had no idea this was that kind of show." He shook his head. "I'm sure I will be getting calls from everyone's parents on Monday."

The lobby was still packed with people when group "D" made their way out. The actors from the musical were greeting members of the audience and signing copies of the show's program.

"Penny, I want to meet them!" Louisa cried. "I want to ask Dr. Frank N. Furter if he's friends with The Rubettes or Mud." She was certain he must be, given it was the same genre of music.

"Ok. Let's move away from the group though," Penny whispered in Louisa's ear, "so they don't think we're little kids with a school."

She grabbed Louisa's hand and led her slowly away from Joan. Louisa followed, but once they were a few feet away, Joan turned toward them. "Stay close, girls," she called out.

Louisa frowned and dragged her feet as she and Penny rejoined their group.

"I know. Let's tell them we have to go to the bathroom," Penny suggested. Louisa nodded gamely.

"I have to go to the little girls' room, Joan." Penny stood dramatically crossing her legs, like she couldn't hold it in any longer.

"Okay," Joan said. "But take Louisa and Cindy with you."

Penny and Louisa locked arms with Cindy, and the trio tromped off to the bathroom. Once there, Louisa put her hand on Cindy's shoulder. "Cindy, when we get back out to the lobby, we're going to say hi to Dr. Frank N. Furter and see if we can get an autograph." She held Cindy's chin and pulled her face closer to hers so she would understand. "But away from the class and Joan so they don't think we're with the other kids from the school. Okay?"

"I hope he's not scary!" Cindy's green eyes widened. "Was he a vampire?"

Louisa chuckled. There was nothing scary at all about the actor, like in a scary movie. However, his erotic character had *literally* exposed her to a world she was petrified of. Despite her fear, though, she was driven to see if he knew any of her favorite bands.

The girls popped their heads out of the bathroom. Joan stood off to the far left, talking with Cody and a few other students. Louisa grabbed Penny's and Cindy's hands, and they slinked into the line to meet the actors. An usher stood near the performers, moving the meet and greet along quickly. With only one other group in front of them, Louisa gaped at the actor who played Dr. Frank N. Furter closer-up in the brighter light. His dark, erotic character in the show flashed in her head again. She didn't know what she would say to him in person—or how to even talk to him. She fretted that she would make a fool of herself.

When the three teens finally approached him, Louisa's breathing quickened. She hung her head low, afraid to look him in the eye. To her surprise, though, the actor's manner was nothing like his character's. He was friendly and asked them where they were from. Raising her head, Louisa smiled at him but remained speechless. She wanted to ask him about the bands she loved but "Ah . . . ha . . . ehh" was all that came out of her mouth. Penny carried the conversation, grilling the actor, asking where he'd gotten his lingerie from and who did his makeup.

After what seemed like a lengthy interrogation from Penny, the usher pushed the girls along. Penny and Louisa scurried off to a corner of the lobby to read what Dr. Frank N. Furter had written in the programs he'd signed for them.

Louisa lifted her head after reading his message to her and turned to Penny. "'Keep smiling' is all he wrote to me."

Penny looked perplexed after she read hers. "Mine says, 'Don't grow up too fast. These are the best years of your life.'"

Louisa was a little disappointed she clammed up in front of him but was still thrilled she met a *real* actor. Once she came down from her high, she looked up from her program at the crowd around her. Suddenly panicked, she grabbed Penny's arm. "Where's Cindy?"

The crowded lobby made it hard to find their classmate. The two girls ducked low to remain inconspicuous while they searched for her. Louisa spied the ladies' room sign, and she took Penny's hand, pulling her back into the bathroom.

"Cindy!" Penny shouted. "Are you in here?"

Louisa crouched to see if she could spot any feet in the stalls. Nothing.

"What are we going to do?" Louisa fretted. "Let's separate."

Penny scurried over to the exit doors when they went back into the lobby, while Louisa peered back in the theater. A few stagehands were working on the scaffolding, but still no Cindy. When she spun around to head back into the lobby, Joan was standing right behind her. "What are you doing?" she asked.

Louisa had to think quickly. "Oh, I just . . . I just wanted to get one last look at the stage." She swallowed hard. "It was such a good show."

Joan glanced around her. "Where are Penny and Cindy?"

Louisa swallowed again. All of this quick thinking was exhausting. "They went back to the bathroom to fix Cindy's makeup."

Joan chuckled. "Okay. The crowds are thinning out now, so you have a little free time left. I want you to get the group together and meet back out in front of the theater in twenty minutes."

Heading back into the lobby, Louisa spotted Penny by the exit doors and ran over to her. "We have twenty minutes to find Cindy!" she cried. "She's not in here. Let's go see if she wandered outside."

The two girls hit the streets of London. The West End had a variety of pubs, restaurants, and shops. It had erupted in a sea of bodies as actors from the surrounding theaters packed the streets for a quick pint or a bite to eat after their evening performances. Louisa scanned the busy sidewalks, hoping she'd find Cindy. She felt responsible for her new friend since she had talked her out of wearing her glasses. She and Penny desperately moved along, peering in the windows of each establishment. Cindy was nowhere to be found.

Up ahead, Louisa spotted Cody walking in their direction. "Cody!" she yelled. "Have you seen Cindy? We lost her!"

Cody shook his head and joined the girls' search party. The three continued for another block before coming upon an old brick pub. Lively music and laughter drifted out into the street. "Do you think she would have wandered in there?" Louisa asked.

"Let's go check it out anyway—sounds like a party inside," Penny touted, and she dashed toward the door.

A thick cloud of cigarette smoke obscured Louisa's vision when they walked in. As they made their way in farther, the savory smells of prime roast beef lingered, competing with the stale scent of tobacco.

The pub was packed with an eclectic mix of people. Glasses clinked together, and rowdy chatter filled the room. A group of elderly men was tucked in one corner, singing "The Drunken Maidens." On the other side were several tables filled with diners.

Louisa surveyed her surroundings, but Cindy was nowhere in sight. Straight ahead was a long, elaborate mahogany bar accented by brass floor rails lined with people. Some were standing; others were sitting on stools. The chanting of "Dricka! Dricka!" from the far end caught Louisa's attention. She grabbed Penny's hand and motioned for Cody to follow, and the three pushed their way through the crowd toward the ruckus.

At the end of the bar, a group of Swedish students stood in a circle, clapping and yelling, "Dricka! Dricka!" Louisa struggled to break through the wall of young men, burrowing her head into the gaps between them. Once she was able to see the center of the chaos, her breathing stopped.

There Cindy stood, misty-eyed and chugging a pint of beer, led on by the cheering crowd. Louisa smacked Cody's arm—whose attention was focused on a long-legged waitress serving one of the tables. "Cody, you have to go in and get her."

Cody peered over to where Cindy was. He stood there a minute, smirking while he watched her guzzle.

Louisa nudged him. "Go!"

His look intensified as he plowed through the crowd and grabbed hold of Cindy's arm, yanking her out of the circle of students as if she was a toddler out of control.

"Halla!" the group of rowdy blonde Swedes yelled angrily.

"Let's get out of here!" Louisa cried.

They sprinted to the exit, with Cody pulling Cindy by the arm.

"What were you doing, Cindy?" Penny yelled once they were outside.

Cindy let out a loud, hearty belch and looked at Penny. "I was trying to be like those men at the medieval place who made you laugh the other night." She tucked her chin in, releasing another belch. "I thought you would like me better if I was like them."

Louisa shook her head, feeling ever more responsible for her new friend's behavior.

The four teens hustled back to the King's Road Theatre, where their bus was parked. Most of the other classmates had already formed a line to get back on. Joan stood, tapping her foot and pointing to her watch when Louisa and her friends approached the group.

"I know, I know," Penny said. "We just wanted to see some of the beautiful architecture in this part of town."

Joan raised an eyebrow, studying them, and nodded for them to get on.

Cindy laughed uncontrollably the entire ride back, causing Louisa to fear the gym teacher would discover her friend's drunkenness. She and Penny took turns covering Cindy's mouth to keep her quiet.

Once the girls made it safely to their room, Louisa stood in front of Cindy, sitting on her bed, and grilled her about how she ended up at a bar.

"I don't really know—*hic*." Cindy giggled between hiccups. "How I ended up—*hic*—there." She took a large gulp from the glass of water Penny had given her before continuing. "I thought I was following you to walk around outside. But once I got into the bar, I think it was two of the actors from the show—*hic*."

A heavy rap on the bedroom door sounded, taking the attention off Cindy. Louisa went to open it, expecting it to be her gym teacher coming to scold them. To her relief, it was Cody. He peered around her, appearing anxious to get a glimpse of Cindy. "I just wanted to see if our barfly was okay."

Cindy looked up at Cody with a hazy smile and waved. "Hi, Cody! Thank you—*hic*—for saving me."

The hovercraft ride home the next morning was as jerky as the ride over. Louisa and Penny found the same seats up front, away from their seasick classmates. The area was extremely quiet, and most of the passengers around them rested with their eyes closed. Louisa stared out her window. She was almost in a trance, watching the white crests of the rhythmic waves scatter apart into a mass of bubbles again and again while the infectious songs from *The Rocky Horror Show* played in her head. The melodies provided continuous waves of exhilaration, even if she didn't know what the hidden meaning was behind the lyrics.

Leaving aside the novelty of Rocky Horror, she still found herself missing the bands postered on her wall at home. She was a little disappointed they hadn't run into any of her groups in London but was satisfied just to see the giant billboard advertising The Sweet's new album. Laughing to herself at her crazed paparazzi behavior in front of group D that day, Louisa knew she must have looked like she was off her rocker. Still, when it came to her music, nothing else mattered, even her image. She would walk into a room of people with her clothes on inside out and toilet paper dragging from her shoes for the bands she loved.

The class arrived at AIS just as night fell. Louisa hopped off the bus and spotted her mom in the blue Peugeot and headed over.

"Louisa! Louisa!" Cindy ran up to her side, wide-eyed with excitement. "Guess what?" She caught her breath for a moment. "Cody asked me for my phone number!"

Confused and speechless, Louisa stopped in her tracks and blinked at Cindy. Her first thoughts were anger. How did this nose-picking girl manage to reel in the cutest guy in school while she was only capable of making a mess of her love life? What love life? She never had one to begin with. Then her rage slowly softened and the jealous spiteful thoughts dissipated, gradually replaced with a hint of saintly virtue—just like the beloved "Little Nell." Louisa knew she had played some part in leading this girl out of her insufferable ways and it felt good. She smiled at her friend while patting her hand.

After, she said goodbye to Cindy and hopped into the car, genuinely happy for her friend. Between the fun events of the week and doing a good deed, she felt content. Maybe this trip was a good idea after all. It certainly helped her forget the main reason why she had signed up for it to begin with.

On the car ride home, Louisa told her mom all about the White Cliffs of Dover, The Old Curiosity Shop, and the Yorkshire puddings she ate.

"I can make you Yorkshire pudding sometime." Her mom smiled. "Your grandmother used to serve that on Christmas Day when I was growing up."

They drove along silently for a while until Louisa spoke again. "Mom?"

"Yes, honey?"

"What's a transvestite?"

Slamming on the brakes, her mother brought the car to a screeching halt and turned to her with a menacing look. "*What* did you say?"

Louisa hesitated, confused and fearful. "Ah-ah-oh. I don't know. I think I'm saying the word wrong. Never mind."

Her mom gave her a funny look, shook her head, and continued driving.

In silence, they approached the main street in Schilde. As the car idled at a red light, Louisa feared her mother was still testy about the whole transvestite thing. Nonchalantly, she turned her head toward her mother, who stared ahead, intently focused on the traffic light. Her expression did not appear angry. Relieved, Louisa let her shoulders relax. Her eyes drifted past her mother and out the window, and everything went still inside her.

Standing out in front of the music shop was Mathis with a girl whose beautiful curly red hair ran down to her waist. The two of them smiled at each other, and Mathis leaned in to hug her. The sight of them together brought on a piercing pain to Louisa's heart, stinging so hard she thought she would scream. She clamped her hand tightly over her mouth to keep it all inside.

The traffic light turned green, and the Peugeot drove away.

TRACK 17

"DADDY COOL" – BONEY M.

MAY 1978

For days, Louisa was in a state of disarray, boiling with jealousy, hurt, and anger. But time moved on. Her rekindled friendship with Penny Hallsworth continued, and she felt the best way to get over Mathis was a good distraction. So she started dragging her friend down to Antwerp to meet her Moroccan friends.

Judy was doing some rekindling as well. Gui was back in her life. She'd told Louisa seeing the hurt on Mathis's face had reminded her of what she had done to Gui when she'd kissed Bob Dylan at the dance. How did her sister do that? Again, was it magic? Judy's power over boys was a complete conundrum to her. All her sister had to do was snap her finger and Gui was back. Louisa knew she could never accomplish that kind of command in her life.

With frequent trips down to Antwerp easing her despair, another distraction helped Louisa forget her woes: the buzzing hype of the Eurovision Song Contest. The event was held in Paris that year at the Palais des Congrès, and it was all the rage with her. Most of the songs didn't fall into the genre of the music she obsessed over and were a little too tame for her ear. Yet Louisa had developed a true love for the European culture by then, like she was one of the locals. She felt it was an obligation—no, an honor—to cheer on not only Belgium but also her surrounding neighbors.

The night before the Eurovision finale, her dad announced they would spend the next day with Phil and Michelle Alexander and their family. Louisa's family had known the Alexanders for over fifteen years. Lyle and Phil had worked together at Union Carbide when they all lived in Buffalo, New York. Coincidentally, Phil and his family had transferred to Brussels a few years after they arrived in Antwerp, and the kids Reah and Alex were the same ages as Louisa and Judy.

The families had already spent many Saturdays together. They would alternate between going to the Alexanders in Brussels or to the LaPlantes in Antwerp. The adults would play tennis while the teens found ways to amuse themselves at the house. After the grown-ups returned from their match, they would venture off to a restaurant for dinner, making it an all-day affair.

Instead of a typical tennis outing this time, Patty and Michelle coordinated the day's events. The two families would do some fun sightseeing around Belgium's tourist spots, then have dinner at a restaurant in Brussels.

When Louisa's father announced the itinerary for the next day, she protested, practically in tears. "Dad, tomorrow is the finals for Eurovision! We *can't* go!"

Her father gave her one of his stern looks that could quiet a room. "We will be home in plenty of time to see your Eurovision."

Intimidated by his tone and harsh expression, Louisa piped down. Inside, however, she was fuming—stome sightseeing!

Saturday morning arrived, and the LaPlantes headed down Bremboslann to meet their friends at the itinerary's first stop. "Where are we going?" Teddy asked from the car's back seat.

Their mom turned to face him. "It's a surprise. And you'll love it, Teddy!"

Disgust filled Louisa upon hearing her mother's response. She was already dreading the day since it interfered with her music. And now this. Another one of her mother's surprise outings.

An hour later, the car arrived at their first stop. After Lyle parked the car, Patty turned around to face all three of them in the back seat. "Do you know where we are?"

Louisa looked at her sister and brother. Their vacant expressions showed they had no clue either. Nothing about their surroundings jumped out; it was only a parking lot.

"This is Waterloo!" Patty proclaimed.

Waterloo? Louisa's forehead wrinkled in confusion. The only thing she knew about that was the pop hit by ABBA. She always thought Waterloo was a breaking-up expression people would use, *Wa-wa-wa-wa Waterloo couldn't get away from your smell of poo*—but was it an *actual* place?

They met up with the Alexanders shortly afterward. Everyone made their way to a small, round building selling tickets to get into the battlefield memorial. Once the group of Americans were through the gates, they approached a huge cone-shaped artificial grass hill standing well over a hundred feet tall. Sitting on top was the Butte du Lion, a cast-iron monument of a large fierce feline. Louisa continued to try to connect the dots between the ABBA tune, the mountain, and the memorial, but shook her head, confused.

The families trekked to the top of the mound where the Butte du Lion greeted them. Louisa tapped her foot impatiently, frustrated that everyone seemed to be taking their time reading every word on the monument's plaque. As far as she was concerned, they had come, they had seen, and they had conquered. The battle was over. Time to move on to the next stop. *Fast.*

Once Lyle's long, drawn-out explanation about the history of Waterloo ended, the group made their way back down to the welcome center and into the gift shop. Louisa and Judy both purchased a silver Butte du Lion for their charm bracelets. Thanks to all the charms Louisa accumulated with her family's traveling in Europe, she had just enough room for the trinket to fit on the chain.

Before they headed to the next stop, Louisa and Reah ventured off to use the bathroom. The girls entered the building and followed the signs that read "Toilette," which led them down a long dingy hallway. Rounding a corner, Louisa was overcome with a horrible reek of urine. A New York subway ride she took with her uncle Bub once years ago came immediately to mind.

They continued on around another corner and into a brightly lit bathroom. A quick glance revealed the wall to their right was lined with ten urinals, with men occupying each and every one.

At first, it was surreal to Louisa. Was she seeing things? She had never been in a men's room before. She turned to Reah and saw the look of shock on her friend's face. They spun on their heels and darted out of the bathroom, laughing all the way back to their parents. "We can't find the ladies' room," Reah cried to her father. "We followed the sign but ended up in the men's room."

Mr. Alexander explained to them, "You have to go *through* the men's room to get to the ladies' room. It's on the other side."

Reah crossed her arms over her chest, appearing appalled. "I'll wait."

Louisa didn't have the luxury of time, though. She made her way back in, went down the dark hallway, and entered the stinky "urinal central." She tried not to look as she passed the men doing their business. At one point, an older man turned his head over his shoulder while he was busy relieving himself and smiled at her. Louisa averted her eyes briskly.

When she finally made it through to the other side, her shoulders dropped. It felt like she'd crossed her own Waterloo battlefield just going through the men's room.

Inside the ladies' room, the foul stench dissipated, and Louisa finally felt safe. She entered one of the vacant stalls and soon discovered something essential was missing: a toilet.

Puzzled, she stood there for a minute, searching. Her confusion continued as her gaze dropped to the floor. In the center was a small hole similar in size to a shower drain. Was this the toilet? Either way, she had to go, so it would have to do. She squatted and did her business in the small hole.

Once finished, she walked out of the stall and looked back, cocking her head to the side. With all the odd rules in this part of the country, she decided not to tell her family or the Alexanders about the odd toilet, just in case it wasn't the proper way to pee when visiting Waterloo.

Afterward, the LaPlantes piled back into the Peugeot and proceeded to the next destination on their itinerary. Teddy, of course, asked, "Where are we going now?"

"Don't ask," their dad growled in his own loving, paternal way. "You'll see when we get there."

The Alexanders were already waiting for them in the parking lot when they arrived. After Louisa and her family hopped out of the car, Lyle strode purposefully over to Mr. Alexander. "Did you know you were going over the speed limit?" he griped. "I had a hard time keeping up with you."

Mr. Alexander jokingly patted him on the shoulder. "Okay, Grandpa Moses." Observing her fathers heated words with Mr. Alexander, Louisa inwardly laughed. She was always joking with her sister and brother about how slowly her dad drove. It just seemed funny to see an adult calling him out on it.

A dirt path led the families to a small bridge crossing a creek then circled an old fortress. Once they crossed to the other side, a sign indicated they were entering Fort Breendonk. The day was overcast, and the fortification held the same gloomy atmosphere. Louisa looked up at the stone facade of the defense wall and a haunting feeling of death came over her. She shuddered and hurried over to her parents, staying close by their side.

Once inside the fortress, a stone passage led them to a set of chambers used as dungeons. Louisa imagined the horrors that had taken place in the cells and the eerie feeling following her deepened. The group fell silent as they walked through a courtyard and into a dark, ominous hall with more barred brick cells. A sickly odor lingered and assaulted Louisa's senses. She wondered what was wrong with this place. It was nothing like the other sightseeing trips her parents had taken them on. Versailles was so colorful and bright. The Notre-Dame cathedral had its vast stained-glass windows, and Luxembourg was home to statuesque medieval castles. But Fort Breendonk was chilling and forbidding.

The next room highlighted the fort's history from the early 1900s. In a timeline, photos displayed small artifacts, military clothing, and other items. While they moved along, the images became increasingly disturbing, showing the horrible abuse that had taken place in the fortress during World War II. Louisa had learned a little about the horrific torture during the Holocaust from history class as well as her family's travels throughout Europe. But she'd never seen the reality of it in actual photos of the suffering captives. Her stomach churned as she cupped her mouth and slowly backed away from the display. How could people have done this and taken photos of it?

Louisa couldn't look anymore and darted out through the exit. Once back in the parking lot, she leaned against the Peugeot and folded her arms. The horrible images flashed in her head like a rapid strobe light and wouldn't go away.

Eventually, the others followed. They all cheerfully chatted and appeared unaffected by what they had seen inside. What was wrong with everyone? Why wasn't anyone else horrified by this Fort Breendonk?

The ride was quiet as her unease turned into anger. Minutes went by until she could no longer hold her fury. She leaned toward her parents in the front seat. "What was that all about? Why did you bring me there?" she yelled. "That was the worst thing I ever saw. What did I ever do to you? I haven't done anything wrong lately."

She had never raised her voice to her parents—especially her father—when she'd been angry at them before. Inhaling deeply, she sat back, then leaned forward again. "I haven't been grounded in months. I've been good. So why? I'm so angry at you both!"

Her dad chuckled under his breath and remained quiet.

"Louisa, this is a part of history," her mother explained. "Not everyone has the opportunity to see this type of history preserved."

"I don't care. I felt like Hansel and Gretel, and you and Dad were bringing me there like I did something wrong. Did you see what they did to the
poor people in those large ovens in the photos?" she bowed her head. "I just
want to go home so I can watch my Eurovision."

"It was a concentration camp!" Teddy spoke up in a high-pitched, spirited tone. "Just like the game we play, Escape from Colditz. They had the
execution walls and the cool torture chambers, just like the game does."

Louisa couldn't believe those awful rooms were on the board game they
had played. Maybe her brother's mind was getting a little warped. She sat
back and let out a satisfied huff now that she'd blown off some steam.

Continuing down the highway, it seemed as if the mood was getting
back to normal. But it wasn't too long before Lyle began ranting to Patty.
"Phil is acting like he's an Italian race car driver. Why is he driving so fast?"
Louisa could feel a rush in her stomach as the car accelerated. She scooched
forward to see what was going on. Her dad sat hunched over the steering
wheel, holding it in a death grip. His heavy, labored breathing fogged the
windshield, as his foot pressed down hard on the gas pedal. Leaning back in
her seat, Louisa elbowed Judy. The sisters shared a silent laugh, then broke
out singing, "Daddy Cool," a song they had heard on *TopPop* a few years
back. Judy sang the first line of the lyrics, followed by Louisa with the next
verse. Playfully, they made up their own words and belted out together,
"*That's our Daddy cool!*"

Four verses in, Lyle turned around threateningly, his eyes ablaze.
"Knock it off, or I'll bang both of your heads together!"

Gasping, Louisa covered her mouth and shot a sidelong glance at her
sister. Ever the calm one, Judy, seemed unintimidated by her dad's outburst
and sat silently, her shoulders shaking with her muffled laughter.

An hour later, the LaPlantes rolled into the capital city of Belgium in
the historical center. Once parked, Mrs. Alexander led the families along
the red cobblestones of old-town Brussels. They descended a steep, narrow
stairwell leading to a restaurant built from dark stone.

As they strolled inside, Louisa spotted a clock above the reception desk;
it was already 5:00 p.m. Her fear of missing Eurovision increased. At this

rate they would never make it back in time. She pestered her mother, who continued to reassure her, "We'll make it home with plenty of time, Louisa. Not to worry. We have an early dinner reservation." Her mom's expression changed to one of zealousness—the same look she'd give Louisa whenever she tried to coax her into something. "Guess where we are? This is a restaurant with a live puppet show. You'll love it."

Louisa pursed her lips. She just wanted to forget about her mother's "Muppet Show" and get home—now.

An elderly woman greeted them at the reception desk. "Bonsoir." The group followed her into a rustic, cave-like room with a low vaulted ceiling and only eight dinner tables. The patrons' attention was drawn to the back of the room, where a puppet theater stood.

Louisa took in her surroundings. After the earlier destinations that day, she might be able to warm up to this cozy restaurant. Maybe there was hope for this stop on her mom's day of disasters. All looked safe. What could possibly go wrong here?

The group was seated at a long table directly in front of the puppet stage. While the others picked up their menus, Louisa, not feeling hungry, checked out her surroundings. Above were large rustic wooden beams running parallel to the vaulted ceiling and hundreds of antique marionettes hung from the rafters. Some were dressed as knights; others were in colorful medieval gowns or Victorian-style attire. She couldn't help but think of how the room reminded her of the *Creature Features* butcher shop in Schilde, the way the puppets dangled like freshly skinned cows.

"Louisa, what are you going to get for dinner?" Reah asked. "I think I'm going to have the steak au poivre."

Louisa nearly gagged. Beef was the last thing she wanted, what with the "puppet meat market" hanging overhead. The safe bet was a bowl of French onion soup.

The conversation continued back and forth while they ate. Still, Louisa was more interested in the puppets. She marveled at how many were hanging above and tried counting them but lost track at a hundred. Directly overhead was an especially interesting marionette in a reddish-orange

Victorian gown with ruffles, sequins, and an embroidered gold hem. The puppet's face was a porcelain baby doll. Louisa found it odd she was dressed in women's clothing while her face was that of a very young girl. Fascinated, she couldn't take her eyes off it.

Finally the curtain went up, and the Marionettes appeared on the small stage, singing, dancing, and dueling in a lively manner. The performance was in French, so Louisa had a hard time following what was going on.

Her attention soon returned to the puppet above her with the porcelain face. She squinted to get a better look at the eyes, but with the lights dimmed for the show, it was difficult to see. She could have sworn one of the eyes was opening and closing slowly, as if winking at her. She tried to be rational and convinced herself a draft was causing it.

Louisa turned from the puppet, attempting to ignore it, focusing instead on the show. But the feeling like she was being watched grew.

Back on the stage, two knight marionettes were dueling for the fair maiden who was standing off to one side. The battle went on for a few minutes until one of the duelers pranced over to a cannon and lit it. Out came a poof of smoke with a *bang*, causing most of the audience to flinch, and the room quickly filled with smoke.

After the air cleared, Louisa sensed movement from above. She looked up, just in time to see the baby-faced marionette plummet from the ceiling and crash right in front of her on the table. She jumped up in her seat and let out a blood-curdling scream, causing the diners to stare in alarm. A waiter dashed over, all apologetic, then picked up the marionette and ran off with it. Everybody at the table was laughing—everyone except Louisa.

The excitement eventually was abated and the bill was paid, Louisa and her family headed to the car to get home in time for Eurovision. "Lyle, follow me and I will get you out of the city." Mr. Alexander insisted. "It's a problematic area to drive in and you are bound to get lost."

Louisa's dad shook his head and walked away, looking determined to navigate out of Brussels on his own. Clearly he'd had enough of trying to keep up with the Italian race car driver.

An hour later, the LaPlante family was still circling Brussels' old streets, trying to find a way out of the city.

When they finally did arrive home, Louisa pushed past her sister, who was in front of her on the walkway. "Move it, Judy, there is no time to spare." She ran into the house and turned on the TV, her heart beating full throttle.

Plopping down on the floor, she sat inches from the screen. The TV's display came into focus; the camera scanned over a large audience clapping and screaming. And then the credits came up, closing the show. The program transitioned right into the evening news in Dutch.

What? Louisa gaped, unbelieving. All the hurdles she had to jump over to get home on time and then this. Could this day get any worse?

After the rest of her family retired to bed, Louisa stayed in the living room in hopes that some kind of summary of Eurovision would come on the TV. She had to know who won. Instead, all she could find was an American detective show called *Baretta* dubbed into Dutch. When the clock on the wall hit 11:00 p.m., she was still wide awake and wondered if she'd ever be able to fall asleep. Once she got over her bitter disappointment at missing Eurovision, the day's events resurfaced, haunting her and making it impossible to forget—first the face of the smiling older man at the urinal flashed in her head, then the horrible photos of the torture at Fort Breendonk, and the grand finale plunging demonic puppet at the restaurant.

She trudged into the kitchen for some milk, hoping the distraction would help. After she downed the glass, she made her way back into the living room, dropping on the couch. Her mind wandered back and forth from the smiling urinal man to the marionettes hanging from the ceiling and how they resembled the prisoners in some of the concentration camp photos. Agitated, she sprang from the couch. If she started having nightmares about naked puppets in prison, her parents were in for the lecture of a lifetime.

The tough, streetwise detective speaking Dutch on *Baretta* couldn't dispel her disturbing memories of the day. Even his talking white cockatoo was fluent in the language, but that still was not enough to entertain her.

"*What to do, what to do?*" she asked herself. She needed to go to a happier place. Music would do the trick.

Her Rubettes record came to mind, and she ran down a mental list of their hits. When she got to "Little Darling," she hardened and right away thought of Mathis. That was *their* song. The broken-hearted feeling came flooding back all over again. An image of his sad face at the bus stop in Antwerp materialized, followed by an even more disturbing vision of him smiling and hugging the girl with fire-red hair. *Ugh!* Why did she go there? Now she felt even worse than she had before she'd started her imaginary record player exercise.

TRACK 18

"FANCY PANTS" – KENNY

JUNE 1978

I t was a typical wet Belgian afternoon on a Tuesday. But the weather wasn't enough to damper Louisa's spirits because Tuesday was AVRO's *TopPop* night, which always made it a reason to celebrate.

She stepped off the school bus along with her brother and David, who was staying for dinner. Fancy-free, she bounced down the hall to her bedroom to drop off her schoolbooks. After tossing her bag on top of the bed, Louisa could hear faint weeping coming from her parents' bedroom.

Quietly, she cracked their door open and found her mother lying on the bed. Her teary eyes were red and swollen.

"Mom, are you all right?"

Patty jumped up quickly and brushed the tears away. "Hi, honey. How was school today?" Her smile seemed forced. "It's just these darn allergies in spring."

Louisa walked over to the bed and gave her mom a tight hug as if she believed her. But her mom's explanation didn't convince her. The last time she saw her weep like that was when the family had to put down their seventeen-year-old Siamese cat, Haji Baba, the year before they moved to

Belgium. Louisa decided not to press the issue and tried to convince herself that if it was really bad news, her mom would have told her. Still, she hated seeing her like that, and it made her a little leery.

After dinner that night, the entire family gathered around the TV to watch *TopPop*. The disco scene was on fire by then, and it ruled the show.

Throughout the soulful, up-tempo beat of the dance music coming out of the TV, Louisa had the feeling David, who sat across from her, was up to no good. Ever since the show started, she sensed him staring at her but would avert his glance when she turned to him. Was there something wrong with him? Or maybe he saw something wrong with her. She glanced down at her feet, giving herself a once-over; inspecting her legs, up past her stomach, until her chin was tucked in, looking at her chest. *Nothing wrong here.*

Dropping her head down, she inspected under the seat of the wingback chair she sat in to see if they planted a whoopee cushion. Nope. Nothing there. Perhaps they had put itching powder in her bedsheets or Vaseline on her bedroom doorknob. Louisa stiffened at the thought of that and was on high alert in fear of the boy's antics.

She watched as David nudged her brother. The two boys stood up with mischievous grins and ambled to the entrance of the great room.

"Hey, Louisa!" David yelled out over the noise from the TV. "Did you hear the news?"

Completely puzzled at this point, Louisa peered intently at them. Maybe it wasn't a prank at all and only a funny joke David was going to tell her. But the words that followed out of his mouth were no laughing matter.

"The Rubettes are coming to Antwerp on tour in August!" Covering their ears, David and Teddy darted out of the room, as if to avoid what they must have known would follow.

"*What*?" Louisa screeched at the top of her lungs, springing from her chair. "Oh my gosh! Really? I don't believe it! And it'll be in the summer." She stamped her feet in excitement. "I don't have to worry about getting up early for school the next day! Whoo-hoo. This is great! I can try to get a tan before the concert!"

Briefly pausing for some air, she looked at her sister and her parents. "I'll grow my hair longer. I have three months to do that! This is great. I know Penny will want to go. My life will be complete now. This is great! I gotta go call Penny right now!"

She bolted out of the living room, waving her arms frantically, with the feeling she could take off into the sky. Once she shared the exciting news with her friend, she ran back into the living room. The concert was all she could talk about: the band, her hair, her outfit, the banner she'd make to wave during the concert. No one could convince her to be quiet.

Judy finally stood up, shaking her head. "Louisa, knock it off. You're acting like Linda Blair in *The Exorcist*." She hesitated before lashing out again. "It's like I can see your head doing a three-sixty and foam coming out of your mouth!"

Louisa giggled and piped down for the rest of *TopPop*. After the show ended, she retreated to her bedroom and pulled out every album by The Rubettes she owned for a music marathon showdown. Their hits blasted one after another from her turntable. She danced, swinging her body wildly as she launched from the floor to her bed several times. Her elation was so high she felt weightless and was walking on a cloud. The ecstatic behavior continued until her father came in with a dark glare that said it was bedtime.

It was early June when Lyle summoned the three teens into the living room after coming home from work one evening. Louisa sat with Judy and Teddy on the Wedgwood blue velvet couch. She was prepared for him to announce another of her mother's adventures to somewhere in Europe.

He stood silently in front of them, looking like he was gathering his words carefully. Finally, he spoke. "Kids, we knew it would happen eventually, and the day has come." He glanced over at their mom, who nodded her head. "We're being transferred back to the States. We'll be leaving Belgium in August . . . to go home again."

It took a few seconds for Louisa to digest this news. Antwerp was the longest she had lived in one spot. This *was* her home. She had planted roots here—or at least made her mark.

Louisa turned to her mother, who stood in the doorway. Her mom's expressionless face seemed to be unaffected by her dad's announcement. No doubt the big news was why she had been crying in her room the other day.

One crucial question entered her mind, though, and had her concerned. *What about The Rubettes concert?* She certainly would have to stay by herself if her family left before the concert. *No way* would she leave Belgium without seeing the band. Her worst fears subsided, when her father continued to explain the family would not leave until the last week in August.

The school year at AIS ended a week after Louisa's father's big news. For her, though, it was like the end of an era. She and Judy each created an autograph book by covering a scholastic notebook with aluminum foil to dress it up a bit. All through her last day of school, Louisa ran around, getting as many teachers and students as possible to sign her book.

Toward the end of the day, after several tearful goodbyes from her classmates, the reality of leaving Belgium settled in. She would miss the small, intimate school—and was already dreading the new, larger one in the States that her father had told them they would be attending. Her class of twenty-four students at AIS would increase to a class of three hundred and twenty-four at her new school in Connecticut.

The final bell rang out at the end of the day, creating a hardening pit in Louisa's stomach. This was it. No more AIS. Her sorrow almost choked her as she and Judy cleaned out their lockers for the last time and headed over to the gym building. Their mom had made appointments for them at the salon to get haircuts and was picking them up at school.

Once all the other students disappeared onto the buses to go home, the school's grounds became exceptionally quiet. While they waited for their mother, the girls wandered about AIS's empty halls. They talked, reminiscing about the students and teachers they had met who had come and gone. Judy reminded her about their first dance and how Louisa had been petrified to go into the gym. "You've come a long way since then, sister."

"Gosh, Judy, we've grown up here. So many memories. I don't want to ever forget AIS." Louisa lowered her head and walked away from her sister.

Sitting down on the hall floor, she leaned back against the lockers, reading what her classmates had written in her autograph book. When she finally turned to the last page, there was a note Cody Conlon had written:

Remember the music.
Remember the fun.
Remember the homework that never got done.

Louisa sat silently, taking in everything she had read. She pulled a pen out of her purse. On the inside of her book's front cover, she wrote, "The best years of my life," and drew a big heart around it.

The Peugeot pulled away from AIS, and Louisa turned to the rear window, gaping at the red brick kastel building and its front steps. She recalled her first day of class there four years earlier and how foreign everything had seemed. Yet it had become a second home to her, and now she was leaving it forever.

Back at the house, Louisa trudged to her room to mope in private. Her focus was drawn to the posters of her rock shrine and momentarily her glum mood perked up. "Hi, guys," she waved. Plopping onto her bed, she became absorbed in her thoughts of what was to come. They planned to fly to the States the following week for her aunt's wedding and return in late June. She worried she had only two months left before her time in Antwerp would end.

Did she really want things to end here? Or would a new adventure await her in the States? Louisa knew she had no control over the upcoming move and came to the realization she had to make the best of what little time was left—to leave Belgium with a bang. Once she vowed to make this summer the best one ever, her excitement grew. "No boundaries," she promised herself.

Upon the family's return from the States a few weeks later, Louisa anxiously called Penny so they could plan the greatest summer they would ever have.

They talked about trips to Antwerp, the pool, the beach, and other fun things, all the way to the grand finale: The Rubettes concert in August.

One afternoon in early July, she was at Penny's house, reclining next to her friend in a lounge chair on the terrace overlooking the Hallsworths' manicured gardens and enormous Olympic-size swimming pool. The high sunlit clouds floated against a clear blue sky. It was a beautiful day— by Belgium's standards, and she had been swimming and sunning herself with Penny all day long.

The girls snacked on Boursin cheese spread on dark brown German bread and orange Fanta soda in a chilled tumbler that the maid brought out to them. While Louisa nibbled away, she turned to Penny. "I want to do something big before I leave." She gulped down a swig of soda. "I just can't put my finger on it. I know we have the concert, but I've been to one of those already. I want something different that I've never done before. Something to impress my new friends in the States, you know?"

Penny leaned forward and placed her elbow on her knee and her chin in her hand. The vacant look on her face told Louisa something was processing inside her head. "Louisa, I know we've been to some of the bars, but you always went home before dark because your parents said to be home early. Have you ever experienced the real nightlife in Antwerp?"

Louisa leaned in until she was inches away from Penny's face, copying her friend's posture. "Well, what do you mean?"

Penny looked around, as if making sure no one was listening, and whispered, "You haven't ever been to a real disco yet. I heard they are wild after dark. We could try and sneak into one. We could get all dressed up."

"Yes, but my parents won't let me stay out past 8:00 p.m. on my own," Louisa pouted. "They're strict like that."

Penny moved over to Louisa's lounge chair and sat down next to her. "I could say I'm sleeping over at your house, and you could tell your parents you're staying at mine. Then we can be in Antwerp all night long."

Louisa squinted with apprehension. She'd have to go into a home for delinquents if her parents ever found out. But wouldn't that be the icing on the cake, a night of adventure she could brag about to the future friends she wanted to impress when she returned to the States?

Her doubts melted away, and an eagerness took over. She nodded and smiled at Penny. "Okay, let's do this. And soon! Time is running out, and I have less than two months before we leave Belgium."

The girls retreated to Penny's room and outlined their plans, from what they would tell their parents to what they would wear and the places they would go in Antwerp. Penny was fluent in the local language because she had lived in Antwerp since she was a baby, so she pulled out the local paper and read up on the events that were happening when they would go. There had to be a good, genuine reason to tell their parents why they were going to the big city, to make their plan immaculate.

The morning of the big night out, Louisa snuck into Judy's room and grabbed her sister's passport, who was then sixteen. In case she was asked for identification, she wanted to have something. She was a little nervous about her actions but knew this was her last hurrah in Antwerp and wanted everything to be perfect.

She entered the living room where her mom sat. "So Penny is meeting me out in front of GSC. She made all the plans for the day in Antwerp. I don't even know what they are. I think she said there was a carnival…or something." Louisa inhaled deeply. "And then we'll go back to her house for dinner and I'll sleep over. You don't even have to drop me off or pick me up. I'll take the bus back the next day. Isn't that great?" She turned away from her quickly, to avoid any eye contact that would give away her big lie.

Strolling down Bremboslaan to catch the bus into Antwerp, Louisa swung a duffle bag with a change of clothes for later from her hand. Fear competed with regret as she thought about how she'd lied to her parents. She kept second guessing herself, debating whether she should really go through with the plan, but finally decided it was too late now. She had to finish what she'd started. Besides, what could possibly go wrong? This was going to work. Their plan was bulletproof, as far as she could tell.

When she got off the bus in Antwerp, Penny was waiting with her own overnight bag on a bench in front of the GSC. "This is going to be so exciting!" Penny hooted. "No curfew!"

Regret overcame Louisa, and she put on a false smile for Penny and hoped her true feeling didn't show.

The girls rented a locker at the train station and stuffed their overnight bags inside. They spent the afternoon at a renaissance festival at the Grote Markt, which was a historical square in the center of Antwerp. Throughout the day, she and Penny laughed and poked fun at the traditional medieval dress, music, and dancing. Louisa finally let her guard down and relaxed, forgetting how wrong this all was. Fantasizing that she might actually be in a *real* disco within hours overtook her guilt.

The sun was still high in the sky when the girls headed back to the train station in the early evening. They retrieved their bags from the locker and grabbed a bite to eat across the street at the GB Quick, Belgium's answer to McDonald's. Once they finished Quick's version of a Big Mac, they went to the restaurant's bathroom to get dressed for the big night.

"This is so funny," Louisa said while she changed in the small stall next to Penny's. "I can't believe we're dressing in the GB Quick." She looked around the cubicle and giggled. "Let's be *quick* about it before someone comes in."

When Louisa was ready, she emerged from the stall and found Penny standing by the sink, dressed to kill in a red silk off-the-shoulder dress with matching pumps. Her friend could have stepped out of a scene from *Saturday Night Fever*.

Louisa took a deep breath and cat-walked toward Penny wearing a Gunne Sax baby-blue off-the-shoulder dress with lace ruffles. At the hem, more accent lace cascaded for a few layers, and underneath she wore white stockings and flat sandals.

"What did you do, walk out of *Little House on the Prairie*?" Penny asked with a silly grin.

"What's wrong with this? I wore it to my aunt's wedding last month." She spun around, fluffing out the dress like she had a petticoat underneath.

"It's very . . . wholesome. You look like an innocent angel."

Louisa put her hand on her hip and looked Penny up and down. "Well, you look like the devil in your *red* dress." The two teens laughed and proceeded with hair and makeup.

Once their transformation was complete, they headed back to the train station and dropped off their bags in the locker. When they walked through the lobby, Freckle Face was standing at the bottom of the grand staircase. "Hello, ladies." He eyeballed Penny and her flashy dress.

"We're going upstairs for a beer in the restaurant," Louisa said. "Where is everyone tonight?"

Freckle Face smiled. "I'm right here. I'm all you need."

Louisa playfully pushed him on the shoulder and giggled. The girls climbed up the steps to the restaurant, with the Moroccan trailing behind them.

"So where are the two of you going tonight, all dressed up like so?" Freckle Face asked after they sat at a table with their beers.

"Out on the town!" Penny roared, holding up her goblet for a toast.

The boy leaned in with his eyes still fixed on Penny. "So guess what? There is a new disco at the end of Statiestraat everyone is going to. They never check whether anyone is old enough to be in there."

Louisa smiled, feeling relieved. *Good.* She wouldn't have to use her sister's passport after all. She poked Penny in the arm. "Let's go check it out."

Out in front of the club a young door attendant stood letting people through. When the two girls approached him, he gave Louisa the once-over and asked, "Hoe oud ben je?"

Louisa turned toward Penny for a translation.

"He's asking how old you are," Penny whispered. "Give him the passport."

Louisa reached into her purse, and rummaged around for it. Her hand shook as she opened it up and handed it to the attendant. She tried not to look at him; she didn't want her terrified expression to give her away.

Instead, she turned to Penny and tried to act breezy. "So guess what I heard? Nancy got caught kissing Kevin behind the kastel building."

"What are you talking about?" Penny asked.

Wide-eyed, Louisa repeated her story, trying to get Penny's attention so she'd follow her lead. Still, Penny didn't catch on and shrugged with her hands up.

The door attendant examined the passport carefully, and his eyes met Louisa's. He stared at her for a moment, then handed the passport back and nodded for them to go in.

"I was just trying to keep the conversation going so he wouldn't know I was nervous," Louisa said in a hushed voice as they walked away. "Why did he ask only me for identification anyway?"

Penny halted, looked her up and down, and sneered. "Well, maybe it's your *Laura Ingalls* dress."

Inside the disco, the layout was long and narrow. Black carpeted walls and dim lights magnified the psychedelic colors flashing to the rhythm of the music. As the girls made their way through the packed nightclub, Louisa spotted her Moroccan friends on the other side, standing against the wall. Everyone was out that night: Striped Pants, Said, and Cointreau, as well as Baldy, Big Nose, No-No Guy, and Funny Face—the last four being Moroccans she'd met later on. She continued giving them nicknames, even if she wasn't struggling with pronouncing them. It was just funnier that way.

"Let's go over to the corner of the bar," Louisa shouted into Penny's ear over the pounding music. She locked arms with her friend. "We can get a beer and make some new friends tonight."

Penny smirked at her. "Yeah, let's do some *fox* hunting!"

Soon after, two young Belgian men began practicing their limited English on them. Penny, in humor, pretended she did not speak the local language, just to see them struggle with what they were trying to say.

"Hey," Penny said to the two lads. "They asked Louisa if she was old enough when we came in."

One of the guys turned to Louisa. "Really?" He laughed. "They let *all* people in this place. This is very funny they ask you of this."

She frowned at him and turned her attention toward the Moroccans across the room. Her gaze went to Cointreau, who stood with a girl with short strawberry blonde hair. Louisa became curious as she observed the two. The blonde had made several attempts to get him to dance, but Cointreau kept shaking his head. Eventually, she reached down and grabbed his hand. Cointreau briskly stepped away from her. His eyes darted across the club to Louisa, and their gazes met.

Embarrassed, Louisa snapped her head away. A subtle jealousy came over her but she wasn't sure why. She knew she didn't want to go steady with him but found herself not wanting him to like anyone else either. Nudging Penny, she pointed out the girl. "I think Cointreau has a girlfriend." Both girls laughed lightheartedly.

The night continued on, and Louisa's nerves were finally in a calm and relax state. The only *real* problem was the music—she didn't recognize anything the club was playing. "I wish they had better songs." She pouted to Penny. "Will you go ask them to play 'Fancy Pants' for me? I don't think the DJ speaks English."

Penny put her hand on Louisa's shoulder. "But, Louisa, the song *is* in English."

Louisa scratched her head and thought about what she asked Penny. When it struck her, she quickly glanced around the room, embarrassed. "Duh! I'm such a spaz. I'll be right back."

On her way to the DJ booth, she strutted past the Moroccans but didn't acknowledge them. She knew she was acting aloof, but didn't want any drama with Cointreau to ruin her big night out. Still, when she passed, it made it hard not to look over because she could sense his deep fixation on her.

After making her song request, Louisa gave in, glancing over at Cointreau on her way back. He and the blonde were arguing, and the girl flew off in a rage to a far corner of the club. Louisa quickly retreated heading back to the bar.

"He's got the song and will play it next," she announced to Penny. "Yay for us!" She took a gulp of her beer. "Let's dance when it comes on."

'Fancy Pants' started with a loud upward glissando slide on the keyboards. The sound of it always reminded Louisa of a western saloon where a brawl was about to begin. A steady drumbeat and sharp electric guitar followed. The music ignited the crowd as it vibrated out of the huge speakers. Everyone began jumping up and down to the rowdy pulsation.

Louisa ran out on the dance floor, pulling Penny with her. Throwing her hands up in the air, she moved wildly and chaotically. The humorous, animated expression on her face matched her mindless, clumsy dancing. At one point, she and Penny were face-to-face, bouncing up and down and yelling the lyrics to "Fancy Pants" as if they were having a contest to see who could sing the loudest. All at once, Louisa bent over, dropped her head, and snapped it back up to fluff her hair, catching Penny in the mouth with the back of her head. The girls broke out in laughter. Louisa couldn't help but feel like she was in a *Laurel and Hardy* episode as she rubbed her throbbing head vigorously and Penny felt her mouth as if to check whether she had any teeth left.

It was at that point Louisa spotted Cointreau out of the corner of her eye, slinking closer to the edge of the dance floor. She could feel his burning stare again but tried to ignore him.

Meanwhile, the DJ segued into a disco song she didn't recognize, but both girls' spirits were high, and they continued dancing.

Feeling a little clammy from sweat, Louisa tossed her head down to fluff her hair again. When she flung it back up, Cointreau was standing right in front of her. Hesitant at first, she decided as long as Penny was with her she was safe from any of his advances. So the two girls continued dancing, with Cointreau be-bopping between them.

Louisa found herself in a dreamlike state between the glory of finally getting into a real disco and the beer she'd drunk. She was feeling quite cool and was all the rage. Playfully, she spun around in her glee and kept twirling blissfully. As she circled back to Penny and Cointreau, something heavy unexpectedly hit her from behind, knocking the wind out of her. The weight pushed her down to the dance floor, and she felt her body slam hard to meet the vinyl.

Disoriented, she remained on the floor as a huge commotion transpired above her. What was happening? Who was on top of her? Pain radiated up her leg like little knives sticking her. Some time passed, yet she remained underneath the heavy weight while the ruckus above continued. Nothing seemed to be getting any better. The loud music and the flashing disco lights continued. Why hadn't someone helped her? This was urgent. She felt like she was suffocating and on the verge of passing out.

Just as Louisa gave up hope she'd ever get out of the situation alive, a strong hand gripped under her arm and pulled her up, prying her out from the clutches of the person who had been on top of her. As she stood up, the only thing visible was the club's dark carpeted walls. Everything else around her spun around and around. Someone was pulling her away. All she could do was follow whoever it was and trust they would guide her out of the bad situation.

Once things came into focus, Louisa found herself standing outside the disco. Everything finally stopped spinning as she raised her eyes to see who had rescued her. Standing in front of her was the biggest surprise of her life—Mathis.

Trembling, she took a deep breath and let it out slowly. Had she died? Mathis looked down at her leg, and she followed his gaze. Spots of blood seeped from her knee and through her white stockings. He untied a blue-and-white bandana hanging from his belt loop and handed it to her.

The disco door flew open, and Penny ran out, carrying their purses. "I can't believe that just happened!" she shouted.

Louisa slowly regained her composure. "Why was I down on the dance floor? And who was on top of me?" She shook her head. "It all happened so fast."

Penny crinkled her nose, looking puzzled at Mathis. She turned back to Louisa. "It was the blonde Cointreau was with. She was in a complete rage. Maybe she was jealous of him dancing with us."

Louisa examined her bleeding knee. "I need to sit and get this cleaned up."

"Who's this?" Penny asked, her attention back on Mathis.

Louisa turned toward him, still confused as to why he was there. "Penny, this is Mathis. I told you about him. He's from the record store. Remember? He doesn't speak English."

Penny walked over and stood with Mathis conversing in Flemish while Louisa looked fixatedly at him. She had never seen him outside the music store like this, except for the brief moment when he'd seen her kissing Cointreau. It was the first time she'd heard what his voice sounded like in a flowing conversation.

"He asked if Cointreau was your boyfriend." Penny nudged Louisa and smirked. "I told him *no*."

Quickly forgetting the trauma she had just gone through, Louisa grabbed Penny's arm. "Ask him about the girl I saw him with. The one with the long red hair."

Penny's focus returned to Mathis. It seemed like their discussion went on forever. All Louisa wanted to know was how he would respond.

When their chat finally ended, Mathis mildly smiled at Louisa. "Dat was mijn neef, Andrea."

"Louisa, he said that was his cousin, Andrea," Penny explained. "Her family had surprised his family. They'd been living in Tunisia for five years and came home for Mathis's mother's fiftieth birthday."

Louisa's heart did somersaults in her chest. Her spirit soared, and the angst she'd been harboring for months that Mathis had a girlfriend finally dissolved.

"Come on, Louisa. Mathis said his house is only a few blocks from here. He'll get you something for your knee."

The girls followed him into a residential area with Louisa limping slightly. "Penny, ask him what he was doing there at the disco."

The two conversed back and forth in Flemish again. Moments later, Penny turned back to Louisa, chuckling. "He said everyone gets in there. They never ask for identification."

Giving her friend a mocking smile, Louisa let out a snort of contempt.

They entered a small grass-covered square surrounded by old brick townhouses and two park benches positioned in the middle. Louisa hobbled over to sit and examine her knee. The pain was steady now that the shock of what had happened was wearing off.

"He's going to his parents' apartment to get something to clean you up with," Penny said.

Mathis disappeared into one of the brick townhouse. When he was out of sight, Penny turned to Louisa with her hand over her heart. "You should have seen it, Louisa. Mathis came out of nowhere and swept you away from that girl on the dance floor. Cointreau was trying to get her off you, but it was *Mathis* that got you out of there."

Goosebumps surfaced on Louisa's skin. She had her very own Lancelot. Quickly, she pulled off her dirty white stockings and put them in her purse before he came back.

In no time Mathis returned with first aid equipment. He gently blotted Louisa's cut with a towel. All the while, his eyes never strayed from hers as he bandaged her up. Even when he and Penny conversed in Flemish, his eyes remained on her.

For the rest of the night, Penny acted as their translator. Mathis explained he'd be studying English the next school year and was anxious to learn the language. When Penny relayed this to Louisa, all she could think of was having a real conversation with him. It was the first time she'd ever fantasized about actually talking to a boy. But then again, this was no ordinary boy.

The night felt like a dream. Louisa was so afraid she'd wake up and find none of this had really happened. If she had to go through the horror again of what had occurred at the club to get to where she was now—sitting on that bench with Mathis—she would have done it a million times.

The dark evening sky transitioned to a hint of daylight building on the horizon. Birds chirped above, leaping back and forth from trees to rooftops. It was time for the girls to head back to the GSC, get their bags, change, and clean up to take the bus home.

Louisa grinned at Mathis with glowing eyes. "Danku vel, Mathis. Dag."

He returned the smile. "Dag, mijn Louisa."

The girls made their way out of the little square. Once they were a few blocks away, Louisa's shriek of happiness practically bounced off the surrounding apartment buildings. She grabbed Penny's hand and kissed it several times. "Thank you, thank you for being the best third wheel ever. I just learned so much about him."

Later that morning, Louisa made her way up the front walk in a bouncy step to her home, deliriously high from the evening. Putting aside the mishap in the club, she wanted to hold onto the rest of the night forever in her heart. As she approached the front door, though, her ecstasy vanished in a flash. Her mother stood on the threshold with a flaming red face and menacing glare.

Louisa quickly learned, Penny's mother had called earlier that morning, wondering what time her daughter was coming home. She stood in the living room, facing her mother and father as if on trial. Her parents deliberated while sitting on the couch and delivered the verdict: She was grounded—*for a whole year!*

"What about The Rubettes concert?" Louisa pleaded.

"Not negotiable!" her father growled.

Storming off to her room, Louisa slammed the door. She fell on her bed, grief-stricken. "This was supposed to be the greatest summer ever," she cried to herself. "And The Rubettes, what about them? I have to go to the concert. I'll never get the chance again."

And then there was Mathis. A flash of realization hit her that he didn't even know she was moving. She hadn't told him yet. She had to meet with him and let him know.

Fighting back the welling tears, she jumped off the bed and grabbed the blue-and-white bandana he had given her. It still had droplets of her blood on it, but that didn't matter. It was something of his. She climbed back into bed, curled into the fetal position, kissing the bandana, then held it close to her heart. The tears she fought started pouring down her cheeks. She repeatedly chanted to herself that she had to see him, somehow. There had to be a way.

A heavy weariness engulfed her after the all-nighter. It felt like sand was being poured on her eyelids. She struggled to stay awake so she could brainstorm a way to meet with Mathis. She didn't want to wake up and not have a plan.

The exhaustion finally took control. She started to drift off, but before her thoughts faded to complete darkness, an image of Mathis extending his hand to her emerged. Semiconscious, Louisa pictured herself reaching out to him and managed one last weep. "I'll do anything to see him again."

TRACK 19

"TEENAGE RAMPAGE" – THE SWEET

MAY 2018

"**P**inch me! Am I dreaming?" Louisa exclaimed to Judy from the ladies' room at the Brussels Airport. "I still can't believe we're here in Belgium." Splashing some cold water on her face from the sink, a calmness enveloped her now that her feet were touching the ground again. No planes to think about for the next eleven days.

The sisters met up with their mother, outside the ladies' room, and they headed down the same corridor they had walked decades earlier. After retrieving their bags, they boarded a train for Antwerp.

The rhythmic clack of the locomotive nearly lulled Louisa to sleep after the exhausting flight. She sat up wide awake, though, when the announcer said in perfect English, "Antwerp Central Station, next stop." Things had certainly changed since the 1970s.

The train doors opened, and they stepped onto the GSC platform, standing with their suitcases at their feet, just like they had forty years earlier. Louisa examined the station's interior, waiting for the memories to resurge. The historical terminal had been upgraded since her last time here. But the famous clock was still there, smiling down at her as if to say, "Welcome home."

"I think I'm having a déjà vu." Judy laughed. "Wait! It was a lifetime ago the last time we were here."

Heading under the clock and into the main lobby, Louisa looked back at the glorious grand staircases as they exited. Her surroundings were familiar, yet nothing particular came to mind. It was like the station refused to release her childhood memories. But she knew formative moments from her adolescence took place there, and the excitement of plunging into her forgotten past churned in her stomach.

They hailed a cab which brought them to a brick apartment building in old-town Antwerp. Across from the apartment was a cobblestone square lined with eighteenth-century bourgeoisie buildings.

"Mom, this is so cute," Judy said. "But how'd you find out about this place?"

Patty scowled. "I know how to use the intranets, Judy."

Louisa shook her head. *Here we go again.* "In-*ter*-net, Mom. It's the internet."

Inside, the wide plank flooring, high ceilings accented with fine art deco crown molding, and a marble fireplace gave the apartment a classic European character. Although the structure was old-world, the furniture was contemporary, with simple lines and quiet colors. The small, plain kitchen had a bistro table tucked in a corner by a window looking out onto the old streets of Antwerp.

Louisa settled into her room and unpacked. She couldn't believe she wasn't tired with hardly any decent sleep. A round clock on the wall with a Belgium flag behind its hands showed it was 11:00 a.m. A giddiness filled her when she realized they had the whole day to go down memory lane. But when she entered the kitchen, her mother and Judy suggested a nap first.

"Really?" Louisa balked. "We can sleep when we get home!" She curled her lip, disappointed, and headed back to her room to wait while they took a siesta. While she lay twiddling her thumbs, she daydreamed about what the day would bring her. Before long, she dozed off, dead to the world.

Waking hours later, she peered out the bedroom window. Warm orange and red sunlight softly graced the side of the Cathedral of Our Lady. Realizing that it was early evening made her cry out, "Crap! It's sunset. We slept all day." She ran through the apartment to the other bedrooms. "Mom!" she yelled. "Judy! Wake up. It's almost night. We screwed up. This is going to mess us up for the rest of the trip now. We should *never* have taken a nap. Bad idea you guys."

At dinner that evening, their mom clinked her chalice of De Koninck beer against Louisa's and Judy's. "Cheers to me!"

Judy's eyes narrowed. "Mom, you didn't even give us a chance to do the honors ourselves."

All three of them ordered moules et frites, which came with a variety of tasty mustard sauces. The restaurant they were dining in, the Rooden Hoed, was known for having the best mussels in town. From its exterior medieval facade to the dated interior, the inviting establishment had served the public for centuries and carried a rich history. Louisa and her family had eaten there on their final night in Antwerp forty years earlier. Now, her mom had decided it would be the first restaurant of their inaugural night back in the country.

"So, Louisa." Judy nodded to their mother. "Mom and I were talking before the trip. You've gone through a rough time the past few years and haven't been yourself lately. This trip was a big step for you, with the whole not-flying thing and the divorce." She put her hand on top of Louisa's and smiled. "So we'd like to reward you."

Wary, Louisa wondered where her sister and mother were going with this. She'd thought this trip was about her mother's achievements, not her woes. "Sister, what's up? This is Mom's moment to shine."

Judy winked at Louisa with the corners of her mouth curled. "Well, we can't say what it is yet, but we have a couple of surprises in store while we're here, and you're gonna love them. We're talking pure memory lane stuff here."

Hearing this made Louisa cringe, she wanted *no more* surprises. Other than flying, this was her worst fear about going on this trip. Surprises always left her feeling uneasy and having no control. Whenever a family dinner or event needed to be organized, she had always been in charge of the coordinating—or she'd refuse to be involved at all. It had become an ongoing joke with her family and friends, who often referred to her as Julie McCoy, the cruise director from the '70s TV series *The Love Boat.*

Louisa sat with her mom and Judy the next morning in the living room, drinking coffee and planning the first stop on their itinerary. "Okay, girls," Patty said. "Where do we want to go first?"

Louisa faced Judy, whose eyes were flashing. "Bremboslaan!" they shouted in unison.

While the sisters waited in the kitchen for their mother to get ready for the day, Louisa asked Judy, "I'm curious, what are your memories of Belgium? Do you feel like you remember everything from when we lived here?"

"It's weird, because I remember the timeline of the four years." Judy appeared to struggle with what she would say next. "But I forget what I really thought about the whole experience."

Louisa nodded. "What I remember is how impressionable I was at that age. But even more so, how the world seemed so innocent to me back then."

Judy shook her head laughing. "I just remember it being so *dark* all the time. Did the sun ever come out when we lived here?"

They drove up the Turnhoutsebaan in their rental car, Louisa playing copilot and Judy doing the driving. Once the car went through the third roundabout, Louisa recalled that back in the '70s, the road had been one straight line from Schilde to the center of Antwerp. But the endless roundabouts constructed since they moved were ruining her memories and had her miffed. "Well, these rotaries weren't here before," she grumbled. "This isn't how I remember it."

After what felt like a wild roller-coaster ride, they finally rolled into their old hometown of Schilde. The GB market, where they had done their grocery shopping, was now a much larger supercenter called the Carrefour. The familiar small market setting with bike racks in front had disappeared.

"I know, I know." Judy pointed. "We take a right here, and then our Bremboslaan will be up ahead."

Louisa pressed her nose against the window, trying to capture every detail of her childhood stomping grounds. "Look at the trees," she said, amazed. "They're so big now. It's almost like an enchanted forest in here."

When they turned onto Bremboslaan, the trio started hooting and hollering with excitement. Arriving at the house they had once called home, Judy pulled the car over to the side of the road.

Louisa anxiously hopped out first and stood in front of number eleven Bremboslaan, analyzing everything that had changed on the exterior. The shutters had been removed, and the French doors had been replaced with regular long windows. To the right, the cast-iron Victorian tower mailbox that had greeted them every time they pulled into the driveway was gone, replaced with a small modern black mailbox.

She walked over to the left side of the house, where some of the bedrooms faced outward. At one time, they'd looked out onto deep, thick woods. Now, that side of the property abutted another home.

Louisa took Judy by the hand. "This is where all of those boys would stand when they came to your window in the middle of the night," she whispered. "Do you remember that?"

Judy stood silently, looking at what had been her bedroom window. A calculating smile swept across her face, looking like it had all come back to her.

After reminiscing, the sisters headed toward the front of the house again. Along the way, they found their mother hunched over, pressing her nose against the window that used to be Teddy's "lab." "Oh no! They took down that spacey brown-and-orange wallpaper Teddy had in his room."

Louisa peered inside. The room was bare as a bone. "There's nothing in there." She glanced around the property. "Our home is vacant."

"I think it's for sale." Judy pointed to a red and blue sign off to the house's right that read, "Te Koop."

Louisa's thoughts raced. How cool would it be if they could get a realtor to show them the inside of the house? But she hesitated to suggest it—she wanted to remember her home as it had been before. She was already rattled by all the changes, from the grown trees to the renovations later owners had made.

Wandering back to the road, Louisa stood there, wistfully taking one last look at her old home, hardly believing she had lived there for nearly four years. "Okay, let's go into Schilde center!" she cried, breaking the silence. She was anxious to move on. They had a lot of ground to cover.

When the ladies drove up to the grand church, Louisa noticed some more disappointing changes—the dilapidated frites stand across the street was no longer there.

"How sad," she whined. "That shack was iconic to Schilde. Where do the people get their frites met mayo now?" A discouraged feeling began to settle in her. It wasn't that she expected everything to be like it was, but one small remnant that remained the same would have been nice.

They continued on and drove toward the Turnhoutsebaan to see the main strip in Schilde. Louisa leaned over and turned the radio on in hopes the music would pep her up. First, a loud, annoying commercial in Flemish blared from the speakers. She hit Seek, and the radio found lively polka music.

She hit Seek again. This time, heavy metal guitar riffs emerged, prompting her to bolt upright in her seat. Flowing out of the speakers was the song "Teenage Rampage," by The Sweet. The nostalgic souvenir she'd hoped for had arrived. It was as if the tune was held captive and waited years for someone to turn on the radio and set it free. "Don't you remember this one from when we lived here, Judy?"

Her sister shrugged. "Nope. That was your department."

Louisa cranked up the volume. The shrillness of Brian Connolly's stratospheric vocals sent her blood coursing, bringing out her inner rebel. The unbridled spirit she used to feel whenever she'd heard the song as a teen was coming back. Singing along, she remembered every word as if she'd learned the lyrics yesterday. Her hair fell across her face, and she dramatically flung her head back and forth to the amped-up guitar. When the music finally ended, Louisa took a deep breath. She was amazed by her recall. "Just like riding a bike!"

In the center of town, they passed several charming cafés and stores. Judy parked the car and turned to Louisa and Patty, "Let's walk around and get a closer look at everything and see if we remember any of these shops."

The three popped into a café and ordered a dainty pot of tea with some sugary treats. Louisa sat across from Judy at a small table and noticed her sister squinting at something over Louisa's head. Her stare made Louisa feel self-conscious, as if a bug was crawling on her. Moments passed and Judy continued gawking. Louisa finally swept her hand over the top of her head. "What? Do I have something in my hair?"

Judy nodded toward the window behind Louisa. "Isn't that where the record store was across the street? You always went in there." She lowered her eyes, looking directly into Louisa's. "Don't you remember? You had a crush on that Belgian kid. What was his name? Magnus?"

Louisa swung around in her seat and peered out the window. A small, unoccupied brick building was across the street. It appeared to have been a store in the past, with large display windows on either side of the entrance. Her eyes followed farther down the main street to the Carrefour, which used to be the GB market. Maybe it was where the music store had once been.

All at once she felt the café fall silent. It was as if the front door blew open and a wave of rumination swept in, consuming her. She closed her eyes and recalled thumbing through bins of albums. A sharp pain in her gut impaled her when it became clear who her sister was speaking of. Her eyes opened. "No," she snapped. "His name was *Mathis*."

It caught her breath that his name had rolled out like it was yesterday. A name she hadn't said or thought of in decades. She had *totally* forgotten about him.

Louisa left her mother and Judy sipping their tea and darted across the street to see if there was any evidence of the music store. She peered in through the storefront window. Inside were vacant desks and empty boxes scattered here and there. The open space didn't look familiar. Louisa's shoulders sagged, and she sighed deeply as her hopes faded. She wasn't really sure what she expected but a sadness welled up in her when she learned her past was no longer inside the building.

Later in the day, the sisters walked down to the market a few blocks from their apartment in Antwerp while their mom napped. The small shop sold everything from skinned chickens and pigs dangling in the storefront window to souvenirs of the city. Louisa meandered down the aisles and picked up some breakfast items, filling the small basket she carried on her arm. Meanwhile, Judy pushed a full-size cart, loading it with snacks, bottles of wine, and souvenirs to bring home.

"Judy, how are you going to carry all of this back to the apartment?" Louisa scoffed. "You should wait until we have the car. It'll be easier."

Judy turned her head and went down another aisle, ignoring her.

When Louisa finished her shopping, she waited for her sister at the front of the store by the single register, impatiently tapping her foot. Judy eventually rolled up with her filled-to-the-brim carriage to the register. Louisa looked down at the cart and shook her head. "Don't think I'm going to help you carry all of that."

"Chill, little sister!" Judy snarled. "Don't be such a downer. You're on vacation. It'll be an adventure, getting all of this loot back on foot."

Louisa stormed up to the register and placed her items on the counter.

"Where are you from?" the male store clerk asked in English.

Louisa clamped her hand over her mouth. She hadn't realized the ruckus she and Judy were making. "Oh, I'm sorry," she said apologetically.

"We're sisters, and we argue all the time." She glanced back at Judy and nodded to the store clerk. "We're from the US."

The clerk had a Bohemian look, with long curly dark hair tied in a man bun and a florescent-patterned tunic-style shirt. "Oh, I love America. My cousin lives in New York."

Louisa put her items in a bag. "Your English is perfect. Where are you from?"

He stood up tall. "I am from Morocco."

Sparking Louisa's attention, her immediate reaction was to tell the clerk about her Moroccan friends from the train station, but she hesitated. How mature would that look trying to explain to him her days at the GSC in the 1970s. She wouldn't even know where she would start her story. Or even what the story was.

Judy, bold as ever, didn't hold back. "Do you know Striped Pants?"

Louisa elbowed her sister. "Judy! Shhh."

When they exited the store, Louisa let loose the laughter she had been holding in. She slapped her sister's arm. "I can't believe you asked him about Striped Pants."

Judy was unfazed, though, shrugging like it was no big deal and headed down the street.

Trailing behind her, Louisa looked up into the early evening sky, absorbed in thought. Her recollections of the Moroccans had been stirred and the vague stories swarmed around in her head. What was the big deal with them anyway? To this day, the word "Moroccan" still set off butterflies in her stomach, yet what was that based on? She could barely remember them.

On day three, Patty had an appointment at AIS to speak with the secretary, Gabby, about the upcoming Women's Club luncheon. She had arranged for a tour of the old campus as well. Unfortunately, they couldn't go inside to see their former classrooms because school was still in session.

While the three strolled with Gabby through the pathways outside leading from one building to another, Gabby explained, "We have over four hundred students enrolled now, and that number increases every year."

"Wow," Louisa exclaimed. "Our little school is no longer." Her bottom lip jutted out, and she wandered away from the others. Stopping at a brick building across from the kastel, Louisa remembered it was once called "building one."

This was where her adventure at AIS started over forty years earlier. An image of her classroom materialized in her mind, and for some strange reason the girls' restroom. She chuckled, recalling why: this was where she had her first puff of a cigarette.

As she rounded the corner to the side of the building she spotted a stone slate on the ground with a plaque. Reading it, she discovered it was a dedication to a student that had passed in her class in 1980, just two years after she had moved back to the States. Penny had written to her about his passing when it happened, but seeing the reality of his name on a memorial made her feel like it was just yesterday when she had heard the news. A sadness overwhelmed her as she stared intently at the memorial. Eventually her moistened eyes peeled away from the stone. "Too young," she muttered to herself walking away.

Heading back to the car after their tour, Louisa felt like an oppressive cloud was hanging over her. Between the small, family-like feel of AIS no longer being there and her fallen classmate, she urgently needed a diversion.

"Hey, let's go into Grand Central, to that restaurant we saw when we came through the other day, for a real Belgian waffle. That place has been there forever," her mother suggested. "That will cheer you up, Louisa. It's such a beautiful train station."

Louisa smiled, aware that her mom was speaking of the same restaurant she hung out with her Moroccan friends drinking beer. Her glum mood faded as excitement built to see what had become of the old hang-out.

The ladies hiked up the GSC's grand staircase. Inside the restaurant, the recessed high ceiling was broken into intricate squares, accented with elegant wainscoting and gold detailing. Large floor-to-ceiling mirrors were framed with hand-carved crown molding.

Amber accent lighting brought a warm, soft glow to the room. The clock in the center wasn't quite as large as the clock in the station lobby, but it was just as breathtaking. Louisa wondered if it was the same place. Had it been renovated? Or was it the same, and she just hadn't appreciated its beauty when she was a teen? Now, it seemed like one of the most magnificent rooms she'd ever seen. The restaurant could have been a room in Versailles.

After their meal, she took one last look back at the room as they exited. This couldn't be the same place. And she certainly doubted any Moroccans were still going in there, buying beers for underage girls.

That evening, the quest for their next meal consumed them once again. Louisa and Judy determinedly scouted out a good old-fashioned, dilapidated frites stand for old times' sake. It seemed the little run-down huts were almost nonexistent now. Their exploration brought them to the Grote Markt in old-town Antwerp.

"Wow," Judy said when they walked into the historic square. "This is a real blast from the past. Don't you remember when Mom and Dad used to drag us here to sightsee?"

Louisa drank in her surroundings, admiring the sixteenth-century square with its Baroque-style gilded houses and Gothic city hall. She remembered the Grote Markt itself, but nothing connected with it came to mind.

Off in one corner, she spotted a giant white cone with large papier-mâché French fries poking out from the top. The word "fritkot" was written across the display. "Look, Judy!" she exclaimed. "They have frites."

The two sped over to the fritkot. The building's exterior had an unassuming charm, with round bistro tables hand-painted in soft pastel shades of green and purple on a terrace out front. The place, though, was far too nice to be called a frites stand.

"I want it dirtier and dumpier," Louisa cried. "Just like when we lived here."

Judy rolled her eyes and grabbed Louisa's arm. "C'mon, beggars can't be choosers."

Minutes later, they stepped back onto the terrace of the restaurant with three packages of frites to go. Louisa admired the dwindling sunrays as the evening lights flicked on, illuminating the Grote Markt as if the entire square was on a single light switch.

Her eyes landed on something in front of her she hadn't noticed earlier: in the marketplace's center, accent spotlights at the bottom lit up the iconic Brabo Fountain. Louisa stood clutching her chest at the striking sight.

The statue itself showed the Roman warrior Silvius Brabo hurling a human hand. It always reminded Louisa of an Olympic athlete tossing the javelin. The foundation of the monument was adorned with mystical creatures. Louisa recalled the story of Brabo and how it was significant to Antwerp's history. The legend was that Brabo defeated a wretched giant called Druon Antigoon. The giant would extort money from people who wanted to pass over the bridge of the Scheldt River leading into Antwerp. If they didn't pay him, he'd cut off one of their hands and throw it into the river. Later, Brabo bestowed the same fate upon the giant after defeating him. Thus, the statue represented Brabo's victory over the ogre.

Louisa staggered over to the fountain with her head looking up at the warrior. A strong awareness of something that she couldn't put her finger on almost brought her to her knees as her body went limp.

"What is it?" Judy asked.

Louisa shook her head, trying to lose the peculiar feeling. "I don't know what that was." She stood there a second longer, taking another look at Brabo. "I guess . . . I guess I just had a monument moment."

Back at the apartment, the ladies squeezed in around the tiny kitchen table to enjoy their nostalgic dinner of frites with mayo and De Koninck beer.

"Louisa, tomorrow is your first surprise," Judy said while they ate. "We have to get up early because we're taking a train."

Louisa's gut reaction was to take control and demand to know the exact plan. She paused, though, as a warm feeling enveloped her. For the first time in years, she didn't feel the need to know the plan—or even what the next step was. Something about the last few days in Antwerp had put her into a totally different frame of mind.

The LaPlante women headed to the GSC the following morning. Standing there waiting for the train, Louisa casually looked up at the schedule and it read Amsterdam. What could possibly be there that would be a surprise? She didn't recall anything from her youth, except for the grizzly Winter Warlock-flasher. She was sure they weren't revisiting that experience. Although, that would *certainly* be a surprise.

They exited Antwerp and the city gave way to suburbs, the flat green landscape became accented with windmills. Louisa peered out the window at the passing scenery. The droning of the train chugging along caused her thoughts to spin around in her head. The lyrics of Leo Sayer's "Train"—the song that had inspired her to hop on a plane bound for Europe—came back to her. She remembered how she and her family had arrived in Antwerp on the train forty years earlier and how she had returned on the same tracks just a few days ago. She had always been fascinated with the GSC itself, as well as with the Moroccans who had hung out there. Now, on this train to Amsterdam, she couldn't help but think it was all connected somehow. Would something life-altering happen to her today? Maybe the train was going to lead to her salvation. Or maybe she was overthinking things again to create some stimulation in her dull, pathetic life.

When they arrived in Amsterdam, the train stopped, and the doors opened. Louisa noticed her mother looking around when they hopped off, like she was expecting someone. "What next?" she asked her mom.

The throng of departing passengers kept her in one spot for a minute. Once the crowd thinned out, Louisa looked straight ahead, and a heartwarming feeling rushed through her. There in front of her stood a true blast from the past—*Anneke Verstraete*. Louisa had stayed in contact with her Belgian friend over the decades. She always felt Anneke was her only living link to her extraordinary days of living in Europe. Ironically, her semi-scandalous friend had become a missionary after college and moved to Amsterdam years ago. She now worked as a counselor for newly released criminals from prison.

Before the trip, Louisa had texted her to tell her she was coming to Belgium. Anneke had replied that she'd be away on business. Now, Louisa discovered it was all just another one of her sister's surprises. And a wonderful surprise it was. Maybe there was room for the unexpected in her life after all.

"Anna-Banana!" Louisa yelled. "Oh my gosh; it's you!" She ran up to her friend and gave her a huge hug. When they released each other from their embrace, Anneke skittishly glanced around at all the people staring.

The group went up an escalator and out into the scenic streets of Amsterdam. "I have a special surprise for you all today," Anneke explained. "I made an appointment for lunch. It's just a few more blocks, and I will explain what the surprise is."

The restaurant was located right on the water. Ducks and small boats silently drifted past as they sat at their table. All four women nibbled on a gooey caramel-filled Dutch treat called stroopwafel.

"Let's order some drinks!" Patty suggested. "How about some rosé?"

Two bottles of wine later and lunch finished, the handsome waiter with wavy blonde hair came over with the check and asked Judy, who had ogled him throughout their meal, "Are you going to a coffee shop next?"

Judy furrowed her brow and did not respond. The waiter shrugged and walked away.

"That was an unusual question to ask," Patty said.

"Oh, Patty, he's asking if we're going to one of the cannibal bars," Anneke said, smiling. "There's one right across the canal. See the sign? Do you want to go in?"

Louisa erupted in laughter. "Anneke, I think you mean *cannabis*. Cannibals are people who eat people." Anneke's face went expressionless for a moment, but soon she joined Louisa in laughing. Grabbing a pen from her purse, she asked Louisa how to spell cannabis so she would remember not to make that mistake again.

Patty peered across the canal at the shop. "I always wanted to try some of that mary-wanna."

"Hey, when in Amsterdam, do like the Dutch, right?" Judy laughed.

Anneke looked at her watch. "Well, we have an appointment with the Van Gogh Museum in two hours. This is your surprise. It's a very *special* art exhibit."

Louisa right away was reminded of her days living in Belgium and all the touristy places her parents had dragged her to that she had no interest in as a teen. Ever since, she'd stayed clear of museums. She took a large gulp of her wine, thinking she would need it—or maybe something stronger—if she was going to spend the afternoon at an art exhibit. "Well, then we have time to do like the Dutch," she said, trying to entice the other women. "Let's go find out what this *'cannibal* shop' is all about."

Louisa, feeling good from the rosé, waltzed through the door first of the "coffee shop" with the others trailing behind. Up front, a regular bar was serving alcohol. The lights were dim, and the feeling was very relaxed. Five young men sat at a table on one side. They looked up at her and the others as if they were lost. In another corner, two older men were sipping coffee and smoking cannabis.

"Oh, so they really do serve coffee here," Judy said, nodding her head at the older men. "It must be a front."

They made their way to a counter at the back of the shop. Reminding Louisa of an ice-cream parlor, a glass display case held various cultivars and strains of marijuana, each with a name placard.

She explained to the young man behind the counter what she was looking for.

"How much tobacco do you want it cut with?" the clerk asked.

Louisa placed her hand on her chest. "No! I don't smoke cigarettes. None, please."

The clerk scratched his head. "Are you sure? Typically, the cannabis is prepared with tobacco to cut the intensity of the effects."

Louisa wondered how intense it could be. They were only going to sample a puff from the little gordita so they could say they did it. "That's okay. *No* tobacco, please."

The women settled in at a table and lit up their purchase. Soon, all four of them were hacking.

"Don't you girls ever tell your father about this," their mom warned. She glowered at Louisa and Judy while taking a puff, sticking her pinkie finger straight up in the air like the fat joint was a dainty slender cigarette from the 1920s.

Louisa chuckled. "Mom, you're in the kids' club now! This is what it was like for us growing up, in fear of you and Dad finding out our little secrets."

The table of cannabis novices was getting loud with hacking, laughing, and the sound of camera shutters. It was evident to the other patrons Louisa's group was a bunch of silly Americans taking advantage of something illegal back home. Laughter could be heard coming from all around the room.

"Okay," Anneke finally said. "We need to go to our appointment now. I'm not too sure how to get there, so we need time."

The ladies headed out the door, passing the two older men, who were still drinking coffee. "Enjoy your day," one of the men said, snickering. "Good luck."

Louisa gave him a strange look. Good luck? What was that supposed to mean?

Anneke navigated through the streets to the museum, walking in the lead with Judy beside her. Louisa strolled along behind with her mom, peeping into the windows of the Delftware souvenir shops.

The sidewalk narrowed as they turned down another block. Louisa noticed her sister lock arms with Anneke. Judy's pace had become significantly lethargic and elongated.

"Sister, what's up?" Louisa teased. "Why are you walking like that? You look like a stegosaurus."

Judy turned to her with a cloudy, glazed look in her eyes. Louisa recognized that spacey look from their younger days of experimental mischief. Her sister was stoned out of her mind. A deafening laughter echoed, shattering the quiet street.

Louisa had no clue what was so amusing, but she couldn't stop her hysterics—not even the loud snort that came out of her nose. Her mother joined in on the meaningless laughter beside her.

Anneke, who appeared frustrated with the nuttiness going on, turned around. "Okay, we need to stop being so silly. We can't go into the museum like this. It is a *very* serious place."

They wandered down a few more streets until Anneke halted. She turned around, her face beaming, "Patty, do you remember when you made me that sandwich with the funny brown stuff a long time ago? It was very special. I'll always remember it." Anneke rubbed her tummy in a circular motion. "I feel hungry again. I could go for one of those American sandwiches right now."

Louisa suddenly realized Anneke was also flying high. Her friend seemed unsure where she was going as she examined her surroundings. Judy unlocked arms with her and turned to face Louisa and their mom. "I don't think I can walk anymore. My legs won't move, and my head is spinning!"

Anneke pointed to a little square straight ahead with park benches surrounded by shops and small outdoor cafés. "Let's go sit. I think my legs are broken too."

Louisa shuffled into the square and stood in front of Anneke and Judy as the two plopped down on the bench. Inching her head up slowly, Anneke yanked on Louisa's shirt. "I don't think we can go to the museum," she muttered. She rested her elbow on her knee and used her hand to hold her head up. "My feet are sparkling, and I feel funny."

The "mary-wanna" was apparently having little effect on Patty, though. "I'm going to hit the jewelry shop over there while you all are resting," she said and wandered off.

Louisa stepped back to get a better view of her sister and friend on the bench. Judy was on one end with her head between her legs. On the other end was Anneke, looking like Rodin's *The Thinker*. She found the scene hilarious and pulled out her cell phone for a selfie with the bench's two human "bookends." If she ever needed blackmail material on Judy, she had it now.

Time crawled slowly, and nothing changed. Judy and Anneke remained on the bench, incapable of walking or keeping their heads up. Louisa realized she would have to start playing nursemaid since her buzz was much milder. "Okay, you two," she said. "I'm going to the store over there to get you some water, so don't you move." She chuckled. "I guess you can't move anyway, so we're good."

Returning to the square with bottled water, Louisa hesitated when she spotted two nuns sitting between Judy and Anneke, eating ice-cream cones.

She glanced over and smiled at one of the nuns as she walked up to Judy. "Here, sister. Drink some of this. It will help."

Judy could barely hold her head up. Slowly, Louisa poured water into her sister's mouth, though most of it dribbled down her chin to the ground.

Louisa could feel the nuns watching her every move. She turned to them, "My sister had too much Gouda cheese and doesn't feel well." She felt like she had to explain to them what was going on. They only nodded and continued their licking.

A long low groan came from Judy as her head remained tucked in between her legs. Then she yelled out, "I'm going to be sick!"

At first, her dramatic retching almost didn't sound human. She twisted her body to the left of the bench, and the stroopwafels cookies from lunch spewed from her mouth, splattering onto the pavement.

Louisa turned to the nuns and watched as they dropped their ice-cream cones, dashing away from the bench.

Her lunch now purged, Judy placed her head between her legs again. Louisa moved over to Anneke's side of the bench, handing her a bottle of water. Her friend didn't seem to be doing as badly as Judy. Still, she had a disgusted look on her face as if she had been scolding herself.

Turning back to her sister, Louisa was taken by surprise when a flock of pigeons aggressively swarmed in from above, "cleaning up" Judy's regurgitated rosé-infused stroopwafels. They pecked away at the mess until the pavement was spotless. As disgusting as it was, Louisa couldn't help but laugh; Judy had *literally* tossed her cookies.

After an hour passed, a college-aged girl with waist-length brown curly hair came over from one of the outdoor cafés. "Alles goed?"

Louisa nodded and asked if she spoke English. Then she explained to her about the coffee shop they had gone to earlier. The girl chuckled. "Okay, just wanted to see if you need help. I watch you from the table, and you all look funny."

"How long will I be like this?" Anneke moped, looking up at the girl.

"Just relax and enjoy the ride," she answered and breezily strolled away.

Anneke's head looked heavy as she turned to Louisa. "Godverdomme," she mumbled in Flemish.

The afternoon continued to move slowly as Louisa nursed Judy and her friend, ensuring they were drinking enough water. Eventually, she convinced the two to get up and walk. The process was long and tedious, like they were learning how to take their very first steps.

Finally, Patty returned to the group, wearing a satisfied grin with several shopping bags in her hands. "Are we ready to go to the museum now?"

Judy and Anneke were standing, holding onto the bench for support with pale, queasy faces.

"I just want to go home," Judy moaned.

The group agreed to call it a day and head back to the train station. When they stepped off the square, a sudden round of applause erupted from the surrounding outdoor cafés. Startled, Louisa glanced around. Unbeknownst to her, their drama had been entertaining the patrons seated outside the surrounding cafés. Louisa giggled when she realized what was going on. Still experiencing the effects of the cannabis, she curtsied to her audience as the group disappeared down the street.

On the train ride back to Antwerp, Louisa sat facing her mother and sister, who slept in the seat across from her. She turned to the window, watching the low-lying plains of the Dutch countryside flash past her. Something about being on a train again and the steady rhythmic motion put her in a contemplative mood. The day's events certainly didn't give her any signal on which way she should turn at the crossroads she was facing. There was no way playing Florence Nightingale for Judy and Anneke was her moment of salvation. Letting out an exasperated sigh, she scooched down in her seat and closed her eyes.

The next morning, Patty busied herself working on her speech for the American Women's Club luncheon. Meanwhile, Judy remained in her pajamas, still looking a little out of it.

"I'm going out for a walk!" Louisa yelled. She grabbed her purse and decided to hit the streets of Antwerp and explore some of her old haunts.

It was a beautiful day—by Belgian standards. Golden sunshine peeked out through puffy white clouds. A warm breeze moved through Louisa's hair, stimulating her to do some soul-searching. Maybe the answer was somewhere here in Antwerp.

An urgent need drew her back to the GSC. Feeling sentimental, she wandered through the main entrance and stood at the foot of the staircase, glancing up at the splendor of the vast dome. Memories of her days in the station with the Moroccans were vague and blurry. Small fragments of something or someone would flash in her mind, but they had no substance. It was like a dream full of nonsensical images she couldn't put together. She leaned against the station wall and closed her eyes tightly. Oh, how she wished she could go back and see it all over again.

The grand clock looking down at her marked the passing of time, but still nothing significant came to mind. What was it she was looking for anyway? She could see it in front of her and could almost touch it, but like the air, it was not tangible. *Forget this.* Time to move on.

Louisa walked out of the station and headed a few blocks up toward Statiestraat, where all the discos and bars had been back in her heyday. The street was now a pedestrian zone. All the nightclubs with their flashing lights had turned into shops, quaint cafés, and restaurants.

While she strolled along window-shopping, something occurred to her; she hadn't thought about her colorless world back home for almost three days now. The dark angry life she'd been living, perversely greeting her every morning when she opened her eyes, was gone. Existing like a drooped, dried-up flower seemed to be her fate. But ever since she'd been back in Belgium, she felt revived, like a drought-stricken meadow after a soaking rain. She stood tall again, her face flushed with color.

Louisa paused, catching a glimpse of her reflection in a storefront window. A hint of vigor gleamed back at her and looked her in the eye. She smirked. *Must be something in the water here.*

Continuing on another five blocks, she realized she may have gone too far. The little shops and businesses were behind her now, and she was entering a residential area of apartments and small market squares.

Eventually Louisa looped around to head back when there was nothing else interesting to see. As she turned, something familiar hit her about the nondescript surroundings. In front of her were two park benches in the middle of the apartment-lined square. A mysterious feeling crept over her—one that wasn't so different from what she'd experienced at the tea shop the other day. She walked to the benches, swung around, and looked across to the old brick townhouses. "I've been here before!" she shouted.

Now energized, Louisa pictured the night when she'd been sitting on the bench in her frilly blue dress, with Penny Hallsworth next to her, waiting for something. For what, though? Then it clicked.

Mathis! It was the time when she and Penny had stayed out all night in Antwerp—and this was the spot where they had sat, talking with Mathis until morning.

Oh my god! I can't believe I'm here!" A prickly tingle surfaced on her flesh. With her hand on her heart, she walked over and sat on the bench looking across the street, trying to figure out which apartment Mathis had come out of. Her eyes flicked back and forth between the three townhouse doors. Finally, she recalled which door it had been: the one in the middle.

She took her phone out to check the time. It was still early afternoon, so she decided to stake out the area and see if Mathis still lived there—or if anyone would even come out of the apartment.

Small pieces of her adventures from that night returned to her while she sat on the bench. She'd been scared about what had happened at the disco and exhilarated when Mathis rescued her. It was like watching a good movie, and she was a character in it. She wanted to stay and see the rest, but couldn't remember how it ended.

An hour had passed with no Mathis sighting. Louisa realized she was probably being foolish and decided to head back to the apartment.

Just as she stood up to leave, a young Asian couple strolled up to the apartment building. She stopped in her tracks to see where they were going, hoping they wouldn't enter the middle unit. That was Mathis's door—as if there was any hope he still lived there.

The couple took their keys out and opened the middle door. Disappointed, Louisa crinkled her nose. Well, what did she think would happen? Her gallant knight would come walking out of the apartment and patch her wounds up all over again?

She scuffed a foot kicking some loose pebbles on the pavement as if she'd been defeated. "Silly girl," she teased herself.

All the same, it felt so good to fantasize about something again.

Day six arrived, and Patty's itinerary had them venturing off to the Venice of the North: Bruges, Belgium. Louisa knew Amsterdam shared the honor of that moniker with Bruges—and she also knew for sure they wouldn't be stumbling in on any "coffee shops" in the Belgian gingerbread village, thankfully.

Louisa didn't remember visiting Bruges when they had lived in Belgium. Nevertheless, her mother insisted they had—and several times. To Louisa, all their travels in Europe had gelled together. She still had dreams about roaming the streets of Paris, asking for directions to the Roman Colosseum. For today, though, she *was* in Bruges and would create new memories. Everything about the town was steeped in charm, from the pristine small swan-filled canals to the traditional red brick houses lined up in rows.

After a beautiful canal tour, the women walked the old cobblestone streets. Louisa discovered the town was like the Disneyworld of beers. From the Bruges Beer Experience to gift shops selling all kinds of beer-related gadgets, the foamy amber beverage was everywhere and seemed to rule the village.

The sisters meandered into a shop that had a sign above the door reading, "We stock over 500 varieties of beer." Shelves extended along the length of every wall, packed with bottles all the way to the ceiling. Louisa stood in amazement, she couldn't imagine so many variations in such a small country. To her, it looked like the Library of Congress.

When they walked back out onto the streets, she soon discovered they had lost their mom. "C'mon, Judy. Let's get the search party going."

After endlessly running in and out of souvenir shops, they finally found their mother inside a jewelry store, her head dropped, engrossed in what was in the display case.

"There you are!" Judy scolded. "We've been looking all over for you."

Patty's eyes widened. "Oh! I thought you were right behind me."

Judy gave her an annoyed look and locked arms with her on one side. Louisa did the same on the other arm and chuckled. "Geez, Mom, you're like a kid on the loose in a candy shop sometimes."

The three stopped for lunch at a restaurant characteristic of Bruges, filled with Renaissance artwork on the walls and antique décor from the sixteenth century. They all ordered the house specialty called waterzooi: a hearty, soul-soothing stew that could be ordered with fish or chicken. All three opted for chicken.

Judy took one last spoonful of her lunch, pushed her plate forward, and sat back in her chair. "So, Louisa, surprise number two comes tomorrow, but we can tell you now if you want to know." She gave their mother one of those sneaky looks before continuing. "This is a bonus surprise. You still have the *big* one left for last—if you behave."

Her interest piqued, Louisa sat up erect in her chair. "Please, do tell."

Judy grinned. "Well, sister, we're going to a seventies-style disco tomorrow night in Antwerp. Can you imagine? It'll be just like when we lived there. They're having some kind of costume party too, so everyone is dressing up in the fashion of the era."

The corners of Louisa's mouth curled up. "Oh, this could be serious fun." She turned to their mother. "You're coming to the disco too. Right, Mom?"

Her mother flicked her wrist. "Sure, why not? I love the seventies."

TRACK 20

"BLOCKBUSTER" – THE SWEET

MAY 2018

The ladies headed to the Meir the next day on a quest to find some 1970s-era fashion to wear to the disco.

"What are we looking for anyway?" Patty asked.

Judy giggled. "I don't know, Mom. Anything that pops out to me that says the seventies. Either way, do we need an excuse to shop?"

Their mother halted on the sidewalk. "They had diamonds in the seventies. Can we start in the Diamond Quarter?" she joked.

The trio ventured over to the monumental Innovation department store that had been a fixture on the prestigious Meir since the early 1900s. Its name had changed to Galeria INNO in the intervening years, but it was still the best store to go to for splurging on something special.

In pursuit of the perfect '70s garb, the sisters diligently combed through the racks inside the historic store. "Well, Judy," Louisa said, "I have those flared low-rise hip-hugger jeans. So I'm thinking a *groovy* top is what's on my radar."

Shortly after, Louisa found exactly what she was looking for: a ret-ro-style blouse in a playful pattern of bright yellow, orange, and purple with wide, flowy sleeves. The shirt was made from 100 percent silk and felt like butter to her touch. It was definitely '70s couture. Satisfied with her selection, she flipped over the tag and did a double take. The price read 500 euros. She tried calculating in her head the cost in US dollars but gave up. She knew the shirt was way over her budget. Disappointed, she put it back on the rack and mumbled, "Well, this store certainly hasn't changed." Louisa scuffed out of the Galeria INNO empty-handed, just as she usually had forty years ago.

After a frites met mayo lunch, they continued their search and headed into the touristy section of old Antwerp. There, the sisters found hippy-style tie-dyed T-shirts in a souvenir shop perfect for the disco that cost only 10 euros. Each one had ANTWERP written across the chest in bold white embroidered letters against the colorful swirls. Louisa worried wearing the shirts would make them look like tourists, but then let it go when she realized the money she saved not purchasing the top at Galeria INNO. *More cash to party with.*

Satisfied, Louisa and the others moved along and the afternoon turned into a walking tour. They ended up in the neighborhood called the Cathedral of Our Lady. While dawdling along looking up, Louisa found herself in another one of her "I've been here before" moments. It did not hit her as hard as the other incidents but the stepped gable roofs resting on top of the old red brick houses grabbed her attention. Something about the architecture was familiar, but she couldn't recall what. She dwelled on it for a couple of blocks, but nothing came to mind.

Finally, she laughed it off. Of course, the buildings were familiar—after all, she used to live here. Still, she wasn't convinced that was all it was. Gazing up one last time, she knew there was something more. Something very special.

They strolled past the Cathedral of Our Lady, wandering down a narrow shop-filled street lined with orbed streetlamps and more red brick houses of varying heights. At one storefront window, Louisa came to a sudden halt when she found herself captivated by the store's showcase. *Perfection!*

In front of her was her lifelong dream displayed on a mannequin's head: a rock and roll wig of long blond hair, short blunt bangs, and wispy side layers sweeping forward. She recalled one of the posters above her bed in Schilde—the one of The Sweet, featuring lead singer Brian Connolly and his signature coif. She remembered how she'd tried and tried to copy his style, but she could never capture his look quite right.

Flabbergasted, she craned her neck to look at the store's sign, which read in English "Wigs and Gigs." "I'm going in," she announced.

Inside the large store, there were various wigs, costumes, and tchotchkes of Antwerp souvenirs. It was a peculiar mix of merchandise. The stale mothball scent caused Louisa to scrunch up her nose, but the smell didn't stop her. She was on a mission. Where was that wig? *She had to have it.*

Toward the back of the store, several table mirrors stood on a counter, along with a wide variety of hairpieces. Louisa spotted another mannequin head bearing the same wig she'd seen in the window front display. She snatched it off the mannequin and went up to one of the mirrors. An image surfaced in her head—one of The Sweet singing on *TopPop*. Brian Connolly was dressed metallically as he gyrated to the galvanizing music. His perfect rock and roll locks swung and swayed with every move he made.

Feeling inspired, she firmly brushed her hair back with her hand and slid the wig onto her head. Gaping in the mirror delighted, she felt like a prom queen who had just been crowned. "I have to have this." She turned to Judy who had followed her in to the shop. "What do you think?"

Louisa immersed herself in the moment by twirling around and around like a little girl. She was living her childhood fantasy. Her spinning sharply stopped and she looked back at Judy with a long, serious face. "The lead singer of The Sweet was the original Jennifer Aniston, in my book."

Judy, staring wide eyed and appearing confused by Louisa's erratic behavior, gave a little chuckle.

"What do you think of this, girls?" Patty appeared, standing next to an end cap display, sporting a classic Florence Henderson shag wig on her head. Her body was twisted to the side, one hand was behind her head, and the other on her hip. "I've always dreamed of having a long pixie cut like this, but I thought it was too wild back in the day."

"What was so wild about Mrs. Brady?" Louisa asked Judy.

The two sisters erupted in boisterous laughter.

Louisa and her mom grinned with contentment as they exited the shop carrying their purchases in a big brown bag labeled with "Wigs and Gigs" in bold red letters. Now it was time to head back to the apartment to primp for their big night out—an evening back to the good old days.

After endless fussing, Louisa was on a mission to make sure she lived up to the ideal of Tom Wolfe, who labeled the 1970s the "Me" Decade. She danced out of her room in her flared, faded denim jeans, tie-dyed T-shirt, glam rock wig, large hoop earrings, and an attitude screaming, "Look at me!"

Her mom was more of a mystery when she emerged with the dated wispy, layered wig, a black watch wool skirt, and a white blouse buttoned up to her chin. The collar was dressed up with a vintage marquisate brooch.

Judy, as expected, came out rocking it with denim jeans and her tie-dyed shirt. Her hair was styled in a classic Farrah Fawcett flip. She'd also added a little glam rock touch, putting a temporary glittery silver star tattoo on her right cheek.

As the three '70s throwbacks spiritedly headed out the door, Louisa wore a silly smirk, feeling that it was going to be a *very* interesting evening.

The DJ blasted the Mud hit "Dynamite" when the women walked through the entrance. Hearing the song instantly riled Louisa up, her shoulders swinging back and forth to the crisp electric twanging. She cast her eyes over the club, observing the bright psychedelic colors, the orange vinyl seat cushions, the art on the wall, the ceiling's neon lights, and the spotlights blinking in sync with the music. Hanging from the ceiling, a large metallic disco ball dangled in the center of the dance floor, with a few people already under it dancing. Louisa smiled in approval. The club certainly captured the funky zeitgeist of the '70s.

After checking out the museum-quality décor, they found a round high-top table near the dance floor. "What's a retro cocktail, Mom, from back in the day?" Louisa asked.

Her mom raised a finger to her cheek. "Oh, I don't know." She pondered for a moment then sat up straight. "I think a tequila sunrise was a big one from the seventies."

A waitress came over, decked out in high-waisted flared red pants, a white halter top with a gold chain draped from her hips as a belt, and silver platform shoes. "Welkom," she said, preparing to take their drink order.

"Hi, do you speak English?" Judy asked.

"But of course." The waitress smiled. "What can I get you?"

All three of them ordered tequila sunrises.

Slowly, the pace picked up inside the club. People paraded in, displaying characteristic styles from the '70s like they were walking in on a red carpet. Gary Glitters and Marc Bolan wannabes were present in abundance. One woman wore leather from head to toe as Suzi Quatro. A group of five guys was dressed up like the Bay City Rollers, all in the band's signature Scottish tartan attire.

Throughout the night, every time the DJ played a song Louisa remembered from her days living there, she cheered loudly as if she was watching fireworks and the explosions in the sky were new colors she'd never seen before. The memory of her long-forgotten idolization of the Europop world was returning. She recalled the mysterious way the melodies used to move through her enigmatically, like the lost spirit of a loved one touching her soul. The songs would spin in her head every morning when she woke, and they would lie softly in her heart at night when she went to sleep.

Now, listening to these bands of her adolescence, it was almost like reliving her introduction to Mud forty years earlier. A new excitement for something exceptional in her life roused her. It made her feel younger—and alive.

Louisa rested her chin in her hand, taking in the eccentric crowd and '70s vibe, with a fresh sparkle in her eye.

"Hallo." A heavy male voice made her jump. She turned around to find a man in his fifties with wavy gray hair, skinny legs, and a protruding beer belly eyeing her table.

"Oh, we're all set," Patty said as if the man was a waiter. "We just ordered more drinks with the girl."

"Oh, where are you from?" he asked, looking at Patty.

"We're American," Judy cut their mom off before she had a chance to respond to him. She had a look on her face like she expected the man to kneel before her.

The man glowered at Judy, shook his head, and in a huff left.

"Sister, we're not *all that* anymore." Louisa laughed. "Nobody is going to bow down to us like in the olden days."

"Maybe he doesn't speak English well," their mom said.

A few tunes later, Louisa spotted the same guy making his way through the crowd back to their table. This time, he had a boldness about him as he approached. He nudged between her mom and Judy, extending his hand to Patty to shake. "Hi, I'm Bub Dylan."

Immediately following his introduction, Judy spewed her drink across the table. Looking around with dread filled eyes, she leaned over to Louisa, wiping her mouth, and whispered, "You don't think this could be him, do you?"

Louisa gave her sister a vacant look.

"Don't you remember Bob Dylan and Jerry Garcia from back in Schilde? They all used to come to my window with Gui at night." The concern in Judy's eyes deepened. "Come on. You're the one who brought them home to me like they were Christmas gifts."

Louisa was stunned when it finally hit her. It was vague, but she certainly remembered the names. She could hardly contain herself as she wriggled in her chair—not only because it might be him but also because her sister was in such an uproar about it. She always got such a rise when she saw her perfect sister in a boy predicament.

Judy cupped her forehead with her hand, hiding her face as she slowly sunk into her chair.

Louisa leaned forward to get a better look at the fellow, but his focus was on their mom. "I don't know if it's him. It's too hard to tell. Do you want me to ask if he lived in Schilde forty years ago?"

"No," Judy snapped. "Let it go."

As the conversation between the man and Patty continued, Louisa fixed her eyes on him, trying to see if anything looked familiar.

"Yes, *Bub*," her mother said to him. "We used to live in Schilde, right outside of Antwerp, about forty years ago. Do you know where that is?"

Judy's face went white as a ghost. She grabbed Louisa's arm. "Let's get out of here and dance before he figures out it was me."

Louisa followed her sister, and while they danced, she couldn't help but laugh at the situation and how Judy kept glancing nervously at their table to see if the man was still there. After the song ended, the fellow finally moved to the other side of the bar. Judy let out a huge sigh of relief and turned to go back to the table.

Louisa was feeling sprightly, though. It had been a long time since she had been on a dance floor. "Sister, I need the DJ to play a special song. I want to let loose a little and rock this wig!" She shot a wink at her sister and darted off to the DJ booth. Once there, Louisa carefully contemplated her song choice. Something about the whole '70s scene and being in Antwerp awakened her inner teen and she had to make the right selection. *No mistakes.* Once she finally settled on a song, she was ecstatic to learn that the DJ had it.

Running back to the table, she cried, "Okay, Judy! Get ready for the perfect song. We're gonna raise the roof, sistah!" She pumped her fists over her head.

The song started with a hair-raising siren that filled the room. Several patrons appeared alarmed, with their eyes wide open, shiftily glancing around. Sharp electric guitar followed—and that was Louisa's cue. She flew onto the empty dance floor, jumping around ludicrously. The music possessed her, overtook her body. Her head whipped to the left, then to the right. Her theatrical public display was to The Sweet's rock anthem "Blockbuster."

Judy ran up to her on the dance floor. "Oh, I can't let you make a fool of yourself alone," she said, laughing. "We do it so much better together."

After the extended version of Blockbuster mania ended, the sisters headed back to their mother, out of breath and laughing. Nearing the table, Louisa initially thought they were at the wrong spot. But no, it was the right table. Her mother was surrounded by six men, all sitting in chairs. She looked as innocent as a lamb, hands daintily folded in her lap while she talked to her new entourage.

"Hello, I'm Anen," one of the men said to Louisa. He stood up and politely greeted her and Judy. "We were speaking with your mother so she was not alone. Can we take our picture with you so we can tell our family and friends back in Egypt that we met Americans?"

For the next several minutes, the men took turns snapping endless photos with the LaPlante women. Louisa thought it was funny how these Egyptian tourists made their own souvenirs by taking photos with them. It wasn't so different from her time living in Antwerp and how all the Belgian teenagers were so interested in her and Judy—like they were an oddity. She remembered how that attention always managed to make her feel good about herself, like she was something special. But tonight, it did more, increasing her sense of self-worth for the first time in a long while.

The revelry and music continued on until Patty put an abrupt end to the night. "I think it's past my bedtime. Let's go, girls."

Louisa, depressed the evening was at an end, trudged along behind her sister and mother to the door. As she passed through the exit, a hand clutched her elbow, startling her. She stopped and turned, looking up into the face of the man who called himself Bob Dylan. His beady eyes homed in on her as he carefully raised his hand to her chin. "You're not too young for me now," he snickered.

Louisa recoiled in disgust. The man was so close she could smell his stale beer breath. He leaned over and whispered, half singing in her ear. "Little sister, don't do what your big sister done."

His closeness—along with his cocksure presence and heavy voice—was too much. She pulled away quickly and ran out the door.

At first, she didn't understand what had happened. Then it dawned on her. He *really* was the same guy who called himself Bob Dylan forty years earlier. Memories of the day she'd met him at the frites stand came back to her. He had been too old for her back then, and he'd sung Shabby Tiger's "Slow Down."

She fled the club to catch up to her sister and her mom, who were way ahead. How many years had passed since she'd met the young man who had called himself Bob Dylan? She'd never thought she would actually run into anyone from her teenage years during this trip. What amazed her even more was that he remembered her and the events that took place that day so long ago.

Louisa quickened her pace. What other unexpected things awaited her here in Antwerp? Mystified, she glanced up at the foggy evening sky. And what was the third *big* surprise her sister had in store for her?

Awakening the next day, Louisa felt infused with zest as the songs from the night before spun in her head just like every morning when she'd lived in Belgium. Those musical groups were creeping back into her life like an old flame she'd never gotten over. Of course, she knew her attraction to the glam bands and her obsessive behavior probably wasn't normal, especially at her age—but did she really care? No. It made her happy, and she was entitled to a little wackiness, given the emotional stress of the last two years. She leaped out of bed, wondering what the new day would bring.

The morning sunlight carried a peaceful quietness throughout the kitchen as she grabbed her coffee and sat down at the round bistro table. No one appeared to be up yet. The amusing events of last night—and meeting the "famous" Bob Dylan—played over in her mind as she sat sipping on her coffee. Letting out a quiet chuckle, she put her cup down.

Her glance landed on an envelope with her name written on it, propped up against a wine bottle on the kitchen table. What was this? She looked around the kitchen. Should she open it? She didn't think for too long before she did.

A ticket of some sort fluttered out. Her sleepy eyes strained as she read what it was. Then she blinked twice in disbelief to make sure what was in her hand was real. She wanted to be sure because she was holding a ticket to The Rubettes concert in Antwerp—*in two days.* Her ear-splitting screech could have spooked a deaf man. It was as if the floor had dropped out from underneath her.

Looking up from the ticket she was clutching tightly, she found Judy and her mom peering around the corner from the living room. Judy was video-recording her hysterics on her cell phone. Louisa jumped out of her chair and shouted, "Oh, my God! I can't believe it! This is a dream come true! What will I wear? I need to get my nails done. This is great. This is great!"

Eventually, she calmed down long enough to thank both of them for the *best* surprise ever. "This time, I'm not doing anything to mess it up," she reassured them. "I'll be a perfect angel. No trouble here. Nope."

Judy shot Louisa a quizzical look. "Yeah, right."

"I can't believe The Rubettes are going to be here at the same time as us!" Louisa cried. "How could this really be happening? Are they even still alive?"

Judy and her mom threw their heads back in a peal of lively laughter.

The cheerful spirit from that morning set the tone for the next twelve hours. Today was Patty's big day at the American Women's Club.

The luncheon was held at a stately kastel in a small town called Schoten, about five miles outside Antwerp. The setting was glorious, with a scenic park, gardens, and a moat skirting the castle. Inside, the old-world feel continued, with décor from the nineteenth century throughout. It was like the setting from a Jane Austen novel.

Gabby, from AIS, greeted the LaPlante women when they walked in, reviewing the afternoon's itinerary with Patty. The first hour was a champagne reception with various "tastes of Belgium" to nibble on. From carbonade flamand—a Belgian beef stew, served in elegant crystal tasting glasses—to miniature chicken waterzooi.

The crowd of mostly Americans flowed in, and Louisa was in deep conversation with a woman named Annabel who had moved to Belgium from Kentucky a month earlier. Annabel had recently enrolled her three children into AIS. Louisa found herself envying the mother, starting her adventure of living in Antwerp, while her time in the country had come and gone so long ago. It was the same envy she experienced whenever she got off a seven-day cruise to Bermuda from New York. As she would disembark, sad about going home, she'd see all the excited faces waiting in line to start their vacations. How she'd wished she could join them and do it all over again.

Finally, the big moment came when Gabby introduced Patty LaPlante. Louisa's mom stood and walked to the small podium looking out on a crowd of fifty or so mostly women. The applause went on for a minute before she read a couple of snippets from her book. One excerpt was about the end of the LaPlantes' time in Belgium.

"Lyle and the kids retreated to the car," Patty read, "and I lingered by the French door that led into the garden and pondered. Even though we were going home, I knew I could neither return to the past nor remain the person I had been. I had broadened my horizons irrevocably, and in doing so, I learned to change my perceptions about others and myself. To the extent that I allowed myself to merge into the social and cultural values of the Belgians, I had, in a sense, become a new person."

Louisa was filled with emotion as her tears welled-up. The connection to her mother's words found a place deep in her heart. Just a few short days of reclaiming her past had changed her. Antwerp had awakened her soul and she felt reborn again.

She looked over at Judy, whose eyes were teary, and took her sister's hand. They both proudly continued watching their mom speak.

Patty gave the crowd a little history about the research she had done for the book—without the internet, which was why it had taken her thirty-five years to write the darn thing. She also mentioned the comedy of errors that happened throughout her quest to finish her story—and there had been many.

Once Patty finished her speech and answered a few questions, it was time for the book signing. Louisa watched her mother in her glory, interacting with Women's Club members who had already read the book and those who had bought it that day. Her mom's blissful laughter echoed through the kastel as she engaged with her new fans. Louisa could not have felt any happier for her. Yes, it was a good day—one of the best.

When they returned to the apartment that evening, all three of them were exhausted and headed to their separate bedrooms. After a long hot shower, Louisa put on her PJs. While she brushed out her hair, she wandered over to her bedroom window. A beautiful, glowing aura was coming from the Cathedral of Our Lady, reminding her of a quote her mother had read from her book during the reception. It was from one of the family's last nights in Belgium before they had moved back to the States. They had moved out of their house in Schilde and were in a hotel in downtown Antwerp for their final week.

"After we crawled into bed that night," her mom had read, "I could barely see the golden glow from the steeple of the Cathedral of Our Lady a few blocks away. Now, however, the exterior of the edifice was surrounded with scaffolding in preparation for years of repair and sandblasting. There was an outdoor concert that night, and the bells were playing. I'll never forget it."

Louisa hung on to her mother's words while she studied the cathedral, beholding its radiance. She found herself in a trance-like state as an odd feeling came over her. Something outside called to her as another suppressed memory fought to resurface. Vigorously, she rubbed her head. What was it that needed to come out? Her struggle to rediscover was agonizing as she stood in the window for what felt like an eternity.

All of the sudden, she let out a gasp that sharply emptied her lungs. It was like someone pried her eyes open with a crowbar to wake up and see her past. Memories flooded her—memories of a time she hadn't thought of in a very, very *long* time.

She stepped away from the window dazed, climbed into bed, and pulled the covers up under her chin. Her wakefulness turned to slumber, taking with it the reborn memories she'd just retrieved. Memories of the adventures that had taken place during her final days living in Belgium.

TRACK 21

"TESSIE (I LOVE YOU)" – LEFT SIDE

AUGUST 1978

Louisa rolled her Brussels sprouts from one end of her plate to the other while she sat with her family at the dinner table. She had been batting the green things around with her fork for over ten minutes, waiting for a chance to stuff them down the lamp's tea-kettle spout when her parents weren't looking. All day long she'd been brooding, and her mother's dinner of liver and onions—accompanied by the wretched vegetables—wasn't helping.

Tonight was the night of The Rubettes concert that she was supposed to attend. Instead, she had spent all day imagining what she would have been doing if she hadn't been grounded.

Finally, she shoved the last bite of dinner into her mouth. Her body recoiled, and she gagged at the horrible taste of the sprouts. The repulsed feeling stayed with her and followed her all the way to her bedroom.

Flinging her throw pillows from her bed to the floor, Louisa sat and made herself a cozy nest next to her turntable. She lit two red pillar candles and placed each one on a packing box her mom had given her for the big move. The process of striking the matches had always made her nervous, but she did it like a pro that night.

Her Rubettes albums and 45s were spread out all around her like a group of old friends gathered for dinner. She spent the next few hours spinning them while clipping out photos of the band from various teen magazines and placing them in a scrapbook. To her, it was a way of paying homage to the band.

Satisfied with her Rubettes ritual, she squinted at the pink heart-shaped alarm clock on her nightstand. The concert was about to start. Quickly, she jumped into her PJs, climbed into bed, and placed her palms together in prayer. "Dear God," she whispered, "Please let The Rubettes know I'm sorry I'm not there for them like they are always there for me. Let them know I was stome and did something bad. Tell them to have a good show and to know that I'm there in my dreams and will love them always."

Starting with her forehead, she made the sign of the Holy Trinity. "The Father, the Son, the Holy Spirit . . . and The Rubettes."

Deep in pensive thought, she pictured what she would have worn to the show, how she would have done her hair, and even the concert itself. Her musing almost felt like reality as she transitioned from her make-believe world into an unconscious state of mind.

In her dream, Louisa's hair was the sun-bleached blond she'd worked on all summer long, putting lemon juice in it while she basked in the sun. With her dark, thick eyebrows and golden tan, it gave her the authentic California look she'd craved, just like her friend Jackie. Her fitted denim overalls with brown piping and pink T-shirt underneath were dressed up by several homemade macramé bracelets and neck chokers and a spritz of her sister's Charlie perfume.

She sashayed into the concert hall with Penny like they were on a red carpet. The usher escorted them to the middle of the front row—the best seats in the house—and handed them both an intricate crystal flute of champagne embellished with a bright red heart-shaped strawberry and the words "The Rubettes" engraved on the stem.

Turning around, she glanced up at all the poor souls in the nosebleed seats way in the back. Louisa was a little sad for them, but she knew she'd paid her dues by sitting in plenty of back rows. Now it was her turn for the VIP treatment. After all, it was her dream. Why shouldn't she have the best?

The audience of screaming girls went wild when the group finally appeared on stage, dressed in tight white jeans and red jersey-style shirts. Louisa was so close to them she could smell their heavy English Leather cologne.

The music started, and silver confetti fell from above like twirling snowflakes. The stage's bright lights reflected off the stardust and lit up the concert hall, creating a dazzling diamond effect. She looked up at the band. Their presence was superior to anything else she had known. The overwhelming feeling made her nudge Penny and the two girls hopped up onto their chair to dance to the music, hoping the band would notice them.

After the first song, The Rubettes' lead singer, Alan Williams, surprised the audience with an announcement: he'd bring one of the band's devoted fans up on stage to sing a song with them. He traipsed along the edge of the stage, searching for who he'd pick. Then he stopped in front of Louisa and locked eyes with her. Extending an arm, he reached out to her, and she placed her hand in his. As he effortlessly lifted her onto the stage, she felt like she didn't weigh an ounce.

Louisa shook nervously as her head tilted up to him. She was on stage with glam rock royalty. The bright stage lights shone on Alan, revealing every detail on his face, even his nostril hair. Normally she would have been grossed out, but she didn't care. That nose hair belonged to a member of The Rubettes, so they were sacred.

Sublime guitar, pulsing gently, streamed through the air, followed by the lyrics of a song still managing to make her body quake— "Little Darling."

Louisa looked down at Penny in the audience. Her friend was cheering her on, screaming her name over and over. "Louisa! Louisa! Wake up!"

Penny's last words startled her out of her sleep. Rolling to the side, she discovered it was the next morning—and her mom, not Penny, had been calling out, knocking on her bedroom door.

"It's time to start packing up things in your room," her mom yelled.

Disoriented, Louisa looked around her bedroom and frowned. Now that she had come down from the ecstasy of her dream, it was heartbreaking to discover none of it had been real.

The end of the summer was creeping up fast. Patty was preparing for the move back to the States, packing valuables and going on frantic last-minute shopping sprees, including some large purchases in the Diamond Quarter. One night, Louisa heard her parents arguing in their bedroom. Her father had asked her mother about the outrageous credit card bill from Antwerp's diamond district. "Don't worry, Lyle," her mom answered, "it's just Christmas presents for the next five years."

"They better not be all Christmas presents for *you* for the next five years!" her father threatened in his booming voice.

Meanwhile, Judy continued her romance with Gui. She had told Louisa when she broke the news she'd be leaving at the end of the summer; he didn't take it well at all. "The poor guy broke down right in front of me. I didn't know what to do." Judy, unruffled, chuckled and flipped her palms up.

One evening when her parents were out at dinner, Louisa heard somber music coming from behind Judy's closed door. Curious about the song, Louisa quietly cracked the door open and peeped inside to see what was going on. Gui stood outside Judy's bedroom window with his portable radio, playing a song by the Dutch pop band Left Side. The melodramatic tune about saying goodbye made for a gloomy atmosphere, and tears rolled down Gui's cheeks. Judy reached out to him through the window, and they embraced. Together as one, they sorrowfully swayed to the melody's slow tempo. When the bassline grew prominent, the chorus and lyrics became more passionate and dramatic, and their swaying intensified, holding one another tighter.

Louisa inhaled deeply, stood back, and shut the door. The heart-wrenching scene made her think about Mathis and what the future would hold for them. She still hadn't seen him since her and Penny's all-nighter in Antwerp.

As the days got closer to their departure, the reality that she might never see him again weighed heavy on her.

A few days later, Louisa's mom gave her a reprieve from her one-year sentence and allowed Penny to come over so they could say their final goodbyes. The two girls were lying on Louisa's bed, rehashing their big night out in Antwerp earlier that summer.

"Did you ever see Mathis again?" Penny asked. "I think he's such a fox."

Louisa let her head drop, looking solemnly down at her lap. "No. He doesn't even know I'm moving back to the States. He's going to think I just fell off the face of the earth."

Penny patted Louisa's hand. "Don't worry. Something will work out. You still have time before you leave."

Patty popped her head through the door. "Girls, I'm going out for a while. I've left some ham salad sandwiches for you both in the fridge."

Seconds after Louisa's mother shut the door, the girls ran out of the bedroom to look out the window in the hallway. The garage door was open, and the Peugeot was gone.

They dashed to their bikes and jumped on, pedaling like they were in the Tour de France as they headed down Bremboslaan to the record store.

Inside the shop, soaring string instruments blasted through the speakers. Mozart's Symphony No. 40 was at full volume as if it were a rock anthem. Louisa glanced around the room, looking for Mathis, but he was nowhere in sight. She made her way over to one of the tables with Penny trailing and flipped through the album rack, stalling for time, hoping Mathis would walk in.

"Hallo, my Amerikaan friends," Mr. Janssens greeted them, popping his head up from behind the register, where he was doing some paperwork.

Louisa chose not to beat around the bush as she approached the counter. "Hello. Is Mathis here today?"

Mr. Janssens leaned over and turned down the classical music he'd been listening to. "No, my friend. Mathis goes to holiday for few weeks. He is at Ostend, at the beach."

Disappointed, Louisa trudged back to her friend's side, shoulders drooping.

"How am I ever going to say goodbye to him?" she asked forlornly.

Penny gave her a smug smile. "Listen, Louisa. This is what you have to do. I'll write a note in Flemish to say you're moving back to America. When you get to the hotel in Antwerp the last week you're here, you'll meet him at the Grote Markt in front of the Brabo Fountain." She pursed her lips before continuing. "You just have to ask his father to give the note to Mathis when he returns." Glancing up at the ceiling, Penny had a smoldering look in her eyes and held her hands over her heart. "It'll be great. Two star-crossed lovers meet to say goodbye for the last time. It's impossibly romantic—just like in the movies."

Louisa lit up at the idea. But after further contemplation, her brightened look darkened. "But I'm grounded. How am I going to do that?"

"Louisa, your parents are going to be out every night, going to farewell parties and dinners. You said earlier that Judy was going to sneak out to see Gui for a night on the town with him before she leaves, remember?" Penny nudged her. "You can hitch a ride with her."

Louisa warmed to the idea even more now. "I guess this could work. Judy is meeting Gui on our second-to-last night, so put that in there as the date. But what if he doesn't get the note? Or doesn't come back from holiday before I leave? Or what if he met someone else while he was at the beach?"

Penny went up to the counter, asked Mr. Janssens for paper, pen, and a calendar, then walked back to her. "He'll come," she said confidently. "And Louisa . . . he has eyes *only* for you."

Louisa made her way back up to the counter with the note and told Mr. Janssens her family was moving back to the States. She gave him the note and asked if he would give it to Mathis when he got back from his holiday.

Mr. Janssens agreed, coming around to the other side of the counter. "My friend, we will miss you. Please bring your mother my best." He extended his arm out to her and shook her hand.

Leaving the music store was a plaintive moment for Louisa. She had spent almost four years going to that little shop of heaven. It was the place she'd found the music she'd built her whole life around—and the place where she'd met Mathis. When they returned to the house, her funk continued throughout the afternoon. But knowing—or at least hoping—Mathis might show up on her second-to-last night in Belgium made her cautiously optimistic.

Louisa's long days in confinement dragged on. Except for the heat, she was truly experiencing the meaning of the "Dog days of August." Her cabin fever grew, and she felt like a cooped-up jailbird. Bored to no end one afternoon, she lay on her bed, eyes glued to the ceiling. She was trying to create an adventure she could have that didn't require leaving the house. One thing she had always dreamed of doing since she was little came to mind: making a time capsule. Was now the moment to do it? Or was she just desperately trying to think of something to kill time?

Nevertheless, she could not let the idea go and fantasized about the possibility that someday, somebody would discover a piece of the life she had left behind. Bewildering images flashed in her head—just like in a romantic movie, as Penny had said. Now *was* the time; she was sure of it. Excitement swarmed through her as the idea turned from mere thoughts to the actual task. She browsed for things to put in the capsule.

First, she opened one of her packed moving boxes, looking for a large canister or something to hold the treasures. It couldn't be too big, though, because she still had to dig the hole, and she wasn't sure how she'd manage that yet. She spotted a red and yellow floral tin her aunt Rita had given her years earlier for Christmas for storing her Barbie doll's clothes. Now she used it for her hairbrushes and curlers.

"Perfect," she whispered.

Running around her room, she searched for more memorabilia. On top of her unpacked albums was her autograph book from the last day at AIS, so she grabbed that. Then she spotted hanging in her armoire, the Bay City Rollers pants. *Why not?* She giggled. They didn't fit anymore, thanks to too many helpings of frites met mayo.

Finally satisfied, she looked at all the items she had gathered: her Mud concert ticket stub, the signed program from *The Rocky Horror Show*, various photos she'd taken, and tokens from her travels with her family. In her hands, she held the blue-and-white bandana Mathis had given her during her all-nighter in Antwerp. That bandana meant the world to her—but something compelled her to put it with the other time capsule items. Wistfully, she kissed it goodbye and placed it on the pile.

Once the mementos were secured, she figured she'd have to write a meaningful note to go along with them—and it needed to be a good note. She sat on her bedroom floor, racking her brain for something clever and well-written. Then she remembered what Mr. Scott had said once in English class at AIS: "Less is more." She took out her pen and started writing:

To Whom It May Concern,

I am an American girl, and I lived at this house from 1974 to 1978. This is my personal time capsule of the things I loved and are my whole world. If you are reading this letter, that means you found my tin. Please treasure my items like I did, as if they were your own.

Louisa LaPlante

At last finished, she ran out to the kitchen, grabbed a plastic garbage bag, put all the items in it, and stuffed the pack in the metal tin.

Later that afternoon, her parents headed out to pick up some things at the store. Once their car had disappeared down Bremboslaan, Louisa flew out of her room and into the garage. Gardening equipment that hadn't been packed yet was hanging from some hooks on the garage wall. She grabbed a trowel and traipsed to the wooded area right past the lawn in her backyard.

Standing back looking at the thick woods, she contemplated, waiting for a sign—or *something*—to tell her where to deposit her box. Minutes passed until she remembered the large chestnut tree where she had carved her and Mathis's initials into the bark a few years earlier. She ran to it, at the edge of the woods, and circled its trunk until she found the initials *LL + MJ* on the back.

Louisa dropped to her knees and started excavating. Once the hole was deep enough, she placed the tin into the earth and sat on the ground. Daydreams danced in her head, imagining the next person who might hold her little box of treasures. Would it be a handsome young man like Mathis? Or maybe a girl just like her who loved music?

Safely back in her bedroom, her little expedition unobserved, she decided she wasn't going to tell anyone about her secret—not even Penny or Judy. She wasn't sure if what she had done was juvenile and didn't want anyone poking fun at her.

Days passed, and the dreaded morning finally came when Louisa woke up in the place she'd called home for the last time. Rubbing her eyes, she heard her mother weeping from across the hall. She got up, slipped her bare feet into her fuzzy purple slippers, and tiptoed to her parents' room. Her mom laid in bed, a box of tissues by her side.

Pausing a moment in the doorway, Louisa watched her distress, knowing her mother and she shared the same gloom. From the foot of the bed, she crept up to her mom and climbed into her arms.

Soon, Judy appeared and quietly joined the pity party. Teddy eventually was at the door and climbed in with them as well. The four spooned together in silence while the soft, steady clicking from the alarm clock on the nightstand ticked on. But the morning was growing old, and soon enough, Louisa's dad made his presence known by clearing his throat. She glanced up at him glaring down and knew by the look on his face it wasn't his kind of party. Curtly, he stomped one foot and clapped his hands. "Break it up!" he roared. "We have a lot of work to do today."

Later in the afternoon, the bulk of their belongings were loaded into the moving van, and the movers came back inside to box up some larger items that remained. Louisa stood in the threshold of the kitchen and watched while one worker dismantled the cast-iron teapot lamp. He lifted up the shade from the heavy cast-iron base and a long strand of green cotton candy-like foam trailed along.

The mover called Patty over. The two appeared perplexed at the strange green mold and kept taking turns poking at it. Louisa quietly backed out of the room. She knew all too well what it was: four years' worth of her mother's culinary mishaps.

Lyle's piano was the last item left in the house. The musical instrument had filled the great room with melodies from Beethoven to the Beatles over the years. Once the movers rolled the large Baldwin upright out through the front door, the house echoed with emptiness.

Louisa stood with her family in the great room, which was now completely stripped to nothing except for a few empty hooks on the wall where her mother's décor and artwork had hung. As they huddled together in silence, Louisa reflected on the day they had arrived in Belgium and how she and her siblings had run through the house, exploring and picking out their bedrooms. She laughed to herself, remembering her quizzical reaction to the sink in her bedroom. What was wrong with Europeans? Sinks belonged in the bathroom, right? But in time, she had discovered it was a brilliant idea. These Belgians really knew what they were doing.

Still, she never did learn what the bidet in the bathroom was really used for. So many stories circulated about it in the four years they were there—but her parents had used it for only one thing: a champagne cooler. They would fill it with ice when entertaining guests and had no room in the refrigerator.

Louisa walked out of the house with her family, hopped in the car, and headed down Bremboslaan for the last time. Her home slowly disappeared behind some tall trees as she rolled her window down, hanging her head out. She was trying to capture a last glance of the street she knew so well, hoping it would remain in her memory forever. Would she ever be back again? It felt so final to her.

The Peugeot passed the GB market and headed up Turnhoutsebaan for their last seven days in Belgium.

TRACK 22

"THE CAT CREPT IN" – MUD

AUGUST 1978

The hotel where the LaPlantes were staying was in the middle of Antwerp's center. The first few days in the city were hectic. Patty had planned a few "last hurrah" day trips to Ghent and Bruges for them while Lyle was at work, finishing up last-minute business.

One evening, the Verstraetes invited the family over for a farewell dinner at their place. Louisa had not seen Anneke in months. Her friends' charade still remained an anomaly to her throughout the past year. She never did question her about the day at the popcorn dance, when she was almost unrecognizable dancing with the older man in the steamy way that she did.

All through the extravagant meal Mrs. Verstraete prepared, Louisa's eyes fixated on Anneke. Her friend sat primly at the dinner table in her most refined manner, as if she was balancing a book on her head. She turned to Louisa's dad, "Can you tell me Mr. LaPlante, what your opinion is on your President Carter?"

Lyle leaned in to her and the two engaged in a deep conversation about politics.

Bowing her head, Louisa tried to conceal the building laughter inside. *Oh boy, this Belgian girl is really good.* If everyone at that table only knew what she knew about the saintly Anneke Verstraete.

At the hotel later that night, Louisa quietly waited with Judy for Teddy to fall asleep on the rollaway cot next to their bed. Once she heard his heavy, rhythmic breathing, she knew her brother was asleep. She nudged Judy in the side and they both kicked the covers off, fully dressed. They were ready for a little late night fun with Judy's classmates from AIS.

The two headed to the corner bar across from the train station. The plan was for Judy and her friends to go to one of the dance clubs after a few drinks. Louisa knew she couldn't get into the disco, so when they departed, she headed back to the hotel by herself.

The evening black heavens glowed from the gleaming yellow full moon and the bright city lights. Louisa's clogs clip-clopped on the pavement down the Meir, sounding like horse's hooves as the song "Tiger Feet" spun in her head. Surprisingly, walking the streets of Antwerp late at night by herself was not scary.

Could it be she was finally blossoming into a small version of her sister, who she so idolized? After all, she had a boyfriend, or the closest thing to having one as of yet. And she wasn't throwing one of her usual tantrums about not getting into the club. She was confidently walking the streets of Antwerp like a fierce gang leader and had that same cool attitude as Judy. Maybe she was finally at a good place and was ready to take a step toward the next phase in her life.

Louisa's pace slowed down when up ahead the sound of pounding music echoed from one of the bourgeois buildings. As she approached, both front doors stood wide open, so she stepped up to the entrance and peeked inside. While the building's exterior looked finished and well-kept, the interior was a run-down brick storage room.

It appeared to be a private party. At the back of the room, a band played onstage. The audience circled the room in a slow, flowing, dreamlike state, dressed theatrically—some in brightly colored spandex jumpsuits, others in animal-print clothing. Feathered boas, glittery boots, and large hair accented their vibrant attire.

The band wore the same outrageous fashion. The lead singer strutted through the crowd and persuaded them to clap along. And the song wasn't just any dynamic, upbeat Europop—it was a cover of Mud's "The Cat Crept In."

Louisa had never seen a live musical group that close before except for Exodus, the AIS rock band.

While she watched the lively affair, she found herself marveling at what made this music so special to her. These uniquely brazen glam bands brought her complete serenity, and represented so much about her extraordinary experience of the last four years. Like a best friend, they stuck with her through thick and thin. Their melodies played in her head at night whenever she dreamed about a boy crush. They also brought her comfort whenever high drama hit. The music from these bands had formed her character on so many levels, from how she dressed to how she acted. Most importantly, it had transformed her from a mousy, insecure girl into a confident, free-spirited teen with an "anything goes" attitude.

She learned, though, through the past few years, she was living in an era when anything *did* go. Pop culture had gone from black and white sparks to multicolor fireworks. The music coming out of her radio had grown from a slow one-lane dirt road to a fast ten-lane superhighway. The loud statement of that evolution had brought her many choices and a fresh, exciting take on music. Perhaps this was why she loved these bands so much. They were a part of that movement. Her bands truly encapsulated the dynamic spirit of the times.

She lingered in the doorway, swaying her shoulders back and forth to the music's shifting rhythm. Eventually, her enthusiasm waned as a memory sent a grim wave through her. When she had been in the States earlier that summer, visiting with family and friends, it was evident the other American teens weren't up to snuff on the music and bands she loved. "Who are The Rubettes?" they had asked. "What is Mud? Never heard of the song 'Blockbuster.'" Somehow Louisa knew in time, the world of music she'd experienced in Belgium would fade for her once she moved back to the States and the influences of American life penetrated her.

Slumping her shoulders, she let out a low-spirited sigh and walked away.

The next afternoon, David visited to say his goodbyes to Teddy. Louisa, her mother, and her sister sat with the two boys in the hotel lobby, reminiscing and laughing about their exploits together. "You surely have been our guardian angel, David," Patty said at one point, chuckling. "If Mr. LaPlante only knew the mischief we got into."

David looked at her with respect in his eyes and shook her hand. "Thanks, Mrs. LaPlante, for giving me adventure in my life."

He hugged the rest of the group goodbye. As he headed to the door, David raised a finger. "I've got one for you from the band Mud, Mrs. LaPlante." His hips swiveled in a circular motion several times as if he was swinging a hula hoop around his waist, then he started singing Mud's hit song "Secrets that You Keep."

Before exiting the lobby door, he spun back around one final time, still singing, his hips jiggling. "Mr. LaPlante's losing sleep over the secrets that Mrs. LaPlante keeps!" The glass door closed as David continued singing, his voice fading with each step.

The countdown had started. The LaPlantes had only three more days left in Belgium. Louisa's parents' farewell parties and events continued almost every day and night, which made it easy for her to sneak out again with Judy. One night they headed to Statiestraat for their own farewell party with their classmates and the Moroccans.

Penny was there and no longer grounded—she was off her sentence for good behavior, which made Louisa scoff when she heard. After all, Penny was the original master of disaster in terms of "brilliant ideas."

Louisa stood with her friend out in front of a bar on the corner of Statiestraat and GSC. They were cooling off after a few hours of dancing while the rest of the crew were inside. "Louisa, are you all set to meet Mathis tomorrow?" Penny asked.

Louisa's eyes brightened. She patted her heart. "Yes! I'm so psyched. I hope he shows up, though. What if he stayed on holiday longer?"

It was a warm August evening, and Statiestraat was bustling with activity. As the two girls continued their conversation outside, Louisa spotted Cointreau walking up to the entrance where they stood. When he met eyes with her, he turned his head away coldly and smiled at Penny before going inside.

"What was that all about?" Louisa asked, stumped by Cointreau's behavior.

"He's just in a spazzy mood tonight. Forget about him anyway. You have a date with a Belgian fox tomorrow," Penny crowed.

At the end of the evening, Louisa and Judy said their final goodbyes to their friends outside in front of the bar. The moment was bittersweet as the hugs and kisses were being exchanged with the large group of classmates and the Moroccans.

Eventually the sisters turned to make their way back to the hotel when Striped Pants, looking like he was bursting with confidence, swaggered up to Judy and flicked his head so his perfect hairstyle swooshed back. He grabbed Judy and dipped her while planting a long wet kiss on her lips.

Louisa watched as her sister's hands flapped in defense for a second but fell limp as she gave into him.

When he finally lifted Judy back up, her flashing eyes were wide open. Looking around at the audience of her friends that witnessed the scene, she shoved the Moroccan away in a huff and turned to Louisa to leave.

The entire walk back was in silence. Louisa saw, though, despite her sister's vexed attitude, there was a sparkle of delight that shone in her from the kiss. It was a sparkle that Louisa had come to know *very* well.

Once they reached the hotel lobby, the girls took off their shoes and quietly crept past the hotel clerk at the front desk, who was fast asleep in a chair.

After they cleared the night watchman, they hopped into the elevator and both relaxed.

"Hey, Judy, what was up with Cointreau? He wouldn't even look at me tonight."

Judy pushed the button for their floor and turned to Louisa. "He's in love. Or so Striped Pants said. With you. He's mad at you for going back to the States." She shook her head and pulled out the keys to their room from her purse. "It must be a European thing. Did he really expect you to stay here with him? You're just a kid!"

Puzzled by what her sister said, Louisa stood in silence.

When they walked into their room, Teddy was still awake, watching TV. He held his hand out, palm up, waiting for his payment for not squealing. Louisa and Judy scowled at him as they deposited their coins in his hand. Their brother gave them a devious smile of satisfaction and turned back to the TV.

After the girls put their PJs on, they lay in bed, chatting with the covers over their heads about the events of the night. "Wow, that kiss Striped Pants gave me was the *best* going-away present ever." Judy said as she turned to Louisa. "Do you think that was the last we'll see of our Moroccan friends?"

"I don't know, Judy. But I think I'll remember our time with them forever."

Louisa tried to sleep after her sister dozed off. She found herself dwelling again on the finale days and how much harder it would be to leave Belgium than she'd expected. Then her mind wandered off to her date with Mathis the next night. It would be the first time they would be alone together. Would she be nervous with him and make a fool of herself? He was the last person she'd want to look stome in front of.

An image of his gentle winsome smile flashed in her head, causing shivers to ripple up her spine. But what if he didn't come? That would be her worst fear. He'd been put right up there on a pedestal with her music for the last four years. Could she ever leave Antwerp without seeing him one last time?

The worrying, the questions, and the fantasizing continued until Louisa finally fell asleep right as daybreak ushered in her second-to-last day in Antwerp.

TRACK 23

"IF I HAD WORDS" – SCOTT FITZGERALD AND YVONNE KEELEY

AUGUST 1978

Teddy had already vacated the room when Louisa eventually woke up. As she stretched her arms above her head, Judy still lay next to her with her mouth hung wide open, snoring in a soft consistent pattern. "Sister," Louisa whispered. Judy didn't budge. Louisa leaned over and plugged her sister's nose with her fingers, forcing her to breathe through her mouth—that did the trick. Judy woke with a sputter, clearly annoyed.

"So what's the scoop for tonight?" Louisa eagerly asked. "I have to meet Mathis in the Grote Markt at nine."

"Did you really have to wake me up for that?" Judy rubbed her eyes. "Okay, okay, I'll call Gui and ask him to meet me there too." She rolled over, away from Louisa. "Let me sleep some more, will ya?"

Louisa remained in a tizzy the entire day. Her emotions were all over the place: from nerves and excitement to worrying that he might not show.

That evening, her parents were having dinner with a group of coworkers from Union Carbide. Before they left, Patty came into the teens' room.

Judy was in her pajamas, Louisa had just come from taking a bath, and Teddy was seated on the floor, eyes glued to the TV. "Here's some money to get some frites." She kissed the top of Teddy's head. "The stand is only a few blocks away."

"Okay, Mom," Judy said. "Thanks. I'll probably go to sleep early. I'll send Teddy out to get the frites."

Once her mom left, Louisa ran over to the window in her towel, still dripping wet. She watched as her parents walked away and disappeared down the street. Her heart pumped with energy. Now it was time to get ready for the greatest evening ever.

The girls scurried around the room, trying on outfits. They tossed clothes back and forth above Teddy's head as he sat on the floor watching TV in the middle of all the chaos, oblivious to what was happening around him. Hours later, Louisa and Judy stood in front of the mirror hanging on the back of the bathroom door. Louisa had chosen a white halter top and lightweight seersucker pants in pale blue-and-white checks. Her hair was pulled back into a long, high ponytail, and she let out her bangs in a curtain flip. Judy was wearing faded blue jeans with a pale-yellow peasant blouse. Her shoulder-length hair was loose in natural waves. Around her neck was a brown rawhide leather cord that all the girls at AIS wore. Once tied in a tight knot, the cord typically remained on a girl's neck for months—or until the leather disintegrated from wear and tear.

Leaving the room and entering the hotel lobby, they passed the clerk who had been there all week. Louisa faintly giggled, wondering what he thought about her and Judy's comings and goings at all hours of the day and night.

The sun didn't set until well after 9:00 p.m. in August, so a bit of light was still in the sky as they headed down to the Grote Markt. "Now remember," Judy stopped on the sidewalk with a serious face, "if we get caught doing this, you weren't with me. I don't want to be responsible for your cause too."

Louisa knew she probably shouldn't be going out. The consequences she would face if she were caught would be severe. However, it was her last chance to see Mathis—and if another year was added to her sentence because of this, the sacrifice would be well worth it.

They soon neared the square. Unlike the rest of the city, the area was quiet. Only a few people were walking around, enjoying the beauty of the historical architecture of the famous medieval guild houses. The buildings encompassed the marketplace, and in front of the houses were trees, cafés, and park benches. The Brabo Fountain stood stoutly in the middle of the square.

Louisa pointed to the iconic monument and jumped up and down. "There's Brabo!" Her pulse quickened. "Penny told Mathis to meet me there in the note."

Scanning the Grote Markt, Louisa spotted Gui standing by a bench on the outskirts of the square. She nudged Judy, and the two walked over to him. Louisa could tell he had been crying again by his reddened eyes. "What a marshmallow," she whispered to her sister.

Judy turned sharply. "Don't knock it until you've been there," she snapped.

Louisa stifled a laugh. It was just that she wasn't used to seeing older boys cry all the time. Her sister walked up to Gui with her arms open wide, ready to console him. They came together in a pitiful hug that tempered the humor Louisa found in the situation. She turned away and walked around, searching for Mathis. But he was not there yet. She made her way back to Judy and Gui.

The three stood in the center of the square, waiting to see if he would show. After fifteen minutes, Judy threw her hands up in the air. "Okay, sister. I don't want to burst your bubble, but I don't think your Dream Boy is coming. We're going to meet some of the others from the gang down by the river. You can either wait here for someone who may *not* show or come with us."

"No. I'll wait a little longer. I'll just go back to the hotel if he doesn't come." Trying to act like it was no big deal on the outside, Louisa held an expressionless face. But deep inside, the anxiety was burning. Her worst fear was coming true.

Her sister slipped down an alleyway with Gui as Louisa sat in solitude. A few minutes later, a street musician entered the Grote Markt, carrying a guitar case and folding chair. Louisa watched him as he walked into the middle of the square. He sat down, pulled out his instrument, and strummed a solemn song she recognized as "If I Only Had Time." It was one of her mother's favorites. To her, though, the melody always induced the stabbing pain of sorrow. The haunting notes always made her dwell on how fleeting life was and how quickly happiness could be taken away.

Eventually, Louisa grew restless. She plodded over to the Brabo Fountain and scanned the area to make sure she hadn't missed Mathis on the other side. To her disappointment, only a few tourists were wandering—but still no Mathis. She returned to the bench and sat down to watch the musician some more while she waited.

The next song the musician played was one about heartbreak called "Love Is Blue." Plucking down heavily on the strings, he played the melody in a Flamenco Spanish style. His technique produced a robust, rounded, passionate tone. Louisa's eyebrows gathered in disarray. Did this musician know she was being stood up? It was like he was directing all of these songs at her.

She finally let out a heavy sigh. *Enough is enough!* She rose from the bench to head back to the hotel. Her brooding started her head spinning. Maybe there was a good reason why he hadn't come, and she imagined all the possible scenarios. Had his father not given him the note? Or maybe he stayed longer on holiday? Either idea was easier to swallow than he just didn't care. She stepped off the main square and glanced one last time at the Grote Markt and then came to an abrupt halt.

On the opposite side of the square, she spotted Mathis rounding the corner from an alleyway. Beams from the golden sunset bounced off his wavy blonde hair, as he entered the square and waved at her. Louisa watched riveted. She studied every detail about him as he approached her. His white flowy linen shirt accented the sun-kissed tan he had from the beach. The blue denim jeans he wore were faded, and frayed strands in the hem hung over his Bohemian leather sandals. When they met in the center of the square, a light summer breeze brought a refreshing clean scent of soap from Mathis that exhilarated her senses. Butterflies fluttered in her stomach, and she almost thought she'd throw up. It was all terribly romantic, but Louisa realized she'd forgotten something: the language barrier. Where would they go from here without Penny translating for them?

Mathis, however, came prepared. He had a way about him that made her forget the barrier. Holding out his hand, he greeted her. "Hallo, Louisa. Come with me."

Louisa put her hand in his and felt a rush as their two worlds merged.

Mathis led her out of the square. She had no idea where they were going, but at that moment she would have followed him to the edge of a cliff on a stormy day. They strolled down one old cobblestone side street after another. Louisa absorbed the sights, smells, and sounds of old-town Antwerp as much as she could. But it was difficult to focus on anything except Mathis. She couldn't take her eyes off him—nor did he avert his gaze—as they walked. They remained silent, but the look on Mathis's face and the smile he gave her spoke volumes.

They made their way over to a small ice-cream booth nestled between two outdoor cafés. Mathis stepped aside so she could choose which flavor she wanted. Louisa looked at the older woman behind the booth and pointed at the chocolate one. "Alstublieft."

Speaking to the lady in Flemish, Mathis held up two fingers, ordering the same thing.

It was a sultry summer evening, so the chocolate delights melted fast. They each licked their dripping ice cream, trying to keep up, but things got out of control. It was cute at first, but soon chocolate dripped all over their hands and clothes. Louisa didn't know what to do. Should she toss the ice-cream cone in the garbage? Before they could do anything Mathis's ice cream fell off the cone and plopped right on top of his shoe. He let out a hearty laugh, and Louisa followed, shaking all over. All at once, her scoop splattered to the ground, triggering even harder laughter between the two.

They ditched the rest of their cones in a nearby garbage bin. The dinky napkins they got from the ice-cream booth weren't nearly enough to clean up with, but Louisa paid no attention to the chocolate stains on her white halter top, and she and Mathis carried on to their next stop.

The night was in full swing, and the city was lit up. Mathis led her over to the Scheldt River and up to Het Steen. The medieval fortress, which had greeted centuries' worth of ships coming and going, was illuminated with spotlights for anyone who wanted to enjoy its beauty. Louisa followed him up the drawbridge leading to the main entrance, and they sat down together on a stone pillar railing.

Staring up at the evening sky beyond the fortress, Louisa admired the backdrop of scattered twinkling white stars. She contemplated whether or not to say something to Mathis in Flemish Penny had taught her. Would she get it right though? Finally, she decided, what the heck. "Een prachtige nacht," she said with a hint of doubt in her tone.

"Ya," he replied.

Alarm bells sounded in Louisa's head. Ya? Yes. Yes, what? What had she said? His response didn't seem right to her. She feared she'd said something stupid. Or maybe Penny had played a joke on her and taught her to say something fresh to him. But when she looked at him sweetly smiling, he did not appear to be laughing at her.

They continued sitting on the railing, gazing up at the stars with their legs swinging back and forth. Louisa's feet kept hitting his accidentally. Finally, Mathis hooked his foot around hers and looked deeply into her eyes.

The warm moment was quickly broken when Louisa recognized familiar voices in the street. She turned to see Judy coming up the fortress's bridge with Gui and her entourage. The last thing she wanted was to be hanging out with Judy and her fan club, and especially not sharing Mathis with anyone else. She yanked his arm so they could get away fast. They jumped over the opposite side of the railing, landed on the pavement, and ran down by the river to avoid being seen by her sister.

Once Louisa realized Judy had not seen her, the two teens made their way back through the narrow alleyways. They roamed for blocks until they met the bright lights and noisy sounds of a small street fair. Vendors were lined up one after another, some with game carts and others selling deep-fried treats. Louisa wandered with Mathis through the carnival, listening to lively bells dinging to celebrate winners of ring toss and laughter echoing from the bumper cars. Soon, the sounds and smells dissipated, and the bright lights dimmed while the two walked on.

A few blocks later, they came upon a small park where people picnicked on the lawn as an orchestra prepared for a concert. Violins and other instruments whined away as the performers warmed up. Across from the park was another square lined with outdoor cafés. Louisa's feet were getting tired, so she steered Mathis toward one of the cafés to get a soda.

Once they settled at a round bistro table outside, she grabbed his hand playfully and taught him how to thumb-wrestle—something she was quite good at, or so she thought. Mathis apparently was privy to the game as well and soon was crushing her. After losing her third match to him, Louisa gave up. The two teens silently met each other's eyes again across the table.

Mathis leaned over and took out a red poppy from the glass vase between them. The poppies of Flanders could be found everywhere at that time of year, and Louisa knew the delicate flower represented hope, something she was surprised she had retained from all of her parents' sightseeing. As Mathis reached across the table and put the poppy in her hair, she thought of the deep emotions the flower held for Belgians and the pride she felt while wearing it.

"Yo!" a new familiar voice shouted off in the distance.

Louisa jolted out of her romantic trance and looked up. Cointreau and Said were at the café entrance. The Moroccans looked like they were waiting for other people to join them.

Sinking into her chair, Louisa hoped they wouldn't see her. Mathis's eyes followed hers to the source of her alarm. He pulled on her arm, and they got up from the table, staying low and hunched while they crept to the other side of the café. Louisa kept glancing back to see if the Moroccans had spotted her. Then her eyes met Said's dead-on.

She and Mathis darted out of the café and down the street without looking back. When they were far enough away, the two broke out in laughter until they were out of breath once again. Louisa couldn't help but wonder why, as big as the city was, she was running into all these people she knew. Didn't the world know she was on her first date with the boy of her dreams? A little privacy would be nice.

Mathis held his finger up signaling he had a plan. He took Louisa by the hand and led her in a new direction. In the distance, she saw the Cathedral of Our Lady. Its beautiful architecture was undergoing a significant renovation on the outside. Several scaffolds rested against the cathedral's elaborate facade. The luminescence coming from the edifice entranced Louisa. It felt like she was headed toward an ideal place that didn't exist.

Mathis ushered her up to one of the scaffolds and carefully looked both ways, as if making sure no one was around. He nodded, letting her know it was okay to climb up. It was all so excitingly dangerous to her. He had protected her in the disco months before, and she felt like her gallant knight was watching over her once again.

They climbed up the ladder slowly. Louisa went first, with Mathis following. At first, she thought it was chivalrous of him to let her go first so he could catch her if she fell. But then she realized he probably wanted to get a better look at her from another angle and blushed. As they climbed higher, Louisa was drawn in by the old eclectic roofs of the buildings now below her. Something whimsical struck her about the stepped gables silhouetted against the moonlit evening sky. They rose up like a staircase on each side and met at a chimney like a cherry topping on a cake.

Eventually, the pair reached a platform and crawled over to the edge where a metal safety bar was set horizontally. They dangled their legs off the side and rested their elbows on the bar. Louisa looked out at the scene in front of her. It was the most beautiful view she'd ever seen—joyful Antwerp, lit up at night. It radiated all of the beauty the city had to offer. In the distance, she could hear the finale of Saint-Saëns's "Organ" Symphony No. 3 being performed by the orchestra she and Mathis had seen warming up in the park earlier.

All at once, the sound of an organ boomed from inside the cathedral, making her jump. She listened for a moment and realized the majestic instrument was playing along with the outdoor concert. Far too large to be moved, the organ broadcast its notes into the park to join the other musicians. She only knew of the classical symphony because the melody was adapted into a pop hit called "If I Had Words". Louisa briefly recalled the performance she had seen on *TopPop*. The video set was in a house of worship with a duo singing from an altar to an audience of uniformed schoolchildren in wooden pews. They dramatically waved their hands back and forth to the glorious melody over and over again.

While the soaring sounds of the concert continued, Louisa sat overwhelmed by everything Mathis had shown her that night. If she knew anything about him by now, it was his passion and pride for Antwerp. Every place he'd taken her—the iconic fortress, the quaint side streets, and now the incredible scene at the cathedral—proved it. It was magical. She was seeing Antwerp through his eyes and felt a special connection with him and the city.

She turned so she was face-to-face with Mathis. He brought her hand up to his lips and softly kissed it. She couldn't take her eyes off him as he put his hand under her chin and smiled. Louisa knew what was coming next—and for the first time, neither fear nor dread was present. She felt eagerness and desire instead.

The two gently came together as one and connected for their first kiss. Louisa could hardly breathe as her heart pounded like the rumbling of a bullet train. But it was so much more than that. The sincerity and tenderness of the moment were things she'd never experienced before. It was so much deeper than she could have ever imagined. The rocketing whistle of the train running through her heart sounded off *choo-choo*. *Finally*, she understood what all the fuss was about.

Mathis put an arm around her, and she put her head on his shoulder. They remained at the cathedral, gazing out over the rooftops of Antwerp. Louisa never wanted the moment to end.

It was nearly 2:00 a.m. when they walked back to the hotel and sat on a bench outside the lobby doors. Mathis took the dirty napkin from the ice-cream mess out of his pocket, placed it on the bench, and wrote something on it with a pen then placed it in Louisa's hand. "Dag, mijn Louisa."

Louisa looked up into his soft eyes. "Goodnight, Mathis. Thank you."

She tiptoed into the hotel lobby, taking her shoes off as she crept past the night clerk, who was again sitting upright in his chair, fast asleep.

Once she was safe in the elevator, she pumped her arms, swung her hips from side to side in exhilaration, and murmured, "This was the greatest night of my life."

Before heading inside her room, she opened the napkin and read the note in the light. It was in Flemish but she noticed he had written out some numbers that she was able to identify. Did Mathis want to meet her tomorrow, on her last day in Belgium? She'd have to ask Penny to translate for her the next day.

TRACK 24

"ELOISE" – BARRY RYAN

AUGUST 1978

The following afternoon, Penny snuck up to Louisa's hotel after her mom left for another farewell luncheon. The girls lay on her bed, and Penny translated Mathis's note out loud. "'Sorry I was late,'" she read. "'Meet me at Brabo tomorrow night at twenty-one hundred hours.'"

Louisa's face lit up. "Yay! He wants to see me again! Penny, I finally kissed a boy for real, and I liked it. The night was so magical. Just like you said it would be." She sprung up in bed. "Remember what Mathis said to us that time we stayed in town all night? That he would be studying English in school? He and I can write to each other when I leave."

Grabbing a pen and some paper from the nightstand, she handed it to Penny. "You'll have to tell me how to ask him for his address. It'll be great! I can go to my new school and tell everyone I have a Belgian boyfriend."

After Penny wrote the note for Mathis in Flemish, Louisa said her final goodbyes to her first and best friend from AIS. "Good luck tonight, Louisa. Make it the *best* night ever!" Penny exclaimed. "And don't do anything I wouldn't do." She playfully winked at her with a lopsided smile and exited the room.

In the early evening, Louisa and her siblings were in their hotel room packing their bags for the early morning flight to the States the next day. Their mom pranced in with a look of delight on her face. "Kids, your father is taking us to the Rooden Hoed for dinner tonight, for one last meal at our favorite restaurant. Then we have a *big* surprise after that."

"What?" Louisa shouted, jumping to her feet. "What do you mean, a surprise? What is it? And how long will it take?"

Her mom looked startled by her reaction. "You'll have to just wait and see." She exited the room, leaving Louisa stumped.

At the Rooden Hoed that night, Louisa barely touched her moules and frites, fearful of her parents' plan after dinner. Her mother finally shared where they were going over dessert. "One of your father's coworkers gave him front-row seats to the opera *La bohème* as a going-away gift." She turned to Louisa. "It'll be *just* like the rock opera, *Jesus Christ Superstar*, we saw in London a few months ago that you liked so much."

Louisa almost cried out loud at the news. This wasn't good at all.

Later at the opera, she sat slumped in her chair, fuming as the singers belted out Puccini's lyrics: "Sì, mi chiamano Mimì." Judy leaned over to whisper in Louisa's ear. "Some going-away gift," she said sarcastically. "They must not have liked Dad much."

Louisa's anxiety boiled over inside. She kept leaning toward her mother, pretending to readjust herself in her seat to see the time on her mom's watch.

During intermission, the sisters brooded in the bathroom over how much longer *La bohème* would go on. It was already 8:00 p.m. Louisa knew there clearly wasn't enough time, with half the opera left to go. "I can't believe they sprung this so-called surprise on us on our last night here," she griped. "From this day forward, I'm so done with surprises."

After the curtain closed and the applause died down, the family headed back to the hotel. Louisa glanced up at the clock behind the hotel desk when they entered the lobby. By then, it was 9:30 p.m. She prayed Mathis would wait. She'd be there soon.

When they got to their floor, Lyle followed the three teens into their room to review a checklist of all the things they'd have to do before leaving in the morning. The way he methodically weighed every word before speaking meant Louisa had to wait another twenty minutes before he finally left.

The sisters stuck their heads out into the hall. They tiptoed quickly, carrying their shoes, went down the elevator, and passed the hotel clerk to head out into Antwerp's streets.

As they entered the Grote Markt, the clock outside a café in the square read it was 10:00 p.m. The same musician who had played there the night before was strumming tear-jerk love songs again on his guitar. The only difference was tonight he had reinforcements: a male singer with a gothic-vampire look about him. His dark hair was long and unruly, and his voice was intense. It bounced off the historical guild houses, shattering the quiet of the square.

Louisa spotted Gui sitting on a bench, once again with tears rolling from his eyes. Judy walked over to him, while Louisa headed away and up to Brabo Fountain. She looked around the monument. Mathis was nowhere in sight.

Circling the square fearfully, her chin trembled as the looming tears blurred her vision. Why didn't he wait?

She walked back over to Judy and Gui, glancing bitterly at the two hugging and comforting each other. She felt terrible about envying her sister, but she couldn't help herself. How much she wished Mathis was there and she was in his arms again. Her anxiety sent her pacing back and forth along the cobblestone square, refusing to accept the fact she wasn't going to see him one last time. Trudging back over to Brabo, she looked up at the fountain, remembering the happiness and exhilaration the statue of the Roman warrior held for her just the evening before. Now, the mythical character brought her pain and sorrow. Her empty gaze fell to the ground.

On a rock at the base of the statue, she spotted a bouquet of red poppies bunched together by twine. She picked up a small piece of paper lying on top of the flowers. The note read, *"Dag, little darling,"* with a heart drawn around the words.

Shattered, Louisa turned her attention to the singer. He was theatrical, dressed in a flowing, ruffled white poet shirt with black pants and riding boots. With his arms extended out in front of him, he clenched his fists tightly as his body jerked with every harrowing lyric. His severe singing charged through the air, piercing Louisa's heart. It was as if the vocalist's powerful performance of complete loss echoed her pain.

A somber aura rolled into the Grote Markt like a silent fog. Lost in her sorrow, Louisa stood alone with her arms at her sides. The poppies dangled from one hand and the note in the other.

The melodramatic performer continued singing through the nearly empty square about his devotion for Eloise and how he waited for her every night, but she never showed up.

The next morning, Louisa peered sightlessly out the plane window before takeoff. Whenever she thought about Mathis, she felt a thousand knives piercing her. The pain was as fresh as the evening before. She finally came to the realization if this was that love thing everyone raved about, then, *No thank you*, send it back to where it came from.

Looking down at her charm bracelet, she studied the dangling Sabena airplane her mother had bought that day they had landed in Belgium. Next to it was the German stein charm, followed by an Eiffel Tower and other monumental tokens of her travels with her family. The past four years hung from her arm.

Louisa's life in Belgium flashed before her—the music she idolized, AIS and her friends, the Moroccans, the train station, her travels throughout Europe, and of course, Mathis. It already felt like a distant memory, and they hadn't even left the ground yet. Overcome with sadness, she blinked, allowing the tears that built in her eyes to roll down her cheek. She looked over at her mother, who sat next to her, weeping as well. Her mom took her hand and turned to Louisa. "Don't worry, honey," she said. "We will be back someday."

TRACK 25

"CRAZY" – MUD

MAY 2018

When Louisa woke the next morning, her muddled thoughts left her in complete confusion. Who was she? Where was she? Had she gone off the deep end?

She rose in her bed, examining her surroundings and muttered, "Okay, girl. Back to the present. Get a grip already."

After pouring herself a cup of coffee, she sat at the kitchen table with Judy and told her all about the blast of memories from their final days of living in Belgium. "Sister, it was so weird that so much came back to me. It was like somebody put me under hypnosis and opened a Pandora's box in my brain that had been closed for so long. I guess I always knew the memories were there, but I just forgot that I knew." She looked down at her cup, mystified. "I keep asking myself if it was all just a dream."

Judy appeared puzzled. "What was a dream? That we ever lived here, or the memory blast from last night?"

Louisa leaned forward in her chair and looked at her sister straight in the eye. "Both."

Once Judy left the kitchen to get ready for the day, Louisa sat alone at the table. She was still pondering how she could have forgotten so much about something that was so special to her. When exactly had Antwerp and everything about it lost its magic? She could still recall when they first moved back to the States. Her first friend in the neighborhood was Diana, who had lived next door at the time. Diana knew all the ropes in the neighborhood and who was who. She showed Louisa and Judy off and told the locals they were French—which was, of course, a fabrication. Nonetheless, the three girls would sit on the green electric utility box at the end of the LaPlantes' driveway so all could see the new European girls in the neighborhood.

It was just like when they lived in Antwerp; they were seen as an oddity. Similarly, the local boys, who had seemed curious about the "Belgian import thing," treated Louisa and her sister like they were more "experienced" than the other girls in the neighborhood. But Louisa knew, for her, that was completely not true.

However, months later, the novelty wore off for the locals, and they stopped driving by the electric box. Eventually, Louisa and her sister were seen as normal American teenagers, influenced by American culture once again. The Belgium experience and all its glory had dwindled.

Louisa put her elbows on the table and her head in her hands, frustrated. How had she let go of the best years of her life?

No day trips were scheduled on Patty's itinerary that day. Instead, the ladies decided to relax and recharge for the concert the next evening. The sisters ventured out in the afternoon and hit a local salon to get a manicure for the big event. While Louisa sat there having her nails painted, the memories from the night before still resonated. It was like the past was following her around everywhere she went.

By evening, she still couldn't shake the feeling. What were those repressed memories that rose from the grave trying to tell her? She lay in bed, rewinding what she remembered over and over again like a surveillance tape being reviewed for a crime. Finally, after endless tossing and turning, her head cleared, and she grew sleepy. As she drifted off, though, something came back to her, and she bolted up in bed. "The time capsule!"

Fully awake and bursting with driven emotion, she ran down the hall to Judy's room. She stood over her sister's bed and tried to shake her awake, but Judy didn't budge.

She remembered a little trick she had used when they were teens. Taking two fingers, she pinched her sister's nose so she couldn't breathe. Judy swatted her hand away as if Louisa were an annoying fly buzzing around and asked, "What's wrong?"

Louisa drew a breath. "C'mon, sister," she whispered. "We're going on a little adventure tonight."

"What? Are you drunk?" Judy sat up.

Louisa quietly explained all about the time capsule, trying to persuade her to go back with her to their house. Judy finally softened a little. "But why does it have to be tonight? Can't we wait until the morning?"

"No. We have to go now while Mom is asleep. She'd never allow us to do this. Tomorrow's the concert. So it *has* to be tonight when it's dark and no one can see us. Besides, the house is vacant. Remember the 'For Sale' sign?" A mischievous grin expanded on her lips. "C'mon, sister, it'll be like old times, when we used to sneak out after Mom and Dad went to bed." Her grin deepened. "It'll be a good story to bring back to our girlfriends at home."

Judy finally relented, probably knowing she could not win this one. The sisters crept past their mother's room, carrying their shoes. They went into the kitchen and grabbed everything they could find to dig with. Their excavating tools were limited at the apartment, so they had to improvise.

Hurrying, they hopped into the rental car and headed up the Turnhoutsebaan, carrying two large metal spatulas, an ice-cream scoop, and a couple of butter knives.

Once they were on Bremboslaan, Judy shut the car lights off as they approached the house. "I still can't believe I let you talk me into this. You're out of your mind."

"What did you say to me the other day in the store?" Louisa mocked in an animated voice. "'Chill, Louisa. You're on vacation. It'll be an adventure.'"

Judy rolled her eyes, looking defeated. "I'll have to be more mindful about what I say to you."

They parked in front of their old house, grabbed their cellphones, and turned on the built-in flashlights. Hunched down low, the two stealthily moved across the front lawn like two cat burglars. Once they were in the backyard, Louisa halted, assessing the area. It looked smaller than she remembered. She thought it would be easy enough when they had left the apartment, but she realized she really had no clue where to find the buried box. She just figured it would come back to her, like everything else magically had done over the past few days.

After they looped around the same trees three times, Judy whispered, "I thought you knew where it was!"

Louisa stalled for time. "Give me a sec. I didn't realize it would be so different. The trees are so big now. I'll find it." While she snaked in and out of the woods for the next several minutes, she could feel her sister's eyes watching her every move, distracting her.

"That's it!" Judy yelled. "I'm going! This is madness." She headed back to the front of the house and disappeared.

Louisa, however, had no intention of leaving until she had found what she had come for. Completely focused, she continued searching despite the flashlight not being bright enough, which made things difficult. Walking back to the lawn, she turned facing the woods and tried to remember that day forty years earlier. The trees' black branches, silhouetted against the moonlit evening sky, all looked the same. But then her eyes landed on one tree that was different—a chestnut tree.

Louisa hustled toward it. Letting the flashlight's beam fall low upon the trunk, she circled it, looking for the carving. She went around once and found nothing. *This had to be the one.* Circling it again more slowly, she moved in closer, hunched even lower this time, examining every nook and cranny of the trunk. Still nothing. She threw her hands up, at a loss over what to do next.

After an exasperated sigh, she stood upright, holding the flashlight much higher this time and began another loop around. Narrowing her focus, she squinted at one spot that caught her attention—and there it was, the initials *LL + MJ*. Louisa drew in her breath, astonished that her life from so long ago was still visible on the trunk, which had moved up much higher as the tree grew.

She squatted down, took one of the knives, and hacked away at the ground to break it up. Seconds after, her attention was broken when she felt a hand on her shoulder. She jumped back and screeched. Turning around, she found Judy standing over her.

"I found it, sister!" Louisa cried out. "Help me."

Judy hastily kneeled on the ground. The two scooped the dirt away, digging about four inches down without reaching anything.

"It couldn't have been that deep," Louisa shook her head. "Cripes, I was only fifteen when I did this." Still squatting, she waddled to another area of untouched ground and started burrowing there. Judy, however, appeared to be losing interest again and stood up.

Louisa couldn't give up now, she had come so far. She continued digging frantically. Sweat beaded on her face and dripped down her neck. With her hair hanging over her eyes, sticking to her wet forehead, she panted breathlessly.

Discouraged, she raised the knife above her head and plunged it down hard. The unmistakable clink of metal hitting metal reverberated in the air.

Louisa looked up at her sister, dumbfounded. She'd found it! Judy darted over to her side, wrapping her hands tighter around the ice-cream scoop she'd been using. They dug together, faster and faster, laughing excitedly. When enough dirt had been removed, Louisa reached down into the ground and grabbed the tin. She pulled it up and fell out of her squat, landing butt-first on the ground.

Astounded at her accomplishment, Louisa sat with the time capsule on her lap. She caught her breath for a second, then lifted the lid off the tin, carefully pulling the plastic bag out. The container had rusted and corroded over the years and was in a delicate state now.

She plunged her hand into the bag. Out came the foil-covered autograph book. She gently brushed her hand across the front cover. "Everything in this box was my whole world—no, *is* my whole world."

A flood of emotions warmed her when she recalled that was exactly what she had said when she buried the tin. She put her hands on her head as the tears tumbled down her face.

Squatting beside her, Judy softly stroked Louisa's hair, calming her.

"Maybe I'm having a meltdown." Louisa cried, wiping away the sweat and tears from her face with her sleeve. "I'm acting like a little school-girl." She looked up at Judy. "I think I'm having one of those midlife crisis thingies."

Louisa stared at her sister with drooping eyes silently, then out of nowhere, a humorous feeling bubbled up inside her. She exploded in laughter. How ridiculous was this! Here she was, having a meltdown in the middle of the night, in the backyard of her childhood home, digging up a box of her lost treasures. She had dirt on her face and was sweating like a pig and crying about it like a baby. Why was she crying? The whole situation was *downright* hysterical.

Soon, Judy joined in, and they howled together in laughter.

"C'mon, silly sister, let's get out of here." Judy slowly stood up.

At the same moment, a sudden snapping sound of branches came from the dark woods behind them.

Louisa looked wide-eyed at her sister as every hair on the back of her neck stood up. Judy raised a finger to her lips, and they turned off their cellphone flashlights.

"What was that?" Judy whispered.

Louisa tried to focus her eyes on the darkness, straining to see what was out there. Her eyes darted back and forth through the trees several times. Then they fell upon a tall figure illuminated by the moonlight—a man in a long coat and wide-brimmed hat lurked about fifty feet away.

Louisa grabbed Judy's arm. "Let's get out of here!"

The dash back to the car felt like it was in slow motion. Louisa's lungs were burning. She wasn't sure if she could make it without stopping to catch her breath. Finally, though, they made it back safely inside the rental car. Judy frantically locked the doors as Louisa sat motionless in the passenger seat. "Who was that?" Louisa cried. "That was so freaky!"

Leaning over, Judy started the car. The headlights beamed down Bremboslaan, lighting up their surroundings. Louisa looked out across their old front lawn and spotted the man she'd seen in the backyard. The trench-coated figure walked off the grass and down the road, heading straight toward them.

She grasped Judy's arm. "Drive!"

"I can't move!" Judy screeched, looking utterly incapacitated.

Louisa's mouth hung wide open. Her eyes were fixed on the figure slowly coming closer and closer as he reached their car. He sauntered along the curb and looked down at Judy as he passed by her side window. Louisa could barely keep her eyes open. She felt like she was watching a horror flick and was peeking through her fingers at the scary parts. This was it. *They were goners.*

The stranger tipped his hat to Judy while passing and said, "Goeienavond."

Louisa's eyes followed him through the car's rear window, and she watched him disappear down Bremboslaan. When she discovered he was just someone out on a walk with his tiny poodle, all her fear subsided, and she inhaled a deep gulp of air. Moments after, she busted out in uncontrollable, stress-relief laughter.

They continued replaying the scene the whole drive back to Antwerp. "You should have seen your face!" Judy shouted.

"The only thing that went through my head was that it was a curse," Louisa joked. "All because I had dug up the forbidden ancient treasure."

Once they arrived back at the apartment and cleaned up, Louisa climbed onto her bed and lifted the lid off the rusted tin. She reached into the plastic bag and took out the foil-covered autograph book. Placing it to one side to read later, she rummaged through the other items.

First, she pulled out a stub or receipt that was so weathered she could barely read it. The only thing it could have possibly been was a bus ticket into Antwerp from Schilde. Next, she yanked out a broken teaspoon. Why was that in there? She couldn't recall any funny stories behind it but laughed anyway. Surely its story was a good one.

She didn't recognize many of the other items in the time capsule. But she did remember her hot pink hairbrush, which was still loaded with her hair. "Ewww!" she cried out in disgust, tossing the furball to the floor.

A little farther down, Louisa found a piece of blue-and-white fabric. She tilted her head quizzically as she focused on it. Then she remembered—it was Mathis's bandana.

A vivid image of his face appeared in her mind. She cupped her hand around her mouth, shocked she was holding something that belonged to him. To her, it almost felt like he never existed.

Feeling downhearted, she slid off the bed and walked over to the window. Her love story with Mathis and the delicate innocence of what they had shared were all returning to her in greater detail. Those treasured memories of him warmed her cold, lonely heart that night just like when he had saved her from harm's way in the disco decades ago.

She leaned out the window getting a better look at beautiful Antwerp's evening glow. "Where are you tonight, out there in this great big world?"

Climbing back to bed, she grabbed the bandana. It smelled musty, but she didn't care. She curled up on one side, clutching the cloth of her past close to her heart and falling fast asleep. Just as she had done decades ago.

TRACK 26

"DON'T LET THE MUSIC DIE"
– THE BAY CITY ROLLERS

MAY 2018

The next evening, the sisters chatted in the kitchen, waiting for their mother to get ready for The Rubettes concert. Louisa was so fired up that she'd been dressed and ready to go three hours earlier. She sat at the table, anxiously holding her concert ticket like it was the winning golden pass to Willy Wonka's chocolate factory.

When Patty finally rolled into the kitchen, she wore one of those clever looks that meant she was up to something. In her hands, she carried two floral gift bags stuffed with pink tissue paper. "Okay, girls," she said. "I want to let you know how special this trip has been, and it means the world to me that you came along for the ride." She handed them each a bag.

"Mom, what have you done?" Judy cried out.

"Just open it," Patty said sitting down with them at the table.

Louisa straightened her posture, tearing into the bag through the tissue paper. She pulled up a jewelry box that stood on dainty gold-leaf Queen Anne legs. The lid was browned from age. It appeared to be an antique and featured a hand-painted scene of the outside of Antwerp's train station over a hundred years earlier.

Louisa studied it, noting the signature dome she knew so well. "Mom, this is absolutely beautiful. Where did you get this?"

Patty smiled. "Just open up the lid."

Louisa lifted the top. Inside was a piece of her past she hadn't seen in decades: her charm bracelet from her travels living in Belgium. She glanced at Judy, who held up her own charm bracelet.

"Oh, my God." Judy said, looking amazed. "I haven't seen this in years. I forgot all about it."

Louisa slid to the edge of her chair as she flicked through all her charms. "I don't remember ever wondering where this went—or that it was even missing. How long have you had this, Mom?"

"A long time, honey."

Studying each charm, Louisa tried to recall the story behind each of them. When she was halfway through the chain, she spotted a new addition to her family of charms she'd never seen before. Her eyes zoomed in on it. It was a tiny silver replica of the Brabo Fountain statue. Even more remarkable was a small diamond inserted into the charm at the base.

The statue had such special meaning for her now and she knew then she'd never forget the story behind it. But it left her mystified. Could her mother have known about the memories it held for her? No, she *couldn't* have, or could she?

Louisa leaned over and squeezed her mother in a tight embrace. She and Judy helped each other put their bracelets on before they headed out the door. It was almost curtain time.

The Rubettes concert was being held in a small historical theater with traditional box seats along the sides that had once been for royalty and the wealthy. The vaulted dome ceiling was illuminated with lights, displaying a heavenly mural full of angels. Hanging from the dome's center was a huge crystal chandelier. The heavy red velvet curtains, crested with carvings of medieval knights detailed in gold, were closed.

Louisa embraced the ambiance, but the elegant theater made the experience less like a rock concert and more like an opera. She was getting the feeling she'd been here before. After carefully scrutinizing the venue with Judy, she remembered why. The sisters got a good chuckle when they discovered what it was: their parents had taken them to this very theater to see *La bohème* on their last night in Antwerp, way back when.

Eventually the lights dimmed, and the curtains slowly lifted. Judy clenched Louisa's hand. "This is it, sister," she whispered. "The moment you've been waiting for most of your life."

The room went completely black, and the audience fell silent. Amplified voices sang "Yeah, I can do it!" in perfect a cappella harmony from the stage. This was followed by driving guitar before the band launched into all-out rock and roll music.

The lights came back on, flashing in a strobe effect to the beat of the catchy song. Louisa's eyes were riveted on the stage as The Rubettes stood epically tall, ready to give the audience the show they had come for.

She exploded out of her seat, dancing and clapping wildly. Fortunately, they were in the last row. She was free of worrying about her idiosyncratic dancing blocking anyone behind her.

A few tunes in, the band eventually mellowed a little and played one of their slow ballads. When Louisa sat back down to take a break, she found herself struggling to get a better look at The Rubettes. She wanted to see how the band members had aged. Still, she wondered if they ever looked out into the audience and noticed how their fans had changed over forty-something years. As she looked closer, it occurred to her these were the same people who shaped her life as an adolescent, and amazingly were still there for her, playing the songs she loved so much—*needed* so much.

The music soon picked up again, and Louisa was back up dancing along with her sister and mother. As she threw her hands up in the air to clap along she noticed Judy was slowly slinking back into her seat. Her sister reached into her oversized purse and pulled out a folded sheet of poster paper. She laid it out on her lap, brushing her hand across it and unfolding it to reveal a large banner. It read: "Alan Williams, I would sell my entire family for you." Louisa's jaw dropped when she saw what was written. "No way!" she shrieked. "You didn't!" She nudged their mother, who glanced down to read the sign, chuckling before returning her attention to the stage.

"Judy, this isn't a Marilyn Manson concert!" Louisa glanced around to see if anyone was watching them.

Judy's crazed expression said she had an agenda, and Louisa knew nothing would stop her. Judy stood up and held the sign above her head, proudly waving it back and forth.

The band segued into one of their bubblegum smash hits, 'Sugar Baby Love'. Alan Williams pranced around the stage, getting the audience involved. As he sang the saccharine-sweet lyrics, his head lifted, and his gaze went to the back of the theater. Louisa could see his beaming smile even from afar as he pointed to the audience in the last rows, serenading them all.

"I love you, Alan!" Judy screamed from the top of her lungs.

Louisa shook her head, laughing. She had no idea if the singer could really see the sign, but Judy appeared to be living out her fantasy regardless.

Once the last encore ended, Louisa sat down with Judy and their mother while she caught her breath from all the singing, dancing, and laughing. Judy leaned over to her. "Hey, they didn't play that song you loved by them. I forgot the name of it. Remember?"

Louisa caressed her chin, thinking.

Judy pushed Louisa's shoulder as her tone heightened. "C'mon, you know! The one Magnus got you that forty-five of when we lived here. You must have played it a million times. You always walked around the house, singing it."

Louisa stared blankly, trying to remember. Magnus? *Did she mean Mathis again?* All at once, an image of a banana yellow 45 label featuring The Rubettes flashed in her head. "Oh, my God!" she cried as it came back to her. "It was 'Little Darling'. I forgot all about that one." Trying to recall the melody in her head, though, was a struggle. There was nothing there but the title of the song. "I can't remember how it went." She paused before gritting her teeth. "And, Judy, his name was Mathis!"

The theater slowly emptied, and Judy suggested the three of them go out for a cappuccino and some delicious Belgian chocolate. She twirled a lock of hair around her finger. "There was something about the lead singer and the way he sang 'Sugar Baby Love' to me. It made me want something sweet."

Patty stood up. "Let's go to that cute outdoor café across the street."

Louisa grabbed her purse to get up, when her attention was diverted to a song that started playing over the intercom, inexplicably grabbing her. She remained seated as her mom and sister scooched out to the aisle. "Go get a table. I just want to hear this song. Order me a cappuccino."

Judy rolled her eyes and locked arms with their mother, and they left.

Louisa saw the irritated look on Judy's face and knew her sister was probably tired of her perpetual preoccupation with music, but she was relieved when they were gone. Something about the poignant melody and words moved her, and she needed to hear more.

"Echoed voices from the past
Recall the songs I thought would last
And say 'Those times will never die'
And the love we share's the reason why
I remember all those days gone by
I remember all their faces,
The old familiar places
Don't let the music die,
No, our song could last forever
Don't let the music die,
Don't let the music die
And though we've said goodbye,
We could spend our lives together,
So as time goes by
Don't let the music die . . ."

Enraptured in the moment, Louisa sat with a vacant stare. The song made her think of her lost adolescence. And she found it ironic that she'd lived the lyrics they had sung that past week.

The theater was empty now, except for the roadies packing up the band's equipment. She remained silent, still digesting the song.

After some time, she shrugged and picked herself up, heading over to the café. Strangely, though, while she crossed the street, she sensed something had followed her out of the theater, like the presence of something unattainable and it was trying to catch up to her. She whisked around and looked. Nothing was there.

Once she found her mom and Judy's table, she could see they were clearly in high spirits after the show, laughing. "They were so good!" Judy raved. "I can't believe what a fox the lead singer still is. Or at least from our nosebleed seats."

"I think that was my first rock concert," Patty said, laughing. "I don't know what took me so long."

Louisa sat down, still marveling at her mysterious encounter in the theater. She had never heard the song before. And why had it impacted her like it had? She trembled a little, worrying that she was having another one of those "aha" moments. She wasn't sure she could handle any more.

Her mind drifted back to her time and adventures in Antwerp over the past week. She was bewildered at all the memories that had come back to her and the music she had left behind forty years before. But was it the music evoking the memories or the memories making her love the music? Either way, they were both pushing her, as if they wanted to open her eyes to see something.

Confused, she glanced around the table, wondering if anyone was watching her. Judy and her mother continued chatting about the show, unaware of her restlessness. Then the odd presence which had followed Louisa from the theater finally caught up to her. It hovered right over her head, fueling her angst.

She rested her elbows on the table and propped her chin in her hands, struggling to contain herself. Everything around her became clouded over.

She glanced at her charm bracelet dangling from her wrist as it slowly slid down her arm toward her elbow. Her mind continued flipping back and forth, recalling something her mother had written in her book: "These indeed had turned out to be the happiest, saddest, wettest, wildest, and most extraordinary years of my life, and I did not want them to end." Louisa felt so connected to that sentiment. But this was more than a mother-daughter bond going on. Her mother's words were provoking her to do something—but what?

The trip was coming to an end. Time was running out for her to find the answers to the questions harping on her. What would happen when they left Antwerp? Would all of the memories and music just go away again? The thought of that scared her. She didn't want to say goodbye to one second of the past week and return to the pathetic person she had been before. And if that was the case, then what had this adventure been all about?

She was silent while her mother and sister continued raving about the concert. Time passed in stillness as she waited. She knew something was coming and it was going to be big.

Just then her arms dropped to the table, as her senses filled with a peculiar rhapsody and the music from her adolescence spiraled around in her head like a cyclone funnel. The songs were scrambled like a word puzzle, creating a muffled static buzzing as the indistinct music played over and over again. Gradually, the sounds fused as if the different tunes were being woven, and soon they became one melody: "Don't Let the Music Die."

Louisa gasped when the answer she'd been waiting for finally revealed itself.

She launched out of her seat, overcome with an explosive passion. "I get it now! I know what I'm supposed to be doing with my life." She looked around the café and realized heads were turning toward her, so she lowered her voice. "Those musical groups didn't just *make* my life forty years ago. They also *saved* my life today. I just don't want to ever let go. I need to keep them alive in my heart."

Louisa turned to her mom, admiring her as she took her hand. "Mom, I know what to do next. I'm going to write a book too, about my experience forty years ago. My three amigos—Mud, The Rubettes, and The Sweet will be there. No—better yet, all my favorites will be there."

She took a deep breath. She had worked herself up into a state of trembling excitement, but her passion was beyond her control. "They rocked my world then, and they still do. I just want to keep them alive in my soul so I'll have them with me always." She clenched her hands into fists and raised one arm in triumph. "Those days of the best music ever are back to stay—for good this time." Her eyes were wide open, and she felt fulfilled, exhaling deeply.

Judy stared wide-eyed at her, as if Louisa maybe had finally lost it. "A-Aha. Okay, sister. You can do whatever you want."

Patty, however, nodded slowly, wearing a smug expression of approval. Louisa understood what that look meant. She knew her younger daughter had finally gotten it, as she had forty years earlier.

Louisa realized it really didn't matter how she interpreted living in Belgium in the 1970s—whether it was the iconic places, the music, or the memories. What mattered most was what she'd gotten out of that experience and how she'd carry it with her for the rest of her life.

"*You'll never forget it,*" her mother had said to her right before they'd moved to Antwerp. "*This experience will change your life forever.*" It might have taken Louisa forty years to realize the truth of those words and let them in, but she knew at that moment her mom had been right. Going forward, her life would never be the same.

TRACK 27

"LITTLE DARLING"(REPRISE)
– THE RUBETTES

MAY 2018

On their last morning in Belgium, Louisa awoke and felt purpose was back in her life. "This'll be a great day," she chirped. Her energy made her spring out of bed and skip down the hallway in pursuit of her morning coffee.

For their final day in the country, Patty had arranged one last trip. The trio hopped onto a train at the GSC heading for Brussels and had an early lunch in the glorious Grand Place, the capital city's version of the Grote Markt.

On the train back to Antwerp, Louisa told her mom and sister she was taking a sabbatical from work and would return to Belgium in a couple of months. She needed to be close to what had inspired her to go on the biggest adventure of her life. And she was certain writing about her passion from forty years ago would be the next chapter.

The ladies hopped off the train in Antwerp and made their way through the GSC. Louisa strolled through the bustling terminal and glanced around at her surroundings. It became evident the station of her youth, which held so many cherished memories, was no longer there. Back in the '70s, she and her friends would play guessing games, trying to figure out what the Flemish signs and posters advertised. Now, most of the billboards were in English. The single frites cart was gone too, replaced by several restaurants, chain stores, and cafés. Even the smell of cigarette smoke mixed with fried food had disappeared, and the travelers rushing past her were different; almost everyone spoke in English. And most evident, there were no more young Moroccan men standing at the grand staircase, looking for adventure.

Louisa pulled Judy aside. "I still can't believe we didn't see one Moroccan boy hanging out here like in the old days. Where did they all go?"

Judy glanced around and shrugged. "I guess it's true. You can't go back."

After they exited the GSC, Louisa was taken by surprise; directly in front of the station was a huge flea market. Tents were everywhere, selling everything from clothes and souvenirs to antiques.

"Wow!" Judy said. "This wasn't here when we came through earlier. I can't believe they set it up so quickly."

The afternoon was still young, so the three decided to indulge in one last shopping spree before going home.

The market was bustling with shoppers and activity. Louisa went from tent to tent with Judy, trying on scarves and hats and theatrically posing while they took pictures of each other dressed in the merchandise. At one point, Judy glanced around and griped, "We lost Mom again, sister."

A few vendors down, Louisa spotted their mom. She nudged Judy and they went over to lecture her about disappearing again. As they neared, Louisa noticed her mother's mouth hanging wide open, and a look of disbelief clearly on her face. "Mom, what is it?" she rushed over to her.

Patty stood in a small booth selling knickknacks and antiques. In her hand was a rose-tinted French Picardie drinking glass. "I don't believe it. I found my glass. This is incredible!"

On a table next to her was a set of four matching Picardie tumblers, lying in a case lined with light blue velvet.

"Mom, they're nice." Judy laughed. "But is there a story behind this special glass?"

Their mother looked eager to tell, so Louisa and Judy moved in closer.

"Do you remember when we took the tent down to the French Riviera with Teddy's friend David?" Patty asked. "That horrible trip in the rain? Well, anyway, there was that run-down house we went into. Remember when the policeman came?"

Louisa squinted, trying to follow her mother's story.

"Well, when Teddy and I were exploring the deserted house, I found a rose-tinted Picardie glass just like this one, right on the ground. I took it. And for years, I tried to find one in this color so I could have a set. It would've been a great story to tell whenever I served something in them to guests. Needless to say, I couldn't find it in this color. So I gave up. I still have the glass somewhere in a memorabilia box at home." She looked pleased with herself as she held the matching glass up to the light, twirling it in her hand.

"Well, Mom, I guess this trip was a good idea after all," Louisa teased.

Patty went over to an elderly woman who was selling the glasses and began telling her the same story. Whether the merchant spoke English or not was a mystery. She just kept nodding while their mom carried on.

The sisters wandered a few booths down to a large retro electronics tent selling old radios, phonographs, old rotary phones, and other small electronics. The area was packed with shoppers and lively '70s music flowed from a vintage Thorens turntable. It grabbed Louisa's attention, prompting her to bop her head and feel playful as she and her sister browsed through the dated hair dryers. "Hey, for dinner tonight, we should go to the Rooden Hoed again," she suggested. "It was the last restaurant we ate at on our final night living here."

Judy crossed her arms. "No. I don't want to go there again. Let's do something different."

"Judy, we have to," cried Louisa. "It's tradition!"

Her sister's face contorted. "Louisa, why do you have to be like that? You're always controlling everything. We always have to do what *you* want to do."

"That's not true, Judy. It would mean a lot to Mom too. She's all about tradition, unlike you. Sometimes I think you are so different from Mom and me!"

Judy's glare at Louisa was pure evil. "Louisa, you're not the boss of me. And I don't think I like how you said that, like I'm not in yours and mom's little writer's club."

Amused that her sister was making such a big deal over nothing, Louisa chuckled. "You're such a booger face, sistah!"

Judy scowled, practically baring her teeth, and swung her foot back, kicking Louisa in the middle of her shin.

"Ow!" Louisa hollered. "You did *not* just do that."

The bickering continued back and forth, with their voices getting louder. Eventually, the electronics merchant ran over to them. "Hallo. Can I help you?"

Judy dashed out of the tent in a flash, leaving Louisa alone with the merchant and a startled audience of shoppers staring at her. She averted her eyes downward, not wanting to look at the merchant or anyone else. "Sorry," she spoke softly. "My sister and I do this all the time." Briskly turning away, she shot out of the tent without looking back.

Once Louisa felt clear of the spectators, she spotted Judy three booths down. It was probably a good idea to stay away from her sister for a while. So she meandered into a small booth selling soaps and perfume.

The calming lavender fragrance from a diffuser brought her adrenaline down as she inhaled deeply. Meanwhile the retro music from the electronics tent drifted to where she was, and the lively beat prompted her to tap her foot. The good mood she had earlier started to return as she continued sampling the assorted scents of jasmine and rose.

After purchasing some handmade orange blossom soaps, her gaze drifted out of the tent and she spotted Judy walking farther away from her. Louisa felt bad they had quarreled. She didn't want their last day in Antwerp to be like this. It was time to make amends.

As she exited the soaps tent, a familiar, haunting melody filled the entire market, cranked to the highest volume. It abruptly brought her to a standstill as chills surged up and down her spine. Looking around frantically, she wondered where the music was coming from. Her focus went to the busy electronics tent, and she was drawn back in. As she entered, she spied the Thoren turntable spinning and walked over to it. Her eyes closed, and her entire presence felt like it was being swept up into a cloud of ecstasy. A warm, ethereal feeling washed over her, as she swirled around and around, absorbing every distinct detail of "Little Darling" by The Rubettes.

Louisa placed one hand on her cheek, letting her jaw drop open in astonishment. What was happening? Then it all came back to her. It was the same spiritual musical intoxication she'd felt as a young teen living in Antwerp. That magical feeling finally found its way back home to her heart. It was the most glorious high she'd ever known.

When the song ended, she didn't want to open her eyes. She wanted to stay there and live in the song forever. But she soon realized how foolish she must have looked, and laughed, almost snorting in disbelief.

Her head dropped, while she savored the warm feeling running through her that felt like the first few sips of a hearty Barolo.

Eventually Louisa collected herself and slowly lifted her head. In front of her, she found the proprietor standing a few feet away, the same man who had asked her and Judy if they had needed help earlier. He leaned against a table of merchandise, looking directly at her with arms folded, the corners of his mouth curled up in a goofy grin.

Louisa blinked, looking closer this time. He was rugged looking with a scruffy five o'clock shadow. His wavy hair with hints of salt-and-pepper highlights hung to his shoulders—and then she spotted that familiar dimple, only on the left cheek.

Louisa could barely speak. But she managed to step forward. "Mathis?"

He continued smiling, and he moved toward her, nodding. "Yes, Louisa."

A flutter of nerves ruffled in her stomach from the unique way he still managed to pronounce her name—just as he did when they were teens.

"So many years." She reached out for his hand, and was not sure if she was extending her arm to politely shake it or if she just needed to touch him. Could this be? Was he real? What a handsome man he'd become. Even so, he still had the same gleaming eyes and boyish smile.

He took her hand to shake it but didn't let it go. "Ja, maar Louisa, I never stop remembering you." Mathis finally had gotten English down; the lines of communication between them were open at last.

Louisa tried to be casual while she explained what they were doing back in Antwerp while glancing down at his hand to see if he was wearing a wedding ring. She never wanted anything more than to see an unadorned finger, and she soon discovered . . . it was. Her eyes closed, and she tipped her head back in relief. Realizing then Mathis had caught her in the act, she laughed, and soon he joined in as well. Just as they had done when they were teens. They still managed to understand each other when no words were spoken.

While the two continued their conversation, Louisa glanced over his shoulder at the train station's large glass dome. Her gaze shifted to one side of the stone building and found a sign reading "Central Station" in large gold letters. It acted like a backdrop behind Mathis's head, creating a halo effect over him.

At that moment, Louisa realized there really was something about the *train* phenomenon that acted as a catalyst, pushing her. It picked her up from derailment in life and put her back on the tracks. It was true: you can't go home again. Little had remained the same in Antwerp. But this trip back along the tracks gave her the faith to believe in the treasured music she knew from forty years ago and the memories that went with it. She only needed to let them do their job and remind her of the person she'd once been and lead her to where she needed to go next. And now, as a bonus, those same tracks had guided her back to her first love. This time, Louisa wouldn't do anything stome by letting either of them go.

Smiling, she watched as a flock of pigeons sitting on the grand clock's ledge outside the station peacefully lifted upward as if their work was finished. They slowly disappeared into the cloudless azure sky.

Yes! Louisa's heart rejoiced. It truly was a beautiful day—by Belgian standards.

The End